FIFTH MEMBER

Claire Rayner

FIFTH MEMBER

A Dr George Barnabas Mystery

MICHAEL JOSEPH
LONDON

MICHAEL JOSEPH LTD

Published by the Penguin Group
27 Wrights Lane, London w8 5tz, England
Viking Penguin Inc, 375 Hudson Street, New York, New York 10014, USA
Penguin Books Australia Ltd, Ringwood, Victoria, Australia
Penguin Books Canada Ltd, 10 Alcorn Avenue, Toronto, Ontario, Canada m4v 3b2
Penguin Books (NZ) Ltd, 182–190 Wairau Road, Auckland 10, New Zealand

Penguin Books Ltd, Registered Offices: Harmondsworth, Middlesex, England

First published in Great Britain 1997
1 3 5 7 9 10 8 6 4 2

Set in 11.5/13pt Monotype Janson
Typeset by Rowland Phototypesetting Ltd, Bury St Edmunds, Suffolk
Printed in Great Britain by Clays Ltd, St Ives plc

A CIP catalogue record for this book is available from the British Library

ISBN 0-7181-4214-4

For Colin Maitland, a most charming outlaw.

ACKNOWLEDGEMENTS

Thanks for advice and information about death, detection, aristocracy, Parliamentary goings-on and sundry other matters are due to: Dr Trevor Betteridge, Pathologist of Yeovil, Somerset; Dr Rufus Crompton, Pathologist, St George's Hospital, Tooting, London; Dr Azeel Sarrah, Pathologist, Queen Elizabeth II Hospital, Welwyn Garden City, Hertfordshire; Mr Richard Bark-Jones, Lawyer, of Formby, Liverpool; Peter Angel, Lawyer, of Kenton, Middlesex; Robin Corbett, MP for Erdington; Debrett's Peerage Ltd; Detective Chief Inspector Jackie Malton, Metropolitan Police; many members of the staff of Northwick Park and St Mark's Hospital, Harrow, Middlesex; and many others too numerous to mention, and are gratefully tendered by the author.

I

'Is she annoyed?' repeated the Member of Parliament for Westleigh. '*Annoyed?* She's bloody incandescent.'

'She can be unreasonable,' said the Member for Central Casterbridge, uneasily aware of how often she herself had missed a two-line whip; she'd only made it to the lobby for this three-line one by the skin of her teeth. 'The man could be ill, or his kids in trouble or something.'

'Sam Diamond ill? The man's made of solid leather. And he hasn't got any kids.'

'Well, you know what I mean. People do have emergencies, after all.'

'Not unless they've paired first, they don't,' said the Member for Westleigh. 'They wouldn't dare. She'd murder 'em. Look, I'm off. Want a lift?'

'Umm. No thanks,' said the Member for Central Casterbridge, glancing at the door of the Chief Whip's office. 'I've one or two things to sort out first.'

'I'll bet you have,' said the other, grinning knowingly, and left her there, painfully aware of the fact that she'd been slotted into the brown-nosing category by her colleague, and not liking it much. But what the hell, she told herself, that's politics. She composed her face into an expression of exhausted but indomitable support and went into the office.

In the event, hanging around did the Member for Central Casterbridge no good at all. Mary Bodling, who had the reputation of being the toughest Chief Whip the Tories had ever had, with bigger and harder balls than any man on the Front Bench, was in no humour for an erratic backbencher with a lousy voting record, and sent her away smartly, while making a mental note to speak to her sometime about the way she did her hair and the sort of clothes she wore. She looked entirely too left wing with that scruffy haircut and heavy boots under a long skirt. Tory women should look like Tory women, in Mary Bodling's opinion, and while she sat in this office they bloody well would. But that was for a later date; right now she wanted to get hold of Sam Diamond and excoriate him. She wanted that very badly.

But however many calls her staff made, however they scurried through the contact lists, he wasn't to be flushed out, and Bodling's frustration had built steadily until now she was scowling like a character in a Disney film, as one of the junior people murmured under his breath to the man at the adjoining desk.

Mary Bodling heard him. She made another mental note to deal with him too in a way that would make life exceedingly disappointing for someone as ambitious as he was; a fact which would have alarmed him greatly had he known. One of the things that made Bodling so formidable was her elephantine memory: she never forgot a slight and never overlooked a peccadillo, though she took swift compliance with all her requests as her just due. The Prime Minister adored her, Central Office thought she was the Angel Gabriel come again, only less namby pamby, and the press loved nothing more than reporting her latest exploits.

It was the press about which she was concerned now. The vote had been an important one involving the Government's response to another piece of Brussels legislation, dealing this time with the importation of costly drugs from European pharmaceutical companies, and journalists had been scrabbling around excitedly looking for more evidence of Government splits on the issue. The fact that the Government had been so nearly defeated this evening for the sake of one vote had sent them baying like so many bloodthirsty wolfhounds. It had been a long time since there had been a hung vote like this, needing the Speaker's intervention to carry the day. The TV and radio people had already had their fun at the expense of the Speaker, who was known privately to be as ardent a Labour man as he had ever been and who must have tasted very bitter gall indeed when he had to give his casting vote to the Government as the rules of the House demanded, and now they wanted to sup Bodling's blood. Tomorrow's papers could be a PR disaster, and Mary had no intention of allowing that, or at least not till she herself had had her fill of Diamond's.

But even his wife, who might be expected to have news of him, couldn't be found. She was, reported the anxious and most junior member of Mary's staff who had been set to work to find her, in Italy on a buying trip.

'Buying trip?' roared Mary Bodling. 'Buying? She'll need to go shopping for a new husband when I get my hands on him.'

'It's stock,' said the wretched junior. 'For her shop.'

Mary, who knew perfectly well what the trip was about, almost snorted her disgust. Alice Diamond, who was altogether too blonde, too thin and too expensive for Mary's tastes, had a wickedly pricey establishment in Sloane Street where she made a great deal of money selling wisps of silk and suchlike to American tourists. Mary had told the Diamonds several times that it was her opinion – which of course should have been regarded by Sam and Alice as Holy Writ – that a Tory wife's place was in her husband's constituency. Why didn't Alice sell nice tweeds and cashmeres down in Hedgington? But Alice had gone on her own sweet way, and now Sam Diamond had defected on an important vote. It was too bad; worse than bad: downright wicked disloyalty than which there was no greater crime in Mary's decalogue. Steps might have to be taken regarding deselection, Mary told herself darkly, and set about harrying her staff again. Last night's vote wasn't the only crucial one that had to be dealt with. There was the NHS Financing Bill to push through somehow, with far more provision for the Private Finance Initiative than ever ('privatization by the bloody *front* door', as its opponents sourly put it) and the fuss about NHS consultants' merit awards, and the legislation designed to protect the House of Lords from the reformers, the Right to Inheritance Bill. All of them mattered and all of them, Mary had told the Prime Minister, would be buggers to get through with a majority as wafer thin as the one the Government currently suffered. And so much bad temper and contrariness on the Lib-Dem benches! So some pretty thorough and comprehensive bullying would be needed over the next few weeks.

Mary set to work with a relish. Bullying, after all, was what she did best.

'All I wanted was a slash,' the man said again, his voice muffled by the way his head was held between his hands. He sat on the kerb, his whole posture one of sick misery. 'I had a few drinks with my friends, and I needed a slash. You know how it is . . .' He peered up owlishly at the two men standing above him. 'And I didn't like to stand out here in the street. You never know who might come by, and, well . . . it isn't nice.'

The two men exchanged glances, amused, and then looked back at him.

'We'll need a statement, sir,' the taller of them said in a soft Scottish accent. 'We'll arrange for you to be taken back to the station to do that.'

'Oh, shit,' the man on the kerb said. 'Do I have to? I feel lousy and I've told you all I know. I went into the alley to pee, and didn't see – see anything till I turned round to come out. I mean, I was desperate. I didn't wait or look about. I just got on with it, and then, after, feeling better you understand, sort of did. Look around, I mean. And there it was . . .' His face went a little paler as he remembered. 'Made me sick, it did. It was seeing it, you see, made me feel awful.'

Durward Street was beginning to fill up with passers-by, even at this time of night. Detective Sergeant Urquhart glanced at them and scowled. Half past one. 'Get those gawpers out of here,' he said over his shoulder to one of the hovering uniformed men. 'And then see if we can clear the area of unwanted staff too. The Guv's on his way and I doubt he'll need any uniforms.

Leave just one of the cars, send the others on their way and we'll see where we go from there.'

He stopped at the mouth of the alley and looked back into the dark street. There was a low mist hugging the pavement and he took a deep breath and smelled the river which, though it was a fair bit south, still managed to make its presence felt. Murder, he thought. The Guv'nor'll like this one. Not that he likes people to be killed, of course. Just that he likes oddities. And this one is bloody odd.

'Come on,' he said to Bob Pennington, the Soco. 'This way.'

They stepped over the wet patch left by the man on the kerb, who had now identified himself as Mr Piers Wilson, and was now in the car on his way back to Ratcliffe Street station to give his statement, and went on into the tiny yard beyond. It was little more than a patch of old cracked concrete, some twenty-five feet by forty or so, with dustbins in the corner, a bit of scattered rubbish of the broken-down bicycle and old tin can kind, flanked by dead walls, dirty windows and back doors, the whole a remnant of the way the entire area had been before great swathes of buildings had been culled to make room for a vast supermarket and a couple of blocks of modern flats. But here, the old East End lingered on in the huddle of battered buildings that gave on to the courtyard. The doors were locked from the inside; Mike had had that checked as soon as the patrol car, which had stopped to investigate the man sitting on the kerb rocking and retching miserably, had called in with their find. Calls had been sent out to bring in the buildings' keyholders, since all three of them were clearly used for offices or small workshops, and empty at night; so all there was to pay much attention to was the figure lying on its back to the left of the alley's opening into the yard.

When Mike had first arrived it had taken him a moment or two to assimilate what the patrol man's torch had shown him. He had stood looking down in amazement and with a sort of detached sense of horror, just as he did now, a little to his surprise. He had been in the force long enough to be inured to most horrific sights; but he'd never seen one like this. And it was as revolting to look at now as it had been when he had first seen it, half an hour ago.

A man, portly, well dressed – as far as it was possible to tell – his head thrown back and a great grin disfiguring his face. Only it wasn't his face. His throat had been cut, hugely, gapingly, and the effect was ludicrous as well as horrifying, like a vast mirthless smile. The darkness that was blood puddles showed on each side of the throat, though there did not appear to be as much as might have been expected with so ferocious an injury. 'Lots underneath,' he murmured aloud and the Soco, seeming to read his mind, nodded.

'The other one too,' Mike said then, and took a deep breath. With a conscious effort, he made his glance slide downwards to follow his torch beam. The man's trousers had been pulled away and the skirts of his overcoat flung aside. The underclothes had been ripped and the belly and groin exposed. But that was where normality, if it could be called that, ended. Where the man in life had had beneath his rotund belly an expanse of pubic hair and his genitals there was just a wide, deep darkness, fringed with clotted blood. Nothing else at all.

'Oh, my God,' breathed the Soco and Mike put one hand on his arm, feeling a need to offer a fellow worker in a foul field some comfort.

'That's not all of it,' he said in a flat voice, shifting the beam of his torch up again and then to the left, settling it on the man's outflung right arm. It was there, lying on the point of the shoulder, that the missing parts of the body lay, spread out neatly for all the world like meat on a butcher's slab.

By the time Detective Superintendent Gus Hathaway, head of the Area Major Incident Team, arrived, Bob Pennington had finished. The photographers had recorded every inch of the yard and the alley and the pavement on Durward Street outside, and Bob had taken a sample of Mr Wilson's body fluid, an unusually pernickety step, but one which he felt necessary with so terrible and bizarre a killing. 'Anything could be evidence,' he said heavily to Mike as he stoppered his bottles. 'You never know.

6

And I didn't want the Doc on my back because I didn't collect it if she decides she wants it.'

'Ye've a point there,' Mike said and grinned briefly. 'I'll tell her as soon as she gets here.'

'She coming with the Guv'nor then?' Bob asked.

Mike shrugged. 'Mebbe. Your guess is as good as mine. Will you be wanting to talk to him?'

'I'd rather get all this worked up ready for the morning,' Bob said. 'If I know the Guv he'll want the reports on his desk at sparrow's fart. See you in the nick.'

'Yes,' said Mike and watched him go, glad to see his car passing the Super's as it came swinging round from Brady Street to pull up with a shudder of hard-used brakes.

'What's all this I hear about weirdies?' Gus demanded almost before he was out of the car. He was looking very dapper, Mike thought, with his usually all-over-the-place dark curly hair smoothed down and an expanse of white evening shirt between black satin revers. Gus caught his appreciative glance and reddened slightly. 'Bloody hospital dinner,' he growled. 'Another one of those buggers of professors discovering something and gettin' an award. You'd think they had more'n enough bleedin' diseases to get on with without discovering new ones. I came straight here.'

'And – er – the Doc?' Mike murmured.

'Sent her home to change first. She's wearing a dress that cost her the best part of three hundred quid and if you think I'm going to let her muck that up you've another think coming. She won't be long. So, fill me in.'

Mike did, swiftly and with much graphic use of language as well as gesture. Gus listened, his eyes glinting in the meagre light from the one remaining set of rotating blue lights.

'Getaway!' he said. 'You're makin' it up.'

'Would I do that, Guv?' Mike shook his head. 'Come and see for yourself. Soco's finished. We just need the doctor and then ... anyway, come and see.'

'Well,' Gus said, when he stood beside the body and stared down. 'Well, well, well.'

'Yeah,' Mike said, sliding a sideways glance at him. 'That's what I said. Or something like it.'

'Makes you hold your knees together, don't it?' said Gus. 'Jesus, what a thing to do to a bloke.'

'What I can't fathom,' Mike said, 'is why.'

'Hmm?'

'I mean, I ask myself, why should someone do a thing like that? Cut off his wedding tackle. All right, take it away or something, but arrange it all neat and tidy like that, on his shoulder? It's crazy.'

'Arranged on his shoulder,' Gus repeated. He looked vague. 'Yeah. That's just what he did, isn't it?'

'Look for yourself,' Mike said. 'I mean, it's not that he, well – threw them up there, is it? That's arranged, sort of planned, I'd say. Wouldna you?'

'Now you point it out, maybe so.' Gus seemed abstracted. 'It reminds me of . . . Oh, so you're here at last!'

'I'd have been here sooner if you hadn't been in such a sweat over my dress.' The figure which had materialized beside them was wearing jeans, a loose sweatshirt with 'Buffalo' written on it in faded letters, and battered trainers. Her hair, which was thick and dark and as curly as Gus Hathaway's but much longer, was piled on her head and pinned in an untidy but beguiling knot. She was wearing large round glasses and carrying a square attaché case which she stooped to set on the ground beside the body. 'What's the story?'

'Look for yourself,' Gus said, pulling the torch from Mike's hand. 'Mike, go and organize some lamps here, will you, so Dr B. can see what she's doing. I'll give her the details.'

Mike lingered, clearly torn. 'Are you sure you wouldna – that the Doc wouldna prefer . . .' He subsided as Gus turned and stared at him.

'Prefer what?'

'Well, maybe some help. From one of – from a chap, mebbe, from the Home Office back-up team. I mean, it's a very nasty –'

'Mike, go and take your mealy-mouthed wee kirk notions away and fetch those lights. If Dr B. couldn't handle this, she

8

wouldn't be in the business, right, George?' And he almost leered at the tall woman as she looked from one to the other.

'What is all this?' she demanded. 'Give me that torch, Gus. Let me see what the hell it is you're all on about.'

'Mike thinks it might upset your nice female susceptibilities.' Gus grinned ferociously. 'Me, what knows you so well, has no such fears. I'm not sure you've got any female susceptibilities at all, whatever they may be. You even have to be nagged not to ruin as handsome a dress as you've ever had by changing it to come to a scene of crime, hmm?'

'Oh, Gus, do shut up,' George said. She grabbed the torch and turned its beam on the body at their feet. She made it travel from one side to the other, slowly, letting it linger as it illuminated the horrible grinning throat, but making no sign or sound in response. The beam moved on, downwards, and then stopped as it reached the belly and she saw the mutilation; that brought out a short sharp intake of breath and Gus, at her side, said sardonically, 'As they say in the movies, dolly, you ain't seen nuthin' yet. Up and a bit to the right – no, your left, it's the corpse's right – yeah. That's it. What do you think of that, then?'

There was a short horrified silence and then George said, her eyes wide and her voice low, 'Jesus. Jesus H. Christ.'

2

Even with the Tilley lamps rigged up and filling the yard with painfully white light, there wasn't a great deal George could do at the scene. She made a cursory examination of the body and then supervised its packing into a body bag ready to be taken to her mortuary.

'If you don't take care that head'll come right off,' she said. 'The neck's as damn near severed as makes no matter, and the weight could – that's right. Support it. Hmm. I'd better collect some blood from that mess. He can't have a great deal left in him that'll be any use for testing.'

She busied herself with bottles and labels, crouching over the clotted patch on the concrete that had been revealed by the body's removal, as Gus organized questioning of the keyholders of the adjoining buildings and had the area cordoned off till daylight would permit a more thorough examination.

'Not,' he said, 'that I expect to find all that much. Mike did a good job, and so did the Soco. The answers to this one won't be here, I don't suppose.'

'He certainly isn't dressed like a local wino,' George said. In her years as both Home Office forensic pathologist for the area and also resident pathologist at the Royal Eastern Hospital, locally known affectionately as Old East, she had become accustomed to the detritus of dead bodies left stranded in the neglected old houses, on patches of waste ground and beside (and in) the river that defined the southern border of Shadwell.

This one was certainly of a very different ilk. 'Have you an ID yet?'

Gus shook his head. 'Soco made no attempt to look for a wallet or anything else. Left it all to you. I wonder why?'

'I wonder,' George said sardonically. 'You want the job done tonight, I take it?'

'It's up to you, dolly.' Gus sounded unconcerned, but he was watching her carefully, she knew. 'I'll have to make a night of it, I imagine, and it'd help to know who the bugger is as soon as possible. Praps you could do the prelims – clothes and that – and leave the full PM till tomorrow?'

'So much for our romantic anniversary,' she said and his eyes glinted in the lights.

'Once I've got the incident room set up and put the fellas to work, I'll be able to catch up on my sleep,' he said. 'Like, tomorrow afternoon? And maybe you could get all your part of the job done by then too, and leave Alan and Jerry to hold the fort for you while you – um – do the same?'

'The whole point of an anniversary is that it happens on the date the first event happened on,' she said. 'Not the day after. By tomorrow I'm back into the old routine, my friend. All the romance'll have gone.'

'Not quite gone, sweetie. Leave it to me, and you'll be amazed what I can drum up for both of us.'

'Goddamn it, Gus, do you ever think of anything apart from sex? Here we are with as weird a killing as any we've ever had, and all you can do is plan for –'

'Nookie.' Gus leered horribly. 'It's what refreshes me for the job in hand.' He turned then irritably as a voice called him. 'Who's that?'

'Me, Guv.' A man came out of the darkness of the alley into the yard and George felt her face stiffen as he, for his part, gave her the sketchiest of nods, barely looking at her. She had never been able to get on to anything but the most frigid of terms with Rupert Dudley. He'd been a sergeant when they'd first met and almost from the beginning she'd managed to step on his toes. In two separate cases on which she and Gus's team had worked, she had reached the answer before Dudley, a professional let-down for which he'd never forgiven her. Now he was an inspector, because Gus thought highly of him and had worked hard to get him on his team; but in spite of that George still couldn't like the man. Discussion of or comment about Rupert Dudley was one of the few no-go areas between herself and Gus. So now she bit her lip and listened owlishly.

'Hello, Roop,' Gus said. 'You didn't have to turn out of your bed an' all. We've got most of Ratcliffe Street's CID here, as well as some of my own people from area office. You could have stayed in your bed.'

'My patch, Guv, my case,' Rupert said, primming his lips a little. George was maliciously amused. Gus would persist in calling him Roop in spite of appeals not to, and Dudley, hating the diminutive as he did, never failed to react. 'Of course I'm here. I came as soon as I'd heard. And I wasn't in bed. I was out. It's Mrs Dudley's birthday. Now, listen, I got here in time to see the body loaded in the van, and I took a look at him. I think I have a notion who he might be.'

'That's handy,' Gus said, suddenly exhilarated. 'A local toff of some sort, is he? Or just a spraunced-up chancer?'

'Local, my foot,' Rupert said, with a certain relish. 'National, more like. In fact he might even be international, seeing his job, as I recall, was to do with export . . .'

'So?' Gus said sharply. 'No riddles, if you don't mind.'

'MP,' Rupert said. 'Something to do with the Department of Trade and Industry, I seem to remember. Sam Diamond. I'm pretty sure that's who he is, though he doesn't exactly look the way he does in his pictures in the paper, or how he was when he came to speak to Mrs Dudley's Ladies' Lunch Club. She was President last year, so she got me to turn out. You know how these things are . . .' He blushed a little and it was visible in the poor light. 'So, I met him. That's why I'm so sure.'

'An MP?' Gus said. 'Oh, for crying out loud! That'll put the fat in the barbecue and no error! We'll have every lousy hack in Wapping here. Christ Almighty, that's all we're short of.'

'I'll work tonight,' George said quietly into his ear. 'See you at home.' And then, more loudly, 'Good morning, Roop,' and smiled sweetly at Dudley as she passed him. That'll show him, she thought and felt rather better.

As she drove through the almost empty streets she was smiling a little. It had been a good evening up till now, and even this case wouldn't spoil it. It was clearly going to be a real honey of a job; a bizarre style of murder and a V I P victim to boot. She shivered a little with agreeable anticipation of the work that was to come, tracking this one down. It was exactly the sort of puzzle she, and she knew Gus too (though he would never admit it in so many words) enjoyed.

The day had started well. The carpets she had ordered all those months ago for their house in tiny Constom Square, just off Shad Thames on the other side of the river, had arrived early enough in the morning for her to get them properly laid and the furniture arranged as she wanted it: the rewards of a rare day off she had allowed herself. The bedroom had looked lovely when Gus had come home and he'd been enchanted by it. Just as she had meant him to be.

Moving into a house so old – Gus said 1815 wasn't that old, but for a girl from Buffalo, George had told him, it was old enough – and so dilapidated had been a challenge, almost as much of a challenge as actually living together. But they'd done it, after that last case on which they had worked together and which had left her with such a loathing of her little flat in Bermondsey that she had had to move. Gus had decided to sell his handsome and costly shiny new flat in one of the more elegant of the new Dockside blocks over towards Wapping, and they had invested the shared result and a good deal more besides (George insisting on paying her full whack even though Gus had more than enough money in his own right to buy the place outright without a mortgage since he had inherited his father's considerable fish and chip shop empire) and set up a joint home. Six months of what amounted to connubial bliss without a wedding ring had been smoother than George had expected, but not without its fireworks, of course. No one could live all the time with Gus and not have fights, for heaven's sake. Especially as he maintained that it was she who caused the friction while he was, of course, the most emollient and easy of men.

So they had their bad days, but today had not been one of them. At last the house was beginning to look as they both wanted it, from the long living room, with high windows at both ends and white walls, good modern paintings, a scarlet carpet and black furniture, which occupied the whole of the first floor; down to the snug wood-panelled dining room and pretty stone-floored kitchen on the ground floor; up to the two floors of bedrooms with the attics used as studies for each of them. For the first time in her professional life George had real space in which to work but she'd had no time since they'd moved in till today to do any professional work on the book she'd been planning about her more interesting past cases. Now, this after-noon, once the bedroom was straight, she'd actually had the chance to go up to her study and organize her desk; a major step forwards, and she had glowed with it all the time she was showering and dressing in a very special new dark emerald silk slip of a dress that clung to every curve and yet seemed some-how to make her seem better shaped than she knew she was. Her hair had gone just right, agreeing to be arranged in a most elegant knot at the back of her neck, and she'd been able to use her contact lenses without shedding a single excess tear. And the dinner hadn't been all that bad: Professor Caversham had made quite a short speech, for a professor; the food had been surprisingly good for hospital eats; and the wine had been remarkably good for an establishment that usually spent as little money on entertaining its staff and guests as it possibly could.

And then a call on Gus's mobile phone had told them a body had been found on the Ratcliffe Street patch and had, as Gus put it, cast a blight on the rose. He had been determined she should go home and change out of her dress before joining him to investigate. She, in her usual impetuous fashion, hadn't given a damn; dresses could always go to the cleaners if they got a splash of blood or mud on them. But Gus wouldn't have it. And the maddening thing had been she had known he was right. It was a delicate dress which had cost her more than she'd ever spent on a single garment in all her life, and anyway, she needed her emergency kit to take to a scene of crime. Going home made sense. It had just infuriated her that Gus should take it upon himself to tell her so.

Well, she'd deal with Gus later, she thought now as she guided the car expertly into her small space behind the path. lab, so that she could let herself into the building with her own private keys instead of trekking all the way through from the front of the hospital. Old East was a great rambling place, and a lot of time could be wasted plodding its myriad corridors and walkways. Right now I have a tricky PM to deal with, she told herself and felt a small frisson of excitement as she considered Roop's words. A Member of Parliament! Well, that would certainly cause a hullabaloo and there was little George enjoyed more than a hullabaloo. It added spice to the usual round of accidental deaths, battered wives and men slicing each other to pieces in pub fights which was all that had come her way lately. To have another case to work on with Gus would really be fun.

'Darling,' Mattie said, 'it's not *like* him, honestly it's not. I'm truly, truly worried. I mean, there's no reason –' And she reached for her glass and, because her hand was shaking, knocked it over and swore.

Susan Napper, hearing the clink as well as the loud, 'Shit!' guessed wearily what had happened and said loudly, 'Mattie! I've told you before. He's just been held up with business at the House. He'll be home soon, I'm sure. As long as you're certain you didn't have any – disagreements. You remember what happened last time . . .' She let the words hang in the air.

Mattie sobbed and then sniffed thickly and at her end of the phone Susan's gorge rose. She grimaced and made a soft sound. Beside her Marcus stirred and lifted his head blowsily.

'Whassamarrer?'

Susan didn't even bother to put her hand over the mouthpiece. 'It's Mattie. David hasn't come home yet and she's worried.'

'Tell the silly bitch to stop fussing,' Marcus grunted into his pillow. 'Course he's not in a hurry to get home. Bloody woman's always pickled out of her skull.'

'Oh, I'm not. Soos, honestly I'm not!' Mattie wailed into Susan's ear. 'Tell Marcus I'm not pickled.'

'My dear Mattie, you're imagining things,' Susan said with great briskness. 'Marcus said nothing of the sort, he just said you were – um – sick with worrying, no doubt, but there's no need. And I agree with him. David works hard at the House, you know that and –'

'But he said he'd be home by midnight!' Mattie wept. 'He said he would. I cooked supper for him and everything. I've been trying so hard to be – not to – well, you know – and he didn't come and I had to – Oh, shit!' And she hung up the phone with a clatter and burst into even louder tears before getting to her feet, awkwardly avoiding the patch of wet carpet where the glass had fallen, and going to fetch the bottle from the kitchen. She'd put it there and taken her glassful into the living room, in the forlorn hope that she'd be too lazy to go and get another drink when she'd finished that one, but it wasn't going to work. Not if everyone thought she was fussing over nothing. She'd been dry for almost a month and he had to go and choose tonight, when she'd actually managed to cook for him, to be late. Why should she bother to try, anyway, when people thought she was drunk when she wasn't?

This time she brought the bottle back with her to the sofa and sat and emptied a glassful of vodka before picking up the phone again.

Gus was busily organizing the preparation of an incident room at Ratcliffe Street nick for the morning when he heard. Mike Urquhart had good naturedly agreed to help him, though he had every excuse to go home now if he really wanted to. Neither Rupert nor Gus would have stopped him because he'd worked almost half the night before over a hit and run which he'd successfully tied up. But he stayed, and that was why he happened to be within earshot when the call came in. He had been collecting extra stationery from the cupboard which happened to be tucked into a convenient corner of the Control Room when he heard the woman police constable on duty taking it.

'If you could speak a little more slowly, madam. You say you expected him at what time? Nine o'clock. I see. Well, couldn't he have been held up at his office? It does happen, doesn't it? We're always hearing of men who have to put in a lot of overtime and – yes, madam, I do agree, it is getting late. Hmm? Well, it's after two. Er, maybe he decided to stay at the office till morning not to disturb you?'

The PC caught Mike's eye on her and put her hand over the mouthpiece under her chin. 'She's smashed out of her mind, Sarge, this one. Swears her husband's run off and wants us to go and find him, right now. I've tried to soothe her till the morning when maybe she'll make more sense even if she has the hangover she deserves, but – What? Oh, yes, madam, I'm still here.' She pulled her hand away from the mouthpiece and listened, her eyes staring into the middle distance, clearly unimpressed with her caller.

'Well, madam, I don't think we can do more. An adult man not getting home at his usual time isn't the sort of situation we'd normally deal with in the small hours. Perhaps if you call again in the morning after you – after you call his office and see if they know? Where does he work, by the way? Oh! The House of Commons, I see.'

Mike, who had been about to leave, came back from the door and stood over her. 'Ask her what his job is there,' he hissed.

The PC looked startled, but obeyed. 'Er, madam, what does your husband do there?' she asked obediently and listened. 'Oh? Member of Parliament, I see, madam.' She looked up at Mike with her brows raised and the corners of her mouth turned down. 'I see. Well, I'll make a note of the matter and we'll see what we can do. Could I have your full address and phone number again, madam? No, I took it down, but just to double check.'

'What was that?' Mike demanded as soon as she cut off the call. 'When it's a Member of Parliament you don't treat it like the usual business of a fella after a bit of illicit nookie and a drunken wife in a tizz.'

'I didn't know before that he was an MP!' The girl sounded aggrieved. 'She didn't say. Sorry, Sarge, but I mean, I never thought to ask, "Is he an MP?" I mean, you wouldn't, would you? And anyway, even if he is –'

'MPs aren't like other citizens,' Mike said. 'Who is it?'

The PC looked down at her notebook and snickered. 'Sounds like a real Barbara Cartland hero, he does. David Caspar-Wynette-Gondor with two hyphens! How's that for a mouthful? His wife's name is Marietta. Blimey, there's a name to go to bed with. Marietta Caspar-Wynette-Gondor.'

But Mike had gone, almost running along the corridor to the office he shared with Tim Brewer. There had to be a copy there, surely . . .

There was, and he breathed a sigh of relief as he found the small blue booklet marked *Vacher's Parliamentary Companion* and leafed through the thin pages covered with very small print indeed, praying that the copy, dated 1989 – which was about normal for half the reference books on the shelves – wasn't too out of date. It shouldn't be: unless the man had got in on a recent by-election he should be listed. If he really was an MP, that was. The constable had said the woman who rang in was drunk, and fantasist drunks weren't unheard of in the dark night watches at Ratcliffe Street.

But she clearly wasn't a fantasist. There he was. The Hon. David Caspar-Wynette-Gondor, Member of Parliament for Bilkley Town. Bilkley Town? Mike thought, staring at the page. Where the hell was that? He'd need another reference book for that, and he grabbed the AA book lying on the top of the bookshelf. Not the most detailed of guides but it would serve his purpose.

Bilkley, it appeared, was a sizeable market town in the Midlands. Not too far away from London; a plum seat, he suspected. Not that that mattered at the moment. The first thing he had to do was to tell the Guv that there just might be another MP to worry about.

3

The headlines of the late editions of the morning papers were almost hysterical with excitement. There hadn't been a decent murder or rape to occupy the press for some weeks, and now to get one that combined horror with politics was almost more than they could have prayed for. Everyone and his sister had been interviewed, with Mary Bodling well represented as expressing deep regrets at the loss of so able and remarkable a man as Sam Diamond, an ornament of his Party and always so utterly reliable and loyal that she had in fact feared last night that something terrible had happened to him when he didn't appear to vote on the issue of pharmaceutical imports to the UK from other European nations about which he had cared so deeply – indeed, her inability to find him, she assured the *Clarion*, had made her determined to involve the police herself this very morning – and if only she had done so last night! – but of course by then the police had made their dreadful discovery; and so on and on *ad nauseam*.

The reports made much of the fact that Diamond's throat had been deeply cut and George, reading the papers as voraciously as anyone else, even though she had all the inside information anyone could possibly want, checked carefully that there was not a word about the other mutilations to the body. Well done, Gus, she thought, to have kept that quiet. Let the public know about that and the mind boggles at what the reaction might be.

She had done the post-mortem well before six a.m. even

though she had had to wait for Danny, the mortuary porter, to respond to the call to his room in a lodging house a couple of streets away. He came, grumbling furiously, of course, but eagerly enough. The rate of overtime he was paid for these special out-of-hours jobs more than compensated him for the loss of his sleep, but he wouldn't miss any opportunity to make George's life a misery if he could.

He couldn't this morning. She was altogether too fascinated by the job in hand to pay any attention to him, and after a while Danny too became so interested that he stopped his complaining and just watched, avidly.

On the other side of the PM room Mike Urquhart leaned against the wall with his arms folded, not watching. Anyone watching his steady, if glazed, stare would have assumed he was observing every movement of George's hand, but he had retired behind his eyes and was thinking his own thoughts. Indeed he was almost asleep.

'Major vessels of the neck severed,' George dictated into the microphone over her head as she probed carefully in the blood-boltered mess beneath Sam Diamond's chin. 'Exsanguination, however, not as complete as I would have expected. Hmm . . .' She paused and then, using her forceps as delicately as if she were handling living tissue, lifted the flap of skin to the left side of the neck, and peered at it more closely.

'Danny, hand me a wet swab,' she commanded, and, taking it from him, began to clean the skin of the blood stains that obscured its original colour. It had a yellowish waxy tone now, though George suspected that in life Sam Diamond had had a rubicund look that would match the roundness of his jowls and the soft double chin that was almost a triple. He had been, she was sure, what would have once been called a plethoric man. Someone with too much of everything, particularly blood and gall.

She pulled her mind back from its wanderings and concentrated, difficult though it was beginning to be at this hour of the morning after a long busy day, and a hospital dinner (was that only a handful of hours ago? It felt like half a lifetime) was not conducive to sharpness of intellect.

But then what she had thought earlier came back into her mind, and her wits did sharpen. Somehow the body had more blood left in it than she would have expected from the degree of damage to the major arteries of the neck. If they had been cut while the heart was still beating, the loss of blood would have been greater; but there were still areas of pooling in the cadaver that suggested that perhaps the heart had stopped. Indeed, had stopped some considerable time before the throat was cut.

The skin emerged thick and dimpled from her careful washing. She pulled on it gently to try to give it the same tension it would have had in life, jerking her head at Danny to bring round the big magnifying glass she had on a swivel arm above the table for close examinations, and peering through it.

'There!' she said after a while. 'I was right. See it Mike, come and look!'

Mike started, blinked fast several times and shook his head to clear it. 'Whassa – Is something wrong, Dr B.?' His Scottish burr sounded unusually strong.

'Not wrong.' She sounded pleased with herself, even a little excited. 'Just interesting. Look. Through the glass, where my forceps are pointing.'

Obediently Mike looked. 'What's that?'

'You tell me what you can see,' she said. 'Then we'll find out if your opinion about what it might be matches mine.'

'Well, there's great pits there – it looks verra strange all magnified like that – and it's a horrid colour, like old soap, and – Ah! Now I see,' as George tilted the glass a little more and pointed again with her forceps. 'A sort of scratch. Well, not a scratch so much as a – a depression. Half-moon shaped and yes, there's another, and another. Mmm! The last one is a scratch, too, isn't it? The one nearest the middle. I mean it's broken there, the skin . . .'

'Anything else?' she demanded.

He peered again. 'Am I imagining it or is there a bit of blueness there? Not a lot, but . . .'

'You're not imagining it,' she said jubilant, now. 'Which proves

21

I'm not either. Here and here and here.' Again the forceps moved, tracing the outline of a smudge of faint colour and then, as Mike straightened his back, she said urgently, 'Surely you can see what that suggests?'

He stared at her and bit his lip. 'I'm not sure.'

'Here,' she said, impatient now. 'Look at it with the naked eye. You can still see it but not so clearly. Look.' Again she pulled gently on the skin flap to the left of where the gullet had once been, and he bent and looked. This time when he straightened his back his eyes were bright.

'Strangled,' he said. 'The man was strangled. Manually strangled.'

'Got it!' She was absurdly pleased with him. 'If they're not the indentations of fingernails, and faint bruises – hard to see now because there's been so much damage and blood flow they've lost their original depth – in the sort of configuration that suggests a right-handed man stood behind him and gripped him with his right hand only, and managed to choke him, I'm the Queen of Romania. He'd have fractured the hyoid bone, I've no doubt, bringing the pressure of his fingers over the midline, but I can't prove that because the whole larynx is so chopped about that it's impossible to say what happened there or when. But it certainly seems to me that this man was dead before the slicing up happened. Now, why should someone do that, do you suppose?'

'Why does anyone kill another person? Isn't that what we have to find out?'

'No, I don't mean why kill. I mean why kill him twice? He was dead. There was no need to spend time slicing him up and risking getting himself covered in blood as well as interrupted, caught by the police, even.'

'A good question!' Mike really was fully awake now, and able to think clearly and concisely. It was the last flicker of energy he'd have before crashing out to sleep the rest of the day away. 'Is there any other evidence you can suggest that might help answer it?'

'I've some more to do here.' She reached above her head for

the camera that hung there on its jointed arm, and with speed and considerable dexterity shot several angles over the area on which she was working, and then picked up her scalpel. 'Danny, get me a specimen bottle. I want to take this section of skin and hold it as evidence. Mike, watch now, to make sure the chain of evidence is safe, and observe precisely where I'm taking it from. You'll want to make notes. I'll dictate, shall I?'

They worked on until at last she'd finished with the head end of the body completely, including the skull and brain. 'That's all that's there,' she said. 'Now, let me see what's happened to the viscera.' And there was, she knew, a note of relish in her voice.

Around them the big bright room glittered with its chrome fittings and the sparkle of water as Danny splashed away with his hose to get rid of the excess body fluids that obscured George's view, and the taps in the big basins dripped mournfully. George was supremely and single-mindedly content. She had no more to ask of life than a complex puzzle and a different sort of P M from the usual; and this job offered both, in abundance.

At length she stopped work, stretched her back, and grinned at Mike. 'Well, no more surprises. He had a hearty meal before he died – about an hour before, no more. Lots of wine with it, too. I'd say. The specimens' – she jerked her head at the row of labelled jars and bottles that Danny had arranged on the side – 'will tell us how much. I'll get Jerry working on them tomorrow. I don't know exactly how old he was, but I'd guess about forty, though his heart and mesentery both show some excess fatty deposits, and I suspect his arteries do too. I'll look at those in more detail later. His liver was all right. Nothing marvellous in terms of health. I suspect he was a heavy drinker. Another few years and he could well have been in trouble.'

'More than this?' Mike said and grinned, and she grinned back.

'You know what I mean. For the rest, well, the testes and penis together with a sizeable amount of fat and skin and other connective tissue from the supra-pubic area were removed. The bladder has been breached but the lower gut is intact. What more can I tell you?'

'Why he – the killer – should have arranged the – made the display on the shoulder,' Mike said. 'It's really weird. I canna understand that at all.'

'It's quite a common mutilation in sexual crimes,' George said. 'I've come across it before. Without the shoulder arrangement, however. There I agree with you. That *is* weird. Because usually, they take them away.'

'Why a murderer should remove such organs, in both senses.' Mike shook his head. 'I mean, chop 'em off and then take 'em away. That really gets to me.'

'I told you, it's not that rare. I've heard about plenty of murderers in other parts of the world who've taken away trophies of their victims. A man in China used to take away some female parts – he killed several women. And others have taken tongues and ears and –'

'I'd rather not know,' Danny said very loudly. 'I mean, Dr B., you've brought some right nasty stuff into my mortuary over the years, but this is about the nastiest. And rude with it. As a decent sort of bloke what does his job to the best of his ability I don't think I should 'ave to be exposed to more than is necessary in the way of 'orror. And the way you're talkin' is 'orrors, and I'll thank you to stop it. I wouldn't want to 'ave to discuss this with the Union, you know.'

'Oh, Danny!' George opened her eyes wide at him. 'I keep forgetting what a delicate flower you are. Do forgive me. Not another word, or at least not here. O K, Mike, I've done, so you can head for bed. Don't worry about writing your report at once. I'll be talking to Gus about all this before you see him. And then, tomorrow – I mean later today sometime – we can all sit down and think about what we've got here. Because it really is one hell of a puzzle.'

Gus didn't get home, in spite of his plans. He snatched a few hours' sleep after dawn on the old sofa in the shabby office that had once been his and which was now Rupert Dudley's, while the bulk of the uniformed branch of Ratcliffe Street, as well as most of the CID, went on searching for David Caspar-Wynette-Gondor, or CWG as everyone was already calling him. And woke about eleven a.m.

'Right,' he cried, bouncing out of the office like an excited three-year-old. 'Where is everyone? Time for a rundown on progress. Joe, fetch me a bacon sarnie and two cups o' black coffee and a cherry Danish from the canteen and do it yesterday. I'm bloody famished. Margaret, is George – Dr B. here?'

The DC looked up and shook her head. 'No, Guv. She phoned and said call when you were ready for her and she'd come right over. She's at home.'

'So call her. And tell her – I mean ask her nicely if she'd bring me a plain suit and shirt and tie. I can't prance round looking like a battered penguin all day.' He tugged irritably at the collar of his dress shirt as the DC giggled and reached for the phone.

'Roop? Where's Inspector Dudley? And Mike Urquhart? And what about Tim Brewer? What the bleedin' 'ell is everyone doin', for God's sake?'

'There's a big search on for the missing MP, Guv.' A PC came over to put a sheaf of paper in his hands. 'There's been a big push on him. You said before you went to sleep you wanted everyone to –'

'Yeah, yeah,' Gus said, remembering. 'OK. Put a call out, get the most up-to-date stuff you can and call 'em in. I want a meet, so that we can really thrash this out properly. Just swanning around picking up stones here and there and looking under 'em isn't going to find him, for Gawd's sake.'

The two constables lifted their brows at each other in exasperation because that was exactly what everyone else had said last night when Gus had sent them all out; but that had been the way he wanted it, so that had been what they had done. To have him complaining now because they'd obeyed orders was a bit rich; but then the Guv always had been like that and probably always would be.

The sandwich and coffee arrived, together with a doughnut ('All the Danishes gone, Guv,' said the PC nervously). Gus grinned lasciviously at the doughnut which was dripping with jam and pallid with sugar.

'What a pity,' he said, sinking glittering white teeth into the sandwich and gobbling it at amazing speed. It was less than fifteen minutes later that George arrived, with a suit and shirt for him over her arm, and by that time he'd finished the food. ('One of these days you'll get an ulcer,' George said resignedly, knowing it would do no good to try to change the eating habits all his years in the Force had taught him), and had also managed to get a shower, so was wearing just his dress trousers and unbuttoned dress shirt over his damp skin.

'Yeah, I know,' he grunted as he grabbed the clothes and retreated to Inspector Dudley's office, away from the interested stare of two constables. 'But it'll be your naggin' as much as fast eatin' as'll do it.'

By the time he emerged, slick, clean, even shaven – he'd helped himself to the electric razor Dudley kept in his desk drawer – and properly dressed, the rest of the team were coming in, uniforms and CID men, all looking decidedly crumpled and exhausted. Some of them had been up all night and they looked sourly at Gus's perkiness.

'It's all right, it's all right!' he chided them. 'Once we've thrashed out what's been going on and come up with a strategy, you lot can go and get some sleep. I've got some extra people coming over from area, so we can take the heat off you a bit. I just need a bit of info on how things are going so far. There's coffee an' toast coming up from the canteen for all of you. Don't make a mess on the bleedin' floor.'

The roomful of people relaxed and settled. Gus had long had a reputation for taking good care of his men and women. He pushed them as hard as they could be pushed, but he knew when to stop and smooth them down and make them feel good, and George, sitting quietly watching him, glowed a little as she recognized, yet again, the skill of the man.

She'd never imagined she would fall so ridiculously in love with such a one: rough, noisy, fast talking, and very much a Londoner. ('I got more front than Brighton,' he used to boast to

her. ('Believe me, ducks, I know 'ow to put meself about a bit!')
But there it was. She, as deep dyed an American (though now
with a certain London gloss to her speech and style) as he was
a cockney, made him an unexpected partner.

It had happened even though she hadn't meant it to. Now
they were living together and most of the time enjoying it.
Maybe marrying wouldn't be such a bad idea at that, she found
herself thinking, and then pushed the thought away. It was a
suggestion that Gus brought up lazily from time to time, and
she knew she'd have to face it properly one day, if only because
she knew, at gut level, that both of them wanted children. But
not yet, and certainly not now. Now they had murder on their
minds. And she, George Barnabas, a forensic pathologist but by
no means a policeman, had as good an idea to throw into their
pot as any of them. And she hugged to herself her expectation
of the consternation that would be caused by what she had to
say.

'Right!' Gus called the big crowded room to order as Rupert
Dudley came in, his suit as uncreased as though he'd spent the
previous night in his bed instead of out of it in the streets. 'Let's
have a rundown on the situation. First, as a reminder to one and
all, who are we looking for?'

'David CWG,' said one of the sergeants.

'Caspar-Wynette-Gondor,' said Rupert Dudley reprovingly.

'The initials'll do or we'll be here till Easter,' Gus said and
there was an appreciative murmur of response.

'Right. David CWG, MP for Bilkley Town. Aged forty.
Labour Party. Quiet sort of chap. Neither very ambitious, nor
very lazy. An average backbencher they say,' Dudley said, a
touch stuffily, clearly feeling himself put down.

'Who says?'

Dudley grimaced. 'The Tory Chief Whip. Woman for a
start. There's a piece of holy terror and no mistake. But several
other MPs say it too, even their own Whip. Wife's a different
sort.'

'Oh?'

'A lush. Couldn't be lusher. Swears she's been dry for a month till last night, but when he didn't come home, it pushed her over the edge and she gave up trying. Now she's right out of her skull, and useless for questioning. You couldn't blame a man for skipping out on someone like that.'

'Except they've been married for fifteen years and there's never been a whisper of gossip about him and other women.' Tim Brewer put that in. 'Which doesn't give us much in the way of leads.'

'Hmm. So what have you all been doing?'

They told him, one after the other, of enquiries to all CWG's known colleagues and friends, calling them out of their beds at the crack of dawn to the irritation of many. Of visits to all his known haunts in restaurants and clubs. Of calls to his family, his barber, to *everyone*. No one knew a thing and all claimed to be worried.

'"It's not like David," they keep saying,' Tim Brewer reported. 'Everyone kept telling me what an easy-going regular sort of bloke he is.'

There was a little silence then and Gus stared up at the ceiling, his eyes half closed. 'You know what this could mean, don't you?'

A short silence and then someone at the back of the room said bravely, 'Another killing, Guv?'

'Yup,' Gus said. 'Another killing. I'm not one for going off half cocked on these things as well you all know, but there are features of the murder of Sam Diamond' – he jerked his thumb over his shoulder at the huge pinboards that had been put up with the meagre information so far collected written on them – 'that makes me think we might have a serial killer out there. One MP dead in a very fancy fashion and another missing. You can't help wondering.'

'Do we start dragging the usual bits of the river, Guv?' Dudley asked. 'We could get the river patrol at it tonight – better then, to stop a lot of fuss and comment. And there are the commons and the parks –'

'You won't find him there,' George said loudly. One or two people jumped, startled. She had been totally silent till now and they had forgotten she was present. After all, the pathologist wasn't usually part of such meetings.

'What's that?' Gus said.

'I said you won't find him in the river or on a common or a park or such a place. I think I know exactly where he'll be. And he'll be very dead. And what's more, he'll have been strangled before his throat was cut.'

There was a sudden silence, so thick it was almost a palpable weight.

'Really?' Rupert Dudley grinned at her over his shoulder without any humour, his eyes glittering. 'Quite sure, are you?'

'No,' George said. 'Not totally. But enough to say I think it's worth looking in Spitalfields. In the neighbourhood of Hanbury Street, I'd suggest.'

4

This time they showed their amazement by breaking into an excited buzz of chatter, which Gus allowed to continue as he stared at her, his face crinkled with puzzlement.

'Yer what?' he said at length. 'Why Hanbury Street? What do you know about Hanbury Street that we don't?'

She grinned at him, delighted with herself. 'Only that it's been there a long time,' she said.

'But what's that got to do with – Shut up, you lot! Christ Almighty, a man can't hear himself think! Right. That's better,' as the room quietened and they all turned to stare at George expectantly. 'Now, Dr Barnabas, will you do us the kindness of explaining?'

'A pleasure, Superintendent,' she said, amused at his attempt at formality. 'I did the PM last night, as requested, and I found some interesting things.'

Gus looked round. 'Where's Mike Urquhart? I want his report on that PM. Why didn't I get it this morning? Wasn't he attending as coroner's officer?'

'He was,' George said, 'and he made notes. But the man was out on his feet. I told him I'd report this morning for him and he could give you his written report later.'

Gus glared at her, opened his mouth to complain about her interference with his staff and then, seeing the glint in her eyes, thought better of it. 'Good of you to be so concerned about him,' he said sardonically. Someone in the room snickered and Gus glared again.

'I'll read you the rough of my notes,' George said quickly. It had been fun to get them all startled that way, Gus in particular, but now she had to be businesslike. 'Here we go. A well-nourished man – in fact, over-nourished, running to fat. Age uncertain but I'd suggest about fifty. In reasonable health, and no signs of illness. His injuries, now. The throat had been cut by about six or seven pretty savage blows from a smallish knife. Not a heavy one, but very sharp. The neck vessels and other structures were severed. The larynx in particular was severely damaged – he'd tried to get through it and then, because it resisted, had to go through the trachea. The cervical spine had been nicked by the knife in several places but had held its integrity, otherwise it was very close to a decapitation.'

'Jesus,' said someone. 'That must have been bloody painful.'

George lifted her head to see who had spoken but failed, so she said it to the room at large. 'No, not in the least. He was already dead when his throat was cut.'

'Bloody hell!' said Rupert, startled enough to speak to her directly without a sneer. 'Already dead?'

'Yes,' George said. 'He'd been manually strangled. I found the indentations of fingernails and the remains of bruising under each of the indentations. One of the indentations had been scratched, too. I've sent the specimen of skin for micro-photography, in the hope that you might eventually get a suspect and be able to match the injuries to his right hand. I got photographs in situ, as well, of course. The trouble is obviously that any suspect just has to cut his fingernails and there you go – the indentations won't be worth a dime as evidence. And, of course, no prints. Even if there had been a hint of one, which as you know is rare on skin, though not entirely impossible, it'd have been washed away by blood – and I had to remove the blood to see the skin and that would have removed such traces too. But I had to do it, of course.'

She waited for Gus to complain but he just nodded.

'The rest of the injuries, well . . .' She looked up at Gus who hesitated, thought for a moment or two and then turned to the rest of the people in the room.

'We've got some tricky business going on here,' he said. 'Only a handful of people know what I'm about to let Dr B. tell you: last night's patrol car team, and the people who came to the scene at Durward Street. And not all of them know this detail. Those that do have already been warned to keep their lips tightly buttoned, because this information absolutely *must* be kept quiet – both because it's the sort of information we're going to need to weed out the wrong suspects and the nuts who'll come rushing to confess in the usual way, but also because we don't want to start a public fuss. I just want you all to know that if a single whisper of this gets out of this room I will find out who did the whispering – and never think I couldn't – and deal with them *personally*. Is that understood?'

There was a little movement of excitement and eagerness as people looked at each other and then at Gus.

'Is that understood?' he repeated, looking from one side of the room to the other, catching the gaze of one person after the other, constables and inspectors, men and women. There was a ragged murmur of assent and after another moment Gus nodded, satisfied. 'I trust you,' he said and turned to George.

She described the rest of the injuries in the most colourless tone she could manage, trying to make it sound as normal as sunrise for a murderer to remove his victim's genitalia and arrange them neatly on the shoulder. They all listened in complete silence. Not until she finished did someone stir and mutter, 'What a way to get back at someone who screws your bird,' and there was a nervous giggle that released the tension. Gus made no effort to control the laughter, letting the wave of sound slide across the room and die of its own accord.

'A very odd case, ladies and gentlemen,' he said then with a slightly portentous air. 'A tricky problem for us. And it explains why we're so anxious about this other Member of Parliament. It's not just that he's an MP and all those buggers are vulnerable these days, it's the fact that this first murder has all the stamps of a serial killer's work. Peculiarities like this aren't part of your average domestic, after all.'

'They were for Wayne Bobbitt,' someone said and again there was laughter, but this time Gus was quick to stop it.

'Not the same thing at all,' he said. 'This man was strangled and then mutilated in a particularly gruesome fashion. So, you have to think serial. It stands to reason. Right, Dr B.? You're the pathologist, you know how these buggers' minds work.'

'I'm not a forensic psychiatrist,' George said. 'Yet. I've taken the courses, but I haven't done the exams or done much work in the field. So you'll need to get a second opinion. But for what it's worth, I agree. This looks like a serial killing with more than one bizarre feature.'

'Three,' Rupert said. 'Strangled first, and then throat cut. And then – then the other thing.'

'I can think of another,' George said. 'If you'd like to hear it. It's the one that tells me the place to look for CWG is Hanbury Street.'

'Let's have it then.' Gus went and perched on the edge of one of the desks so that he could swing his legs. He seemed more relaxed now, and she knew why. His entire team was hanging on to every word uttered; and that was the way he liked them. The more interesting they found a case, the harder and better they'd work.

'I was thinking as I finished up the PM that I'd heard of a similar sort of action before. The removal of genitals and the displaying of them on the shoulder, that is. Another serial killer, and one that caused a lot of excitement. He didn't always remove the genitalia, mind you, but that was harder for him, seeing his victims were women –'

'Blimey!' someone said from the back of the room. 'I know who you mean!'

George glanced up and saw the look on the face of a young woman police constable who was sitting well to the back. She was in uniform, and her face went pink as she realized that George had identified her.

'Well?' George said.

The girl mumbled and went pinker than ever. 'I – I don't know, of course,' she managed. 'I was just sort of guessing.'

'It's all anyone's doing at this stage.' George was encouraging. 'I'd be more grateful to hear what you think. If it matches my idea, then I'll feel more – well, I'd like a match. So, who did that make you think of?'

'It sounds so silly,' the girl said. 'Now I think of it, I mean. Melodrama and all that.'

'No,' George said, greatly encouraged herself. 'Come on, lady, spit it out. Don't be afraid of this bunch of guys here. No need to apologize for having an imagination.'

'Oh, dear,' the girl said miserably. 'I suppose – well, I thought, Jack the Ripper.'

There was a guffaw from a couple of the men standing near her, but George jumped to her feet. 'No joke, fellas. Because I thought exactly the same thing, and wondered if I was being stupid. But I'm not so sure we are, as you'll see. Uh, what's your name?'

'WPC Julie Bentley, ma'am,' the girl said.

'Right, Julie, let's look at the facts.' George almost ran across the room to the big pinboard which had fastened to it a map of the area, with a pin with a red flag on it attached to a point over to the right of the area covered, just above a major road.

'Look, this is where Sam Diamond was found,' she said. 'Durward Street, just behind Whitechapel Station. OK. I have here a map of this same area when the Ripper was at work. It's dated 1862 and the murders happened in the late 1880s, but I don't imagine the street had changed that much in the twenty odd years.'

She held up a small paperbacked book. 'I read this a little while ago. It's by a chap called Bruce Paley and he's got a great theory about who the Ripper was. Not that that's what we're concerned with, of course. But it's well researched, and believe me, it really made me think. Look, the first Jack the Ripper murder, the first one they were sure was his, that is, happened here.' She produced the map illustration in her book. 'Just where –'

34

'Can we get that blown up so we can all see it?' Gus demanded. 'How long would it take?'

'I can fix it, but it'll take a while,' Dudley said. He reached for the book.

'Let me explain first,' George said. 'And then of course you can have it. It's your book anyway, Gus – Guv.' She looked at Gus over her shoulder. 'I, um, borrowed it. You remember, you bought it after we saw that TV programme about the case.'

The people in the room, all of whom were in on the open secret that Gus and George lived together, grinned at each other, delighted with the Guv's discomfiture, but George rattled on. 'OK,' she said. 'Here it is. You'll have to take my word for it till the map's been enlarged for you. I can tell you that the first murder happened on a street called Bucks Row which was just north of Whitechapel Station. Bombed, I guess, or just pulled down. There's been a lot of building round there, with the new supermarket and stuff. Anyway, as best as I can tell the body was found where Bucks Row used to be. Isn't that too much of a coincidence? The appalling neck injuries. The genitalia removed and arranged on the shoulder the way the Ripper did – and in the same street or as near as dammit. That's why I think you ought to look for CWG around Hanbury Street, up near the old fruit and vegetable market, because that was where the Ripper's second victim was found. If I'm right and you find him there, it means we've got a copycat murderer who is more than a hundred years out of date.'

Again there was a silence and then Julie, clearly emboldened by her previous efforts said, 'But the Ripper killed women. Prostitutes. This is a man. So's the missing one. And they're both MPs.'

'Some people regard them as prostitutes,' Tim Brewer said thoughtfully and a great shout of laughter went up in which even Rupert Dudley joined.

Gus grinned widely. 'You've got a point,' he said. 'Dr B., doesn't that push your theory in the mud?'

'It could,' George said readily. 'Of course it could. I wouldn't dream of saying I was right for sure until we had another victim.

But if we do, and it's where I said it would be, well then, we'll have to consider it possible, won't we?'

The speed with which the search was reorganized and recommenced was remarkable. George sat in the big incident room as the briefing was given, listening to Rupert Dudley giving detailed instructions about who should go where and how they should comb the area, enjoying the crisp efficiency and much impressed by Dudley though she would not have let him know it for the world. Gus had left this straightforward chore to him, while he himself went to report back to the Commissioner, who was taking a great deal of interest in what was going on. And even Gus had to admit that it was natural he should. 'It isn't every day,' he said dryly as he went to find a quiet phone, 'that you get someone stalking members of Her Majesty's bloody Government.'

George agreed, and after a while found she was listening with only half her mind while considering with the others just why someone should want to kill MPs. Was this killer – if she wasn't running ahead of herself and there really was someone after MPs in general and not just Sam Diamond in particular – why would anyone have it in for such people? That they were among the most despised members of the community in these cynical days, George was well aware; it had been a long time since nations had offered deference and respect to those elected to govern a country. But that was a hell of a long way from setting out systematically to kill them.

Stop it, she told herself. You're jumping to absurd conclusions. There's no reason yet to suppose this is more than a one-off killing. And yet –

'Inspector Dudley,' she said as the last group to have been given their instructions began to leave the room. 'May I come along too?'

He looked at her dispassionately. 'What for?'

'Well, if I'm right and you do find him and he's dead you'll have to send for me anyway. If I'm already there you'll save time.'

'And if you're wrong,' he pointed it out wearily, as if speaking to a fractious nagging child, 'you'll just be in the way. As long as you've got your bleep switched on, as it should be, I can get you if I need you.'

'All the same,' she said, biting back the angry retort she ached to make. 'I'd like to be there.'

'No doubt,' he said and turned to leave himself. 'No doubt,' and went.

She was furious. To be treated in such a fashion by one of Gus's junior people – it was no wonder she hated him so. The man was a sonofabitch and always would be. And she'd be damned if she listened to anything he ever had to say, ever. He didn't want her there? Tough. She'd be there, and what was more, she told herself as she pulled on her coat and headed for the door after him, I'll go in a Goddamn police car, the way I've every right to.

She hadn't, of course. If they wanted to give her a lift some place, then they could, and she'd say thank you, but she couldn't precisely open a police car door and say, 'I'm coming with you.' Not as a *right*.

But that was precisely what she did. Dudley had stopped in the corridor to speak to someone and she shot past him and down the stairs as though King Kong was after her, reaching the station yard as the last two cars headed for the big gates. She sprinted after them and managed to get close enough to the second to thump on the back window.

The car stopped, and a uniformed head poked out of the front window. 'What the f – Oh, it's you, Dr B.'

'Yeah,' she gasped, not needing to act too much. She wasn't as fit as she might be these days. 'I'm coming with you. Roop said that –' And she left it there.

The policeman got out of the car, and opened the back door for her. 'It's a pleasure, Dr B.,' he said courteously. 'Even if Roop hadn't said so.' And she clambered in as quickly as she could, in case Dudley appeared in the yard himself, saw her and hauled her out ignominiously. She was just in time. As the car left the yard and curved away to the left towards Spitalfields she got a glimpse of Dudley at the entrance to the nick, beyond the netted area and slid down a little in her seat. She'd show the bastard!

The car she was in was clearly a police car, complete with blue light though that was not in use at present, and she was very aware of the way traffic on the road made way for it with exaggerated courtesy; and was amused at the way the pair in front enjoyed their superiority. Men and cars, she thought. Babies, every one of them.

But it was only when they reached Commercial Street, passing the huddles of Bengali and Bangladashi people on the pavements and the glittering sari shops and exotic grocery stores with their heaps of vegetables and herbs outside, where women with covered heads and white shawls dickered with shopkeepers in the floppy pyjama suits that were the commonest male attire in these parts, that she realized just how many cars there were on the search. They passed two that looked like private vehicles and then recognized the occupants; it was as though, she thought, a cloud of exploring locusts had descended on the scene.

The radio spluttered in the front and came to busy life. 'Alpha Tango Three, take Brick Lane from Hanbury to Fashion Streets on the eastern side, repeat Brick Lane, Hanbury to Fashion Streets.' And the driver snorted as his colleague responded. 'On way!' into the set. 'Where the bloody hell do they think we're goin'? We've been told once, how often do they have to repeat it for every radio ham to pick up?'

His partner, a more placid person, clearly, was soothing. 'Oh, the bods stuck there in Control need to feel they're being useful, I s'pose. OK. Right here. That's it. Hanbury Street.'

Eagerly George leaned forwards to stare out of the window. It didn't look any different from any other East End street. Here and there the remains of the old buildings, but mostly fill-ins, put up after the Blitz which had battered this part of London most comprehensively. The same sort of people filled the pavements, and everywhere there was bustle and colour. Under normal circumstances George would have revelled in it, but now she was concentrating on looking for alleys or hidden corners where, just possibly, a body might lie unseen.

The driver of the car she was in parked at the top of Hanbury Street where it met Brick Lane. 'We'll start here, on foot,' he said. 'You want to come with us? Or stay here? Up to you, Dr B.'

She hesitated. She'd rather search on her own, to be honest, but they had the radios on them. If she didn't stay with them she wouldn't know what was going on. She scrambled out of the car to join them.

'I'll search too,' she said and fell into step with them as they began to walk along the pavement of Brick Lane. The people they passed watched them with suspicious anxious stares and pulled back to let them pass by. The dislike they showed was so clear that she almost wanted to shout, 'It's all right, I'm not a policeman. I'm just ordinary, like you.' Which was stupid because of course she was with the police and she was, in the watcher's world, far from ordinary.

The search was long and detailed. It was a muggy day, with rain in the air and the moisture seemed to concentrate the spicy scents around them of turmeric and chilli, coriander and cumin, for it was getting close to lunchtime and the little restaurants that spattered the street were all busy. She began to feel a little hungry herself. She hadn't thought of eating breakfast.

Her spirits slowly sank. The two policemen didn't seem to miss anything. They looked under each car that was parked, peered into their interiors, walked through shops to their back premises, pushing aside crates and sacks of stock as their owners watched sullenly, not protesting but sending out waves of loathing, and then moved on to the next few square yards to start all over again. It was laborious and very boring, and George wished for one brief moment that she had heeded Roop and waited at the nick for a call. If a call was to come.

She had come to the conclusion that there never would have been a call and that she was totally, wildly wrong.

She was aware that there were other policemen too, on the western side of the street, making the same scrupulous searches and she watched them out of the corner of her eye, hoping they'd come up with something if her own pair of searchers didn't.

But they went doggedly on getting nowhere except near to the end of their allotted area of search and she plodded on behind them, feeling more and more miserable. Oh, but Roop would enjoy this! She'd come up with a suggestion that had tied up most of the shift on duty at Ratcliffe Street, both uniformed and CID, for hours and got absolutely zilch. He'd crow over her; oh, how he'd crow!

And then the radio on the shoulder of the policeman in front of her rattled into life and she heard the voice, tinny and husky at the same time. 'All units, all units, return to base, return to base, except Alpha Tango Three, Alpha Tango Seven and Alpha Tango Eight. Three, Seven and Eight, to Greatorex Street, between Chicksand and Hanbury Streets on the western side, repeat western side. All other units return to base.'

'Which are we?' George cried, pulling on the sleeve of one of the policemen. He grinned back at her.

'It's all right, Dr B. You can go to the party. We're Tango Three.'

5

The Palace of Westminster was always a maelstrom with messengers rushing about as though they were carrying the fates of nations in their hands rather than gossipy notes about dinner dates, and people standing with their heads together looking deeply portentous as though they too were dealing with matters of vast importance rather than exchanging a little agreeable malice about other people's peccadilloes. But this afternoon was different. Now the people talking together looked avid rather than full of their own importance and the messengers were almost frantic in their speed. This was a real situation, a real anxiety, a real drama of much greater interest than the latest bêtise from Brussels or threats from cash-strapped NHS administrators to blow the whistle on the machinations of the Department of Health.

In the Government Chief Whip's office there was an emergency meeting going on. The coffee was flowing and the people sitting around Mary Bodling's desk looked edgy and excited, but not as despondent as they had been at a previous meeting, held immediately after they had received the news of the discovery of Sam Diamond's body. Then they had been both anxious about what might be revealed about Sam Diamond (more about that than about what had happened to the man, and why, to be truthful) and licking their political wounds, wondering just what the hell they'd have to do to hold on to their paper-thin majority when they were yet another Member down, and considering what bribes could be offered to individual Lib-Dems to keep their Government afloat. Now that threat had retreated with the loss of a Labour member, they could indulge themselves in a little gossip.

'I'd never have imagined David Gondor going in for hanky-panky,' said Henry Bowler, who had opted to handle his passing-over for the Chief Whip's post in favour of Mary by being thoroughly sycophantic towards her. 'Would you, Mary?'

'I never think anything's impossible for anyone,' Mary snapped. 'The more virtuous they look, the more likely they are to be covering up something.'

'You're right, of course,' Henry said.

Steven Wittering, who was a shade more robust than Henry but still liable to give in to Mary's whims without too much pressure, shook his head. 'Mostly I'd agree with you, but Caspar-Wynette-Gondor? The worst kind of Socialist, he was. Committed idealist woolly liberals and parlour pinks, I can handle – we've got enough of 'em in our lot, going around with permanent puddles round their feet, they're so wet. But Caspar-Thingummy-Whatsit wasn't like that. He was so passionate about his political balls that I doubt he knew what the real ones were for. So I think Henry's right. A sexy Caspar-Wynette-Gondor is an oxymoron. They'll find no reason for his ending up as butcher's meat in *that* department.'

'Which only goes to show how little you understand human nature,' Mary said. 'The more passionate they are, and the more adrenaline they get going on the floor of the House, the more they've got left over to get their testosterone up. Believe me, I *know*.'

Henry, contemplating the formidable Mary in a situation in which she might obtain definitive knowledge of the effects of testosterone on anyone at all, managed not to look at Steven, who was, he knew, thinking the same thing. 'Do we know much about his background?'

Steven, whose job it was to monitor the private lives of Labour Party members, on the grounds, as Mary always said, that you never knew when you mightn't need a bit of mud to oil the wheels (she was rather given to mixed metaphors), leaned back in his chair and stared at the ceiling. 'Bit of a maverick. Not really popular with the nuts and bolts of his party, who still don't feel really comfortable with toffs. They're finding it hard enough to cope with the Islington brigade of intellectuals. David double hyphens really give 'em heartburn.'

'What sort of toff?' Henry, very aware of his status as the son of a family of old-fashioned County gentry, who liked to believe he was regarded in his village in deepest Devon as 'the Squire', was ready to scoff. 'Some sort of pickle factory heir?'

'I'd have thought *you'd* know all about him.' Steven was amused. 'I had the impression you'd swallowed Debrett at an early age. No, not a hint of pickle in his blood. Dead blue, it was. He's the Earl of Durleigh's younger brother. Surely you've heard about him? There was an uproar when he joined the Labour Party, just after leaving school. He refused to go to university, went and did a course in bricklaying and plumbing or something of the sort. I told you: one of those passionate socialists.'

Henry was pink with mortification. Not to have known all about a fellow Member of the House – how could he have missed him, knowing as much as he did about the country's peerage? He spluttered something which implied as much, and Steven was kind.

'Don't be embarrassed, old boy. He's played his cards very close to his chest since he got here. I wouldn't have known about him if I hadn't gone hunting it all out for Mary. He worked on building sites for years, while being an active member of his local Labour Party branch – fell short of anything more intense, though it's my guess he'd have been happier with one of the more lefty set-ups. Anyway, a couple of years ago, when you were off sick, remember?' – Henry had managed to break both of his legs skiing, which hadn't endeared him to Mary at the time, but had made his Labour pair very happy indeed –' there was a by-election at Bilkley Town, as safe a Labour seat as you could find in the country and David Thingy-Whatsit got himself selected in spite of Walworth Road pushing for one of their harridans in red nails and shoulder pads, and got in with a slightly increased majority. Not at our expense, happily, the Lib-Dems. And he's kept a low profile ever since. The only things he's done, let me see . . .' He went over to his desk to punch a few keys on his computer. 'Yeah, I thought I remembered it right. He's on the Select Committee looking at the Right to Inheritance Bill. And one of those Committees on building regulations. Works hard in his constituency, too. On the personal side' – more keys were punched – 'nothing really, except for a boozy wife.'

'Oh?' Mary's ears pricked up. She had been sitting with her elbows plonked on her desk, her coffee cup between her hands, thinking her own thoughts rather than listening to her juniors. Now she became alert. 'What was that?'

'Marietta. They've been married fifteen years. No children – ah! Several miscarriages, I have here. Anyway, she's a lush and has been for years.'

'So,' Mary said. 'He must have been wandering after all. And it could be that's why –'

Steven shook his head, still peering at his screen. 'I don't think so. All the signs are he's – was – a devoted carer, stays home to be with her whenever he can. According to my sources' – he smirked a little at that; how many Tories had Labour sources as good as his? None, he rather fancied – 'that's one of the reasons he's been so low profile. He didn't want any job that took him away from his Marietta too long.'

'Marietta! What a name,' Henry said, whose own wife was plain Jane, as befitted the daughter of a baronet, and whose children were William and Emma. Highly suitable. Anything fancier smacked of the gutter to him. 'Some show girl or other, I suppose?'

Steven grinned and switched off the computer. 'Sorry to disappoint you there, old duck. She was a bit of a toff in her own right. Father owned great chunks of Yorkshire. Her brother's got it now, of course, and she got barely fourpence and she's drunk most of that. So there you go. One thing's sure. There's no link with our Sam, thank God. That was the possibility that bothered me.'

'How could there be a link?' Henry said, and Mary looked at him witheringly.

'Very easily,' she said. 'Remember the business of the Gravesend pub?'

Henry reddened. He had indeed forgotten the fuss a while ago when several MPs from both major parties and even one Lib-Dem had been rounded up after a fight in a pub, which turned out to be a well-known gay S and M venue. 'Well, all the same,' he said, blustering a little, 'you'll grant that there doesn't seem to be any link between this fella and poor old Sam of that kind or any other. So we can relax a little. Both sides have to have a by-election and –'

'And going by the polls those bastards could win both of 'em,' Mary said brutally. 'Central Office'll have to put a bit of a bomb behind the constituencies if we're not to be in major trouble. At least we know there's nothing anyone can dig out about Sam. I've checked every inch of him, too.'

'And his wife?' Steven said, and Mary cast him a sharp glance.

'What have you heard?' she demanded.

'Oh, nothing concrete,' Steven said hastily. 'It's just that she – Well, you know, Mary! Looking the way she does, and dealing with the sort of gear she does, I've heard a good many of her customers are – umm . . .'

Henry leaned forwards, avid again. 'Mmm?'

'*Poules de luxe*, they used to be called.' Steven giggled. 'Upper-class tarts, ducky. They're expensive and they spend a lot. I gather Alice does a very nice business with them.'

'Shit!' Mary exploded. 'I told her a year ago that wasn't on! Warned her the effect it might have on Sam's reputation. And she's still at it?'

Steven shrugged. 'I don't know for sure. It's just that everyone knows that if you want something a bit cheeky for your wife – a birthday or whatever, you know – Alice does a nice line in scanties. And it's better than our people going into Soho shops or those Ann Summers-type places.'

'Steven, I've told you before, it's facts we need, not surmise.

But just in case, you'd better put it about I don't want our people buying stuff like that. Scanties? Ye Gods, do people still call 'em that? Anyway, it's got to stop. They're to keep well away from her. It's the sort of thing the *Sun* would make hay with. The buggers are already camping outside to pounce on anyone who comes in or out and the phone has been jammed with bloody journalists ever since Sam was found. All we need is a titbit like the stock in Alice's shop, and there'll be no controlling them. So, see to it. And, Henry, keep an ear to the police, will you? I want to know every step of their investigation. Move both of you. I've got work to do.'

They went. You didn't hang around when Mary had given an order.

'Well, what are they saying, you lot?' Colin Twiley sat on the edge of his desk, staring around at his inner sanctum team: Marcus Napper, slumped in a chair in the corner, looking half asleep; Bryan Naith, sitting as usual slightly aloof, with his hands shoved deeply into his jacket pockets, looking like a walking slum, according to Molly Nidd, who was sitting on the other side of him, herself pin-neat, though her skirt was very short and showed a certain excess of black-tighted leg, and her make-up was just a touch over-emphasized. The fact that these two loathed each other showed in every inch of their postures, each glowering at the other – with elbows, shoulders, even knees. Beyond Molly, Sean Burnell, all six feet six of him, tried to look comfortable and at ease in such august company and only succeeded in looking what he was, awkward and still rather young to be there. No one could argue about the quality of Sean's mind; the boy could be brilliant. The trouble was, that brilliance tended to get him involved with people he couldn't handle, as now. Left alone at his desk, Sean was a treasure; in meetings like this, he was completely useless. So Colin didn't even look at him as he repeated his question, turning his gaze from one to the other of the trio.

'Steven Wittering's been trying to dig dirt about David, of course,' Molly said. 'It's what he does best, that one. But they're all a lot more relaxed now their chap Diamond's got a pair, as it were. I don't think the police have talked to them yet.'

Colin looked hopeful. 'Why should they want to talk to them? Do they think one of their people –'

Molly shook her head. 'I don't know! What I mean is, the police are sure to want to talk to them, aren't they? Just as they'll want to talk to us. About David's friends, about contacts who might be an enemy, all that stuff. I'm just a bit surprised they haven't talked to the other lot yet. Their man was clobbered before ours, after all.'

'Perhaps they're trying to save money,' Marcus said and began to scrabble in his pockets for a cigarette. 'Wait till all the victims are in and then do the interviews in one fell swoop.'

'Don't be stupid, man,' Bryan growled. 'They can't know there'll be another coming along, can they?'

Marcus looked up at him over the flame of the match he'd just struck. 'Oh, dear!' he said mildly. 'Are my irony glands overacting again? Sorry. Though I must say, it did occur to me that this could be one of those serial bods on the prowl. Another Sutcliffe, you know.'

Molly stared at him. 'Jesus Christ! D'you really think so?'

'I didn't till poor old David got it. But then – I mean, dammit all, Molly, use your intelligence! Cut throats, two MPs – who knows what's in the man's mind? He has to be barking mad. Mad enough to be a serial killer.'

'Yes,' Sean said suddenly. 'That was what occurred to me.' He went scarlet as they all turned and looked at him. 'I – er – well, it was a bit – I checked, you know? Throats cut, and something else, I think. I couldn't get anyone to say, but something else happened. I'm sure of it. We'll find out eventually but they're not talking yet.'

'Who aren't?' Colin said.

'The police,' Sean said simply. 'I went over to the station where they're doing the investigation – Ratcliffe Street was the nearest to where they found Diamond's body, so I thought, that'll be the place, and I made out I was a journalist. I just held a dictating machine in my hand. I didn't actually tell any lies' –

he looked very earnest suddenly – 'I just held out the machine and asked questions and they assumed ... And I got the impression ...' He faltered miserably to a close.

'More killings?' Colin said. 'Members?'

'Could be.' Marcus sounded judicious, as though he were discussing a matter that had no personal impact at all. 'It's an interesting idea, putting MPs in the firing line.'

'You might be at the front of the queue, when whoever it is decides to get going again,' Bryan said with a certain relish in his voice. 'So what are you so cheerful about?'

'Aha, we're forearmed, Naith, old boy,' Marcus grinned. 'From here on in, I go nowhere on my own, I keep well away from geezers with knives or who look as though they might be carrying 'em – so don't ask me out for a drink, will you? You could have God knows what stowed in those pockets of yours – and altogether I shall stay firmly in the places where the light is brightest. You'll do the same if you've any sense.'

Molly giggled, enjoying the spectacle of someone else being rude to Naith. 'You needn't worry, Bryan,' she said with a sunny air. 'He'll only go for people with necks they can get at.' She looked pointedly at the tight frayed shirt collar round Bryan's neck, which was circled with tyres of thick fat. 'It'd take the guy half a night to carve through your windpipe, so you're safe as houses. Sean, here, now' – looking over her shoulder winsomely at the thin young man – 'a big Adam's apple like his is a walking invitation, isn't it? I think he should stick with Marcus, to be on the safe side, really I do.'

'Oh, for heaven's sake!' Colin decided it was time to behave like a Chief Whip. He was well aware of the fact that in the House bars and dining rooms they bracketed him with Mary Bodling, calling them the Elephant and the Mouse, and he was trying hard to be bigger and stronger. (He'd foolishly said as much to Marcus Napper, who had looked at him owlishly and said, 'Be careful, old man. You might just turn into a rat.') Now he got to his feet and stood with his legs apart and his arms folded to increase his gravitas. 'We've got better things to do than sit here making bad-taste jokes about murderers. David was a good friend of mine and it's disgusting to hear you all being so –'

'Put it down to nerves, old man,' Marcus murmured. 'Like medical students, you know. The only way we can handle the horror is making disgusting jokes. I was very fond of David too, but it doesn't help to go around weeping and wailing and gnashing the old teeth, does it?'

'What we have to talk about,' Colin said, refusing even to look at Marcus, 'is our representation on the Committee for the Right to Inheritance Bill. It's the first step to reorganizing the Other Place and the Leader wants it done our way and done fast. David was worth his weight in gold on it: we'll miss him dreadfully. Oh, shit!' And he made a sharp sound, half sigh, half hiss. 'Well, any ideas?'

'I'll take it,' Marcus said. 'I know a lot about it, and I know how David felt. I can carry his baton for him. Glad to do it. And I wasn't making light of his killing, Colin, believe me. Just – I mean, Mattie phoned us that night, remember? The girls are each other's best friends. Susan looked after Marietta from time to time. Well, you'd expect that, wouldn't you? So . . .'

Colin looked dubious and bit his lower lip, staring at Marcus. 'Well,' he said. 'It's up to Walworth Road, of course, more than it is to me. I'll see what they say. And other names will have to be put forward. Don't hold your breath on this one. And then he was on the Building Materials Committee as well. And the one on the Employment of Casual Labour on Building Sites.'

'Richard Fallon has done a lot of good stuff in that area, I think. We could put him up. Or how about that chap who used to be with the cement people – what's his name? Garton? D'you reckon to him at all?'

They settled to sensible discussion at last, and were all into their arguments – because they could never meet without arguing – when the door opened and a secretary put her head round. She was alight with excitement, and almost hissed at Colin, 'Mr Twiley, there's a Detective Inspector Dudley and a Sergeant Urquhart from Ratcliffe Street police station here to talk to you, and I can tell you they've sent some other policemen along to

49

the Chief Whip's office for the other lot. Is it true what they're saying happened to poor Mr Caspar-Wynette-Gondor? Did he really have his throat cut from ear to ear like Mr Diamond did? I mean, it's very worrying, isn't it? It could be anyone of you next, couldn't it?' And she held the door open as the two policemen came in.

6

The four policemen met as arranged, in the lobby leading to the St Stephen's entrance of the House, to compare notes. They could have gone back to Ratcliffe Street separately, but as Gus said when Inspector Dudley pointed that out, 'As soon as we get back we'll get bogged down in what they've all been doing. And I want us all to get a proper debriefing before we do that. So, we'll wait. In fact, we'll have some lunch. How's about that? See what we can get in the seat of Government.'

In the event, they had to go out of the building to find a pub; it was made very clear to Gus when he talked to the constable on duty in the main lobby that access to the dining rooms was controlled by the Members, and not very generously at that.

'You've got to be a guest of one of 'em, Super,' the constable said. 'They have to sign you in and all that, and they don't really like doing it. But I wouldn't bother if I was you, really I wouldn't. It's like school dinners without the taste.'

'You've eaten in one of the dining rooms then?'

'No, sir. Only in the staff canteen, down in the bowels, like. Now I bring sandwiches. I've just been told about it – often.'

'Thanks for the warning,' Gus said and stared around the lobby with its knots of people looking rather small and incongruous among all the green and red and gold pseudo-medievalism Charles Barry had inflicted on London a hundred and fifty or so years ago. Odd to think that when the first Ripper murders happened, this place had only been here forty years or so. The

Ripper might even have seen it all being built. And now Ripper murders might be happening again.

He gave himself a small shake and pushed the notion away. The fact that George had made a strong case for the connection didn't mean it was true, any more than the fact that he had felt a genuine frisson of horror when they'd found David Caspar-Wynette-Gondor's body. The slit throat, the mutilation above the legs which had been spread wide with such an air of sexual mockery had made him feel like the most raw of rookies: sick and even frightened. Who could do such a thing? But he could not, must not think in that unprofessional way. He was a copper with a job to do. He had to find out all he could about the people involved with each victim without making any premature judgements about who might have killed them. The basic rules of detection had to be followed; conclusion-jumping was a futile exercise. He looked at his watch, chafing as he waited for Inspector Dudley and his sergeant to appear.

'They won't be long, I don't suppose,' Mike said soothingly. 'I think they had more people to talk to than we did. I've been told they have a lot more bodies in the Whip's office on the Government side than on the Opposition's. What did you think of them, Guv?'

'Not sure.' Gus sat on the bench that ran right round the lobby and rested his head back against the wall, letting his gaze move across the ornate ceiling as he talked. 'They seemed straight enough. Admitted they were as worried about the politics of the killings as the personal aspects. Didn't seem to be hiding anything. Answered the questions easily enough. What do you think?'

'I wasn't sure about that bloke Napper. I think he knew more than he was letting on.'

'Really? Why?'

'Well . . .' Mike hesitated. 'He was a bit too jokey. Flip. Didn't seem to take it seriously. Twiley was genuinely upset, I thought, as was the woman. But Napper was too offhand.'

'And the others. Naith? What about him?'

Mike looked disgusted. 'What a slob! How do people like that get to be in Government? Looks like he hardly ever washes, for a start, and gave us barely more than a grunt when we talked to him. Not my idea of what a Member of Parliament should be.'

'Did you feel the same about the young one? Burnell?'

Mike's face cleared. 'Oh, aye, he was well enough. Young, you know, and a bit scared of the older ones, but a bright lad. I'd vote for him if he was a candidate. Of course he's just a research assistant right now. But it's my guess he'll go further. And he'll do well. He felt honest . . .'

Gus laughed. 'Oh, Mike, Mike, what an innocent abroad you can be in spite of all your experience! An honest politician? It can't be!'

Mike flushed. 'Ye might as well say there aren't any straight coppers, Guv,' he said stiffly. 'And that's no true, as ye well know.' Mike always got more Scottish when he was annoyed and Gus patted his knee in a cheerful manner and grinned at him.

'I stand rebuked. Ah, here they are, and about time too. Have they told you their life stories, then, Roop?'

Dudley scowled. 'It was like pulling bloody teeth out of hens to get anything from them. They came on like villains off the estates; wouldn't say a word if they could help it and wanted to get their legal wallahs in before they talked. I ask you. Just for preliminary enquiries!'

'They say being in Government makes you paranoid,' Gus said. 'Look, let's get the hell outa here. I need a beer and a sandwich. We'll find a pub.'

Once they were settled with lager and ham sandwiches in a dingy smoke-scented saloon bar ten minutes' walk away, they compared notes. In spite of taking longer over his questioning, Dudley had least to report. 'The Chief Whip, Mary Bodling – she'd put the fear of God up the Angel Gabriel, I can tell you – did most of the talking. OK. Diamond had been a Member of Parliament since the 1983 election, coming in after local government and Conservative Party business for donkey's years. One of the pillars of the Party, to listen to her, though I got the impression she's not so keen on his wife. We'll go to see her as soon as she gets back. She's been in Italy and she's flying home today. Runs a shop in Sloane Street, by the way. Wouldn't be caught dead in the constituency if she could help it.'

'Which is?'

'Hedgington South, the other side of Dorset. There's an adult son, who lives and works in Australia, so he's right out of the frame, like the wife.'

Gus grinned. 'Don't tell me you thought this could be a nice domestic murder, Roop?'

Dudley looked down his nose. 'I don't exclude anything till I have all the facts,' he said stiffly. 'The fact is that most murders are committed by members of the family or other close contacts and –'

'Yeah, yeah, I know,' Gus said. 'And you're right, of course. What about the close friends, then?'

'They were vague. I got the feeling that in politics people don't have friends as much as allies. They shift around all the time, depending on what the issues are.'

'And what issues was Diamond involved in?'

'Well, Brussels. He was a devout anti-European,' Dudley replied, and then added unexpectedly, 'He'd have got my vote on that issue.'

'Really?' Gus looked amused. 'I didn't have you down as a Little Englander, Roop. I didn't think you were into politics at all, come to that.'

'I'm not a Little anything and I'm not all that much interested in politics. It's just that when some jumped-up idiots in there' – he jerked his head in the general direction of the Houses of Parliament – 'do things that muck up the way I live, I don't like it. It was bad enough when they changed our money to make us fit in with Europe, instead of making Europe fit in with us, and charged us a packet for the privilege. Now they're trying to turn us into an offshore island of some European United States. Bloody Germans!'

Gus blinked at the illogicality. 'Well, I see what you mean. I think. Maybe we'd better not talk about anything but the case, eh? I wouldn't like to fall out over such things with you, me old mate. So, carry on. He was a Euro-sceptic, then. Anything else interesting? Any campaigning?'

'I got the impression he was more a reactor than a bloke who started things,' Dudley said. 'Let me see.' He riffled the pages of his notebook. 'I've got the list here. He was a member of the committee looking at the new Bill to do with inheritance.'

'Was he, by God?' Gus said, a little startled. 'Interesting, as you'll see. Anything else?'

'Yes.' Dudley looked at him sharply. 'Why the surprise?'

'I'll explain later. Go on.'

Dudley returned to his notebook. 'He was also involved with an investigation of some sort into building regulations. Also the NHS. There's a Select Committee looking at the way drugs are brought in from Europe and he was very active on that. For the rest . . . nothing special. They were all surprised he missed the vote the night he was killed because he was usually reliable. That Mary Bodling still looked pissed off, as though she didn't think being murdered was much of an excuse for such behaviour.'

Gus laughed. It wasn't often that Dudley managed to be funny, and Dudley was pleased with his reaction. For a moment he looked agreeable, which was very far from his normal expression, and that seemed to affect the whole group. Both the sergeants relaxed and Gus lifted a hand to order some more beer and another round of sandwiches.

'Right,' he said quietly when they had been served and left alone by the hovering barman who was far too interested in their conversation. 'Let Mike give you the rundown on our chappie, David of the fancy names. Go for it, Mike.'

Mike went for it. 'David Caspar-Wynette-Gondor,' he read from his notebook. 'Aged forty. Brother of the Earl of Durleigh –'

'Blimey,' Tim said. 'Shouldn't he have been in the House of Lords, then?'

Mike looked at him scornfully. 'He's not the Earl. His *dad* was, and now his brother is, so he's the House of Lords Member, of course. I've got quite a bit about his family. David was the youngest. There are two older brothers, twins. One of them of course is the Earl. He sits regularly in the Lords, unlike some of 'em who turn up for tea and a bun and the few quid they get for attending and then beetle off before there's any voting. The Earl's a true-blue Tory. Very high Tory, in fact. Goes in for the huntin' shootin' fishin' bit. Strong supporter of blood sports altogether. He and our CWG were poles apart. David joined the Labour Party very young, refused to go to Oxford like his brothers, learned to be a brickie instead and worked on building sites and so forth. Active in the Union, a hunt sab. at weekends – once even interfered with his brother's hunt – *he's* an MFH of course. I mean, he would be, wouldn't he? The brother, that is. Our chap married one of his own sort though. Well, not entirely his own sort though she'd been a friend from childhood on. Not one of your landed gentry from time immemorial. His brother-in-law sits in the Lords too. He inherited his Lordship a few years ago, but his dad was the first Lord Hinckley. He made money out of engines, apparently, and was very Tory, but this Lord sits as a Lib-Dem. He likes to attend sometimes, not as often as the Earl, but oftener than some. It's funny really. The whole political scene is like one family.'

'Well, that could point to a common-or-garden sort of murder, then,' Dudley said. 'With everyone at everyone else's throat.'

Gus shook his head. 'No it doesn't, Roop. We asked about that. It seems they're all on very good terms in spite of politics. David and his wife didn't see a lot of her brother, but only because she doesn't want to. It seems her father owned a lot of Yorkshire but he had strong views on being landed gentry. He left all the land to his son, and the big house and most of the cash on the grounds apparently that he believed a woman ought to marry her money, so he left her just a bit. She's drunk most of it, according to the cove in that Whip's office. David got on well enough with Hinckley, his brother-in-law, and apparently was as close as he could be to his own brothers. The three of them, according to Marcus Napper – he says he knows so much because his wife was a friend of CWG's wife – he says the three are, or were, rather, close mates. They never let politics come between them. We'll have to talk to the wife of course, but apparently she's been knocked for six by losing her David. She's been checked into a drying-out clinic over in Harrow. I'll see if I can talk to her tomorrow, though it'll depend on her state, of course. I'll check with her doctor before I go. For the rest, well, there isn't a lot. CWG was active on the Building Materials Select Committee –'

'What?' Dudley said and sat up very straight. 'The same as my bloke?'

'That's not all,' Gus said with satisfaction. 'He was also involved with the Right to Inheritance Bill, which is apparently being used as a lever to reform the House of Lords, if they can get it through. The Labour Party are very keen on it, and none keener than our David. It started out as a Tory Bill, of course, designed to strengthen the Lords, but the Labour people on the Committee have been making a hell of a running on it.'

'Well,' Dudley said. 'That *is* interesting.'

'Just what we thought when I heard your bloke matched our bloke,' Gus said. 'We're going to have to do a bit more digging around in political waters, Roop, whether you like it or not.'

'I want to start with the families,' Dudley said, his chin up. 'And do me a favour, Guv, and drop the Roop, will you? It's setting my teeth on edge.'

'Sorry,' Gus said. 'And after that?'

'We'll see where that leads us,' Dudley said, still obstinate. 'I want to talk to the son in Australia. The fact that he isn't here doesn't mean to say he mightn't have involved himself in some way. The wife'll give me a lead on him. I'm arranging to have her plane met later – one of the women constables can do that, together with you Mike or Tim here. They'll see what she says on the way in from Heathrow. It's always a good time to get 'em on the hop, when they're a bit fagged from a flight.'

'Play it straight,' Gus said warningly. 'We don't want anyone accusing us of cutting corners. This one's a very spicy hot potato and don't forget it. Did you see that crowd of press outside the St Stephen's entrance? They're after all they can get, however slight, to build into something huge. Don't take any chances.'

Tim Brewer looked hurt. 'Here, Guv, whenever did you know me to bend the rules?'

'Well, I hope you do sometimes, for Gawd's sake,' Gus said. 'If you don't you'll never get a bleedin' result. I'm just tellin' you to go very easy on this one and walk on eggshells.' He dropped his voice even more. 'We're walking on the buggers right now. Don't look now but if that isn't that bastard from the *Clarion* over at the table in the corner, then I'm the Duchess of York.'

'You've got the toes for it, Guv,' Mike muttered, and Gus snorted. The pressman at the table in the corner looked over longingly as the four of them laughed loud and long.

They left five minutes later, still seeming to joke like a quartet of ordinary lunchers. But Duggie Rowe from the *Clarion* wasn't fooled. He knew Gus by sight, and suspected that he knew Dudley too. He'd certainly seen him at the scenes of various crimes; now, as the engraved glass doors swung closed behind the little party, he pulled out his mobile phone. The sooner the editor heard what he'd managed to pick up (and careful as the policemen had been, he'd still managed to pick up a good deal because the ear-whistling tinnitus that made his life a misery sometimes had forced him to become the best lip-reading journalist in the business, an asset he exploited for all it was worth) the better.

'I'm going to Heathrow,' he told his editor when he managed to get through. 'Alice Diamond'll be back from Italy tonight and the Bill are meeting her. With a bit of luck, I'll be to her first and see what's what. OK?'

'Oh yes,' clacked the little voice in his ear. 'Very much OK.'

7

George was perched on a high stool in the middle of the main lab, watching Jerry finish off a batch of slides as Alan Short, working on the other side of him, completed the assays for the afternoon's Endocrine Clinic. What she was about to ask of them was, she knew, outrageous. If she were in their shoes it would make her mad as hell; but all the same she had to ask them. She wished, just for a moment, that she was one of the autocratic sort, like many of the other consultants at Old East, who simply told their junior staff what they were going to do and then went and did it, no matter how much extra work it made for them. But she couldn't be like that, not ever. A natural Democrat all the way through to my middle, I am, she thought. Goddamn it.

'Um. Jerry,' she said as he tidied away the last slide and cleared his work area ready for the next job. 'I want to talk to you. And you too, Alan.'

Alan looked up as Jerry, his head on one side, swung himself up on to his high stool, crossed his knees and folded his arms and looked at George. 'Well, now,' Jerry said. 'What d'you reckon, Alan? Is my bet going to pay off, or isn't it?'

'I don't know why I let you talk me into it. It's like taking pennies from a beggar's bowl, that's what it is.'

'Then you agree I'm going to win?'

'What are you two going on about?' George demanded, a little pink because she feared she knew the answer perfectly well. 'I just want to talk to you!'

Jerry put the finger in the middle of his forehead and made a face like the Scarecrow in *The Wizard of Oz*. 'Aw, let me think, even though I haven't got a brain. Aw, the little lady wants to talk to us about . . . I know, Tin Man! She wants to go away and leave us! She wants to take her little basket and go off with Gus – or do I mean Toto? – and find . . . Now, what *does* she want to find?'

'Um,' said Alan and struck an awkward tight-jointed pose. 'Could it be nasty murderers? Rippers with knives? Oh, if I only had a heart it would bleed with the horror of it all.' And he pretended to weep.

'Oh, bugger the pair of you,' George said crossly. 'I'm not that transparent, am I? But – well, it's just that this really is one hell of a case, and they only found the second body because I told them where it would be. And I have a notion that if they take good care to stake out the place I'll show them then they'll get the man before he can kill again. You have to admit it's an important case. Is it any wonder I want to be bang in the middle of it? And I can't be if I have to be here all the time. I just want to concentrate on it, and leave the Old East stuff in your capable hands . . . please?'

'Oh, wowie!' Jerry said. 'The control! The strength! The sheer power she's putting into our hands! I love to see a woman grovel, don't you, Alan?'

'She's not grovelling enough,' Alan said with a fine judicious air. 'I want to see some real begging.'

'And you can go on wanting, because you'll get diddly squat!' George retorted. 'OK, OK, I get the message. So I'll do the case and I'll work here as well. I've done it before, and I can again, so to hell with both of you.'

'Oh, come down out of the rafters, Dr B.,' Jerry said, laughing. 'Of course you can. It never occurred to me you wouldn't. That's why I made the bet with Alan, silly sod.' He grinned at Alan. 'I'll take my winnings in beer next time you and Jane can get a babysitter. And don't fret, Dr B. I'll see to it you get a full report every day of what's happening here and who did what, to whom, with which.'

He jumped down from his stool and made for the little office in the corner. It had once been the domain of Sheila Keen, his predecessor as chief technician, but no one ever spoke of her now. Not after what had happened last year. Jerry had had it painted in bright yellow and totally refurnished it with pieces he bought out of his own pocket: an old roll-top desk, an armchair and a scrap of crimson carpet, all found in a Bermondsey street market. Now it was very much his and it was as though Sheila had never existed.

'Look, let me lend you my mobile phone. I shan't need it much for the next little while and if you have it with you all the time I'll be able to contact you in an emergency. Though I doubt anything'll turn up that Alan can't handle. Right, Alan?'

Alan, who although he was George's registrar and as such nominally in charge of the pathology department when George wasn't there, but who much preferred to do his own medical work than be involved in administrative details, grinned contentedly. 'Right, Jerry. And he *is* right, Dr B., we'll cope fine. I don't blame you for wanting to spend all the time you can on this case. If it were mine I would. So, you go ahead and don't worry. I'll do the routine PMs – it's only the forensic stuff I'll leave for you – and I can call you on Jerry's phone about that if necessary.'

'Boys, I love you,' George said fervently and took the phone. 'I'll keep this switched on all the time, I promise – oh, is that the spare battery? Great. I'll see I keep it charged up.'

She was almost at the door when Jerry called after her. 'Just one thing, Dr B.! We expect you to come back and give us every gory detail there is so that we're a step ahead of everyone else.'

'Ghoul!' said Alan.

'You bet,' Jerry wriggled his shoulders. 'I love to have my flesh creep.'

'I promise,' George called back over her shoulder as she headed for her own office to fetch her coat and her emergency bag. 'Every bit of it!' And then she ran. There was no time to waste.

*

At the nick, the incident room was busy with everyone, it seemed, making phone calls, but there was no sign of Gus. She felt flat and cross; she had imagined how pleased Gus would be when she told him that she was free to help in any way at any time and now she couldn't tell him, she was as disappointed as a child watching the ice-cream van drive away. She looked round for Mike Urquhart; in Gus's absence he was always a good source of information about what was happening; but he too was out. She bit her lip with irritation. She'd just have to wait till people came back from wherever to report on what was going on out there; and she ached to be out there with them.

'Where is everyone?' she said with a casual air to the woman PC at the desk nearest the side of the room where all the pinboards were. The girl, who had just cradled her phone, looked up, and George recognized Julie Bentley and grinned with relief. 'Hi, Julie, I didn't realize it was you.'

The girl leaned back in her chair, equally pleased to see George. 'Hello, Dr B.! They're out on various things – Roop and Tim are interviewing the Tory MPs at the House of Commons and the Guv has gone with Mike to talk to the other lot – the Labour ones. After that, they're going to the political party headquarters.' She riffled some papers on her desk. 'Here we are. Central Office, 32 Smith Square. That's where Roop and Tim are going. The Guv and Mike are going to 140, Walworth Road. John Smith House, it's called.'

'Did they choose them because of their political feelings, I wonder?' George perched on the edge of her desk. 'I'd have expected Roop to be a Tory, wouldn't you? And I know Gus isn't anywhere near being a Tory, so . . .'

Julie shrugged. 'I've no idea. Politics is so boring, isn't it?'

George looked at her a little sadly and shook her head. 'Is it? It shouldn't be. The way politics works controls the way *you* work. The way we all work.'

'Oh, I dunno,' Julie said. 'The brass here, they're always politicking with each other but it makes no difference to us poor oiks who do what matters, the real work. I can't be doing with politics. It's just people talking of stabbing each other in the back or cutting each other's throats.' She grinned bleakly. 'Anyway, it's got nothing to do with life and the way people feel, has it?'

George shook her head. 'You're wrong, Julie, truly. Never think that politics isn't to do with real life and real feelings. Because it is – and it can make people do appalling things. Even violent things.'

'Well, I grant you it seems to make 'em do violent things to each other. Politicians, I mean. Two with their throats cut – it makes you wonder, doesn't it? And now they're all in a state.'

'Who are?'

'The politicians,' Julie said. 'We're having to call every damn Member of Parliament to check, let me see, "if they've had any reason to be alarmed by behaviour they might have noticed".' She had glanced down at a sheet of paper which clearly bore her instructions. '"Or have become aware of anything which might be of use to our inquiries."'

'All of them? You're phoning all of them?' George said, awed.

'Damn near.' Julie sounded gloomy. 'Though we're getting some help from the AMIT team, and some local forces are dealing with their areas for us. Still, it's a lot of work. There're over eleven hundred in the House of Lords and six hundred and fifty in the House of Commons.'

'And they all have to be asked,' George said thoughtfully. 'And that means, of course, warned . . .'

A sort of rustle went through the room as everyone bent closer over their desks. It was as though a cold wind had blown over a field of ripe wheat, and George looked over her shoulder to see that Roop and Tim Brewer were back.

She sat still, letting her shoulders slump a little. The last thing she wanted was any sort of run-in with Roop before Gus got back. She wouldn't put it past him to make her leave the incident room. Anything he could do to sideline her he would, she knew. And she slid from the desk into the chair beside Julie and slumped even more.

But it didn't work; he spotted her at once and said something to Tim who looked across at her, seemed to try to argue with Roop and then, with a resigned shrug that didn't escape George, came towards her as Roop went over to the far side of the room to bend over a pile of faxes, his back firmly turned.

'Hello, Dr B.,' Tim said wretchedly. 'All right, are you?'

'Fine. Or I was till you two got back. The sooner someone runs that man over with a Sherman tank the better off we'll all be,' George snapped. 'And you can quote me!'

Julie giggled and bent her head assiduously over her desk.

'I wish I could,' Tim said, more miserably than ever. 'But what can I do? He says to ask you kindly to wait in the Guv's office, because . . . Well, just kindly to wait there until –'

'Like hell he did,' George snapped. 'He said, "Get that bitch out of my sight. Put her in the Guv's office or somewhere."'

'Oh, Dr B., do me a favour!' Tim said, almost pleading. 'I don't want to get mixed up in a row between you two. I haven't time. I've got to go to Harrow in a minute.'

'You don't have to get mixed up in anything,' George said with a sudden lightening of spirits. 'Here's Gus now.' And she stood up and went marching across the room to stand at Gus's side. The fact that he had made a beeline for the small pile of faxes that Roop was reading pleased her mightily.

'Hi, Gus,' she said, putting a hand on his sleeve in a manner that was clearly meant to be proprietorial. She saw a muscle in the corner of Roop's mouth twitch. Great, she thought, he's good and mad. She stood even closer to Gus, sliding herself between them as Gus obligingly made way, till they flanked her.

'Busy morning, Roop?' she said. 'Poor old you. Gus – Guv, I mean' – she saw from the corner of her eye that Roop had noticed, and pressed on – 'I have some important information for you. Can we talk?'

'Sure.' He looked at her and grinned. That she was up to something was very clear to his experienced eye. She was looking particularly fetching at the moment, he thought, for her eyes were glittering even more than usual, and her curly hair was springing over her forehead in a way that made her look more like a schoolgirl than a woman well into her thirties. 'Talk on, dolly.'

'Oh, we'd better go to your office,' George said sweetly. 'Roop thinks I'm in the way here, don't you, Roop? He sent Tim over to tell me to wait in your office, so let's go there, shall we?' And she linked her arm in Gus's and half pulled, half led him towards his room on the far side.

'Hey, what's goin' on here?' Gus protested. 'You two sparrin' again?'

George looked shocked. 'Would I spar, Gus? I ask you, would I?'

Roop hadn't waited. He was gone to talk earnestly with Mike who had found himself a vacant computer terminal as soon as he had come in, and had been punching keys busily ever since.

'I'll say you would,' Gus said, sounding resigned and irritable at the same time. 'You two never have got on. But if he's been really unpleasant –'

'Not really,' George said, relaxing now. 'It was just that he tried to shove me out of the room. Listen, Gus, I've been thinking. If it's as I suspect – and I think you do now too – that this is a serial killer using an MO based on Jack the Ripper's cases a hundred years ago, you're going to need a Ripper expert, aren't you? And that's me. So I've arranged time off from the hospital to –'

'Who says it's you?' He had let her lead him into his office and now he sat on his desk as she closed the door behind her. 'You're an expert after reading one book? One I'd already read and could as easily read again? Do me a favour, ducks.'

'No, it's more than that,' she insisted. 'I've read more since then. I mean, when I read Paley's book after seeing that programme, I went off and bought everything I could get my hands on. Why should you waste your time mugging it all up when I already know it? Let me in on the investigation properly and not just as a pathologist, hmm? I told you I've fixed it at the hospital so I can get away. I'm in touch by phone.' She patted the breast pocket of her jacket. 'And I could really be useful on this case. Didn't I help you find CWG? No one believed me, but there he was.'

He sighed and stared at her, his eyes partly glazed, and she let the silence stand, knowing he was thinking seriously. After a while he looked over his shoulder through the glass wall of the office to where Roop was now sitting at a computer console of his own, and shook his head. 'Roop'll go ballistic if I do, of course. He likes everything by the book.'

'Who's the boss around here?' she said softly.

'Believe it or not, he is. This is his patch, his nick. I'm just visiting, as it were, from Area.'

'Oh, come off it, Gus! You're the Superintendent on this case, you can decide how things'll go. And I know your team is in on this case. I know you like to keep all your people happy, but there are limits. If you say I won't be any use to you, fair enough, but –'

He shook his head gloomily. 'Oh, you're useful enough, you old bag, as well you know. You've solved a couple of nasties in the past and I dare say you could bring some brain muscle in here, 'n all. It's just not –'

'Yeah, I know,' George said. 'It's not the usual thing to have the pathologist hanging around so much. Too bad. Now can we talk about what we should do next?'

'Do I have a choice?'

'Sure. Listen and find out or don't and miss out.'

'Some people call it feisty,' he said to the ceiling. 'I call it bloody big-headed.'

'So I'm big-headed,' she said. 'It's only because I've got a lot of brains in there. Can we talk about the case now?'

He threw his hands up as though in despair and she grinned at him.

'OK. Now, here's the way I've been thinking. We've got two bodies so far, both showing close resemblances with the Ripper cases of over a hundred years ago. Now, what matters, I think, isn't so much what matches in the MO, but what's different.'

He was listening, his head on one side and his eyes very bright. 'The dog that didn't bark?'

'Kinda. And there were different time lapses between the Ripper cases and ours.'

'I'm not sure I see what that has to do with –'

'Nor am I. I'm just thinking aloud. Let me go with it, huh?

OK, different time lapses.' She reached into her pocket and pulled out a notebook and opened it. 'Look, here we go. The first real Ripper murder happened in high summer: 31 August. There'd been a couple of nasty knifings of prostitutes in the spring of the year 1888, but they weren't like the later versions and anyway, prostitutes were always getting themselves killed in those days. It was an occupational hazard.'

'Still is,' Gus murmured.

She ran on. 'So, 31 August. Then just over a week later, another. But then, around three weeks after that, a double event. Two on the same night, 30 September. After that pair, there was one more about six weeks later. They were all at weekends, by the way. Fridays or Saturdays or Sundays. And that was it.'

'So?' He was puzzled.

'So, that's one other difference from our cases. This is the end of October. Then there's this business of displaying the genitalia on the shoulder –'

'That really is *horrible*,' Gus said with sudden violence, and George looked at him wryly.

'I wonder if . . . Well, never mind.'

'Wonder what?'

'Would you be so put about if it was a woman? I know you hate all murders, truly I do, but I have to say you showed a bit of, shall we call it fellow feeling over what's been done to these two guys.'

He made a face. 'I can't deny it makes a man clamp his knees together when he thinks about it, but let's not get into any of this man versus woman talk. *Please?*'

'I agree,' she said. 'Back to the point. In fact it was only in one Ripper case that happened. The display of viscera, I mean. The first. After that, it was different. In three of the cases the genitalia were taken away altogether. In another the heart was removed, and in one there were no mutilations at all, apart from the slit throat, of course. Anyway, the total was that in one case genitalia – together with other viscera – were displayed on the shoulder. In two cases the uterus was removed altogether and was never found, and in others a heart and a kidney were

67

removed. Although the mutilations were undeniably gross, the bit about displaying removed genitalia has kinda gone into folklore. Even I thought that had happened every time. It wasn't till I read Paley's book a second time and made some notes I realized I was wrong. Well, it seemed to me, maybe our killer has the same folklore in *his* head and that's why he did what he did.'

Gus shook his head and sighed. 'Disgustin' the way I make my living,' he complained. 'Why can't I just be a jolly fish-and-chip shop bloke, and settle down to frying some nice bits of halibut and keep away from all this horror?'

'Because you're greedy and you want to do both,' she said a little absently, still studying her notebook. 'And you do. Gus, it seems to me that what our man is doing is making a statement. He's not just out to gratify himself in some weird fashion the way the Ripper was. The way most serial killers are. He's more –' She stopped. 'More calculating than that. He did what he did for effect.'

'But serial killers always do it for effect!' Gus protested, interested again. 'Look at how often they send letters to the investigating police or phone up and taunt them, or send letters to newspapers.'

'That's part of the pleasure. They do that because they want to add to their underlying enjoyment. Which is the killing. In this case I'm not convinced the killings are done for pleasure. I think it's more to do with making a statement or revealing a truth. *Something.*'

'I think you're jumping to conclusions,' Gus said. 'Our two victims are MPs, and because of that, you think political statement. And because you've been right about where we'd find the second body, you think you've got a political serial killer. But maybe there's nothing political at all about these deaths, and no one's trying to make any statement at all? Maybe these fellas cheated on their wives or screwed a friend out of money and that's why they were killed? Why did they agree to go to the places where they died? We've not been able to identify any reason for either of these fellas to be in the East End, remember.

And maybe we won't find any more bodies. That'd smack your Ripper theory right on the head, wouldn't it?'

'Yes,' she said, and lifted her head from her notebook. 'We need more bodies, don't we?'

'Jesus!' Gus said. 'I thought my work had coarsened me, but you!'

'I can't deny I'm fairly comfortable around corpses,' she admitted. 'But that doesn't mean I want people to be dead, if that's what you're implying.'

'No, of course I'm not. It's just that you sounded so dispassionate.'

'I'm not really, just passionately interested in an academic way, which is different. And I'd like to stop the next killing if there's one in the pipeline. Wouldn't you?'

'Does the Queen have problem children? Do me a favour! Of course, if there is one in it.'

'I think there is. I'd like us – just you and me, not the whole damn force, which costs a bomb and'll make Roop say horrible things if we don't find anything – to go and do a bit of prowling on our own account. So far the killings have been close together. He – the killer – is ignoring the time lapses the original Ripper used. So let's look now. You never know what we might find.'

'Hmm,' he said, looking over his shoulder into the incident room again. 'We'd be quicker and maybe safer with a few bodies with us.'

'And we'd be more likely to frighten off anyone who might be lurking around too,' she said. 'He could be getting ready to kill again, but if he sees a lot of Metropolitan flatfoots swanning around, it'll send him off somewhere else where I can't work out the address.'

'What address?' He stared.

'Henriques Street, of course,' she said. 'As far as I can tell, comparing the old maps with the contemporary one, it's where Berners Street used to be. And Berners Street was the site of murder three. Are you game?'

8

'I can't really say,' the barber said, setting the clippers to the neck of the man in front of him with a flourish of his wrist. 'I ain't here all the time. I just stand in for a mate when 'e goes off to an 'oliday. You'll have to talk to people what're 'ere all the time.'

Gus shifted his gaze to the mirrored reflection of the man in the barber's chair. 'Do you come here often?' he asked.

The man, thick necked, red faced and in his fifties with a skull that was shaved halfway up the back of his head, snickered. 'I'm sittin' this one out, ta.'

'Very funny,' Gus snapped. He reached into his pocket for his warrant card and flashed it at him. 'Superintendent Hathaway, OK? And I'm not askin' you for a bloody waltz, just a little chat.'

'Well, how was I to know?' the man said and slid his eyes sideways to look at George. 'Saw the lady, like, and thought you was just – you know, nosin' about.'

'She is my colleague,' Gus said, painfully aware of the fact that George had no warrant card and should therefore not really be taking part in police enquiries, not this way, anyway. 'So. D'you know these parts well?'

'Should do. Used to live 'ere. Before all the Pakis moved in and changed it all. So I've gone to Chigwell. Nice place, Chigwell.'

'So why are you having your hair cut here?' Gus demanded.

''Cos I work 'ere, don't I? Over in the Market. Got a nice little shop there – all done up fancy since the fruit and veg went, it is. And I like to go where they knows me, see? Can't get a decent 'aircut in Chigwell.'

Gus looked unbelieving. 'But this bloke says he isn't usually here, just standing in for a friend. So what are you doing here today?'

The man in the chair sighed theatrically. 'You can't even 'ave a bleedin' 'aircut these days without the filth getting interested, can you?' he said to the barber's reflection. 'I ask you, you'd think they 'ad better things to do, wouldn't you?' He shifted his gaze back to Gus. 'I didn't know till I got 'ere that Alfie wasn't here, OK? And I looked like a bog brush, it's bin so long since I had an 'aircut. So I let Fred here do it, right, Fred?'

'S'right,' said Fred. 'Only I'm Gary.'

'Yeah, Gary. Whatever.'

'I see.' Gus pulled out his notebook and scribbled. 'I'll take your name and address if you don't mind.'

The man gave it sulkily, and Gus wrote it down, snapped the rubber band round his notebook and turned, ushering George in front of him. They left, banging the barber-shop door behind them. 'Bloody fool, I am, letting 'em rile me,' he muttered. 'I didn't mean to let on we were police at all. He just got up my nose.'

'It's all right. No harm done,' George said soothingly. 'I'd have been irritated too. Now where?'

'Where's left?' Gus said gloomily. 'We've been in and out of every corner there is down this miserable bloody street.'

Indeed they had, buying things they didn't want in scruffy tobacconists and sweetshops and groceries, and peering at 'To Rent' and 'For Sale' signs as though they were would-be tenants or buyers of the battered property they were admiring and, all the time, looking as carefully as they could into every corner and every doorway where it was possible that something or somebody might be hidden.

The most obvious place had been the site next to the shop where they were now standing: a small piece of waste land covered with heavy foliage, branches and grass which was almost waist deep in places, fringed with massive bushes that added patches of gloom to the edges of the area. It looked like a perfect hiding place for any number of bodies, George had pointed out as soon as they'd seen it. There was even easy access via a section of broken wooden fence giving on to the street. But Gus had shaken his head.

'Look at it,' he said. 'It's been trampled all over. Our fellas went through with the proverbial nit comb when they were looking for CWG. If there'd been a body here they'd have found it.'

'If it had been there at the time,' George said, still looking over her shoulder at the waste ground. Somewhere across the other side a dog was barking and she had to raise her voice. 'When did they stop searching?'

'When we found CWG in Greatorex Street. That was, what? About twelve, I suppose. Before lunch, anyway.'

'That's right,' she said slowly. 'I did that PM in the afternoon, yesterday afternoon.' She lifted her head then. 'Gus, that dog sounds hysterical. Is it hurt or something?'

Gus turned his head irritably. 'I've got enough to worry about without being a branch of the RSPCA,' he snapped, and then stopped, his eyes widening.

'Yes,' George said. 'That was what I was thinking.'

'Goddamn it,' Gus said. He turned and went back into the shop, pushing the door open so violently that the barber whirled, clearly terrified. The man who had been in the chair was on his feet now, being brushed down.

'You could have told me about the bloody lorry that was here yesterday afternoon!' he roared. 'There was one, wasn't there? Or was it a van?'

Gary stared. 'Lorry? I didn't see no lorry –'

'You must have heard one, then. You can't tell me you noticed nothing yesterday afternoon. On the waste ground.' And he jerked his head to indicate the direction.

'Oh, shit,' the barber said in a resigned voice. 'How often do I have to tell you? I didn't see nothing out of the ordinary. There was no lorry and no van, I've told you.'

'No cars parked there?' George had come in behind Gus and couldn't stop herself from asking questions. 'Aren't parking places popular round here? I'd think lots would use that patch.'

''Ow often do I have to tell you? I ain't usually here!' Gary sounded exasperated. 'All I can tell you is there was no vehicles yesterday. All right?'

'That dog.' Gus shifted gear abruptly. 'Was it barking yesterday?'

For the first time Gary looked interested. 'Barking? I'll say it was. Driving me barkin' too, it was. It wouldn't shut up. It went on 'alf the night. I'm stoppin' in Alfie's flat upstairs this fortnight he's away, so I heard it all night. Ruined me telly, it did. I had to turn it up loud and then the neighbours on the other side banged on the wall. Bleedin' dog! Coulda killed the bugger, I could.'

'What time did it start?' George asked.

'Eh?' Gary rubbed his head, thinking. ''Ard to say. About . . . Let me see . . . I'd just popped down the bettin' shop to pick up the winnings from the four-fifteen at Ripon. Nice little tip I had, at fourteen to one, come in lovely, and it wasn't barkin' when I went, but it was by the time I come back.'

'Who was here while you were at the betting shop?' Gus cut in. 'And where can I find him?'

Gary looked uncomfortable. 'I'm on my own here. And, well, business was a bit slack so I took a chance. Put up a notice on the door and locked up. I wasn't gone that long.' He sounded defensive.

'How long? Oh, come on, man. I don't give a donkey's fart how long you were gone. You can sort that out with your pal Alfie when he comes back. Just tell me what I need to know. How long?'

''Bout an hour, I suppose. It was a nice little win and I met a coupla mates and we went for a quick wet.'

'And when you came back were there any cars parked then?'

Gary crinkled his eyes, trying to remember, and then shook his head. 'I didn't notice. Didn't look. Why should I? I didn't even worry that much about the dog then. Like I said, why

73

should I? But it went on and on. Didn't stop till well after the pubs closed.' He shook his head. 'I was about to go out there with a hatchet, I swear, but I s'pose its owner heard it at last and come and fetched it. An' now the bugger's out barkin' again. It's enough to drive a man barmy.'

The newly shaven skull beside him grinned. 'You ought to live down our way, mate. They sell more muzzles there than anywhere in the country, I swear. All those Rottweilers and suchlike, making a row fit to burst. But it keeps the tea-leaves away, don't it?' And he nodded affably at George and Gus and made for the door.

'I'll be in touch if I need you,' Gus said with a slightly ominous air.

The man winked. 'I'm breathless waitin',' he announced and went, slamming the door behind him.

Gus and George followed him out to the street and as the man turned to go stamping off up Henriques Street towards Commercial Road, Gus led the way to the edge of the waste ground. There was a low ridge between the pavement and the space itself, a row of bricks on which the broken fence had been set. Gus leaned over and looked on to the other side.

'Hmm,' he said. 'It won't have been easy. See? The space is a good deal lower than street level. There are more courses of brick showing down there. So it's about nine inches down: easy enough if a bit bumpy to drive in, but tricky as hell to drive out. You'd have to get a bit of a rev up to give it the power to mount that high step.'

'Not if it was one of those big new cars that look like vans,' George said. 'You know the country sort people seem to use in London these days – what do they call 'em? Four-wheel-drive Range Rovers, Jeeps and Toyotas and so forth. They look like great boxes on wheels, with rails on their fronts.'

'Bull bars,' Gus said. 'Mmm. I know what you mean. Yes, one of those'd manage it.'

'Well, come on!' George said, moving towards the fence, ready to climb through it to the space beyond. 'Let's get looking.'

'Hold it. Eyes first, lady. Then we go in.' He stood at the edge

74

and stared round. 'Tricky,' he said after a while. 'It hasn't rained all week so the ground's pretty hard. And that broken-down foliage and grass could have happened yesterday morning when our chaps were looking for clues. Hard to tell if there's been any traffic this way since then. And I can't see any of the sort of wheel tracks I'd expect if someone had come in here with one of those heavy four-wheelers. Or any other vehicle capable of getting itself out again.'

He squatted then to look closely at the course of bricks at his feet. 'There's nothing here to suggest anything's gone over, though here . . .' He peered a little closer and then, to George's complete delight, took a little leather case from his pocket and unsnapped it to reveal a small but powerful magnifying glass with a tiny, very bright bulb which lit up as he opened it out.

'Sherlock, Sherlock,' she crowed. 'I never thought I'd see –'

'It's a map-reader,' Gus growled. 'And bleedin' useful at times. Shut up.' He peered further then stood up and brushed down the knees of his trousers. 'Some rubber there as though some tyres came close while they were on the hot side, and a bit of rubber melted off. Only on this side, though, not the other. But I can't be sure. I'll take a specimen and you can have it for forensic.'

'I'll send it to the big lab,' she promised and watched as he scraped some of the almost invisible residue he'd found into a small plastic envelope and then sealed it and scribbled on its label. 'Why don't we just –'

'Go in and trample what evidence there might be if there's a body? It'll be too late to look afterwards, so I'm looking now. With your permission.' The heavy irony shut her up and she bit her tongue to keep the questions back.

'Right,' he said at last. 'I don't think there's a lot more that we can do at this point. We'll go in and look and we'll be clever. We'll go round the edges, to avoid going over any remaining evidence that might be here, OK? And we'll see where that dog is.' The barking hadn't stopped; the dog, wherever he was – and he certainly couldn't be seen – was giving tongue for all he was worth.

Gus led the way, holding out a hand to help her over the ledge and she stepped down into the waste land, which was indeed much lower than she would have expected from the look of it; the space had been largely filled with plant growth which seemed to bring it level to the street, and even higher in places. She followed him, picking her way in his wake so closely that for a moment she thought absurdly of King Wenceslas and his page, and then swore as a bunch of nettles swung against her bare leg. That would itch for the rest of the day, dammit.

Gus moved forwards carefully, pushing fronds of ivy and buddleia aside until he had gone round the front of the waste ground, where it ran parallel with the street, and then turned away at a right angle to follow it further in. The dog seemed suddenly to be aware that there were people nearby and the barking became even louder and more frantic.

'He's got something there,' Gus muttered. 'It has to be –' and then stopped short, his hand held out against the foliage in front of him, which looked exactly like the same stuff he'd already pushed down easily. But it didn't move, and he frowned.

'I'll be buggered,' he said softly, scraping at the foliage as though it were a sort of wallpaper, reaching high above his head and dragging it downwards. After a while, as masses of leaves came down, George could make out, beyond it, a much darker surface.

'What on earth?' she said and Gus looked over his shoulder and his eyes glittered.

'If they missed this, I'll murder 'em!' he said. 'I'll break their legs and shove them up their jacksies. I'll –'

'What is it?' She peered over his shoulder and nearly toppled over on to him because the ground beneath her feet was so rough. The dog, which she now realized was immediately in front of them on the other side of whatever it was that Gus had uncovered, made a scrabbling sound and redoubled its barking. From the fence behind them someone yelled; and she looked briefly over her shoulder. It was Gary from the barber shop with a few curious people craning their necks over his shoulder.

Gus pulled at the foliage again and this time it seemed to part like a great green curtain. And George saw, beneath it, vertical panels of creosoted wood. A door. Which seemed to be partly open.

He made her wait till the Soco and the rest of the crew turned up, which they did very soon after he sent his call in on his mobile asking for back-up but without saying why. They heard the howling of the sirens on the cars within minutes, and then one after the other three cars with furiously rotating blue lights were in the street and policemen and -women, some in uniform, were picking their way towards them, following in their path round the side, as Gus bawled at them they should.

Dudley reached their side first and he stared. 'Jesus, what the hell is that?'

'I'll tell you.' Gus sounded grim. 'That is why I called you. That is a shed. A shed that's been here for Gawd knows how long. Long enough for that plant there' – he pointed to the great sheet of leaves and branches which hung over it – 'to grow over it. And your bodies searched here yesterday morning did they not? And did they find it? Did they hell! We've no idea what's in there, waited for you to be on the safe side. But it could be anything, couldn't it? What have you got to say then?'

'Shit!' Dudley's face went a deep brick red and George felt a deep pang for whoever it was had searched here and missed this. 'I'll murder 'em.'

'Much good that'll do,' Gus said. 'Why they didn't push a bit, the way I did, I'll never know. I was trying to get to that bloody dog' – it was still filling the air with its noise – 'and it's somewhere here, so I knew there had to be something more than just a lot of greenery.'

'Which in all fairness they wouldn't know,' Dudley said, trying not to sound partisan for his men. 'Not having a dog to guide 'em, you'd think it was only an ordinary wall looking at it. And that's a Russian vine, by the way. It grows like the clappers. It can cover a whole building so it vanishes in a single growing season. I nearly lost one of my own sheds that way: once it took

77

off, it was like the shed had never been there. It only took a coupla weeks, I swear.'

'Well, that's as may be,' Gus grunted. He was still pulling at the vine and revealing more and more of the wooden structure behind. 'I ain't here for a gardening lesson.' The door creaked and opened a little and George lifted her head sharply.

'There *is* a body in there,' she said. 'That's what got the dog going.'

Gus looked over his shoulder at her. 'Yeah, I thought I got a whiff of it too. Listen to that damned animal, will you? It'll turn itself inside out in a minute. Get one of your bods to call out an RSPCA bloke, will you, Roop? Get the creature taken away – when we can find where it is. You can't hear yourself think in this racket.'

The Soco moved forwards then, beckoned by Gus, while Dudley shouted an order about the dog to one of his men, who promptly reached for his shoulder call system. Gus moved back, making George do the same.

'We're in the way here,' he said. 'You'll get your chance as soon as Soco gets in properly. Then we'll see what's what. Right now, I think you'd better find somewhere to take it easy for a while. He'll be a goodish time yet, and you'll have a nasty job on your hands when he gets done.'

George, aching with impatience though she was, had to agree. That there would be work for her was undoubted. The thick sweetish smell that had filled their nostrils as the door to the hidden shed opened wider was unmistakably that of a dead body. And one that had been dead for some time.

9

Terminal Two at Heathrow was for some reason in one of its occasional fits of lunacy. It seemed that every airline in the world was converging on it at the same time, making the concourse look like an illustration for the Last Trump. People were pushing, shoving, sweating and swearing as they tried either to get in or out and Mike cursed comprehensively as he pushed his way through the mob to find the exit from customs through which arriving passengers from Milan would emerge. It was bad enough that he had to do this job because Tim Brewer had been pulled away to get involved with some business over in Henriques Street (and Mike was already frustrated because he hadn't been told what was going on there even though it was obvious it had to do with this case they were all working on); to find now that the job was going to be complicated by this crowding was infuriating.

The detective constable at his side, Margaret Chalice, looking absurdly young in jeans and sweater and trainers, said breathlessly, 'It's going to be a bugger, this one, Sarge. Finding someone and then talking to them in this sort of crowd is –'

'Does the sun rise in the East?' he snapped. 'Go teach your grandma to suck eggs, lass. I can see that for m'self.'

Chastened, Margaret said no more, but stuck close behind him as he used his considerable shoulders to get his way. It left irate and resentful people behind him, but it paid off. They reached the exit from the Customs Hall just as the first people bearing luggage with Air Italia labels from Milan came through.

'Down by the end of the railed-off area,' Mike shouted above the hubbub. Together they inched their way through the noisy crowd to the point where all the passengers would emerge into the main concourse before scattering. There was a flock of clergymen, in dog collars and even cassocks, some wearing heavy crucifixes, and Mike, a good son of the Scottish kirk, found himself thinking, Catholics, and felt for a moment like a character in a novel. Wasn't it in a Father Brown story that a lot of priests got in the detective's way, and –

He blinked and shook his head a little to clear it. He had to concentrate. He knew what Alice Diamond looked like only from her photographs and that never made for an easy ID. Especially with women. She had only had to change her hair colour or style, or dress differently for that day, and he'd be lost. She could walk right past him and he'd not be sure she was his target.

Again he made himself concentrate. The loss of sleep he'd suffered over the past few days was beginning to demand payment. Keeping himself fully alert wasn't as easy as it ought to be. He looked down at Margaret and said, 'Will you be able to recognize her?'

'As long as she hasn't done anything to prevent me,' she said. 'But you know how it is, if she's done something different with her face and her hair . . .'

'That's what I was thinking,' Mike said glumly, never taking his eyes off the doors through which people were now coming in rather larger numbers, pushing loaded luggage carts and dragging children by unwilling hands. 'We know she's about five five, weighs around nine stone, blonde hair – ah! Would that be – No. Three children with her. Look, you watch the left, I'll watch the right. And for Christ's sake stay alert!'

Margaret, who had an excellent reputation for alertness and suspect recognition, opened her mouth to protest, thought better of it, and watched. And to her gratification saw Alice Diamond before Mike did. 'She's just coming out,' she said softly below the noise of voices around them, so that he could just hear her. 'There, the one in the dark glasses and the pink trouser suit, with the huge pile of luggage on her trolley.'

'Got her,' Mike said. 'Yes, I think – the glasses muck it up a bit. And that bloody hat, but I think you could be – Shit! She's taking the outside lane.'

It was clearly deliberate. While every other passenger aimed at the right-hand side of the railed-off area, since that was where most of the meeters and greeters were, their target had moved sharply to her left, hugging the wall so that she would emerge as far away as possible from the most crowded part, where they awaited her. There was more space there on the left, too, and she was able to move much more quickly. Mike realized at once that she would be out on the other side of the concourse before he and Margaret could reach her, unless they moved fast, and he began to shove to get out of the crowd. Someone in front of him took violent exception to his efforts and turned on him, shouting and gesticulating in what sounded like excited Italian. Mike shouted back, trying to reach into his breast pocket for his warrant card to show the man. That seemed to terrify him, for he shrieked at the top of his voice, and everyone around turned and surged first towards the shrieker and then, seeing Mike with his hand in his breast pocket, surged backwards to get away from him. One man lurched and then almost fell over the bag he had set down at his feet and in steadying himself grabbed at a bystander who happened to be a woman. She in her turn became highly agitated at having a strange man dragging at her clothes, and started shouting too. In the middle of it all, Mike did his best to roar them into some sort of order as he waved his warrant card, now at last out of his pocket, not that anyone of them showed the slightest intention of looking at it or listening to him. They were all much too excited.

Margaret's first instinct was to stay and help him out but she followed her second and wriggled her way through the heaving bodies – not too difficult for someone as thin and wiry as she was – and emerged on the other side just in time to see the object of her search meet a tall man in a dark-green waxed jacket and matching flat cap, looking rather like an illustration from *Country Life*, and throw her arms around him. He seemed un-comfortable about that, and raised both his own arms to take hold of her hands and untwine them from his neck. The action obscured his features, and by the time he had succeeded in extracting himself and had reached for Alice Diamond's trolley, he had turned his back to Margaret and she could not see his face.

She hesitated. Was this Alice Diamond after all? The dark glasses and big straw hat obscured *her* face. Margaret had been quite certain at first, but now she began to doubt. If it wasn't Alice, and she stopped her, it could cause a fuss; people didn't like being intercepted by strangers and asked to prove their identity. They disliked even more being stopped by police if they'd done no wrong. And this woman had not. She was just a murder victim's widow and needed careful handling. Certainly she mustn't be upset. Margaret, uncharacteristically, dithered. If it was Alice and she didn't stop her – but that was not to be thought of. She threw a glance over her shoulder at the fracas which was continuing behind her, with Mike in the middle of it. A couple of airport police were pushing their way through the crowd from the other side now, making authoritative noises, and Margaret turned back to look at her quarry again, satisfied Mike was in safe hands – or soon would be – in time to see her tittuping away rapidly, her high heels almost twinkling as she hurried to keep up with the long-legged escort who was striding away with her trolley.

Margaret made her decision. This had to be Alice; her first impression had to have been right; and she began to follow, trying to get close enough to call her and make her stop; but she was unable to run in the crowd. She could just duck and dive and keep her in sight. Soon, surely, the crowds would thin out and she'd be able to go to Alice, explain who she was and ask her, as she knew Mike had intended to, to accompany them to the station, if that would suit her, to give them some information about her dead husband.

Quite when Margaret realized that she was not the only one following Alice Diamond she wasn't sure, but become aware she did. A rather small man, not much taller than Alice herself, was keeping close behind the couple. He could easily have caught up with them but clearly he didn't want to; when they suddenly stopped so that Alice could reach for her bag, which was on top of the luggage on the trolley, and scrabble in it for something, he stopped too, affecting to study a piece of paper in his hand. Neither of the people in front paid him any attention, and when they started to move again, walking as fast as ever, he too started, again keeping the same distance behind them.

Margaret was intrigued. She could, she knew, make a stronger effort to catch up with Alice and whoever she was with, but the behaviour of the little man just behind them was worthy of observation. And as long as she kept Alice in her sights, no harm would accrue from letting things go on as they were. Margaret could easily speak to her later when it suited her. So they all went on: Alice and her meeter, the little man, and the detective constable in a kind of procession on their way to the car park as the crowds at last began to thin out.

Mike, red in the face with a combination of acute embarrassment and rage, escaped from the airport police at last, and ran to the far side of the exit area. There was, of course, no sign of Alice Diamond, but also – and this was some consolation – Margaret had vanished. With a bit of luck for once, he told himself, she's made contact and asked her to come to the station. Or maybe – he tried to survey all the possibilities as quickly as he could – maybe the woman had got ahead of her and Margaret was following her? Or maybe she had become upset when Margaret spoke to her, and had to be taken away to a rest room somewhere? Or maybe she had agreed to come to the nick and Margaret had taken her to the car, which they'd left parked on the second level of the car park nearest to Terminal Two, and decided to take her back to Ratcliffe Street, leaving him to make his own way there as soon as he could? No, he decided, she wouldn't do that to me. She knows Roop'd have my guts out and made into horsewhips to beat me with if I let myself be left behind. Margaret might be in the car, with Alice, even as he stood here, hesitating, but she'd be waiting for him. The only thing to do therefore, was to make for the car. One way or another, that would be where they made contact. He began to run, following the signs that read 'Car Parks' and this time, thank heaven, people kept out of his way.

Margaret was trying very hard to make the right decision. She couldn't use her call system to tell them at the nick that she'd been separated from Mike, and didn't really want to; it would make them both sound too nerdish for words. Anyway, Mike would get a mouthful from Roop if he found out. She had to cope on her own, use her initiative, and right now she wasn't sure she had quite enough. The little man was standing against the wall, not fifty yards from Alice Diamond, who was standing at the pick-up point in the car park, leaning on her baggage trolley and staring into the middle distance. The man who had met her had gone off, clearly to fetch a car. Now was the time, Margaret thought, to go up to her, introduce herself, offer condolences for her loss and invite her to come to the station to help the police with their inquiries into her husband's murder. But if I do that, the little man would no doubt just melt away – and I don't want him to do that, Margaret thought. What she wanted was to know who the little man was and why he was behaving like this. And once again, she dithered.

Then two things happened at the same time. The double doors through which all of them had come to reach this point swung open again and another crowd of people came out, clashing their trolleys, chattering at the tops of their voices and filling the space around the pick-up with a mini crowd. And Alice looked over her shoulder in a vague sort of way, directly at Margaret, who caught her gaze and immediately dropped her own, hoping Alice hadn't noticed her stare. Almost simultaneously, she jumped horribly as a hand touched her shoulder.

'It's all right,' Mike said softly, looking at Alice's back, for she had turned away again, apparently unaware of Margaret, much to that lady's relief. 'I guessed you'd be at the car. I was on my way there. Why haven't you spoken to her? Something wrong?'

Margaret, grateful for his swift understanding of the need for caution, spoke equally softly under the cover of the surrounding chatter. 'She was met by a bloke who's gone to fetch a car, or so I imagine, the way she's waiting. And there's someone following them. So I thought I'd wait and watch.'

'Yes,' breathed Mike, looking as casually as he could across the heads of the people around him to where Alice still stood beside her mountain of luggage on its trolley and then sweeping his gaze in an offhand way that deceived everyone but Margaret, rapidly identifying the little man who had alerted her interest. 'We'd better move back a little.' Obediently, she let him pull her gently back so that though Alice and the pick-up point where she was waiting were still in sight, there was far less likelihood that she would be aware of them if she turned to look.

A few more minutes passed and then, as a large red Volvo came curving round from the other side of the car park towards the pick-up point, a battered little green van close behind it, Alice seemed to wake up and stiffen.

The two vehicles stopped towards the back of the pick-up area, still very close together, and a third car, a few lengths behind, had to pass them both to cut in front to collect its passengers. There was a considerable bustle as boots were opened and people began to pull cases and boxes and floppy long suiters from their trolleys to load them, and suddenly Margaret gripped Mike's upper arm and breathed, 'Look at that!'

Mike swivelled his head to see what she was showing him and then shook it. 'So?' he said.

'He didn't have any luggage,' Margaret said. She stared through the crowds at the little man who now had a luggage trolley, clearly obtained from the straggle of those left behind by people who had already unloaded and left. He had set it precisely alongside Alice Diamond's, who appeared to pay no attention at all; nor, as her companion loaded some bags into the back of the Volvo, did she show any interest in the fact that the little man had, in the coolest manner possible, slid one of the bags from her trolley on to his.

Margaret started forwards. To watch robbery going on under her nose, being carried out with such smoothness and aplomb that apparently none of the people around had noticed it was happening, went completely against her grain, and Mike had to grab her to stop her. 'No,' he hissed. 'Watch. I've got the Volvo's number. Try and get the van's.' And he gave her a little push.

Obediently she moved casually round to the far side so that she was behind the van and noted its number. 'Bravo two, three, zero.' she muttered to herself, getting it firmly into her memory. 'Yankee, Mike, Lima. Bravo two, three, zero. Yankee, Mike, Lima.'

The car that had been in front of the Volvo and the van at last filled up with all its luggage and passengers and set off towards the exit ramp, and another slid into its place and also began rapidly to fill up with baggage and people. There were fewer bodies around now, and a distinct risk therefore that Alice would see the police staring at her. And, surely, Margaret thought, watching carefully, would see that her baggage was being taken, because the little man had now moved two more sizeable cases.

But Alice didn't see; she pushed away her now empty trolley, quite ignoring the one so close to hers that now had on it three of her pieces of luggage, and climbed into the front seat of the Volvo. The man in the waxed jacket, still with the cap set forwards on his head so that his face was shadowed by its brim, got into the driver's seat, revved the engine and pulled away. And, behaving as comfortably as though nothing at all unusual had happened, the little man pushed his trolley to the back of the green van, opened its door, shoved the bags in, then climbed into the passenger seat of the van which already had its engine running. Its driver had not got out at all, and could hardly be seen behind the streaked windscreen, and anyway was sitting well back so that his face was shadowed. But he had to lean forwards as he put the van into gear and moved off smartly and this time Margaret did get a glimpse of him. Not that it helped much. It was the sort of nondescript face that drove vans all over London, she thought, as she made a conscious effort to burn the image into her memory. He could be anyone. And she stood and watched the van go, as Mike came up to stand beside her.

'Well, well,' he said. 'What an interesting little side show that was! And very unexpected.' He pulled his handset out of his pocket and called the Control Room at Ratcliffe Street nick. 'We'll get those cars traced as fast as they can make it,' he told Margaret. 'And pick 'em up later. It'll be worth it, I suspect. That was as smart a piece of double shuffling as I've seen in years. The question is, just what is it she's smuggling? Because that's what it has to be, doesn't it? She gets the bags through Customs – though you'd think their fellas would take more interest in a pile of luggage that high for one passenger, wouldn't you? – and then gets rid of it even before she's out of the airport. Very nifty.'

Margaret went pink. 'Smuggling? Oh! I thought . . .'

'Robbery?' Mike glanced at her and then, not wanting to add to her discomfiture, away. 'It could have been, but I used to work in Dover before I joined the Met. I got to know their tricks. You did well to keep 'em in sight.'

'But what has it got to do with what happened to her husband, Sarge?' Margaret said. 'Or is it something entirely separate?'

'That,' said Mike as he set off for the ramp that led to the second level where their car was parked, 'that is the question we'd all like answered, wouldn't we?'

Neither of them noticed the man from the *Clarion* leaning against the double doors that led from the main concourse of the terminal, apparently reading a paper as he waited for whoever he was waiting for. He, for his part, watched them go and then sprinted as hard as he could for his own car. He had one hell of a story for the old man this time.

IO

George showered for almost fifteen minutes, scrubbing herself with great dollops of Badedas, which had the strongest scent of all the unguents she kept in the shower room at the mortuary. She shampooed her hair twice and then, when at last she stepped out and dried herself, applied a quantity of rose-scented body cream and a matching spray. She'd rather smell like backstage at a brothel, she decided, than risk any of the smells that the PM had released clinging to her.

She had done some unpleasant tasks in her time but this had really been quite appalling. Once they'd got rid of the hysterical dog, who was scratching furiously at the ground on the other side of the far wall of the shed, where it abutted on to an adjacent alley, and got inside and found the body, it had been a continuous rush of work. She had made what investigations she could there inside the overgrown shed. Gus hadn't wanted to pull down too much of the plant covering that kept out the light, in case that interfered with the collection of evidence, so she'd had to work by the light of Tilley lamps: never easy. But she had been able to see that, badly damaged though the body was by natural decomposition and the attention of wildlife, it fitted the *modus operandi* of the other two.

The body was that of a man, rather older than the other two, she suspected, from what she could see of the hair and a thin remnant of a beard. Both were grey, though it was hard to be certain in the artificial light. The throat had been cut and the external genitalia removed and displayed on the shoulder in what was becoming a familiar manner.

But there had been some differences. She had noted them at the scene and now confirmed them in her careful post-mortem, through which Gus had stood, stony faced, fully gowned and masked, though she doubted that had protected him much from the unpleasantness. Tim Brewer stood there too, also gowned and blank eyed in his turn; it was not easy to watch.

The blows that had almost severed the heads of Diamond and C W G had been assured. The perpetrator had clearly acted swiftly and with a certain degree of expertise. On this body, however, it was different. There were signs of attempted cuts made before the final one: tentative, almost superficial, wounds on the surface of the neck, particularly at the left. And the final cuts were not so savagely deep.

The injuries to the genitalia had also been less assured; in fact, what with the appalling butchery the murderer had inflicted on them, and the inevitable attrition due to the time between the killing and the finding of the body, it had been hard to see the shape of the organs at all. All George had been able to ascertain was that the testes had long since shrivelled and lost all function − not all that unusual in very old men − and the penis was undersized. But it was the neck injuries that gave her most information.

'As before, a right-handed killer,' she said now. 'He stood or knelt behind the supine body and swept his knife, which was very sharp rather than heavy, across the throat. I think the man was already dead, of course, as the other two were. He'd been strangled too. In consequence there was less blood when the throat and abdominal injuries were inflicted. This time the cutting missed the larynx and the hyoid bone is clearly fractured, almost certainly by manual pressure. No sign of a ligature, anyway.'

'No signs of any weapon anywhere, either,' Gus said fretfully, shifting his feet wearily. 'How long has he been dead?'

She shook her head. 'Hard to say. We'll have to wait for the evidence of the entomologist. He got all his samples from the ground under the body, as well as what he took from the body itself.'

'Yes.' Gus blinked over his mask, clearly thrown by the memory of the unpleasantness of the job they had had to do at the scene in Henriques Street, and she looked at him sympathetically.

'It is a bit nasty to think of,' she said. 'But we have to face it. Flies and their behaviour do help date a death. She'll let me know as soon as she can, she said. Meanwhile I'd hazard a guess at something over three weeks. It was pretty warm, wasn't it, last month? Not like now, a bit cooler.'

'Yes,' Gus said. 'Well, no need for details. Let us register the fact that this one died well before the other two.'

'No question,' she said at once. 'And I'll tell you something else. I think he was, well, practising for the others on this one.'

'Eh?' Gus stared, and Tim Brewer moved closer.

'It's not just the tentative nature of the injuries on the neck – they're intention cuts – it's those on the abdomen too. He didn't make such a confident excision. He did a bit of other damage – I'd show you, but I don't think it's necessary.'

'It most certainly isn't,' Gus said firmly.

'But there'll be the photographs. You'll be able to compare them with the others. That's what makes me say this chap was killed as a sort of dummy run for the other two.'

'Which rather buggers up your Ripper theory, George, doesn't it?' Gus sounded disappointed more than anything else, as though he too had accepted the theory. 'If this killing was really the first, and not the third, and –'

'Not at all.' George was thinking fast. 'Maybe he used that shed for a different reason, and only realized afterwards that the Ripper case could be copied because of where the shed is? Or maybe –'

'There's no point in asking that. Not till we see if he does any more.'

'And any more he does.' Tim Brewer's voice made them both stare at him. He had stood stolidly beside Gus throughout, gowned but bravely unmasked, his jaws set and his eyes fixed so firmly on George's busy hands that he was obviously using massive willpower to enable him to be there at all.

'Eh?' said Gus.

'We can't assume he's stopping at three, can we?' Tim said. Now he did look at Gus. 'How many of those Ripper murders were there?'

'Five,' said George.

'See what I mean?' Tim shook his head. 'Do you know where they were too, Dr B.?'

'Yes,' she said. 'It's all documented. Dorset Street, which was just south of Spitalfields Market. And Mitre Square, which is by Aldgate.'

'Yeah, well,' Gus said. 'You've got a point, of course. And I dare say Roop's thought of it too. He's got a lot of people well spread out to cover the whole area by now.'

'I'd have thought it'd be more sensible just to cover the two high-risk ones,' George said as she turned back to the body, nodding at Danny to take over and see it back into its chiller. 'It's a waste of manpower to cover everywhere.'

'George,' Gus said, 'um – Dr B. – stick to your pathology, will you? Let Inspector Dudley decide how to deploy his men.'

'I wouldn't dream of saying a word to him about it,' George opened her eyes wide. 'Only to you.'

'Hmmph,' said Gus and, relieved to see George strip off her gloves as she turned away from the table, turned to go too. 'Then Gawd help me, I suppose.'

Beside him Tim let out a little gurgle of laughter, due as much to his intense gratitude for the ending of the job as the conversation between Gus and George (which of course he would recount gleefully to the entire canteen the first chance he got). Gus glared at him.

'And you can go and write up your report, Sergeant,' he snapped. 'I'll be along later, with Dr B. On your way, now.'

George, dressing now as she remembered, was a little ashamed of herself. It was too easy to make cracks about Dudley and too easy to rile Gus on the subject. She knew that much as she loathed him Dudley was a good copper and a very important part of the team, that Gus thought highly of him, and that he wouldn't do so for small reason. To tease him about the man was wicked. She'd really try to stop it, she promised herself as she rattled the hair-dryer back into its socket and pulled up her hair to pin it on top of her head. Gus deserved better.

She came out of the shower room into the chill of the mortuary corridor and ran up the stairs to her ground-floor office. She was feeling much more comfortable now. Her forecast about where they would find their third body had been correct (even though it had turned out that it had been in chronological terms the first) and that was very encouraging. It shouldn't be all that difficult to track down the murderer, she told herself as she headed for her office door, behind which she knew Gus would be waiting for her as he'd promised. Not with such important victims as Members of Parliament. (And I'll bet this one was too, she thought.) The toughest perpetrators to find were those who killed casually and suddenly and chose insignificant victims like drifters or one of the winos who hung around the back streets of this part of the East End. After dealing with several of those in the past few months, this, she told herself optimistically, should be a doddle. And very, very interesting.

Gus was sitting in her chair, bent over her desk and leafing through some of the documents on it.

'Nosy Parker,' she said without rancour. 'Those things are supposed to be confidential.'

'They are with me,' he said. 'Who am I going to gossip with about' – he squinted – 'acromegaly? Whatever that is.'

'And I'm not going to tell you. Gus . . .' She hesitated. 'I must apologize.'

He leaned back, fanning himself with exaggerated gestures. 'Oh Gawd, stap me vitals, the world's about to come to an end. You, apologize?'

'One more word out of you like that and you'll get none out of me,' she said. 'And don't make it hard for me, sweetie. I'm sorry I was rude about Roop.'

He remained leaning back, looking at her, his mouth turned down a little, then shook his head and sat forwards so that the chair which had been resting on its back legs crashed down. 'Until tomorrow, huh? Or this evening if you see him then.'

George perched on the edge of her desk and put an arm round his neck. 'No, I mean it. I will try to be nice, it's just that he's so irritating. And he should be concentrating on Spitalfields and Mitre Square, you know. It's simply a waste to be looking anywhere else.'

'There you go!' Gus shook his head. 'If it wasn't so funny I'd cry, I swear. Lay off the man, will you? He knows his job! Unless you really do promise me you'll behave I won't let you sit in on any of the briefings any more. And it's getting very interesting. I've heard some strange things about Mrs Alice Diamond, for instance, that'll give you furiously to think.'

She was avid at once. 'Tell me, tell me! And I will lay off Roop, I promise. As long as you help by keeping him out of my way.'

'It's up to you to keep out of his,' Gus said. 'And as for telling you, let me consider.' He looked at her owlishly for a moment. 'Come to think of it, I won't tell you. No, I won't, so don't fuss. Not now. Tomorrow will be soon enough. It's been a pig of a day, one way and another. I've been working flat out ever since this business started and I need a break. So do you. And good old Roop – yeah, yeah, good old Roop – has agreed to hold the fort tonight so I can have an evening off. So, we'll go out to eat, my duck, and then go home and hang curtains.'

She burst into laughter. 'Hang curtains? Sweetie, what a treat! I can hardly wait. Do tell me, I'm dying to know.'

'Then you'll have to die, and I'll get Alan to do your PM. I refuse to talk shop and that's it. So, how about those curtains? What do you say?'

She knew when to give up. It was obvious he'd not say a word about the case tonight, and somehow she'd have to swallow her curiosity till next day. So she thought about the house and the curtains and, almost to her own surprise, shook her head.

'Not tonight. I've had enough interior decorating for the present. Something else, maybe.'

'But I thought that'd be what you'd want to do! We haven't got the place straight yet.'

'Maybe not, but all the same it's no treat to do it when you've got some unexpected time off,' she said. 'Take me to – to the . . .' She cast about. 'The theatre. I'd like that. If we're going to treat ourselves.'

'What a woman,' Gus said, grumbling, but his eyes were bright. 'Always wrongfoots me. Gissa paper, if you've got one.'

'Last night's *Evening Standard*,' she said, going to the pile of newspapers on a chair behind the door. 'I've kept all these to catch up with. Here we are. Now, let me see . . .'

She folded the paper to the Entertainments page and pored over it while Gus sat at the desk, his chair tipped back again and his hands behind his head, watching her indulgently. She looked up and caught his eye.

'You look like a schoolgirl,' he said. 'Great big goggle glasses and all that hair falling around. When are you going to grow up?'

'When you do,' she said and bent her head to the paper again. 'You're like a teenage thug in his dad's overcoat, you are.' But she glowed with pleasure all the same. 'Here we are! How about this, at the National?' She pushed the paper at him.

He looked and made a face. 'Hell no, heavy little number, that. Ibsen's like Marmite for me. Too much spoils the flavour. I want a laugh. Look, how about this one? Lots of culture for you, belly laughs for me. So the critics say, anyway.'

'If you can laugh that hard at Shakespeare, then that's something, I have to say. Will we get in at short notice? It's something of a hit.'

'Leave that to me,' he said confidently. 'I can get anything any time. The Bill always can.'

'OK,' she said. 'I'll believe you. So, where do we eat?'

'My place. Where else? I'll call Kitty and have her save us a nice bit o' turbot.'

'With lobster sauce,' she said greedily, applying make-up with a slapdash hand. 'There, will that do?'

94

'You could very well pass for forty-three,' he carolled, 'in the dark with the light behind you. Come on. I'll call the nick from the car. You can drive.'

It was a lovely evening, she decided. They had been in time to share a drink in the theatre bar before the curtain went up and the seats he'd managed to get out of the box office were bang in the middle of the dress circle. 'House seats,' he'd said with great satisfaction when he came back to her from buying them. 'This really is a huge hit. They're doing it all art deco and sprightly twenties music, so I s'pose that's why. Come on.'

He really is a remarkable man, she told herself as she settled in her seat and relaxed. For all his act as an East End toughie he still had a deep wisdom that emerged just when it was needed as far as she was concerned. He could be as tender and careful a lover as any woman could want. It was true he could also be an overbearing louse at times, but such times were far out-numbered by the good ones. As she let the glow build up inside her she tucked her hand into the crook of his elbow and settled down to have fun.

At the end they came out into Shaftesbury Avenue still filled with laughter and pleasure. 'We did *The Comedy of Errors* at school,' she said. 'I played one of the Antipholuses – or should it be Antipholi? Anyway, I was the unmarried one.'

'Snap,' he said easily. 'I was a Dromio. Well, both of them. We did it as a sort of *doppelgänger* thing, as I recall. You look better.'

'Mmm?' She was standing still, looking up at the dark sky in a search for stars. 'One of these days it'll be dark enough in a London street actually to see a star. What did you say?'

He grinned and took her elbow. 'Not a word, ducks. Just a sideways compliment. You used to be able to see stars when I was a kid. On account of we was too poor to have streetlights down our way.'

'Liar.' She tucked her hand into his elbow and they started to walk towards the Lexington Street garage where they'd left the car. 'How do you mean, I look better?'

'Aha! So you did hear! Trust you! I just meant you looked good right now.'

'Compared with when?'

'You were looking – wrong, somehow before. All tired and wound up. The way you do when you get too involved in a case. It's happened in every one we've done together. One or other of us and usually both end up looking like wet dish rags. This time, it ain't gonna happen. I've made up my mind.'

'So?' she said. 'What are you going to do? Not let me be involved?' She stopped and turned to stare into his face as the other passers-by eddied round them as water passes a rock in midstream. 'You aren't going back on your promise, are you? Not when I've got free time from the hospital to be in on the case from the ground floor. You wouldn't do that to me!'

'It's all right.' He turned her so that they could start walking again and took her arm in a firm grasp. 'I know better than to do that. But I don't want you worn out the way you were last time.'

'Last time,' she said and shivered a little. 'Let's not talk about that. It was awful! Let's talk about the play instead. Twins. Double twins! It's pushing credulity, of course, but what a joy Shakespeare made of it.'

'You're beginning to sound like an English teacher,' he said. 'Trying to persuade a bunch of ivory skulls that they can take an interest in literature, capital L.'

'You're impossible,' she said. 'I try to share some of the stuff I've learned to enjoy with you, and what do I get? Scorn!'

'Oh, I laughed all right. That was a funny production – all that conjuring and leaping about. Like a ballet, almost. And I liked the music. Quite jazzy some of it. But the trouble is I know the story too well. Shakespeare took it from Plautus, you know. The *Menaechmi*. I read it in the original Latin at school.'

'What? You bastard!' she shouted at him and he laughed, letting go of her arm to set off at a trot to run up Great Windmill Street, making her run after him, shouting as she went. No one in the crowded little street paid any attention, of course. Such behaviour was commonplace there.

Altogether a most satisfactory evening she thought much later, sleepily, as he curled up against her and fell into a deep post-coital sleep. A lovely play, a delicious supper and now this. And a great case to get back to tomorrow. I'm a very lucky woman. And then she fell asleep as swiftly as a weary baby.

II

The smell of coffee that filled the big incident room seemed almost as restorative as the coffee itself, George thought, as she watched them trail in one by one, looking weary and with shoulders drooping, only to brighten immediately as they caught the scent and made a direct line for the table in the corner where the two big Cona jugs stood. Gus was always adamant about the quality of the coffee for his team. 'Dust and water might do for residents here, but my lot need coffee with real meat on its bones,' he said. He bought top-quality freshly ground Arabica for them out of his own pocket whenever they had a big case for AMIT. This case, he had already told George, looked likely to cost him a fortune in coffee beans. She had to agree with the wisdom of his attitude; she was herself nursing her second cup, because she had arrived with Gus at Ratcliffe Street nick at an unconscionably early hour. He had been head down over his desk for the past forty-five minutes and all she could do was sit and wait, bursting with curiosity and an urge to be up and at work on what, she was now sure, was shaping up to be the most complicated case of her entire career.

Julie Bentley came and sat beside her, her own coffee cup in her hand. 'Good morning,' she said a little awkwardly, as though she expected to be snubbed; George was, after all, a very senior person compared to a humble uniformed PC, but she relaxed when George greeted her warmly and made space beside her on the desk on which she was perched.

'Hi,' George said. 'How's things?'

'A bit boring,' Julie said, sipping her coffee. George stared at her.

'You find this case boring?' She was amazed. She had thought this girl very bright and worthwhile. Was she going to turn out to be just another airhead after all?

'Oh, no, not the case,' Julie said. 'How could I? The case is amazing. No, it's what they make me do. Just typing lists and putting things into the computer and so forth. I want to get out more and be where it's all happening, not here where all we do is twiddle with the information.'

George relaxed, gratified to find her character judgement hadn't been wanting. 'I know what you mean. It drives me crazy sometimes. Once I've done my PM they want to leave me out of things. Not that I let 'em.'

Julie looked at her sideways and gave a little crack of laughter. 'We'd noticed,' she said.

'Oh, dear.' George made a face. 'Do they gossip sometimes?'

'Not sometimes,' Julie said. 'Every time they get the opportunity, more like.' And laughed again, an infectious sound that made George join in.

'Oh, well, let 'em,' she said. 'What would you rather do than type lists into the computer?'

'Interview people,' Julie said promptly. 'Really investigate. I know the background work matters but it's so bloody dull.'

'Why not ask if you can?'

'I'm not a detective yet. I've put in for a transfer and the chance to learn a bit more and get on in the CID, but you know how it is, especially for a woman.'

'Tell me about it,' George said feelingly and then straightened as the whole room seemed to rustle to attention. Gus had come out of his office, Roop close beside him. Clearly the day was at last under way. George glanced at the clock, 8 a.m., dead on time. She smiled to herself. Gus would deny it vehemently but he could be as rigid in his systems as any bank manager.

'Right, you lot,' he said affably as he stared round. 'Let's get down to it. I want a progress report and then we'll see where we go from here. First off, let's have the picture on the third body.'

'First body,' George murmured, but not so softly that Gus didn't catch it. He didn't look at her but went on as though he had fully intended to: 'Which I have to tell you is in fact the first, since the forensic evidence is that this death occurred well before the other two. Dr B., perhaps you'd like to tell everyone what you found at the PM.'

She looked at him, startled for a moment, and then grinned. Good old Gus. Giving a reason for her presence here, and when she saw Roop's scowl she knew she was right. He'd have happily settled for a written report one of his people could read aloud. But he wasn't going to get it, she thought gleefully, and got to her feet.

'Glad to,' she said. She reached in her pocket for her own notebook in which she had scribbled some salient points when she'd finished the PM yesterday. 'The body we found in the shed at Henriques Street was that of a male, aged about seventy to seventy-five, maybe more, dead around three to four weeks – I'm waiting for some test results to confirm that – grey hair and beard . . .' She went on in as much detail as she could, describing the difference between the injuries on this body and the ones that looked the same but were slightly different on the other two. 'The conclusion I reached,' she ended, 'was that this murder was a sort of dummy run for the other two – the intention injuries and so forth, you see, and –'

'Just the report right now, thanks, Dr B.,' Gus said. 'We'll come to the conclusions later, if you don't mind. And we already have some information about this chap.'

George lifted her head and stared at him, quite distracted from his rebuke by surprise. 'Already?'

'Of course,' Roop growled. 'The fact that you finished work yesterday at six or so doesn't mean I did.'

George opened her mouth to protest that it had been Gus who insisted they take the evening off, caught Gus's glare and subsided. No need to have a row, not if there was news to be heard. 'Sorry,' she said meekly, and Gus rewarded her with an approving nod.

'Right,' Dudley said with relish. He pulled a file from beneath his arm and sat on the edge of a desk so that he could open it on his knee. 'It wasn't difficult, I have to admit. He had a wallet in his pocket and sundry other items which helped with the ID. He is – was a Member of the House of Lords. Jack Scroop. He used to be a TUC swell years ago, and they made him a lord when he retired in 1969. Almost right away he had a row with the Government of the day and instead of taking the whip became a crossbencher.' He lifted his head again. 'For those of you who only read the sports pages of your papers, that means he was a Labour peer on account of they were in then, but changed his mind and set himself up as an Independent where he could make a nuisance of himself.'

'If he retired in 1969 he must have been verra old,' Mike Urquhart said.

'You're right.' Gus was clearly approving of Mike's observation. 'He was. But not as old as you might think. He retired from the TUC when he was fifty.'

'I should be so lucky,' someone said sourly. 'Got a pension did he, as well as a comfy seat wrapped up in ermine?'

'Possibly,' Gus said. 'There was a scandal. It turned out he was gay, had been living with fellas for years. That was more of a thing to fuss about years ago than it would be now, though I dare say the papers do their best to make the worst of it if they can. Anyway, when they found out, the *Daily Express* made such a row that he had a nervous breakdown, or so it was said, and that was it for the TUC. But from all accounts he'd been a good fella so they put him in the Lords.'

'And then he went and thumbed his nose at them and wouldn't do as he was told?' Mike said. 'He must have been quite a bloke.'

'No, he was not,' Dudley said sourly and primmed his mouth slightly. Clearly he disapproved of homosexual lords. 'He was a troublemaker from the start. Or used to be. His' – he sniffed – 'his partner died a couple of years ago. And since then he's slipped out of sight a bit. I talked to some people about him last night . . .' He turned a page of his notes. 'Here we are. He used to turn up at the House two or three times a week before Kenny Powys died – he was the other fella – but afterwards, hardly ever. And when he did, he looked a mess. Unwashed, dressed in whatever he'd found handy when he got out of bed, smelly, the lot. A real mess. People had begun to talk, saying something ought to be done about him. But then he stopped coming altogether so they didn't think about him any more. Till I told 'em last night.' He bared his teeth in a sudden grin. 'One or two people are going to be very embarrassed over this. Not noticing one of your fellow Members has gone potty and then disappeared – it doesn't fill the electors with confidence about the way these people run the country, does it?'

'D'you mean maybe there'll be a fuss and we'll get the House of Lords done away with? Seeing we don't get to vote for them at all, that'd be –' Mike began, and this time Gus did not look approving.

'Serving police officers do not express political opinions, and don't you forget it,' he said, and Mike lifted his brows and closed his mouth a little sulkily.

'We've a few more investigations to make,' Dudley went on, as though no one had spoken. 'I've been in touch with some of his neighbours – he lived in a council flat in Islington, believe it or not – but you have the essence of it. He was a recluse, no one special in his life to notice what he got up to, so when he was killed, no one noticed he'd disappeared. Which was why his body wasn't found sooner.' He did not look at George and she, after a swift glance at Gus, bit her tongue. To point out that it had been her insistence they look more carefully in Henriques Street that had revealed the death would be tactless to say the least.

'Didn't he do any other work?' George asked instead. 'I mean what did he live on? If he wasn't one of these hereditary people who have a lot of money, and lived in a council flat, I'd imagine he had a cash problem. He wasn't particularly well nourished, as far as I could tell, the state he was in' – beside her, Julie gave a little shudder – 'and his clothes were certainly far from expensive. Nothing Savile Row about him.'

'He'd have had his attendance allowance,' Mike said, once again showing an unexpected grasp of Parliamentary matters. 'They get a goodish bit just for turning up and going to sleep on the benches, seemingly. Seventy pounds, I've been told.'

'You've been told wrong,' Rupert said crisply. 'I've checked all that. He could claim a day's subsistence of thirty-three pounds fifty because he lived in London. That covered his travel and his food and so forth. Otherwise all he had was his state pension. Not a lot to live on, but his rent was pretty low. I've got the figures here if anyone wants 'em.'

'As poor as a lord,' someone at the back of the big room said. 'It doesn't sound right, does it? Though if they never do anything, I suppose it's fair enough.'

'He did make occasional speeches, apparently,' Rupert said. 'Always on the same thing. The reform of the House of Lords. He used to go on about them all being descendants of thieves and robbers and that was how they'd got their titles in the first place, which was a bit rich seeing he'd got his from being a rabble-rouser and causing strikes.'

'There's more to trade unionism than that –' Mike began and then bit his lip again as Gus stared at him.

'We're getting off the point,' Gus said crisply. 'The thing that matters is that this was a thoroughly eccentric old fella no one cared much about, who did no Committee work, apparently had no power of any sort, so there was no point in killing him. Or there doesn't seem to be.'

'Unless he was used by our Ripper for a dummy run,' George said, knowing she sounded obstinate and not caring. 'I told you that was how the injuries looked. He sounds to me like the ideal target for someone who wants to try something out.'

'I don't see that,' Roop said. 'Why should anyone take the risk of killing someone just to practise?'

'Why should they take the risk of killing at all?' George's chin was up. 'And killing in this crazy fashion, copying a hundred-year-old series of crimes?'

'We've no evidence that that is what this is,' Roop said. 'It's all surmise on your part.'

'Oh, come on Roo – Inspector Dudley!' she said. 'How can you say that? Am I wrong so far? Haven't we found the bodies just where the original Ripper left his? Isn't the MO a sort of copy of the original one? How much more evidence do you want?'

'It's all circumstantial,' Roop said. 'It'd never stand up in court.' And closed his file to glare at her. She glared back.

'Well,' Gus said, as emollient as he knew how to be. 'Let's leave the matter of Lord Scroop to one side at present. There's more to be done with checking on him and his flat before we can get anywhere. Tim, you do that. Take DC Chalice with you. Now, the next thing. Alice Diamond. Mike, let's hear from you about that situation.'

Mike told them succinctly, with a certain light glossing over of his own problems in keeping up with their quarry at Heathrow, just what had happened with Alice Diamond. They all listened, puzzled and fascinated, and when he'd finished a small buzz of talk broke out that Gus had to settle before he could make himself heard.

'Shut up! If you want to contribute make sure we can hear it. You –' He pointed to one of the CID men at the side of the room who had been muttering busily into his companion's ear. 'What were you saying, Hagerty?'

'Drugs, Guv. It sounds like drugs to me. If they can get the stuff in as normal baggage, they're on to a winner. We'll have to find out why the Customs bods didn't fuss over the amount of baggage she had and then we can follow up –'

'We have checked,' Mike said. 'She's a regular traveller, and she brings in a lot of stuff for her fashion shop as normal baggage. Apparently she prefers to pay the excess baggage charges rather than let it go as ordinary freight – she's done it for years. She has all the proper paperwork for the gear – garments mostly, and some costume jewellery.'

'Do we have proof of that?' Hagerty asked. 'Do the Customs search her bags?'

'I got the impression they didn't,' Mike said. 'They seemed

to know her and be perfectly comfortable about what she's bringing in. They're not stupid, Ray. If she was using her business as a front for drugs they'd have pulled her by now. I reckon it's something else. I just don't know what – yet. I'd like the chance to look round her place, Guv. A warrant maybe? And for the shop as well.'

'What's the point?' Rupert said. 'You said yourself the extra bags were taken off by this other geezer, the one in the van. Has anyone tracked that yet?'

'I've got the info here.' Mike pulled out his own notebook. 'I want to go after him today as well. The vehicle's registered to a Max Hazell. He's got an address on the Wembley Stadium Trading Estate.'

'Then go after him, but leave Mrs Diamond alone at present. I'd rather someone just went and talked to her, but without a search warrant.' He looked round the room. 'Morley, you go with Sergeant Urquhart, talk to her, will you? And I want her treated carefully, understand? The fact that she was involved in smuggling or seems to have been doesn't make her any less a woman whose husband has been murdered. And a husband who was an MP at that. So let's not rock any boats till we have to. OK, has anyone anything else to give us this morning before we break up?'

'Still nothing at Mitre Square?' George ventured. 'Don't you think we should be looking there?'

'I've got a sizeable police presence there twenty-four hours a day,' Rupert said. 'We can hardly do more. It is just surmise, after all.'

'And you're sure there isn't any possibility that there's already a body somewhere?'

He didn't answer, refusing even to look at her, so she closed her mouth. Bad enough she had pointed out that there would be a body at Henriques Street; she didn't have to compound her crime. Maybe she'd go and look for herself, she thought, and, smiling sweetly at Rupert Dudley, said no more.

'I'm still concerned about Alice Diamond.' Mike was stubborn. 'There could well be information there that –'

'You heard what we decided about her,' Rupert said, but Gus put a hand on his arm.

'Tell you what, Mike,' he said genially. 'If you can find a way to have a look round a woman's shop full of fripperies without making any sort of fuss, we'll be glad to see you do it, OK?'

There was a ripple of laughter and Gus shook his head at Mike, who was looking sour now. 'I take your point, Mike,' he said, 'but we've no cause to search that shop and it'd cause trouble if we did. I feel it in my bones. Anyway, she'll be there for a bit yet. We've time to get to her. Right now there's a lot of other more pressing stuff to do. OK, here you are ...' And he was off, detailing each and every one of them with their day's work. Julie, beside George still, sighed deeply when she found herself once again set to work on the computers, checking the incoming data and making sure it was all properly programmed.

'Honestly, as though that was all that important,' she muttered. 'There's Barnett over there' – she jerked her head at another uniformed PC on the other side of the room – 'he's crazy about computers, loves doing the work and gets through it twice as fast as I do. Why can't they let him get on with it and let me go off and do some real work?'

George looked at her and bit her lip, thinking hard. Then she grinned. 'Could you go sick?' she asked.

'Eh? What for?'

'To get out of here.'

Julie looked interested. 'How d'you mean?'

'I agree with Mike. Someone ought to go and look round that shop. Who knows what we might find? I agree with Gus too, though. You can't send Mike thundering around in his size umpteens. But a couple of women, in ordinary clothes, of course, not uniforms – well, that'd be different, wouldn't it?'

Julie looked at her, her eyes bright, then slowly smiled. 'Ooh, Dr B.,' she said loudly. 'I do have the most awful belly ache. D'you think I ought to go and have a word with our nurse about it?'

'Oh, yes,' George said firmly, even more loudly. 'Indeed you should. It's probably dysmenorrhoea, you know. Painful periods. A day's rest should sort it out.'

'Bloody women,' muttered one of the men as they pushed past, and Julie and George grinned delightedly at each other.

'Yeah,' George said. 'Bloody women. Especially when we find things they don't. Go and deal with the nurse, Julie. I'll see you downstairs as soon as you get out. I'll give you a lift home to change. And then, Sloane Square or bust!'

12

George loitered on the kerb, waiting for Julie, who seemed to be having some trouble convincing the nurse in the occupational health department at the nick that she needed to go off duty; certainly she had been gone far longer than George had expected and she was beginning to chafe. She could, after all, visit Alice Diamond's Sloane Square shop perfectly well on her own. But she'd made a deal with Julie so she would have to wait for her; and of course it would look better to have two of them at the shop. One could prowl around while the other distracted attention in some way.

So she was still there when Gus came clattering down the steps on his way to Scotland Yard for a meeting with the Commissioner, who was, understandably enough, getting very twitchy at the rate at which Members of Parliament were being culled. He pulled up in surprise when he saw her. 'I thought you said you had to go to the hospital this morning?' he said. 'Have you changed your mind?'

'Oh, no.' George, accomplished liar though she could be when it was necessary, hated deceiving Gus. 'I just promised someone a lift who's going that way. Er – if they don't come soon, I'll have to go.' She scrabbled for a change of subject. 'Um, what are we doing tonight? Will you be working late? Or maybe –'

'Of course I'm working late,' he said. 'We took last night off, ducky, but there's a limit. Roop's working every night. I can hardly let him if I don't, can I?'

She ignored that. Getting on to the subject of Rupert Dudley would not be wise. 'Is it something I can help with?'

'Help with?' He looked at her thoughtfully. 'That needs thinking about.'

'Well, then, think!' Over Gus's shoulder she saw Julie come out of the station and prayed she'd have the wit to hang back till Gus had gone. She came halfway down the steps looking pleased with herself and George, not even daring to glance at her, went on quickly. 'Let me know and I'll do it. I told you, I've taken this time off from the hospital and I don't want to waste it!' Just in time she saw the pit she was digging for her own feet. 'That's why I'm – um – going in this morning, to check all's well so that I can go on staying away.'

'You sound like Alice in Wonderland on a bad day,' he said. 'All right, I was considering it anyway. I'm going to see if I can wangle an invitation to dinner at the House of Lords. I've put a call into Joe Durnell. He got his lordship when he left the force three years ago. He'll understand, and make sure we get some inside info. You can come along if you like. You might enjoy it.'

'You're on,' she said fervently, not only because she was delighted at the proposal but also because of her relief that Julie had assessed the situation correctly and gone back up the steps to melt into the shadows under the portico. Sensible girl, George thought, and smiled brilliantly at Gus. 'I'll put on my best bib and so forth and meet you – where? At the House of Lords? Or at home?'

'Keep your phone switched on and I'll call you,' he said. 'I must go.' He looked at his watch. 'My meeting's in ten minutes. I'll have to use the blue light to make it as it is. S'long.' And he flicked his thumb and forefinger at an imaginary hat brim and went, belting round to the side of the building to the yard where the cars waited.

Julie came down the steps a few moments later, and without a word followed George as she half trotted, half ran to the side street on the other side of the building where she had left her car. It would never do for Gus to come out and see them together;

and she felt a stab of shame because of her duplicity. He hardly ever lied to her. But then, she argued inside her head as she unlocked the car door and Julie scrambled in to sit low in her seat (clearly fully aware of the need for discretion), he doesn't have to. I don't try and stop him doing things that need to be done, do I?

She pulled the car into the now thick morning traffic and headed away in the opposite direction to the one which Gus's car would have to take when it left the yard, and took a deep breath, and Julie sat up straight and looked at her sideways.

'Does he know where we're going?' she said.

'Of course not. Would I drop you in it? What did the nurse say?'

'I don't think she believed me at first, but it's a hard thing to prove isn't it? Anyway, she gave me a couple of aspirin, and said I could go home if it really was that bad. I felt a right wimp, to tell you the truth.'

'You have to do what you have to do if you want to get on with things,' George said, as much to herself as to Julie. 'Where do you live? The sooner we get up to Sloane Street and back the better. Then you can have a miraculous recovery, and go back to your computer.'

Julie was admirably swift. She left George waiting outside her flat in Wapping little more than ten minutes, reappearing looking a very different person in a short-skirted red suit and high-heeled shoes. George looked at her approvingly.

'You look Sloane Street all the way through to your middle. I feel positively dowdy.'

Julie looked at her and said candidly, 'Well, you're not exactly formal, are you? I like the look, of course, but, well . . .'

George looked down at her black jeans and matching casual jacket over a green shirt, all underpinned with a pair of clean but all the same well-worn trainers, and had to agree. 'Never mind. It gives us a reason to be together. I'm the out-of-towner needing to be dragged up into fashion and you're my advisor. OK?'

'OK,' said Julie contentedly and settled to enjoy her morning.

It mightn't do much for her career, especially if she was caught sloping off, but at least it would give her some experience of real detection. She was a very happy young woman as the car slid its way through the hubbub that was London on this bright autumn day. And so was her driver.

'I wish I could have been at Heathrow and seen what happened the other day,' she said, carefully overtaking a lumpen slow van loaded with planks that stuck dangerously out of its back doors. 'That'd have been useful.'

'Why?'

'You can learn a lot about people just by looking at them. The way they walk, the way they hold themselves. Like what sort of mood they're in and the state of their health. You can spot where they have aches and pains and how long since they had a meal . . .'

'You sound like Sherlock Holmes.' Julie was admiring.

George laughed. 'Not a bit of it. It's straightforward medical training. You learn to look at people as specimens as well as people. As for Sherlock, of course, Conan Doyle based his Sherlock on a doctor he'd worked with, didn't he? He was a doctor himself.'

'If the only way I can get to be a detective is to take up medicine,' Julie said, 'then I'll make a living waiting at tables. I wouldn't do your job for anything.' She shuddered. 'All those bodies all the time.'

George looked happy. 'Mmm. They are horrid sometimes. But very interesting. So interesting you stop noticing the nasty bits. Ah, now, here we are. But where the hell do we park?'

It took them half an hour to find a vacant meter, a sharp five-minute walk away from their target, and then to weave their way back to Sloane Street, but it was still the right side of ten a.m. when they got there. And the shop was closed.

It was a very pretty establishment. The windows were a mock-up of an eighteenth-century shop, complete with one or two panes of thick bottle glass in the corners, but not so faithful to the old design that the contents of the shop were not clearly visible. The window itself held a wisp of peach silk trimmed with double layers of lace drooping over a model of a prancing white horse with Pegasus wings, and a couple of matching panties lay coyly round its feet. There was also a great deal of ruched tulle and silk daffodils and sweet peas clustered in corners. Behind all the whimsy, there was a clear view of the shop's interior, brilliantly lit with spotlights and filled with racks of sugared-almond-coloured garments. There was more ruched tulle and lots more artificial flowers. George leaned towards the window to look, cupping her hands round her eyes to improve her view, and almost snorted. 'God, it looks like a brothel,' she said.

'I've never seen one,' Julie giggled. 'But I suppose you could be right. I think it's rather pretty, actually.'

George shook her head. 'Not my style. Well, now what? We just wait?'

Julie looked at her watch. 'It's five to ten,' she said. 'It's my guess they'll open then. These posh shops often do start late. Their customers don't get up any earlier, do they?'

'I suppose not,' George said. 'What's smartest, do you think? Hanging around waiting or going off somewhere for ten minutes and then coming back?'

Julie considered. 'Going away,' she said. 'It'll make us look, well, anything but posh to hang around.'

'Then we'll wait,' George said. 'Because if she thinks we're just hayseeds she'll behave differently. More relaxed is my bet.' And, folding her arms, she leaned against the shop door.

Julie looked mulish for a moment and seemed about to argue, then shrugged her shoulders. 'It's up to you. I'll just go and look in the other windows.' She tittuped away to stare earnestly at the suits in the adjoining establishments.

She had moved five shops away by the time Alice Diamond arrived. A small sports car, which clearly held a great deal of power under its engine, pulled into the kerb and parked, the driver quite ignoring the double yellow lines, and she got out, unfolding a pair of long legs in navy-blue tights. George watched her, trying to look simply tired with waiting, but not missing a detail.

Much older than she dresses, she decided, watching the woman as she reached into the boot of her car. That blonde hair has to be touched up every week, I suspect. And the clothes look as though they cost a bomb, but she needs pretty firm corsetry under them. It was the face that gave away the most. The make-up was perfect, as George could clearly see when the woman at last locked her car and carried the two packages she had extracted from it towards the door of the shop, but, sleekly applied though it was, the fine network of lines and the soft sagging of a woman of fifty or so showed clearly in the cruel morning sunshine. Yet the effect was good. Just enough eye make-up to make her interesting, enough lipstick to add glamour; she looked both elegant and workmanlike. She is, George decided as she straightened up and made room at the door, an artefact and a credit to her maker, who is, of course, herself.

'Good morning,' the woman said brightly. 'Can I help you?'

'Oh, I just wanted to look about,' George said, letting her American accent slide back. These days she rarely showed her origins except to people with educated ears. Most assumed she was Irish or a Northerner or something of that sort, now she'd been in Britain for so many years. But she suspected that this woman would be attracted by the thought of an American tourist with money to spend.

She was right. The blonde hair bobbed with the vigour of the woman's nods and her earrings seemed to twinkle more as she stretched her mouth wider into a welcoming smile. 'Well, of course, you must come right in! I'm so sorry you had to wait. Coffee at once. Ah, here you are, Maria!' She looked over her shoulder as another woman arrived, a carbon copy of herself in terms of style, but a great deal younger and cheaper. 'We have our first customer, Maria. Do make some coffee, right away, will you? And then I'll see what it is we can do for you.'

'My friend's here to help me,' George said brightly as Julie, seeing the action, came hurrying up. 'But don't worry about the coffee. I just want to look at the stuff. I'm kinda fixing up a trousseau, you know? I'm getting married soon and I thought

I'd have a better chance of getting some really gorgeous scanties here rather than back home in – um – Minneapolis.'

'I'm sure you will,' the woman said heartily, leading the way into her shop. Even more spotlights burst into life as the girl Maria scurried around attacking switches and in no time Julie and George were settled in armchairs, which were narrow, covered in gilt and exceedingly uncomfortable, while the woman chattered at them. 'A trousseau – well, where do we start? Maria, bring the far rack, will you, with the Italian labels. Yes, that's the one. Now, my dear, which colours are you planning? Classic white? Or outrageous black? Or some of the jewel colours that are so in this season?'

'Oh, I don't know,' George said, trying to sound prettily confused. 'What do you think, Julie, honey?' She turned back to the woman not waiting for an answer. 'This is my friend Julie and I'm – er – Vanny.' Her mother's name would fit in better here than her own, she decided. 'Evadne, you know?' And she thrust out her hand.

'I'm Alice,' the woman said, accepting it, and George relaxed a little. Until now she had not been absolutely sure. Now she could really get to work.

And work she did. Alice chattered and displayed, draping nightdresses and teddies and lacy wisps of bras and panties over her arms as Maria handed them to her and after a while Julie, who had been included in all George's chatter at first, realized she was being deliberately left out and responded as George wanted her to. She got to her feet and went wandering about the shop, which meant that the girl Maria had perforce to go with her. George could hear them talking right over in the far corner, and complimented herself on her choice of ally. Julie was clearly making the best of her opportunities.

'It's so hard to know what a man will like, isn't it?' she said artlessly to Alice, who was displaying a slip in a rather sour yellow. 'What do you think, Alice? I'm sure you've more experience than I have, being married and all.' And she looked pointedly at the wedding ring on Alice's finger. 'What does your husband like?'

Alice hesitated for a moment. 'He's dead,' she said.

George opened her eyes wide and clasped her hands together. 'Oh, I am so sorry! Gee, the last thing I would want to do is upset you with questions. Oh, do please forgive me. Um – did he pass away – er – recently? Or have you had time to –'

'Very recently,' Alice said brusquely. 'Now about this colour. What do you think?'

'Oh, I am just mortified!' George put her hands to her face. 'To be so clumsy and ... forgive me. Please, do come and sit down and let me apologize properly.'

She reached for Alice's hand and, in spite of her resistance, made her sit down on the adjoining armchair so that George could look earnestly into her eyes. 'You must be absolutely devastated. And still here at work? How brave of you.'

'Well, life goes on,' Alice said and looked at her directly. Now her face was in repose for the first time – she had been too busy providing sales talk for George to see her properly – it was clear that she was watchful. And there was distress there too, George decided. Her eyes had the faintly puffy look of someone who may have wept, but who certainly had not slept; and she put out a hand and said with genuine concern, 'You're not sleeping at all well, are you?'

'Jesus,' Alice said. 'Does it show that much?' She put her own hands to her face and shook her head.

'I worked as a nurse,' George said. 'I'm trained to see these things. Was it very recent, then?'

'This week,' the woman said. 'Just this week.'

'Then you've had to cope with a funeral,' George said, still sympathetic. 'How horrible for you.'

'No, not yet. Next week maybe. If – Next week.'

'You mean, you don't know? How can that be? The sooner the funeral the sooner you'll be able to pick up the pieces of your life.' She used the cliché deliberately. This was no time for clever talk. 'It kinda puts a full stop to things and you can get yourself together again. I know how it was when my Daddy died ...' Somewhere deep inside shame grew. If this woman was a genuine mourner this treatment of her was obscene. But her husband had been murdered, George reminded herself, and wives usually have more to do with husbands' untimely deaths than most people realize. Also, she had behaved oddly over her baggage at the airport, and furthermore, others had been murdered too. No, even at the risk of hurting her unjustly, George felt she had to go on.

'So when will the funeral be?' she said.

Alice took a deep breath, as though it was easier to talk than fight off this inquisitive stranger. 'There has to be an inquest. And various other things. He was – killed.'

'Oh, how?' George caught her breath and said no more, trusting to Alice to carry the momentum forward. Behind them they could hear the murmuring voices of Julie and Maria; and after a moment Alice seemed to crumple and give in.

'You'll probably have seen it in the papers, anyway,' she said. 'He was a Member of Parliament and he was – Well, it's murder. No need for details.'

'A Member of – You mean like a Congressman?'

'I suppose so,' said Alice. 'Anyway, there it is, I'm on my own now.' She stared into the distance for a moment and George, with genuine concern, put her hand over the curled fingers still holding the yellow slip.

'You have no children? Or other relatives to help?'

'A stepson. He won't care much. He never liked me, anyway. It was really just Sam and me. We had an understanding. I'll miss him.'

'Of course you will. When you love someone –'

'Love?' Alice laughed then, a sharp ugly little sound. 'I'm not sure what love is. I do know we knew and understood each other and didn't make judgements and helped each other out. We had our rows, of course. The last time I saw him we had a hell of a fight.' She took a long shaky breath, and her eyes glazed as she looked back into her memory. 'God, I wish we hadn't. He'd have come round to it all in time. I could have made him see . . .' She blinked then, refocused her eyes, and gathered herself together. She went on, 'He won't be easy to replace. Not with someone who understands the way I do things as well as he did.'

It was an odd turn of phrase, George thought. She sounds more like an employer who has to replace an essential member of staff than a woman mourning the loss of her life partner.

Alice Diamond seemed to realize she was talking too much and suddenly got to her feet. 'But really,' she said with a return of her original brightness, 'I mustn't upset a young bride like you with my troubles! Let's get back to your trousseau.'

'I'm not such a young bride,' George said. 'I've been – well, I've not married before but I've not been lonely, you understand.' She gave her the look that said, 'I'm a woman-of-the-world-just-like-you-so-let's-talk,' but Alice had recaptured her self-control. She just held out the lemon-coloured garment again.

George would never cease being grateful for Julie, who timed matters precisely as she should. She suddenly appeared from between the racks with Maria in tow and smiled brightly at George.

'Um, Vanny,' she said. 'I'm so sorry, but we really have to go. I made that appointment for you to talk to the estate agent, remember? At half past ten.' She turned to Alice. 'We thought you'd be open earlier so we'd have enough time. But we have to go now. We'll be back later. This afternoon perhaps. Though we have to see two flats of course. Come along, Vanny. I really can't let you be late. You always are, and it does make life so difficult, so let's be on our way . . .'

And chattering busily she extracted George from the shop, leaving Alice and Maria staring after them as they hurried away back towards George's car.

13

'It's pronounced "Chumley",' Gus said. 'Bloody ridiculous, but there you go.'

George, who had indeed been trying to decipher 'Cholmondeley' on the piece of pasteboard in her hand, grinned. 'It's no worse than trying to read Sioux City, I guess. What is this event anyway? And how did you get us invited?'

'Fundraisers never mind how many bodies they have at their parties. There's always the chance you'll cough up a few quid. This one's in aid of the Country Sports Association, but never mind. We can pretend to be landed gentry. Joe Durnell's acting as host. They have to have one of the lords to get themselves in here, so he fixed it. Come on.'

He led the way past the little police cubby hole at the entrance to the House of Lords, under the arch into the central square and on to a wide door on the far side. George followed, trying not to be overawed. It looked as though it dripped with antiquity, but she had Gus's word for it that the whole place was not yet a hundred and fifty years old. The smell was old, though, musty and damp with layers of floor polish and sweating people, and the scent enveloped her as they moved through the doorway into the Cholmondeley Room, which was buzzing with activity.

They were introduced to a burly man in his sixties, with suspiciously dark hair, which he wore plastered close to his head like a helmet, and a thin man in the striped trousers and dark jacket of an old-fashioned civil servant. His air of subservience to the burly man made George want to kick him; it was obviously an act, taken straight from Dickens, but he seemed actually to enjoy it.

The burly man, however, who was Lord Durnell, reassured her greatly. He had an accent as comfortably cockney as Gus's, and was clearly quite unimpressed both by the thin man and his surroundings. 'Hope you get what you want, Gus,' he said. 'They're a right shower – get more of a charge out of gutting a bleedin' fox than rogerin' their wives, but what do you expect? Still, they've got a good turnout so you should get some stuff out of 'em.'

George couldn't help it. 'So you're not keen on hunting?'

'Do me a favour! It's never bin my cup o' tea. Barbarian I call it.'

'Then why act as host for them?'

He looked at her admiringly. 'She don't creep around in carpet slippers, does she, Gus? You got yourself a real one 'ere, ol' boy. It's politics, ducky, that's what it is. I do someone a favour and that someone does one for me when I need it, see?' He looked at her earnestly. 'It's the only way you can operate in a place like this, it's so crusty. But I'm doin' all right, so don't you go making hasty judgements about me. I'm not one of them.'

George blushed a little and Gus chuckled appreciatively. 'That's put you in your place,' he said, well satisfied. 'Come on then. Let's get to work.' He nodded affably at Lord Durnell and moved forwards into the hubbub. George followed him and was grateful for the glass of wine someone put in her hand, so that she could stand and sip it as she looked around and listened.

No one seemed to be talking about hunting. As far as she could tell – because words were swallowed by the ambient noise and because when a talker got to an interesting part he tended to drop his voice – they were doing what people who knew each other well always do at a party: they were gossiping about each other. George tried to absorb some of it, but without much success. All she could decipher was that some people were taking hellish risks with other people's wives and some wives were more trouble than they were worth to the Party, and one of these days someone would – at which point, again tantalizingly, the gossips moved away towards the table which acted as a bar in search of refills, and George missed the rest of it.

She went after Gus then, slipping between earnestly talking groups, smiling apologetically for disturbing them, and finally saw Gus at the end of the bar, in close conversation with a rather chubby man with thin pale hair who looked vaguely familiar.

Gus caught her eye and waved at her. 'Come and be introduced, Dr Barnabas,' he said and she took the message that she was expected to behave like a colleague and no more. She primmed her face accordingly and joined them.

'Dr Barnabas, the Earl of Durleigh – Lord Durleigh.'

'Oh, hi,' George said and decided to play the dumb American card again. 'Glad to meet you. Um – what do I call you? Your lordship?'

The round face cracked into a smile. 'Try Richard. I usually answer to that. How d'ye do?'

'Very well, thanks,' George said. 'If you're really asking.'

Richard Durleigh smiled cheerfully. 'I agree with you, it's a rather silly phrase, just as titles and so forth are. But there's not much I can do about it any more than I can about the way we talk here. I was born to it and I'm stuck with it, as the eldest. I couldn't do what my brother did.' His face seemed to tighten and lose some of its chubbiness. 'He was able to do as his conscience led him.'

'The Earl is the older brother of David Caspar-Wynette-Gondor,' Gus said quietly.

George blinked, bit her lip and said, 'I'm sorry,' ashamed of her spiky behaviour.

Richard Durleigh managed a thin smile. 'It's all right. I'm – I'm getting used to it. I can't pretend we were all that close. Miles apart in lots of ways, to tell the truth. Politics can split a family wide open. It certainly did so to ours. But as I told your chaps when they came to interview me, a brother's a brother when all's said and done.'

'Indeed,' Gus said.

There was a little silence as they all sipped at their glasses, looking rather absurd as they moved in unison. 'Are you still wanting to talk to me?' Richard said then. 'Is that why you're here?'

'Oh, no. No, no,' Gus said quickly. 'I – er – I'm an old friend of Lord Durnell and he suggested we drop in. All for a good cause, he said.'

Richard raised his brows. 'Really? I wouldn't have thought old Durnell was interested in country sports. I thought he was hosting this party because he owed one of the chaps a favour. In fact, I gather he's a bit of a supporter of animal rights organizations. I've had some of his stuff in my pigeon-hole, and –'

'Pigeon-hole?' Gus looked alert.

'Mail and so forth. Our names, you see? Very alike. Sometimes his mail goes into my hole and mine into his. I've seen the stuff because they mark their envelopes with slogans. And to tell the truth the temporary secretaries they send us tend to be less than the brightest; they open all the mail in the pigeon-hole and don't check the addresses on it first. So I see quite a bit of his. But it evens out.' He smiled thinly. 'He sees mine in the same way. I dare say he gets fed up with my copies of *Horse and Hound*.'

Someone came up behind George and spoke over her shoulder. 'Evening, Dick. I've been looking for you. There's something I must talk to you about. It's to do with Marietta, I'm afraid.'

George turned her head and looked at the newcomer. He was a slighter version of the man they were talking to, with the same pale hair and round face, but he was a good two inches shorter. George actually had to look down at him, and as she did so she realized where the likeness was that she had recognized earlier in the taller man: this had to be another brother of David Caspar-Wynette-Gondor. Appallingly maimed though the corpse had been, he had the same look as these two, though he had been, she thought, rather younger. These two looked to be well into their forties.

She put out her hand. 'Mr Caspar-Wynette-Gondor?' she said. 'May I offer my condolences on your loss?'

The small man blinked and looked at her and Richard said

quickly, 'This is Dr Barnabas, Eddie. And Superintendent Hathaway of the police. My brother Edward, Superintendent.'

'How do,' Gus said and shook hands. 'I'm sorry too, about –'

'Well, yes,' Edward said a little brusquely. 'It's a dreadful business, appalling. Are you here to talk about it? I've already spent a lot of time with one of your people this afternoon, a chap called Dudley, as I recall.'

'Oh, no,' Gus said. 'This is a purely fortuitous thing. We came because Lord Durnell asked us, and it's a good cause, isn't it?'

'Certainly it is. Are you a hunting man. Superintendent? Or perhaps an angler?'

''Fraid not,' Gus said. 'Town chap all the way through to my middle. Country pursuits are a foreign country to me. But I believe strongly that people have the right to do what they want and if country people feel their lifestyle is being damaged by meddling do-gooders, well then, I'm there at the barricades with 'em. Right is right, after all.'

Edward looked at him for a long moment and then nodded. 'Very estimable, very. Glad to have the support. It isn't always forthcoming on our side of the argument, unfortunately.'

'Really?' Gus said with a disingenuous air that made George glance at him sharply. 'I'd have thought that the weight of country opinion in favour of field sports would be considerable.'

'It should be.' Edward showed some signs of animation for the first time. 'But there are so many incomers now bringing their sentimental townie notions about fluffy bunny-wunnies and good old Brer Fox with 'em that it's hard for the voice of commonsense to be heard, which says that hunting is the best way of dealing with vermin and at the same time provides the best sort of competitive sport there is. Pity you don't choose to come and live amongst us. We need a few more sensible voters.'

Gus set his head on one side. 'Voters? Are you a Member of this august house too, then?'

Edward made an odd sound, half sniff of disdain, half snort of disgust. 'Absolutely not. Not my world at all. Sitting in rows posturing and shouting at each other isn't my idea of how to get things done.'

The Earl looked amused. 'As you see, my brother and I don't always agree on political matters. He prefers the bureaucratic approach.'

Gus quirked his eyebrows and Edward seemed to accept the question.

'Brussels. I spend a certain amount of time there in the EU offices. I'm involved on the agricultural side. Part time, but I probably get more done in the few hours I put in than this lot here' – he made a scornful movement of his head that took in both chambers of the building in which they stood – 'get done in a whole session of Parliament.'

'Not if you count the hours you spend travelling,' Richard murmured. 'You seem to spend more time in the air and on trains than at the desk.'

'And I need more time at home running the place than you can spare, so I can't see that –'

He stopped suddenly and took out a handkerchief and blew his nose with a certain amount of flourish. Displacement activity, thought George. There's a real argument here between them and he nearly gave it away. I wonder what –

Gus pulled her thoughts away. 'Brussels, eh? Must be very interesting?'

'Not in the least,' Edward said, brusque again. 'Very boring. But it's becoming the place where things get done. And I like to get things done, as I say. Can't be doing with inefficiency. Now, if you'll forgive me. I have to take my brother away. We really do have to discuss something that's come up. A matter of some urgency. Dick?'

'Excuse me, Superintendent,' the Earl murmured. 'We can speak again later perhaps.' And he followed his brother to the side of the room where they stood head to head, the shorter one talking at some length, with sharp, almost agitated little gestures. After a little while Richard nodded and followed Edward, who led the way to the door. Clearly they were leaving, and Gus followed them, seeming casual in his movements, but going in such a way that he would be near the door when they reached it; he's on an eavesdropping trip, George thought, and followed him in her turn.

But the two men were too quick for Gus. They were out of the door by the time he got there. He stopped and watched them go.

Lord Durnell, who had moved away from his position as greeter, was standing very close as George came up and he too was watching the brothers. 'You'd never think they were twins, would you?' he was saying to Gus as she reached his side. 'And supposed to be identicals, what's more. But the shorty one looks like he's got the thin end of the pudding spoon, doesn't he?'

'It happens with twins,' George said. 'One gets less nutrition *in utero* than the other and never manages to catch up. And even identicals are changed by their life experience. I guess the Earl's had a better time than Edward has. He certainly looks a lot more cheerful.'

'He won't now,' Durnell said. 'What with his brother being one of your cases and now his sister-in-law playing up.'

Gus cocked an eye at him. 'What's that?'

'I gather from the grapevine that she's made a suicide attempt,' Durnell said. 'Hadn't you heard?'

'No.' Gus sounded angry. 'No, I hadn't. Why didn't they call and tell me? And how did you hear?'

Durnell winked at him. 'I always like a gossip with the lads at the gate when I come in. One of 'em heard it on the radio, I gather. It's natural they should all be agog with fellas from the Other Place as well as here getting done in! I'd ha' thought someone'd have told *you* by now.'

Gus glowered. 'So would I.' He reached into his pocket for his phone. 'I'll call the nick, see what's going on.'

He turned away to the corner to use the phone and George said, 'What sort of man is this Earl? Does he do a good job?'

Durnell looked at her and grinned. 'Good job? Where? His real job, do you mean, or here in the House?'

'What's his real job?'

'Running his estate,' Durnell said. 'He's got a great chunk of

124

Warwickshire to call his own, and he farms a fair bit of it himself. Well, up to a point himself. He's got a good man who does the really heavy stuff. And of course Edward's very involved. I'm told, some ways he works even harder on the place, but he's the younger son, of course, so there's not a lot in it for him. Not that he does all that badly, I imagine. He'll get some sort of salary and Richard's got an eye for money, by all accounts, so it could be a good screw. He's almost doubled the place's worth since his father died, I gather, what with guided tours of the house – he owns Durleigh Abbey – and putting in golf courses where they used to grow wheat. And market gardening too. It doesn't leave him a lot of time to come here, but he does when it's something that affects agricultural policy or things like this.' He waved his hand vaguely. 'Sees himself as a sort of protector of the traditional ways, I suppose. It made life tricky for him with his brother, of course.'

'Edward?'

'No, David. The dead one. He was always banging on about reforming the House of Lords, the way young ones do, though he was a bit long in the tooth for it. I used to think it was the right thing to do when I was a lad. But now I'm here, I can see the good of it.'

'Really,' George said, not wanting to be sidetracked into a political discussion. 'What did Richard do about him then? David, I mean.'

Durnell looked amused. 'Do? What could he do? Got himself on the same Committee, on the Right to Inheritance Bill. It's a label that covers a whole lot of stuff, one of which would be to put an end to hereditary seats here. They'd all have to be like me – it'd be the biggest bleedin' quango in the country.' He laughed fatly. 'Then maybe we'd get some real work done. It's a great help not having to worry about elections – you can concentrate on what's really right and what's really wrong when you don't have voters breathing in your ear'ole all the time.'

George nodded politely. This wasn't really answering her question. 'And I take it the Earl didn't agree?'

'And the rest! They were at loggerheads all the time over it.

So that's the answer to your question about whether Durleigh is good at his job. He does a good job on that Committee here, but that's about it. Just lobby fodder for the Tories, otherwise. He turns out when they put the whip on and sometimes just to be obliging, as long as there isn't something more important going on in Warwickshire.' He shook his head as Gus at last came back, tucking his phone away in his breast pocket. 'He's a canny bugger. Got himself out of cattle ten years ago. Reckoned there was trouble coming over that business of mad cows and how right he was! Though to be honest, it wasn't his idea entirely. It was Edward. He doesn't just work on the estate with his brother. He knows what's what in Brussels with this short-term Commission job of his and though they argue a bit over this and that, they're pretty close.'

'Well, twins,' George said. 'They often are. Are they married?'

'Not to each other though sometimes you'd think they were. Where one is the other one tends to turn up.' Durnell laughed again. 'Edward isn't married. Not the marrying type, you get my meaning?' He leered a little. 'Got a friend what he lives with, I gather. A chap. Still, I suppose it takes all sorts. And these days it's more'n your life's worth to criticize his sort, so there you go.'

'And Richard?' George said, not allowing herself to make her usual retort about people who judged others' sexuality. 'What about him?'

'Oh, yes – and no.' Joe Durnell anticipated her next question. 'No children yet. They've only been married a little while, just a matter of weeks, so I dare say they'll get round to it soon enough. The gentry don't waste time over such things, do they? Though Richard's taken his time to settle down – they have to be well past forty, those two. But now Richard's found his Countess, he won't hang about. He's been sowing his wild oats cheerfully for years, but the time's come when he has to have an heir. And a spare too, if he can. That's what the Royals aim for, so the aristocracy do too.'

'Joe, you're as much of an old woman as you ever were. Thank God!' Gus said. 'Where would we be without you?'

'Well, it's what you came for, isn't it? A bit of background? Is there anything else you're after?'

'I can't stop now to talk any more. I'll call you. What about you, George? Speak now or forever hold your whatsits.'

She smiled at the old man; for all his occasional flashes of prejudice he was a good contact, and pleasant enough. 'Not right now. But if I think of anything, may I call you?'

'Of course. Are you part of the investigating team for AMIT then?'

Gus looked uncomfortable. 'Like hell she is,' he said, taking George's elbow. 'She's the pathologist, but try and keep her out of the rest of it. It's like trying to carve mercury. It's safer to take her around with me to keep an eye on her. And she's useful sometimes, of course.' He looked wickedly at George then. 'And I know the hell I'll get for that comment later on. Come on, George, we have to go. I'm needed at the nick.'

'Why George, by the way?' Joe asked as they turned away. 'Georgina are you? Or Georgette?'

'No,' said George with some force and the old man lifted his eyebrows.

'It was her grandfather,' Gus said quickly. 'He didn't reckon women, but had just one daughter and said he'd only leave his money to the baby she was expecting when he was dying if it was named after him. This is what was born, so her mother called her George. Simple, really.'

'Yes,' Joe said and laughed. 'Is she as strongminded as her mother?'

'Hey!' George said. 'Stop talking about me as if I wasn't here!'

'You see what I have to put up with, Joe?' Gus bent and kissed George's cheek. 'But I'm learning to change my nasty male ways. Thanks, ol' man. I'll be in touch, or maybe Dudley will. One or other of us anyway. G'night.'

'G'night,' Joe said. 'And come and have lunch here sometime, George. The food's not wonderful, but the gossip's the best.'

'Thank you,' George said. 'I think I will. When I've got rid of this one here.' And Joe laughed and watched them go.

14

'Just let me check up on this Marietta business,' Gus said, as he steered the car past a massive articulated lorry from Holland which was trundling noisily up the middle of the Embankment. 'And then we can go home to bed. Or, if you like, you can take the car and I'll come home in a cab.'

'No need,' George said. 'I'm as interested as you are. What's happening?'

'It's clearly the same thing that made the brothers go off in such a rush. It's Marietta, David CWG's widow. She's been tucked away in a nursing home, but it isn't a secure unit, no one's locked in, and apparently she's taken off. I don't know the details, but she left a note of some sort. So I have to get there.'

'Oh, for heaven's sake! And you stood there gassing on with Joe? Why didn't you say it was urgent?'

'Because it isn't. Hinton's on the case, and half the local force in Harrow are out searching for her. I'll be told soon enough when there's anything to tell.'

As though on cue the phone in his pocket rang; he pulled it out and she took it from him. 'You concentrate on driving, I'll transmit any messages,' she said.

'Bossy boots.' But he made no sign of really minding and she put the phone to her ear.

It was Mike Urquhart, much to her relief. It had suddenly occurred to her that it might be Dudley, and if it were, he would

128

probably have refused to tell her what he had to say, insisting on speaking only to Gus. But Mike had no such qualms.

'Tell the Guv'nor they've not found her yet, but they've had a couple of sightings so it shouldn't be long. The woman's out in a nightdress and barefoot, for pity's sake, so she's hard to miss. But there's something more important...' He hesitated. 'It mightn't be anything, but there's been a nine nine nine call from a caretaker in a building in Creechurch Lane. The squad's on the way but I didn't want to waste any time.'

'Oh?' George said, looking sideways at Gus. 'Where did you say?'

Mike sighed softly. 'It's sort of parallel to Mitre Square,' he said. 'But that doesn't mean it's another killing, of course.' But George ignored that and opened her eyes wide as she turned urgently to Gus.

'Gus, there's some sort of panic on near Mitre Square –'

He grabbed the phone from her hands, swerving slightly as he did so and shoved it to his ear. 'More,' he said and listened. And then nodded. 'On way,' he said crisply and flicked the phone off and back into his pocket.

'Gus, tell me, tell me!' George cried. He sighed deeply, not taking his eyes from the road.

'I suppose if this turns out to be a true bill I'll never hear the last of it from you. The caretaker in this office building called nine nine nine, was hysterical but said something about someone being hurt. Mike was in the incident room doing some catching up on his paperwork when the call was relayed in – at least they remembered to report all suspicious cases in the City directly to us instead of just following the usual routine – and Mike remembered what you said about Mitre Square. All right? Now tell me what else he said to you.'

She told him about the progress of the search for Marietta, trying not to sound exultant. It was dreadful to be so pleased, she told herself, if this latest call was another mutilated body found close to where she said it would be. A murder victim was not something to celebrate, for heaven's sake. But at the same time there was the excitement of deduction and being proven right; it didn't bear thinking of, she told herself firmly and turned back to Gus.

'Are we going straight there?'

'Of course. They'll let me know about Marietta, and there's nothing specially odd about that anyway. The woman's off her rocker, so ... Right, here we go.' He reached into the glove compartment for the blue light and siren he used when he was in his own car, as now, and opened the window to thrust it out on to the roof. The noise and flashing opened a path before them as though by magic, and he went careering along at well over sixty miles an hour, clearly enjoying it hugely. For a moment both he and George were supremely happy people, however ashamed both might have been to admit it.

It took Gus and his outrageous driving just seven minutes to reach Leadenhall Street, where he pulled the car round to the left with a screech of tyres and joined the mêlée in Creechurch Lane. There were three squad cars, and even though it was getting late and this part of the City was sparsely populated after office hours, a few starers had collected to see what was happening. More to the point Gus spotted a group of newspaper-men with cameras and swore loudly as he threw himself out of the car, George on his heels.

'How did those buggers find out what was going on here?' he shouted at the first uniformed man he saw.

'Sorry, Guv, but they were outside the nick. They just followed us when we came out. They've been hangin' about there all the time since the first case. We couldn't get rid of 'em.'

'Bloody freedom of the press, and bloody tripehounds who abuse it,' Gus said loudly enough for them to hear him, but the press people ignored the comment, only taking it as their cue to move closer, as he went rapidly to the entrance of the building ahead of them, where most of the action seemed to be. George trotted after him, keeping close.

The press pack clustered round them like a little flock of hungry birds and Gus flapped his hands much as he might have done if they had been. 'I shan't have anything to say till I've been in and had a look round. And I doubt I will even then.' He stopped. 'Look for the PR girl – she'll be over here from the nick, I imagine – and get out of my bloody way.'

'Must be another body, you've got the pathologist with you!' one of them shouted. 'Come on, Super, give us a break. Is it another MP? Has the Ripper struck again?'

'Ripper, my arse,' Gus said sharply. 'Stop putting the words into my mouth.'

'Don't need to when you use such ripe ones all on your own,' someone murmured and Gus glared.

'Will you let me get on with my job?' he roared. 'I told you, get out of the way!' And he pushed them aside and went into the building, dodging a camera and the furry business end of a stick microphone, with George close behind him.

It was an office building, which, George saw as she spotted the long noticeboard at one side, offered shelter to a great many tenants. Gus saw the board at the same time and growled deep in his throat. 'Christ, checking all that lot'll take for ever. And mark my words, no one'll know anything or will have seen anything. Hello, Roo–Rupert. What's up, then?'

Dudley detached himself from the group of plainclothes men standing near the open door of a lift. A frightened-looking man in the uniform of a guard was standing with his finger on the 'Door Open' button and watching them all with wide eyes. Dudley spoke directly to Gus, managing to ignore George completely even though she was standing looking at him over Gus's shoulder.

'Same again, Guv,' he said in a low voice. 'In the basement, by the central-heating boiler, it seems, though I've not been down there yet to see. Something was up with it, the fella went down to check and found it.'

'Same MO?' George asked. 'Throat, viscera and so forth?'

Dudley had to look at her. 'From what the fella said, it could be, but I don't know. Like I said, I was just on my way down to the basement when you arrived, so I can't be sure. Seemingly there's a lot of blood. The caretaker who found it said something about a cut throat.' He spoke unwillingly, as though the words were being pulled out of him with pliers. 'So you'll be –' He stopped and switched his gaze back to Gus.

'If you were about to say I'll be pleased with myself, I'm not,' George said. 'I feel a bit . . .' She shook her head. 'Sick, I suppose.' And she did. The sense of triumph the phone call had created in her had quite evaporated now. That someone else had been killed and mutilated gave her no satisfaction at all. Then she said, almost without realizing she was going to say it, 'I wonder when the fifth will be . . .'

'There won't be one if we can help it,' Gus growled. 'Any idea who this one might be?'

Dudley shook his head. 'Not yet. We've only been here a few minutes. The call went out at' – he looked at his watch – 'About fifteen minutes ago, I suppose. Urquhart called and said you were on your way, so we waited.' He looked at George again then, unwillingly. 'Are you able to deal now? Have you got your gear with you?'

George took pleasure in assuring him that she had. Not for the first time she was glad she kept a spare kit in Gus's car; she never knew when she might need it.

'Then we'd better go down.' Dudley looked over his shoulder. 'Is Soco here, d'you know?'

Hagerty detached himself from the group and came over. 'Evening, Guv,' he said to Gus, and then looked at Dudley. 'I don't know, sir. Ah. Here's Mike. Maybe he knows more than we do.'

Mike Urquhart came across the marble floor of the entrance hall at a trot, a little out of breath. 'I got here as fast as I could,' he said. 'What's news?'

'We know no more than you do. There's a caretaker throwing his heart up in the lavatories, with one of the uniform people with him, and we were about to go down and look. Is there a Soco on the way?'

Mike nodded. 'Shouldn't be more than ten minutes or so.'

'So we can look but we mustn't touch,' Dudley said. 'Right. No need for all of us. You, Tim and Mike and the Guv and me, that's all we need. You can't start, doctor, till the Soco comes, so –'

'I'll come and look just the same,' she said firmly, bracing herself for an argument; Dudley looked at her and after a moment capitulated. He said no more but turned and made for the door of the lift.

The uniformed man standing there was sweaty and pale and Gus looked at him sharply. 'What do you know about all this?'

The man shook his head miserably. 'Not a lot, sir,' he managed. 'I was just about to brew up the first cuppa of the night, you know, now the tenants 'ave all gone, and then we was going to go round together, like we usually do, to check they've all locked up properly. Only it felt cold, so Darren went down to look at the boiler, and the next thing I know he's running up the stairs shouting and looking like – well, I never seen a man so pale. He said there was a body down there by the boiler, what had had its throat cut and worse, and then he threw up.' He looked across the hallway to the door marked 'Stairs'. 'He's in the bog – the toilet now. I never seen a man look so ill. An' I'm not feeling too good meself. Even when I dialled nine nine nine I was feelin' funny.'

'Go and lie down somewhere,' George said. 'Or at least sit and put your head between your knees.' She caught Dudley's eyes on her. 'It'll be less trouble than picking him up if he passes out.'

Dudley jerked his head and one of his uniformed men put a hand on the guard's arm and eased him away as Dudley led the way to the lift.

'I'll go down the stairs,' Gus said. 'See if there's anything on the way down. Mind where you put your big feet, you lot,' he added as the doors closed, and then grinned at George. 'I shouldn't wind Roop up like that. He's the last man to let evidence get touched. Come on.' And he led the way over the hall to the staircase doors.

The air of opulence that had so characterized the hall, with its marble floor and superfluity of pillars and brass trimmings and mock art deco light fittings, vanished abruptly. These stairs were strictly utilitarian, tough stone, rather grubby and echoing. The walls were painted a dull yellowish colour and were decidedly grimy. George looked up at the flights curling up and away, and counted. 'Seven floors,' she murmured.

'And every one of them to be searched. Come on then. I'll take the right-hand side. You use the left. And keep your hands in your pockets.'

'Would I do anything else?' she retorted as together they made their way gingerly down, walking on their toes as far from the centre of each tread as they could.

'Not,' Gus said, 'that we're likely to get much in the way of prints from stone as rough and porous as this lot, but we have to try. Right, here we are. Basement level.'

He used his foot to push the door open – it was unlatched – wide enough for George to go in and then followed her.

The lighting was patchy but clear enough. The space looked as basements usually did: a few piles of battered old furniture; a corner with a work-bench and a couple of elderly tools on display, but a well-padlocked cupboard above it which clearly held better equipment; and to one side a large boiler which was hissing gently to itself. The smell was a familiar one: dust and oil and burning gas.

George started forward but Gus pulled her back, insisting on going first as they made their way round the side of the space where there was undisturbed dust to show no one had walked there ('Make a mental note of that, George, in case you have to give evidence,' Gus instructed. She did) to reach the boiler.

The light was brighter here, but only in a pool, as a shaded overhead bulb threw the whole of its illumination downwards to concentrate on the front of the boiler. It had the usual dials and fittings and George peered at it. It seemed to be working well enough, she thought. It was probably just that they needed to turn up the thermostat if they were too cold . . . and then she saw it. Huddled to the far side and looking like a darker patch of darkness.

Gus had pulled a slim torch from his pocket and directed the beam into the darkness, and at once it sprang into horribly clear definition.

The body was lying, as all the others had, on its back, but this time the legs were crumpled beneath the trunk, the knees pointing awkwardly outwards. The other bodies had had their legs pulled straight.

'He was in a hurry,' she murmured without stopping to think. Gus looked at her sideways, and said softly, 'Well spotted. Yeah. He got the hell out fast. But he still did what he does, or most of it . . .'

He had indeed. For the first time since the case had started George felt a qualm of the nausea that had so profoundly affected the man who had first found the body. She was used to horrors, heaven knew. Wasn't her entire working life concerned with matters the average person found utterly repellent? But there was something about this case that made it worse.

Behind her she heard the hum of the lift, and registered the fact that it seemed to be taking Dudley and the others a long time to descend one floor, but then dismissed the fact as irrelevant. Instead, she stood and stared as Gus made his way to the other side, picking every step as though he was on quicksand, and let the thoughts move through her mind, making no effort to control them.

Is it because these are mindless serial killings that I find this one so chilling? So disgusting? Why should that upset me? Isn't a killing done with – what was the word? – malice aforethought, carried out in order to give the killer some sort of material advantage, more reprehensible than one done, like these, simply to satisfy a deep need to kill in a person with no understanding of why he acts in such a way? She turned the thought around in her mind and then said, almost in a whisper, 'If this *is* a serial killer, that is . . .'

'Eh?' Gus didn't look at her. He was now crouching on his haunches, staring down at the body. She didn't answer and he didn't seem to notice. 'Poor bugger,' he said quietly.

'May I come over?' she said.

'I suppose. Take care where you put your feet. There's a hell of a lot of blood.'

There was indeed. She reached the body's side and looked down at the puddle that was there beneath the head, for the throat had been cut in the now hatefully familiar way, and then at the lower part of the body. There her eyes narrowed and she said, 'I was right. He was in a hurry. One hell of a hurry.'

'Yes.' Gus straightened his knees with a little grimace of discomfort as he came upright. 'Interrupted, do you suppose?'

'Perhaps. In which case you might get a lead. If you can find out who was down here and might have alarmed him.'

Because he hadn't finished. This time the excision of the genitals was incomplete. There had been a start on it: the clothes were pulled aside and there was a knife cut to the left-hand side of the groin, but it had not completed its arc, nor were the genitals arranged on the shoulder. The penis, however, had been sliced off and lay on the ground, forlorn and absurd at the same time. Clearly the killer had intended to do what he usually did, but this time, this time, he hadn't.

Gus took a deep breath of satisfaction. 'You're right. This should get the bastard,' he said. 'We may have to interrogate everyone who uses this building for hours, days, even, but one of them will have seen or heard something. They *must* have done. And that means we'll get this character –'

'Before he tries the fifth one?' George said softly. 'Because the original Ripper did do five killings. And this is just the fourth.'

15

The smell of coffee pulled her up and out of her sleep, nagging at her, though she tried to push it away and sink back into the bliss of whatever it was she had been dreaming. She opened one eye and there it was, sitting on the bedside table, just a few inches from her face: a mug, large, embellished with pansies painted in absurd colours, and steaming seductively. 'I hate you,' she mumbled. 'Go away. Wanna sleep.'

'I know you do. But you've got to wake up because I have to go and I want to talk to you first. Come on, ducky. I put cream in too. Just to spoil you.'

She opened her eyes again and grimaced, stretching her sleepy face to a semblance of alertness. 'You have to go so I have to get up?' she grumbled, dragging herself upright. 'Oh well, now you've done it, give it to me.'

He put the mug into her hands, and she curled her fingers round it and, eyes firmly closed, sipped. It was perfect: strong, hot, unctuous with the cream and with just enough bitter under-tow to give it power. She felt the energy seeping into her as she drank it steadily; an early call that included a brew like this was well worth while. She had swallowed half of it before she opened her eyes again and leaned back against her pillows, still holding the beaker between both hands. 'What's the time?'

'Half eight,' he said. 'I know, I know. But four hours sleep is better than none and you can go back to it after I've gone. I can't catch up till tonight. I wanted you to know that I've already been on to the nick. We've got an ID.'

She sat up, fully alert now. 'What? How? Who?'

'He'd failed to show up at a meeting he had booked, an important one. People had been calling all over London for him. We started to check on missing people and there he was.'

'Then he was an MP?'

'Not this time.'

'A lord then?'

'Not a lord temporal.'

'What does that mean? Stop playing the Riddler with me.'

'A lord spiritual, ducks. Not your sort at all. A bishop, no less. Bishop of Droitwich. Rather a well-known bloke. I can't imagine why I didn't recognize him.'

'He wasn't exactly looking his usual self when we found him,' she said dryly. 'Droitwich? I've heard about him. Isn't he the one who caused all that uproar last year over homosexuals in the Church? Picketing Church House and stuff like that?'

'That's the one. A hard-line traditionalist. Dyed in the wool, in fact. A leading light in the anti-abortion movement too, and anti sex education in schools and –'

'I know.' She drained her coffee mug before pushing him out of the way so that she could swing her legs out of bed. 'Considering the man was a doctor before he got religion, he ought to have known better.'

'That's hardly fair. There are lots of doctors opposed to abortion, aren't there?'

'We all are,' she called from the bathroom. 'I hate it. It's misery for the woman and for the doctor who does it, it's messy, it's risky, it's expensive, but it's a hell of a lot better than the backstreet version the women'd go for if we don't offer them a service, so the majority of doctors opt for a woman's right to choose. Because, she'll choose anyway, so let's give her a choice between treatment by a real doctor and a money-grabbing butcher.' She stopped suddenly, and after a couple of moments put her head round the bathroom door. 'Gus, do you think maybe . . . No, that wouldn't work. Not with the others,' and she went back into the bathroom.

'Get a move on,' he bawled. 'I can't stand conversations like this.'

She did, and emerged from the bathroom five minutes later, wrapped in a bathrobe and rubbing her wet head with a towel. 'Fastest damned shower I ever took,' she complained. 'But since I spent fifteen minutes in the shower last night after the PM I guess it's no crime. Now, why did you call me so early?'

'Because I didn't fancy sneaking off and just leaving a note. Roop called at seven, to tell me about the ID and to ask me what I wanted done first, and, of course, how I wanted to set up the stake-out over in Spitalfields Market.'

She stopped rubbing her head. 'Spitalfields? Oh!'

'Indeed, oh. That's where Dorset Street used to be, the place where the Ripper dealt with his last victim. I'm as capable as you of looking at the history books you know. Dorset Street's long gone and the Market covers the area where it was. So far, the murder sites have been more approximations of the original ones rather than exact, so we have to assume the next one, if he tries it, will be the same. Which means around the Market. And I have to sit down with Roop and plan how we're to use the force we have and how many more men I have to con out of the Commissioner.'

He grinned then. 'Not that it'll be difficult. With the sort of VIPs our chummy's polishin' off, there'll be resources and to spare for the job. Parliament won't like it if their people keep getting duffed up, either. I'm not worried about getting what we need, but I still have to plan. Which means spending the day at the nick. And, no,' for she had opened her mouth to speak, 'you can't come with me. There'd be no point, ducks. It really is the most tedious of routine stuff today. We'll be planning, and collating info we've already got. You take the rest of the weekend off. You never know your luck, I might even be able to spend tomorrow at home. So will most of the team. I don't reckon people work well when they get no R. and R. I tell you what:

organize a decent dinner for tonight, what do you say? You haven't cooked for me since God knows when. It's always me what does it.'

'Like hell it is,' she flared. 'I cook often.'

'When was the last time?'

She blinked, trying to remember. 'Well, of course, if you're going to be petty about it . . .'

'Petty, me? Never. Here, give us a kiss. I'm off. Oh, and yeah, what was it you were going to say when you were in the bathroom?'

'Hmm? About what?'

He was patient. 'You said, "Gus, d'you think maybe . . . No, that wouldn't work. Not with the others." What was all that about?'

'Ah!' she said. 'I was thinking, maybe it was one of these people who disagreed with the Bishop on abortion who killed him. But then I thought that wouldn't make sense of the other killings, would it? The trouble with this affair is we have to think about four killings at once – maybe five eventually – and that's a whole different ball game from thinking about single murders.'

'It's also different when it's a serial killer, the mindless sort. There's no motive that you can get hold of. Well, there is, in a way, but it's so obscure, buried so deep in their weird little minds, that no logical person can work it out. No one can ever second-guess a serial killer, right?'

'I'm not sure . . .' she said, shaking her head. 'I'm not sure at all.'

'What, you mean that it's possible to understand serial killers' motives?'

She looked impatient. 'Oh, that's not so difficult. Once you know who they are. I agree it's not easy knowing before you catch 'em why they do what they do, though some of the profilers do a good job on working out what it might be. And after you've caught 'em, you usually find out. Peter Sutcliffe said he had voices telling him to kill prostitutes, right? No, what I meant was that I'm not convinced this is one of your mad axe-killing types. I keep feeling this is real murder.'

'You don't get anything much more real than cut throats and necessaries,' he said dryly.

'Yeah. What I mean is, this keeps feeling to me like the sort of crime where there *is* a definite motive, a logical and sane reason for what's being done. We just have to work out what that is and we have our killer.'

'There can't be a logical, sane reason for these cases.' Gus had stopped hovering near the door trying to go, but had come back to sit on the bed absorbed in thought. 'Or can there? If these are sane killings done for a sane reason there'll be something in common between all the victims, right?'

'Right.'

'And if we look at them rather than anything else that will definitely provide the answer? Well, we are looking at them. We know they're all Members of Parliament.'

'Both Houses, Lords as well as Commons.'

'Yeah.'

'And all parties, pretty well. No political bias as far as we can see. This isn't an over-enthusiastic electioneering type trying to give his lot an edge on the hustings.'

He grinned. 'It'd make a change from character assassination I suppose, to go in for the more physical sort. No, it isn't party political, not in that way. But could it be para-political? You thought of that yourself: a pro-abortionist having a go at one of the antis?'

She shook her head. 'Violence isn't the ploy of the pro-choice people – and never call us pro-abortion on account of we ain't. I've already told you that. It's the lesser of two evils. It's the antis who've been going in for shooting doctors and clinic people in the States. Never the other side.'

'Well, all right. It's not an abortionist. But could it be something else of that sort? What have they in common, these victims, that might show us a logical motive for one person to kill them all? And why do it à la Jack the Ripper?'

'That's the trickiest bit of all,' she said. She had started to brush her hair, which was drying rapidly in the warm room.

He watched her with pleasure, even though he was still

thinking about the case. The sweep of her arms as she lifted them rhythmically to her head made him feel warm and happy.

'Is he trying to tell us something about the people in treating them so?' she went on. 'Or is he trying to tell us something about himself? Because one thing's certain. Or at least I think so. He's trying to communicate with us. If he just wanted people out of the way, he'd go and kill 'em, right? But doing it this way, and taking such risks to do it, makes it even more obvious. He must see from the papers that we're aware he's copying the old Ripper MO – it didn't take 'em long to sniff it out, did it? – so we know where he'll be next. What is it he's trying to tell us? Or is he just showing off about how clever he is, fooling the police? The way the first Ripper did?'

'You're the medical expert, George,' he said. 'You tell me. Could it be that not all these crimes are being done by the same person? The MOs are the same but couldn't there be an element of copycatting here? Damn. Of course not.' He shook his head. 'The genital mutilation. We haven't let that info get out. But each and every one has had that element. Even this last one, though it was incomplete.' He sighed deeply. 'I wish I could stay home today and talk with you. I think we'd get further, just the two of us gassin', than I will all day with the thundering herd over at the nick. But there you go. The job's the job.'

He stood up and came over to her to kiss the back of her neck, now revealed as she pinned up her hair. 'Take it easy today, sweetheart. I'll see you tonight. And you don't have to cook unless you really want to. We can always eat out.' He chuckled. 'What does an American Princess most like making for dinner? Reservations! Boom boom!' He ducked his head as she whirled and then kissed her cheek. 'It's up to you. See you around seven if I'm lucky. S'long.' He snapped his fingers at the non-existent hat brim and this time he really did go.

By the time he came home she'd really done rather well. She'd been unable to get back to sleep, weary though the night's work had left her. She had opted to do the PM on the body found in Creechurch Lane last night, going straight to Old East to open up the mortuary and once again drag Danny out to earn some overtime, because she had been filled with energy in spite of the long day she'd put in, and it seemed to make sense to get on with it. Gus hadn't demurred. He'd been as eager as she to get what facts there were as swiftly as possible.

It had been a straightforward-enough job. As she had told Gus, 'I'm getting used to bodies with injuries like these,' and she had finished comparatively quickly, a little to Danny's chagrin. He'd hoped for more reward than a measly couple of hours at double time. The only odd thing about the body had been the total absence of any identifying items. He had carried in his trouser pockets a few coins, some five-pound notes rolled up and held in a rubber band, a handkerchief, a comb, and that was about all. Now she knew who he was that made sense; and she had sat at her kitchen table drinking her second cup of morning coffee (which was not at all as good as the first had been, a phenomenon she had noticed before and puzzled over) and thought about the man, trawling her memory.

A traditional Christian, but a bit on the conspicuous side, she thought, that was it. He'd been a young doctor who had Seen The Light and Been Called, as he had announced, to Work for the Poor, back in the 1950s. She remembered reading that about him when he'd made headlines because of the way he'd picketed Church House over the homosexual priest business. Ever since joining the Church he had gone out of his way to live a life of obvious poverty, on the model of ancient saints like St Francis, but had managed at the same time to allow himself to be ambitious and had risen in the Church hierarchy so far that people murmured he'd make it to Canterbury yet.

Well, she had thought, that explains the rather old and shabby though basically clean clothes the body had worn, as well as the paucity of pocket content. But that didn't explain why he might have been chosen as a victim. And she had pushed her coffee beaker aside, pulled the *Guardian* from the other side of the table towards her and seized a red biro to scribble on it.

First, she listed the victims to date, 'SAM DIAMOND', she printed, and then added as an afterthought, '(CON)'. She and Gus had agreed that these killings probably weren't linked with party politicking yet all the same, you never knew . . .

On the next line she wrote, 'DAVID CASPAR-WYNETTE-GONDOR (LAB)' and followed that with, 'LORD SCROOP (IND)' and finally, 'BISHOP OF DROITWICH (JIM LUTTER)'. After a moment's thought she added to that, '(CON)' and looked at it. 'Well,' she said aloud. 'He probably is, with all that traditional Church stuff.' Then she thought again, scratched it out to put '(LAB)' before thinking some more, and crossing that out and putting '(?)'. There was no point in trying to guess, after all. She'd find out later.

Four dead men: what did they have in common, apart from the indignities done to their bodies in death? All of them had been strangled first, she was sure. She had found the same throat markings to suggest that on CWG and the Bishop's bodies, though not so much on the body of Jack Scroop. But he had been dead a longer time, after all. There were good reasons why it was hard to tell. Well, she thought, that's a beginning, and wrote it on her newspaper. Now, what else?

Obviously, they were all part of the Houses of Parliament. Two were elected members, one had inherited his place and the last held his *ex officio*, by virtue of his job. But all members of the same establishment. Anything else? She chewed her biro and got red ink on her face as she pondered.

After a while she wrote tentatively, '? ALL RADICALS'. Certainly CWG was; he ran right against the grain of the way people like him were supposed to behave. A scion of an aristocratic family yet as far to the left as it was possible for a member of Labour to be. Even the Party found him a touch too idealistic for them on occasion. And Scroop? What of him? A trade union man who had been elevated to the peerage to act as a Labour spokesman in the Lords and what did he do as soon as he got there? Refused to toe the line and became an Independent. That's radical! And the Bishop, of course, insisting on making so much noise about things he disapproved of; he certainly displayed a sort of radicalism, when compared with

144

the rather damp liberalism of the Church, which seemed to hate above all people who stepped out of line and made exhibitions of themselves, as Lutter undoubtedly had. He'd been on all radio and TV news bulletins and in every paper at regular intervals for ages. She scribbled down these facts, congratulating herself for sitting through so many news broadcasts and *Panorama* and *Newsnight* programmes when she had been too sleepy to make the effort to change the channels. Some of what she had heard on those august transmissions had clearly gone into her head.

And then she stopped. What about Sam Diamond? He was no sort of radical, was he? A Tory with a comfortable majority and no history of ever stepping out of line. Except perhaps, via his wife ... Again she scribbled. Perhaps having a wife who didn't behave the way a virtuous Conservative wife ought to behave qualified him. Radical by association, that was Sam Diamond.

A beginning, she had thought gleefully and then torn the scribbled page from the paper and attached it to the fridge door with a magnet shaped like a pig. There were things to do right now, and while she did them she'd think some more.

So she did. She spent the day doing domestic things, slowly bringing a little more order to the remaining chaos of their move, even managing to get the curtain material ready for cutting, which was a start, at least. And all the time she pushed the four victims around in her head and tried to figure out what more there was that connected them and whether those connections, should they be studied, could be expected to point towards a motive for their deaths and via that motive, a murderer.

And then, just before seven, when she had checked the chicken casserole she had made, and found it rich, fragrant and a credit to her culinary skills, and had added a dollop of brandy to the fruit salad she had put together (with nuts in it as well of course; to Gus a fruit salad without nuts wasn't worthy of the name), and tidied the kitchen, picking up the mutilated *Guardian* to dispose of it, she noticed a headline she hadn't registered earlier, and stopped to read the article beneath it. And it hit her. Hit her so hard that the moment she heard his key in the front door, she went belting up the stairs two at a time from the kitchen to pull him in and cry, 'Gus! I think I might have worked it out. The why, I mean. Oh, Gus, I really think I might be on to something!'

16

He refused to listen until both of them were sitting on the sofa in the cluttered living room with glasses in their hands. 'I'm no boozer and no one can say I am,' he interrupted when she tried to tell him what she'd been thinking. 'But after the day I've had, I'm not about to listen to a word till I've got a little restorative under my belt.' And with considerable expertise for a non-boozer set about making Bloody Marys for both of them.

'All right,' he said eventually as he stretched himself against the sofa cushions with a sigh of comfort. 'What has the day spent among the fleshpots of home brought forth? Apart from dinner, that is. That chicken – it is chicken, isn't it? – smells fabulous.'

'It's this.' She pushed the *Guardian* at him.

'The "Grauniad"? What is it this time? Have they started producing misprints again? I do hope so, I miss the old days.'

'Read that headline,' she said and obediently he bent his head and read.

'"The Destruction of Democracy",' he said. 'The comment columnist?'

'That's it. Now read the article.'

She sat watching him over the rim of her glass as he read, waiting with as much patience as she could. And when at last he raised his head and looked at her she said eagerly, 'Well? Do you see?'

'I suppose so,' he said slowly and put the paper down. 'This chap is suggesting that there could be some attempt to bring down not only this Government but also the Opposition, so that the whole party system is thoroughly discredited and the electorate will accept all the Independent candidates who will flood the hustings at the next election as a result?'

'That's how I read it too. He doesn't say so in as many words, but the implication's clear. All that fuss over the cash-for-questions affair, and then that business over the nuclear industry and the way so many MPs have been caught with their pants down in strange bedrooms this past few weeks –'

'And you think there's a connection between all this' – he looked down at the paper – 'and our killings?'

'I do. I truly do. Look, suppose you were part of some group which is trying to change the system radically. Trying to get rid of the existing parties and just have Parliament run by individuals who don't act together but do what they think's best for themselves and their constituents – which, as that piece says, could be a disaster because it just opens up the way for some charismatic type to take over.'

He shook his head. 'Ducks, you're talking about a deliberate conspiracy. And I don't think that's on for a moment.'

'Why not? There've been conspirators before in this country – in every country.'

'Oh, sure. But they're itsy-bitsy schemes dreamed up by a handful of lunatics – zealots, then, if you don't like the word – who come up with crazy notions. I just can't see why you're so excited about this.' He tapped the paper. 'It makes no mention of the deaths of our two MPs and a couple of blokes from the House of Lords, does it? He's just floating a notion of his own about what's been happening in the media recently. Journalists are getting smarter and finding out more. And taking more chances publishing it all. But believe me, sweetheart, these people who hang around Westminster and Whitehall aren't smart enough to conspire. They're much too busy looking after their own problems and pensions – and pockets – to make the effort.'

She was stubborn. 'It fits so well, Gus! One of the links between these four deaths is the fact that they were all radicals of one kind or another, but of the old-fashioned sort. There's Sam Diamond who's not one of your top people, the way Tories usually are, but who's got – had – a wife who sells suggestive underwear and appears to be involved in some sort of racket – remembering what happened at Heathrow. Nothing very top peopleish about all that, is there?'

'Oh, I don't know,' he said. 'They stopped being the fancy top-drawer element back when the grocer's girl got to Number Ten. And you can hardly call the Prime Minister top class, can you? That hare won't run.'

'But the others! CWG was a burning hot idealist, a man of the people, who'd throw himself off Everest to protect Parliamentary democracy. And I think the same would have been true of Scroop. A trade union man like that, he'd have been on the same side as CWG must have been. As for Lutter: an idealist all the way to hell and back. They'd be so against any attempt to bring down the two parties, wouldn't they, that they'd be blocks in the way of these people that column is about. Getting rid of them would make total sense.'

Again he shook his head. 'I can see it's an attractive idea, but it doesn't incorporate the other features we've got. Why mimic the Ripper killings, for example?'

'Mimicking? But you're wrong. That *does* fit in! There were definite attempts to hush all that up, weren't there, at the time? People said they thought the killer might be a VIP in spades – Queen Victoria's son, for God's sake! And there were other theories. The main thing we know is that a hell of a lot of the available evidence never saw the light of a court. It was as though the police had orders, and a lot of pressure on them, to drag their feet and not find a perpetrator. Which would make sense if it was a VIP – and in this case I suspect the same sort of VIPs could be involved now and our killer is actually telling us this by using the Ripper MO. Did they call it that then? *Modus operandi?*'

'Probably. And I do see what you mean there.' He sounded judicious. 'But what's the point? If all you're trying to do is get rid of some people who are a political nuisance to you? I grant you that *could* be a reason. I was involved in that business of the Bulgarian chap who was killed with ricin on an umbrella tip when he came out of the BBC at Bush House, so I know things like that happen, but then you just kill 'em where and when you can. You don't expose yourself to appalling risks of being caught just so you fit a hundred-year-old case. And you don't risk covering yourself with blood when you do it. Not just to send an esoteric message in a wacky code, to show us the killings are political.'

She pounced on the latter point. 'They were strangled first, remember?' she said.

'So?'

'So that means there wasn't so likely to be blood in great spurts all over the killer. If you put a knife into a living artery, it's like walking into a fountain. If the heart has stopped though, it's just puddles, if you're careful. And he always stood behind, remember, and so dodged any possible splashes. If he wore gloves and –'

Gus leaned forwards and put a hand on her knee. 'It won't stand up, sweetheart. I can see what you mean, and I can see why you think it. When all the people being killed are involved in politics then it seems obvious there's a political element. But let me offer you a different scenario.'

'So offer.' She was a little sulky. She'd expected if not enthusiasm at least a less dampening response.

'I'm going back to the mad axe-killer idea. Or one of his ilk,' he said. 'It's really the only one that makes sense. Here is a man who is in essence barking mad. He may seem, to his friends and neighbours, as normal as a nice cuppa, but underneath he seethes with paranoid notions. And one of 'em makes him hate politicians. And why not? There's plenty of reason to hate them. Whenever they do surveys of people's attitudes, politicians come higher on the list of those most people despise than even journalists.'

'And policemen?'

He ignored that. 'And as you say yourself, they've had a particularly vicious press lately. Not that they haven't earned it, of course. I can well see why someone with a bee in his bonnet about the buggers already might be tipped over into craziness and start to kill 'em off. But that's incidental to the need to kill in a – in an elaborate repeated pattern. *Who* they kill is far less important than the fact that they kill *someone*. It's pure accident a particular type is chosen – for the Ripper it was prostitutes, for our chummy it's politicians. For another it might be lollipop ladies. It's doing it that gives them satisfaction, not the identity of the person. And there's something else I can tell you about these mad axemen. They love stories about mad axemen. If you look around their pads after you've caught 'em you find all these books about past killers and how they do what they do and where they do it. Our man's one of those, mark my words, ducks. It's going to be careful policework that'll get him, not ratiocination in the booklined study and all that. It's not Sherlock we need. It's PC Plod.'

'Well, I suppose you could say you've got *him*. Every time I look at Rupert I think – OK, let that go,' as he opened his mouth to argue. 'I'm going to disagree with you. Not completely, but a good deal. I know you don't go along with gut feelings and hunches but –'

'Where did you get that idea?' He sounded genuinely surprised. 'I've all the time in the world for them. I think they're evidence of knowledge you've got and don't know that you've got. If you act on them, eventually you trace out the lines of where the gut feelings came from. So I never ignore them.'

'But you prefer to have a logical line of reasoning first. Or at least at the same time.'

'Well, yes, of course. Wouldn't you in my place? But hang on to your hunches, sweetheart. If something else turns up to strengthen 'em, well, then we'll look at 'em. But the one about a great political conspiracy I can't take. And' – he hesitated – 'I'm not trying to come the old acid, but let's face it, ducks, you're a bit of a newcomer to British politics. You need to have lived here all your life and really studied it to make sense of it, I reckon. I'm a cockney born, bred and built in, and I don't understand most of it, mainly on account of I've never had the time to waste on it – party politics, that is. But I know this much: we're designed all wrong for the sort of thing this fella's writing about.' Again he tapped the paper. 'And that you've been beguiled by. It just ain't on. Not here.'

'Wanna bet?' she said. 'Politics are politics the world over. Some places are more honest than others, but I don't for a moment suppose you're not as subject to corruption here as anywhere else. But fair enough' – she raised both hands, for it was clear he was settling down to argue – 'we'll say no more about it. But I tell you, this affair is a hunt not for a madman but for a highly motivated plotter who has good reasons to do what he's doing and that politics may or may not be part of it. You register that, and when the whole thing's over and done with, we'll see who's right. And if I am . . .'

'OK, it's a deal. I say it's got damn all to do with what we'd consider real motives; that we've got a common-or-garden serial crazy here. What do you bet?' She considered. 'I'll take a rain-check,' she said after a moment. 'Wait till it's over and if I win I'll demand whatever I want from you and you'll have to give it to me. And vice versa.'

He put a hand out. 'We'll shake on that. And start saving, sweetheart. On account of this is going to cost you. Now, how about that chicken dinner, eh? I'm famished.'

By unspoken consensus they said no more about the case during their meal, which Gus pretended to be amazed by, making outrageous comments about her usual cooking skills, and afterwards they settled to watching TV, a typical trashy Saturday-night film that they could jeer at. As Gus said when he switched off and they went trailing up to bed: 'It's more fun to watch a lousy flick than a good one. I love picking holes.'

'Mmm,' she said. 'Listen, Gus, tomorrow, are we home?'

He hesitated. 'Not me, ducks. I'm sorry, but I have to put in an appearance. Everyone else is working overtime, so I must too. I got tonight to myself so Roop can go off tomorrow. He's got some special event at his local Church. He's a pillar of the place.'

'Really,' George said a touch waspishly. 'I just wish he'd show a bit more goodwill and loving kindness towards women as a result. Then I'd be more impressed.'

'One of these days you two might be friends,' Gus said and yawned again. 'When pigs fly to the moon to get their cheese rations.'

'Well, I'll come with you,' she said. 'May I?'

He shook his head. 'It'll be boring. Really. We truly are just plodding. I've got men out all weekend hunting down as many people as they can from that office building in Creechurch Lane – they'll get the ones they miss on Monday – and a lot of the others are prowling around picking up stuff on the whereabouts of our victims and the people around them. Once we have all the evidence in, and it's time to analyse what we've got, then I'll be glad to have you along. But till then you might as well –'

'I know. Make curtains. OK, I'll make curtains. Come on. I'm bushed.'

Curtain-making vanished from her schedule at three a.m., when the phone rang. Gus emerged from sleep to grab the handset and growl into it, listen, and then, as George reared up to blink at him anxiously, hang up and say to her with real amazement: 'Would you believe it? The bugger's done it again! How the hell does he manage it? Another one . . . its bloody impossible, but he's done it.'

17

She was still in a dazed state when she arrived at Old East to do the post-mortem. During the journey to Spitalfields Market and the trek through the maze of little shops and boutiques which now occupied the area to reach the storeroom in which the body had been found she had experienced a state of *déjà vu*, the longest-lasting one she had ever known. She seemed to have been so often to places where she had expected to find a mutilated corpse that it felt like a habit now. And the effect of repetition was underlined even more when she saw the body. The likeness was so vivid; and it wasn't just the slit throat and belly and the transposition to the shoulder of the genitalia. It was the face. She looked at it and then closed her eyes and shook her head.

Gus said, 'Are you all right?'

'Of course I am. If you mean, do I feel ill,' she snapped. 'It's not that. It's just that I know him.'

'You do?' He peered at the body again, tilting his head to avoid the dazzle of the torchlight that was being thrown on it by two or three of the uniformed men who were standing there. 'How can you – Ye Gods!'

'It is, isn't it?' she said.

'If you mean, is it Lord Durleigh, you're right.' It was Dudley, who had come up to stand behind them. He had been part of the knot of police at the entrance to the Market when they arrived and had followed them inside. 'I never got to meet him, but one of the others did, and anyway he's had his mug in the papers a good deal since his brother was killed.' He looked down at the body and shook his head. 'Question is, is this just another of the series, and the relationship with an earlier victim coincidental, or . . .' He left the question dangling.

'If it is Durleigh it certainly shifts the emphasis,' Gus said. 'Before they were all linked just by being Parliamentarians, but when relatives start being clobbered, well, it makes you wonder. After all, most murders are –'

'Committed by close relatives of the victims. Yes,' George said. 'But in this case, it can hardly be regarded as one of "most murders" can it? I mean, the whole point of this is that it's one of a series. The link is Parliamentary, surely, more than the relationship? After all, there aren't many close relatives who are Members of Parliament.'

'Yes, there are,' Dudley said, pleased to be able to contradict her. 'There's that father and daughter pair in the Lords and a husband and wife in the Commons, and –'

Gus interrupted adroitly. 'Who found him? And when? Have there been any reasons why this wasn't prevented? We've had more uniforms around her than flies on a pork chop, and yet here he is.'

Dudley was defensive now. 'My blokes have been pulling out every stop. This is – Well, if the murderer turned out to have been equipped with wings and flew here with his victim, I wouldn't be surprised. There hasn't been a single thing missed out as far as security is concerned. It's very difficult during the day, of course, when the place is heaving with shopkeepers and customers and strollers and Gawd knows who, but once the day was over and we could police the entrances properly, and seal the premises to make sure they were empty, there was no way anyone could get past us.'

'But someone did,' Gus said.

Dudley's face mottled with an angry red. 'I'm well aware of that, Guv, and don't think I haven't been goin' spare over it. I tell you, I've talked to every man on the job, had the day people on the phone and several of 'em called back here, to check on what happened. This place was searched with toothcombs.

There was no way anyone would have got in. Or out. I'd have sworn it.'

'Hmm,' said Gus, forbearing to point out the obvious yet again, and looked around him. 'Who found him then?'

Dudley's colour was still high. 'It was a tip-off,' he muttered.

George lifted her head, suddenly alerted. 'What sort of tip-off?'

He looked at her, then at Gus and, thinking better of arguing with her, pulled from his pocket a transparent plastic envelope. Inside it was a sheet of flimsy fax paper. He gave it to Gus, and George came closer and peered over his shoulder.

It showed a drawing of the Market. It was a neat plan, drawn in thin lines, and over one section there was a big cross. That was all. No words had been written, no indication of directions given, just the series of squares and oblongs with a big cross.

'It arrived at Ratcliffe Street,' Dudley said. 'The duty clerk gave it to me and I saw at once it was a plan of this place. I know the layout by bloody heart, I've been over it so often. So, I came here, got the nearest gate open' – he jabbed his finger at the map – 'and headed for the storeroom. It was partly open.' He took a deep breath in through his nose. 'The bastard. That door had been shut with a padlock that was rusted in, it had been locked for so long. You can still see it. No one had a key for it when we searched, but two or three of my men took a close look at it, saw it hadn't been opened since the year dot and let it go.' He looked at Gus, his eyes filled with misery and rage and a sort of fear. 'I have to take responsibility for that. I've always told my people not to go damaging property unnecess- arily and it was obvious to them that no one had been in here or had tried to get in. It never occurred to anybody that someone had been buggering about with the bloody hinges. So they let it go.'

'Ah.' Gus sounded resigned rather than angry. 'So that was it, was it?' He turned to look at the door, squeezing out through the gap to do so. In the light of the torches he could see clearly how the door had been breached: the hinges were the old-fashioned flat sort, attached to the jamb and the door itself on the outside. All the killer had to do was unscrew the flap on the door side, and ease the door outwards. Even though the padlock and the latch and lock on the usual side were rusted firmly in place, there was just enough movement on the rather flimsy door to open a space on the hinged side, enough for a slim person to get through, albeit with difficulty. Once the door was pushed back into place and the hinges refastened with a few turns of a screwdriver, it looked totally undisturbed from the outside.

'Well, it's good he wasn't a fat man,' Gus said, coming back inside and looking down on the body. 'He could never have squeezed in here if he had been. But why should he have done? Why should an intelligent man in possession of his senses agree to go into a storeroom by squeezing through the wrong side of a door?'

'He trusted the person who was with him,' George said. 'Someone had to be with him, obviously. And he gave him a believable reason.'

'The killer,' Gus said a little abstractedly, still looking at the hinges. 'Another thin man.'

'Another thin man,' she had agreed. And now, as she changed into her greens and tied a cap over her head before plodding in her heavy theatre boots into the mortuary where Danny had the body ready on the central slab for her attentions, she tried yet again to visualize what had happened. The Ripper – No, she corrected herself, I mustn't slide into thinking of him that way. The killer had persuaded his victim to go with him willingly with a tale that made it perfectly logical that they should go into a storeroom by a highly illicit method. And that didn't frighten him. She stared sightlessly at the opposite wall. If I were an MP, knowing of the horrible death of my colleagues, would I go to some hidden place of my own free will? Surely I'd think about the risks if such a suggestion were made to me? She shivered a little. Whoever the killer was, he clearly had a great gift for reassuring his victims they were safe in his hands. And he must have done the same with all of them. Or had he?

She stood there, slowly pulling on a pair of gloves and smoothing the latex over her fingers as she remembered. The first one.

Sam Diamond. Why had he gone to that hidden square off Durward Street? Had he too been invited there by someone he knew and trusted? And what about CWG, who had died so near to the same place as his brother? How had he been persuaded to come to Spitalfields? One of Gus's jobs clearly would be to investigate links between the brothers and that part of London – but then she reminded herself: he would have done that already for CWG and had found nothing. If he had he would have told her, of that she could be certain.

She picked up her knife and looked at it, thinking of the job that had been the most disagreeable: the Scroop post-mortem. How had he been lured to that shed on the waste ground beside Henriques Street? Or had he been strangled first and taken there afterwards?

She sighed. She had a job of work to do on this victim; it was no time to be trying to work out the whys and wherefores of all of them. She pulled the big magnifier round on its ceiling fixing so that she could investigate the throat of the man on the slab. Had he too been strangled first? And she bent her head to her task as Danny, yawning beside her, tried to do the mental arithmetic that would tell him what he could expect in his overtime-padded pay packet at the end of the week.

The message she found waiting for her when she had finished was terse. 'Meeting incident room. Ratcliffe Street ten a.m.' read the fax. 'See you there.' It was in Gus's familiar scribble, and she was a little amused, weary though she was as the effect of a broken night's sleep caught up with her. It was more private to send a fax than to use the phone these days, especially when others were likely to listen in to your calls. This way she could turn up and no one would know she'd been invited, so no one could get uppity over her presence; or if they did they'd aim their irritation at her, rather than at Gus. And for that 'one', she told herself as she went to the shower, read Dudley. Not that he'll be quite as full of himself as he has been, now he's been so thoroughly caught out failing in the protection of the Spitalfields

Market site. For a very brief moment she had it in her to feel sorry for the man.

The incident room, when she arrived there, smelling richly of Badedas and with her hair still curling damply over her ears, was still empty. It was barely half past eight, she realized, and shook her head at herself. It was very difficult to keep track of time intelligently, feeling as weary as she did. But not sleepy, she assured herself as she settled on the sofa in Gus's office to wait for him. Not sleepy at all.

She woke with a start an hour and a half later as Gus slammed the door behind him. 'Hi,' he said absently, as though she had been there all night and he hadn't noticed her before, and headed for the phone on his desk.

'Griffin?' he barked when at last he got an answer to his irritated thumbing of the keypad. 'Where the hell are those reports? . . . What? Of course I know it's Sunday, but what's that got to do with the price of eggs? I need 'em *now*! I've got five bloody murders here to handle and I can't do it without the data I ask for when I ask for it . . . Eh? Well tell 'em it's a matter of life and bloody death – yours probably – and get 'em out of their stinkin' beds. Sunday or no Sunday. I never heard they were that religious in Brussels anyway. So move it.'

He slammed down the phone and glared at her. 'Five hours and still nothing! You'd think they'd have found something by this time.'

'Who haven't found what?' she said, yawning hugely. 'You're not making a lot of sense.'

'Interpol,' Gus growled. 'According to his housekeeper he's in Brussels, and I want to know where and with whom. It's not enough just to have someone say it.'

'Who's in Brussels?' George managed to hold on to her patience.

'The brother, for Pete's sake! Who else? Edward C W G. We tried to find him, to get him to do the necessary I D rather than his housekeeper – would you want to show a woman her boss looking like that? But the housekeeper said –'

'I've got it now. He's in Brussels, Gus. It's the middle of

Saturday night. Or it was five hours ago. You can't expect everyone everywhere to run around getting stuff for you at that sort of time.'

'Of course I can. This is a massive case we've got here. We need all the information we can get and we need it fast. I'm convinced I've got to talk to the brother. Check his movements and so forth.'

'I bet you wouldn't turn out in the small hours of a Sunday morning for Brussels police,' she said. 'And why get so agitated over the brother? I grant you that in most murders it's someone close to the victim who did the nasty but in this case we're looking at a serial murderer.'

'But you said this wasn't just a serial murder,' he said and suddenly yawned too. 'The other day –'

'Much good staying up all night has done you,' she said. 'And yes, I know I said that, but I meant that I believe there's some sort of political motive here. As well as an element of serial behaviour. One thing I'm sure it ain't is a nice cosy domestic.'

'Two brothers dead? It could be.'

'Why?' she said. 'You saw the two of them together. They seemed on comfortable-enough terms, didn't they? You're talking like a policeman instead of –'

'Of course I am. I *am* a policeman. And thinking like one is what gets cases solved, ducky, not some airy-fairy flights of fancy.'

'Are you suggesting that's all I offer? Because if you are –'

He put up both hands. 'We mustn't argue. We're both dead on our feet and it's making us as ratty as a pub cellar. I don't suppose it's helping much, either. So let's not talk about anything but work, OK.'

She stared at him and bit back the angry retort that had slipped into her mouth. He was right, of course. It was her fatigue that was making her irritable.

'OK. So, what's next? What's this meeting you've called me to?'

'Just routine. I want us to collate all we've got, and that includes your findings on this case. Durleigh, I mean. I don't want to be kept waiting for your report. Bad enough I have bloody Brussels to contend with. With you here, at least I can get a verbal on the PM. Come on.'

He led the way out into the incident room which now was alive with people. Someone had brought in hot bagels and cream cheese to go with the coffee that was as usual bubbling on the table at the side, and everywhere there were champing jaws. Gus and George joined in and felt a good deal better when they'd finished. Hunger makes a dangerous mix with sleep deprivation, George thought. Gus is right. We really mustn't get personal over this investigation. It's too complex and important to allow such indulgences.

'Right,' Gus said, when at last everyone had settled and mouths were emptied. 'Let's see what we've got here. And it had better be good. Because I tell you, I'm getting madder and madder about this case. Five murders in a matter of days, and a clear view of the MO right from the start. And still he managed to do four more. We've got a lot of fingers to be pulled out here this morning and if they aren't, by God, you'll all be sorry.'

18

The first half-hour of the meeting was, from George's point of view, somewhat tedious. She knew perfectly well that the bulk of police work was painstaking, detailed, dull even. Each victim had to be checked exhaustively: his working practices and colleagues; his family and friends; his tastes, his pleasures; his every activity dug out, listed, collated and compared with the same data from all of the others, as part of the search for a common theme that might just possibly point them in the direction where the murderer might be. That they had been working hard was clear; they all had the drawn look that came from too little sleep and too many sandwich meals snatched on the wing. George caught Julie's eye at one point as a detective sergeant droned his way through an account of the Committees – there were dozens, it seemed – on which the victims had served, and Julie looked up at the ceiling with the classic look of boredom. George smiled back, comforted. She had been feeling guilty about finding it all so dull.

Gus seemed to feel that too, because he pushed the sergeant with questions and then shook his head at him. 'There's nothing to find down that road. We've already considered all this stuff. It's something new we need, a new lead, anything that'll get us out of this cul-de-sac. We've been at this business for five days now, we've got five victims and we're nowhere near finding ourselves a suspect.'

'Apart from Alice Diamond,' George murmured as much to

herself as to the room at large and Gus turned and glared at her.

'Eh? Alice?'

'Well, yes,' she said, very aware of the way everyone was looking at her. 'She did behave oddly, didn't she, at the airport? Or that chap who followed her certainly did. And the way she talked about him –'

Gus cocked his head to one side. 'Talked about him? When? Who to?'

George saw the edge of the precipice just in time. She had not told Gus of her visit to Alice's shop, of course. She had just stored away the information she had collected, sparse as it was, until she could make use of it. Which was certainly not at the moment. 'Oh,' she said artlessly. 'I thought I heard someone saying she didn't seem all that upset.'

It was Dudley who saved her. 'Neither of them were, not the son or her. The son was aggravated at having to come over at all which he had to do for financial reasons, once his father had died, and keeps nagging about when he can go back to Australia, – which he can when he likes, for our part, though I gather the buyers need him here for a while yet – and as for her – well, she talked about her husband as though, I dunno, as though he was just someone she worked with, rather than a husband.'

George, remembering thinking much the same when she had talked to Alice in her shop, actually smiled at Dudley. 'Is that so?' she said. 'What did she say?'

Dudley appeared not to hear her. He was looking round the room for one of his people and then pounced. 'Urquhart, wasn't it you and Morley who've been watching her?'

Mike Urquhart coughed and sat up rather straighter. 'That's right, Guv. But nothing seems to happen. When we talk to her she just says she misses him – Sam, that is – but life has to go on. We've had an obbo on her all week, but she just goes to the shop and then goes home again. Maybe we could put out an intercept on her phone?'

Dudley shook his head. 'Not justifiable. We'd never get a warrant for that. And I'm not sure it'd tell us much anyway. Those vehicles led nowhere, after all.'

Mike looked miserable at that. 'The Volvo turned out to be her own car. No problem there. The van . . .' He coughed and looked embarrassed 'I told you we'd found it registered to a Max Hazell on the Wembley Park Industrial Estate. Well, turned out Hazell was an old bloke, with a small import business, who died three weeks ago. There's a problem of probate because he left no will and no one seems to know who his relations might be, so the warehouse and office and the gear are all locked and the keys held by the solicitor. The van was part of it, but it was kept parked up outside. We checked, of course, and found it. It was locked, no marks on it, but dirty; so many prints you'd never be able to use any for an ID – so that's a dead end. It was just used because someone noticed it was available and easy to ride, I'd say.'

'Is the van still there?' Gus asked.

'Oh, yes, sir.' Mike looked pleased with himself. 'We put a clamp on it so it canna be used.'

'You shoulda left it and put on an obbo,' Gus growled. 'See if someone comes to borrow it again. Now, o' course, whoever it is knows he's been rumbled.'

Mike, scarlet with mortification, blinked and said no more. George felt so sorry for him that against her better judgement she joined in. 'I still think we ought to search Alice's shop,' she murmured.

Dudley looked at her witheringly. 'No justification. If we tried to get a warrant we'd be turned down. And rightly so. The woman isn't a suspect, but a victim's wife. In case you'd forgotten.'

George caught Julie's eye and opened her mouth to snap at Dudley and decided not to. No point, and Julie clearly had something to say. She'd wait and see what it was before going further down that road. Instead she said, 'Well, what about the man you said met her at the airport – not the guy with the van, the other one?'

Mike had recovered. 'He kept himself well covered up. There wasn't much we could do about an ID because he had one of those Barbour coats that cover up everything, and a cap, and he kept his head well down. Isn't that right, Margaret?'

Margaret Chalice nodded. 'I've watched for him most particularly while we've been on obbo, but there's been no sign of anyone like him. And I have to say that it'd be impossible to recognize him again, because like Mike said, he made sure he wasn't really seen.'

'Then there has to be something odd about Alice Diamond.' George could bear it no longer. 'A van borrowed from a dead man and returned, and a man who meets her in a sort of disguise; you can't call that ordinary behaviour, can you?'

'We're well aware of that,' Gus said. 'But as Roop says, there's not a lot we can do at this stage. We'll go on watching her, of course. Mike? Margaret? And keep an eye on those premises in Wembley. Further down that road right now, we can't go. Not till we can get a warrant.'

Across the room one of the faxes pinged and started to spew out paper and the police constable sitting beside it reached for it, twisting his head to read it as it emerged. And then grinned. 'Guv!' he called. 'Something here from Brussels.'

Gus moved with alacrity, threading his way through the tables to join the man at the fax machine and began to read aloud the message on it. 'Edward Caspar-Wynette-Gondor, Officer of the Commission (Agriculture), see photograph attached, has been identified here in Brussels attending meeting in Secretariat General of the European Commission, rue de la Loi, 200 1049 Brussels. Detailed list follows.'

He waited as patiently as he could as sheet after sheet appeared until at last the machine pinged again and he was able to gather up the pages and go through them properly.

'He's been there since – let me see – late on Friday.'

'We saw him at that party at the House of Lords,' George said. 'So it had to be very late. He went off with his brother, remember?'

'I remember,' he said, his head still down over his faxes. 'Here it is. He checked into his hotel, the Prinsenhof, in rue Archimedes, at eleven-thirty p.m., coming direct from the airport in a taxi. By God, they don't miss much detail – I've even got the name of the cab driver here – and since then he's been at meetings.

Hey, look at this.' George had come to stand beside him and so had Dudley. 'He was returning to Brussels! He'd been at the Prinsenhof all week – ever since the previous Monday, and went back to London on the Friday lunchtime. He told the hotel his sister-in-law was sick and he had to go and see her, but asked them to hold his room . . .' He read on, page after page, and then shook his head. 'Well, you have to hand it to them,' he said. 'They've come up handsome. There was I goin' spare because I thought they weren't bothering and then they come up with all this.'

George was still looking at the faxes, with the times of departure from Brussels airport and occasionally railway stations, arrival at the hotel, departure again followed by arrival at the Secretariat and return to his hotel, sometimes via restaurants, with a frown on her face. 'Why is there so much detail?' she asked. 'It's amazing –'

'Hmm?'

'No one knew you were going to want all this information,' she said. 'Why on earth do they have it? Why were Interpol following him like this? It's very strange, isn't it?'

'No,' Dudley said. 'The fella worked in the Northern Ireland Office for a while, ages ago. But they go on getting special obbo to protect them after they quit.'

'Blimey!' Mike Urquhart said in some awe. 'All of 'em? That must cost us a fair bit of dosh.'

'You get more in the budget if you've got politicians who've been involved with Ireland on your patch,' Gus said. 'You ought to know that, Mike, ambitious bloke like you.'

Again Mike subsided. He's not having a good morning, George thought. In sympathy, she chose again to put her oar in. 'So now what? Do you want to hear my report on Durleigh's PM?'

'We might as well,' Gus said. 'There's nothing here for us. Edward CWG has to be right out of the frame.'

'I never saw him in it,' George said and Dudley glared at her.

'Everyone is till we can be sure they're clean,' he said. 'And the first thing you do *always*, is check family connections.'

'Yes, indeed,' Gus said hastily, seeing storm clouds coming

up. 'Let's see what there is to hear about the PM, Dr B. Anything startling?'

'If you mean, anything different from the other four, no.' She turned her back on Dudley and looked round the room at the rest of them. 'The same MO entirely. He'd been strangled and then mutilated. I'd say there was a slightly shorter time gap between the two actions on this occasion – perhaps just a few minutes, because there was a heavier blood loss from the cadaver this time. He didn't want to hang about. But the heart had definitely stopped beating. I've taken all the usual samples, of course, but I don't expect any surprises. All I can say is that if this killer is modelling Jack the Ripper, this should be the end of it.'

There was a little silence round the room as they contemplated the fact that the Ripper cases never had been solved – or at least not by the police force. It was a dispiriting thought, and after a moment Gus seemed to straighten his shoulders to push it away. 'So,' he said very briskly. 'There's not a lot more any of us can do at the moment but keep on the usual plod. But we'll get going tomorrow at top level. It's going to be difficult to get hold of people for interviews on a Sunday, so I'm inclined to treat this as a breathing day. Clean up your paperwork, make sure every single item we have, however scrappy, is on the computer, and carry on the search for connections amongst the data we've already collected. Roop, you go home and get some rest. You look like a dish rag. No, don't argue, I'll need you in better nick tomorrow than you are now, so go home and get some food and some sleep. The rest of you ...' And he settled to instructing various members of the force about what he wanted them to do the next day as Dudley, clearly unwillingly, did as he was told.

George sat there for a while watching Gus and then, catching Julie's eye across the room, made a gesture with her head in the direction of the door. Julie understood at once, got up and went out towards the door that led to the women's cloakroom. After a few moments George, very casually, followed her.

'This won't do, will it?' George said to Julie, who was waiting for her, perched on the edge of a washbasin.

'How do you mean?'

'Well, sitting around waiting for things to happen. I think we ought to do a bit of work together again.'

Julie lit up. 'Oh, yes, please. It was great going to that shop the other day! Where this time?'

'Where do you think?' George said. 'I've got an idea, but I'm not certain that it's quite . . . let's hear your notions first.'

Julie bit her lip, her eyes a little glazed as she concentrated. Then she said uncertainly, 'Well, there is that business of the van. Mike seems to think that it was just sort of accidental that particular van was used by the bloke who picked up the cases. But suppose it wasn't? I'd like to know more about this chap who died. It may be a long shot, but all the same . . .'

'Julie!' George said delightedly. 'You're a lady after my own heart. I was thinking the same. So, what do you say? When do you finish today?'

'Well, it could be up to me, in a way, I mean if I just sort of wasn't here, you know? Roop's the one who notices stuff like who's where – and he's gone off now. So – this afternoon maybe?'

'And it's my bet that Gus'll stay here till all hours,' George said. 'So that's OK. Do you know how to get into locked buildings?'

Julie looked scornful. 'I should hope so. Mind you, we're not supposed to break in, but . . .'

'But – but – but. You're beginning to sound like Roop.'

'Oh, Gawd!' Julie said. 'I can't have that, can I? I'll see you later then?'

'Meet you at the nearest underground station,' George said. 'It'll be more anonymous, I think, than turning up in a car. Can you get the details about exactly where?'

'I'll give you a note,' Julie promised. 'And –' The door opened and another woman constable came in and Julie went on as smoothly as a placid stream. 'Thank you for your advice, doctor. I was feeling a bit worried about it, but it's fine now. But I'll pop in to my GP like you said. Ta ever so.' She smiled widely at her colleague and went tripping away, leaving George to wash her hands in a casual manner before wandering back to the incident room.

Gus greeted her return with gratitude. 'Here, Dr B., would you be able to write your report on the PM here and now? Then we can get it into the computer and that'll complete that section. I know Tim was there and I ought to wait for his report as well, but it helps if I could have yours now, written and not just verbal.'

'A pleasure,' she said cordially, and found herself a vacant computer screen and settled down happily to transcribe her notes. This felt right, like really being part of the investigation team, and she laboured away contentedly, even taking extra care over her spelling and punctuation, which didn't usually concern her too much.

Gus disappeared into his office and stayed there, his head down over his own paperwork, and George watched over the top of her VDU as Julie slipped away from her desk, leaving an old jacket over the back of her chair to make it seem she'd just gone to the ladies room. She felt a stab of guilt about the way they were deceiving Gus; it was a shame really, to use his good heart so; after they'd solved the case, she promised herself, she'd be sure he knew just how valuable young Julie was and how worthy of transfer to the CID, and also how necessary it had been to be a little less than honest with him. And it was a promise she renewed to herself for Julie's sake when another woman PC, passing her desk on her way back to her own, dropped a scrap of paper on it. 'Message I was asked to give you,' the girl said. 'Quietly, like,' and winked.

Wembley Park Station, Metropolitan Line or Bakerloo. Two-thirty sharp. I have full address. See you.

19

Wembley Park station at half past two on a Sunday afternoon was, George decided, a good place to be anonymous. Clearly there was an event on at the Stadium or in some part of the complex, because the trains coming in were full to the point of standing room only, and the small and shabby concourse was buzzing with people. She had worried for a moment that she and Julie would not be able to find each other in the hubbub, but as she reached the top of the stairs from the platforms she saw her standing in front of a map of the London Underground system and staring earnestly at it as though she were trying to learn it by heart.

Julie greeted her warmly when George tapped her shoulder and said loudly, 'Lovely to see you! I'm so glad your mum gave you the message in time.' George grinned. Julie playing detective was rather touching.

'Of course she did. Come on then, let's go.' They linked arms and walked out of the station and across the road to the Stadium side.

'Well,' George said. 'OK, we're just a pair of women out on the razzle for the afternoon. What is it we're supposed to be coming here for? A football match?'

Julie giggled. 'You should be so lucky! No, it's a choral-singing thing at the Conference Centre that's bringing 'em in. Lots of hey nonny nos and so forth.'

'I'll prefer a bit of breaking and entering. Have you got the right gear to get us in there?'

'Would I go equipped? You can get a stiff sentence for that! I've got a couple of skeleton keys, I don't deny, but I hope we won't need them. There are other ways.'

'Go equipped?'

'Police term. Going equipped to commit burglary. If you find jemmies and diamond cutters and so forth on a chap in the small hours it's enough to make a charge even if he hasn't done anything. So you have to be careful what you're caught carrying. My keys don't look all that unusual, fortunately. I got them in the States and they're fixed up to look like ordinary keys. If anyone at work knew I had them I'd be in big trouble. So not a word.'

'I promise,' George said. 'Have you found out exactly where this place is?' They were walking now down a road lined with middling-sized buildings, many of which bore elaborate logos; office buildings and small factory units, George thought. A typical business park. She collected herself: industrial estate in England.

'I've got the address.' Julie reached into her pocket and pulled out a piece of flimsy paper. 'Here we are: Unit Seventeen A. In Lyons Way. It's a spur off this main road.'

They found it fairly easily, and for a moment George's spirits sank. There were few people about; most of the crowd had gone streaming towards the Conference Centre, but the area was by no means deserted. She looked at the building they had reached, a boxy brick structure with blank windows and a very simple sign over the door in paint on a wooden fascia that read '17a EASTWEST IMPORTS 17a' and that was all. Parked in front was a small and rather battered green van.

'We'll be noticed going in,' she murmured to Julie as a man and woman, walking fast, went by. 'There are more people around than I'd hoped, Sunday afternoon and all.'

Julie was looking up at the building. 'Mmm? Oh, I expect it's parking,' she said. 'They'd rather find somewhere free around here than use the paid car park nearer the Conference Centre.

But they won't be interested in us. We just have to be determined and relaxed as though we're entitled to be here. Don't worry.'

'It's not me I'm worrying about,' George said. 'It's you. If I get caught doing what I shouldn't, all I get is a row with Gus. If you do . . .' She let the words hang in the air.

'I know,' Julie said. 'But I'd rather take that chance than go on feeding a computer for the rest of my working life. This'll either show I can be a real detective or it won't. If I am I'll get on in the Force. If I'm not the sooner I'm out the better.' She giggled. 'I can always try my hand at being a private one. Like on the telly. I've been thinking of that. Come on. It's getting late. All these people'll disappear soon – the concert starts at three and it's almost that now.'

And indeed the numbers of people around did seem to have diminished. The last few hurriers were well on their way to the Centre and the area was becoming quieter by the moment. George turned back to speak to Julie, to find she had already crossed the small open paved area in front of the building towards the door. George hurried after her.

'This is a padlock and it's too small for my keys,' Julie said. 'Dammit, dammit, dammit. We'll have to see if there's another way in.' She turned and moved away to the corner of the building and vanished round it. George followed her.

At the side there were only several large, high windows – too high to peer through – but no door. The back of the building was the same. It wasn't till they rounded the third corner and were coming back towards the front that Julie stopped. There at last was a side door but this too was fastened with a padlock and that made Julie grimace. But alongside the door was a lower window, within reach of the top step of the three that led up to the side door.

'That's a lavatory,' Julie said. 'See? That pipe up there by the roof corner with the sort of birds' nest of chicken wire over it? That's the sort they have over lavatories. Something to do with the soil pipe. I bet the window isn't locked. People always forget to lock lavatory windows. And it's sizeable. We can get in there.'

She looked at George's hips thoughtfully. 'Yeah, you can manage it, I think.'

'Thank you,' George said bitingly and then shook her head. 'Getting in through windows? That doesn't sound too scientific to me. I'd have thought your keys would –'

'No use here,' Julie said. She was clearly enjoying herself hugely. The rather frightened young constable of the Ratcliffe Street nick seemed to have been replaced by a very determined young woman indeed. 'Here, make a back for me. I'm going up.'

She shoved at George's shoulders and obediently George bent, tightening her joints and muscles as Julie set one trainer-shod foot on her back and then, with both hands on the sill of the window, hauled herself up. She was heavy, but stood on George's back for only a second or two, the time it took to push in the window.

'Now,' she said in a sort of gasp. 'I was right. I'm in.' She pulled herself up even higher, and as George straightened her back to see, her legs vanished inside. After a moment she reappeared, face up this time, and looked out at George.

'Can you manage to get up here if I give you a tug?' she demanded.

George looked over her shoulder. There was no one around that she could see, just the adjoining building as boxy and as anonymous as this one with matching dead-eyed windows, and a stretch of empty road in front of the building away to her right. It seemed safe enough. 'I'll have a go.' She reached up and, with a tug from Julie (that pulled her arm muscles so much it was days before the discomfort faded), managed to get herself into the window, head first. Julie was ready for her, and she was able to put her knee up on the sill and get inside by reaching down and holding on to the edge of the lavatory pan that was beside the window. She almost somersaulted her way in, but at last there she was, red faced and breathless, but standing on the floor.

'Get us!' Julie said and giggled, excitedly, yet again. She was a great giggler, George decided. 'This is such fun.' She turned, pushed open the lavatory door and went out into the main part of the building.

'I like the way you take it for granted there's no one here,' George hissed behind her. 'For all you know there's a night watchman or someone having a snooze in a corner somewhere.'

'Not with both doors padlocked from the outside,' Julie said cheerfully, making no effort to lower her voice. 'This place is empty as last week's pay packet. Now, what are we looking for?'

'I haven't the least idea,' George said. 'Something. Anything. Information about the man whose place it is. Was, I mean. Some sort of link between him and the people in our case because of the green van and the little man at the airport we all heard so much about. I don't know what I'm looking for but I'll know it when I see it.'

'I know just what you mean,' Julie said. 'How shall we do it? Together, or separately? We'll be quicker separated, I imagine.'

'Then separate it shall be. I'll take this side, you take the other, OK?'

George looked down at her side of the corridor on to which the lavatory door had opened and considered. It was a very long corridor with doors running off it and, after a moment, she walked purposefully to the far end and began to open the doors and look inside, one after the other.

The first one led to a cupboard full of buckets and brooms and the smell of sour floorcloths. She wrinkled her nose and closed the door sharply. The second opened into what was clearly a staff restroom, with shabby old chairs, a battered coffee table well marked with rings from hot cups and a few elderly crumpled magazines and dirty ashtrays, which made the room reek of stale tobacco. Again George closed the door gratefully.

The third door at last offered something interesting. The smell that greeted her here was one that took her immediately back to her childhood: the scent of new cloth. It was like the shop where her mother used to take her to buy new underclothes for school. Even the light seemed the same: subdued, because of the blinds over the windows, and muffled because of the rows of hanging rails, each of them laden with garments.

This then, George thought, was the stuff of the business carried out by Eastwest Imports. She began to edge along the

174

narrow walkways between the rails, riffling the garments as she went. They were an odd mix, she thought: cotton and wool, silky fabrics and crêpe and chiffons, heavy knits, firm cloths. She frowned. There seemed to be no logic to the way they were displayed either. Fripperies that were clearly meant for a female buyer jostled with heavy knitted jackets that not only shouted butch man, but which had the buttons arranged so that they fastened left over right to prove it. Any ordinary business, surely, would sort their stock out so that when orders came in, groups of garments could be collected easily.

Then she stopped and stared blankly into space. Long ago as a high-school student wanting extra money to spend in such fleshpots as Buffalo had to offer, she had taken a Saturday job in a clothing store. She remembered all too clearly now the day she had sat in their stockroom, unpacking the newly delivered items. Dress style 78764PLK, sizes six thru twenty, five colorways each, all to be laboriously checked so that she could make sure all the garments ordered were the ones that had arrived. That was how a clothing business was run; she'd learned that much.

But on these rails there were no different sizes and colourways at all. Each garment was a singleton, one after another. And she ran her hands along the rails again to confirm that, yes, she was right. Each and every one was a single garment.

She stepped back and took an overview, counting the rails, estimating the number of garments there. Five long rails. Each one holding – she began to count the hangers, and then did the multiplication. And stopped frowning, feeling amazement fill her. There were over five hundred different styles of garment here, some for men, some for women and, she could now see, some for children too. She touched one of them, a particularly attractive gingham frock which looked just about big enough to fit a two-year-old and felt a little surge of – what? Some sort of feeling she had no time to consider now. After a moment she turned and went back to the door. It was high time she found out what else this place held.

She met Julie outside, looking for her. 'I've found very little,' she said, looking as woebegone as a child who has found her

Christmas stocking empty. 'Just a workshop of some sort, with sewing machines and so forth and piles of cut-up fabric – and boxes full of fancy labels for clothes. I don't know much about fashion but I suppose that's what they do here.'

'I'll say,' George said. 'Show me the workshop.'

Julie led her back down the corridor to the other end and pushed open a door. George stared around and, as she did so, she saw the whole thing as clearly as though someone were standing there describing to her exactly what was happening, and how.

'Julie,' she said and she was jubilant. 'Julie, this is as fancy a way of making money on other people's backs as you'll ever see.'

'Eh?' Julie said, startled. 'How do you mean?'

'Show me the labels first,' George said. 'So's I can be sure.'

Julie went over to the other side of the room and beckoned. 'They're too big to fetch to you,' she said. 'Come and look.'

George did and found herself looking down at a series of large wooden boxes arranged in neat patterns. Each was full to the top with strips of printed ribbons and paper tags; each box had different ones, but essentially they were all the same. The trimmings that go on garments to tell shop customers about them, what the size is, how to care for them. But above all the designer's name.

'See?' George said, squatting beside the boxes. 'D K N Y. That's Donna Karan New York. And Chanel. And Calvin Klein. And Gucci and Valentine and Yves St Laurent and Christian Dior and Issey Miyake. Ye Gods, is there anyone who *isn't* here?'

'You'll have to explain.' Julie was looking mulish. 'This is a lot of nonsense to me. So what if they're clothes labels? What's that got to do with –'

'Everything,' George said. 'This is crime in a big way, Julie. What happens here is industrial espionage. They get hold of original garments of very expensive designers – probably even before they're properly launched by the companies that own them – and bring them here. Then ' – she looked around again – 'Yes, there they are. Then each garment is carefully unpicked

– I dare say they're photographed first to make sure they get an accurate record, we'll have to find the office where the paperwork is – unpicked and the pieces numbered.' She had picked up a small pile of pieces in the bright gingham and denim similar to that in the little girl's dress she had seen in the other room. 'Next they're sent off with the labels – see? This is OshKosh B'Gosh: wonderful kids' clothes from the States, very expensive but gorgeous and beautifully made. They send it all off to little workshops around the country, I suppose, where they copy the garments exactly, put in the labels and there you have it. The finished clothes are sent to another place on another business park somewhere, so that they cover their tracks, and then sold off as originals with a huge mark-up. And the actual designer gets nothing.'

'Wow,' Julie said after a moment. 'Are you sure?'

'No, of course I'm not. But what else can it be? I found the rails of originals inside – some of them are amazing – and I'll bet there's also a place here where they've got fabric – cheap copies of the materials the originals are made of.' She fingered the gingham fabric on the table. 'This is shoddy stuff, cheap and full of dressing compared with the dress I saw and handled in the other room. Come and see for yourself. And then let's see if we can find the office. There has to be one, for heaven's sake!'

She showed Julie the other room, and as she reached the end of the last rail, where she hadn't been before, she yelped with excitement. 'I should have been all round when I was in here before. Look!'

There was another door. Julie pushed it open and shot through and then they both stopped on the threshold and stared.

'Well, you were right,' Julie said after a moment. 'I've never seen so much cloth in one space in my life. Not even in John Lewis's, when I went to buy some curtain material for my mum.' The room was massive, with all the walls filled from floor to ceiling with shelving, and each shelf packed with rolls of fabric of all colours, sorts and weights. It was here that the scent of new fabric was strongest and George took a deep breath of satisfaction.

'Yes,' she said. 'I was, wasn't I? And now let's see if there's an office in the same sort of place on the other side of the building.'

They almost ran down the long corridor, this time, and at the far end counted back the doors until they identified the one that corresponded with the room with the rails. They found themselves in another room, just like the one in which they had found the fabric pieces and the boxes of labels. This one was equipped with knitting machines, however, rather than sewing machines, and boxes of brilliantly coloured yarns stood on the tables. George went in and ran her fingers along the yarns and shook her head. 'Shoddy again,' she said. 'Cheap man-made fibres.'

'These labels are different,' Julie reported, almost head first inside a wooden box. 'Look, Pringle and Kaffe Fassett and Coorgie.'

'I'll bet they are. This is the knitwear workshop. But look over there.' She pushed past Julie and shoved at a big rail, covered with a vast yellow dust sheet, that was standing in the corner. 'Going by the other room there should be a door. Ah, here it is.' She tried to push open the door she had found but this time she was stopped. It was locked and she looked over her shoulder at Julie and grinned. 'Time for your skeleton keys, sweetheart,' she said. 'Nothing's ever wasted, is it?'

Delighted, Julie pulled her bunch of keys out of her pocket. George peered at them. They looked very ordinary to her, car keys, Yale keys, deadlock and luggage keys, and she said as much.

'Not a bit of it,' Julie almost crowed. 'Have a look.' She took one of the deadlock keys in both hands, twisted and pulled and the barrel of the key seemed to split and open. Julie made a folding movement and there, suddenly, was a classic skeleton key, the slender ends and hooks neatly fitted in the barrel, with the false part bent back to double the handle end.

'Brilliant,' George said. 'Go for it, Julie.' And she went back to look at the stuff on the tables, leaving Julie to fiddle with her keys.

As she stood there, the door that led to the corridor opened.

She lifted her head to find herself staring in frozen horror at a man in a guard's uniform, holding a large stick in his hand. And peering in from beneath his raised arm was the face of an old woman who was standing behind him, staring avidly, with a small dog under her arm. The dog, when it saw George, began to yap furiously and tried to jump out of the restraining hold. George jumped back and in so doing hit the sheet-covered hanging rail which moved round smoothly on its wheels to its previous position. So at least, she found herself thinking as she stood and stared back at the two people in the doorway, trying not to grimace at the dreadful noise the small dog was making, at least he can't see Julie. Which is a silly thought, really, she told herself in an oddly abstracted way, because of course they'll find her in a moment or two. And there goes the poor kid's career, and it's all my fault.

20

The guard lost his patience with the dog before George did. He turned to the old woman and said sharply, 'If you don't mind, madam, I'll take over now. Just take your dog away with you. Can't hear meself think.'

The woman looked affronted. 'If I 'adn't 'ad to take 'er out for a bit of exercise, I'd never 'ave seen this one climbing in, would I? If it 'adn't been for my Cherry Pie 'ere, you'd never 'ave known nothin' about it, and now you want to chuck me out? Well. We're not goin' no place till I see this one properly arrested. I'm waitin' 'ere till the coppers arrives, I am.' Since she had to shriek to make herself heard above the noise the dog was making, the effect was ear shattering and George covered her ears with her hands. But she was grateful for the din. If Julie was making any sound behind the screen, at least she wouldn't be heard.

'There's no need to get into a state over this,' she said to the guard, raising her own voice. 'I'm here on police business. A bit unorthodox, I grant you, but police business all the same.'

The old woman glared at her venomously. 'If you believe that you'll believe anything,' she said to the guard. 'What sort of police business 'as people slidin' in through winders, tell me that? Oh, yes, I saw you with your rump in the air, *an'* I'll give evidence in court about it, just you see if I don't.'

'There'll be no need for any evidence giving because there'll be no case in court. Not over this, anyway.' George was still listening – or trying to – to the space behind her. How was Julie coping? Had she opened the door; had she got in? Somewhere deep inside her head she prayed that she had.

'So you say,' the old woman began, and now the guard lost his temper.

'Out you go,' he said. 'You done right gettin' me, but I've called the police and now you can be on your way. Yes, I mean it. You can wait outside if you want to talk to the police yourself and maybe they'll want a word anyway, but right now out of here you go.' And he walked further into the room and closed the door firmly behind him, leaving the old woman and dog outside, both yapping furiously.

'All right, then.' The guard was a plump rumpled man in late middle age, clearly not very fit and sweating nervously. 'I've sent for the police so don't you go getting clever with me. I only come in because I was afraid – because of the risk you might take off again before the police got here.'

'Is that what the old witch said?' George smiled at him. A little charm, she thought, to oil the wheels. 'Well, she had a point. Or would have if I'd been a criminal. But I'm not. I'm one of the team on the new Ripper murders. You'll have read about them, of course, or seen the news on the TV.'

His eyes widened. 'Eh?' There was fear there as well as excitement and she shook her head kindly.

'It's all right,' she said. 'No bodies here. But we have cause to suspect that – well, I can't say too much. You understand how it is, being in security yourself?' She smiled as bewitchingly as she knew how.

He looked doubtful. 'Why should you be looking around here on that case? Wasn't all those murders done in the City?'

'Indeed they were.' She looked admiring as though he'd said something of great wisdom. 'But we have cause to suspect a link between this business and some of the people on the periphery of the case.' And she nodded confidentially at him, and he nodded back, clearly not certain what the periphery might be.

'Have you got the proof you're right in what you say you are?'

She smiled even more widely and reached into her pocket – at which he flinched slightly, but bravely stood his ground – and pulled out the police pass she carried. 'Here you are. See? I'm a pathologist.'

He looked at the pass and then at her. 'Why on earth should a pathologist be climbing into windows? That doesn't make sense at all.'

She smiled another of her special smiles. 'Well, of course I should leave it to the Superintendent or the Inspector, but well, you know how it is with bosses. They never want to listen to the ideas other people have, so I thought I'd follow up a hunch of my own. I dare say you do the same in this building, from time to time!'

'This ain't my building,' the man said. 'I work next door. The old girl came and called me out when she saw you climbin' in.' He sniffed. 'She's a bloody pest. Lives up the top of the road but always comes down here to walk that horrible dog, but really so's she can snoop. She knows I'm keyholder for a few of the buildings around, seeing my company's the only one what's got twenty-four-hour security surveillance.' He said it with a hint of pride. 'Anyway, I didn't believe her first off, to tell the truth. She's such an old Nosy Parker she causes more trouble than you'd believe. But she went on and on, was so sure, I didn't have much choice.' He looked at George and for a moment produced a sort of shamefaced grin. 'It was easier to do what she wanted than not, if you follow me. And here you are after all, so she was right, damn her! Anyway, the police'll be here soon and you can sort it out with them.' He lifted his head sharply and listened. 'Is that a siren?'

It was. Even above the continuing yapping from the corridor outside she could hear it and now all her fears for Julie came back.

'You stay here,' the guard said. 'If you budge out then I'll – Well, just you stay here. I'm going to fetch 'em in –' He went out and closed the door firmly behind him.

At once George shot behind the screen, afraid she would find Julie still crouching there, but to her huge relief, she wasn't. She pushed on the door that Julie had been trying to open and it held fast. Her spirits lifted.

'Julie.' She bent to hiss through the keyhole. 'Can you hear me?'

There was silence and she risked making more noise and scratched on the door panels. After a moment there was a soft scratching in reply.

'Keep out of sight if you can,' George murmured, her lips close to the keyhole. 'With a bit of luck they won't look in here.'

Behind her the door of the main room opened again and she shot out, knowing her face was red and unable to do anything about it. The uniformed policemen who were standing in the doorway stared at her and she stared back. She knew neither of them, but then, why should she? They were local.

'I'd be grateful if you'd put in a call to Ratcliffe Street nick,' she said as easily as she could, leaning against the bench beside her with both hands in her pockets. 'Ask for – let me see – Superintendent Hathaway or Inspector –' She stopped and thought, Dudley? Heaven forfend. 'Sergeant Urquhart, who are all from the Ripper team. They'll tell you who I am.' She pulled her hand out of her pocket and held out her pass.

The smaller of the two policemen came towards her and took the pass, stared at it and then at her. 'Are you telling me that you're one of the Force?'

'No,' she said. 'Just one of the team. I'm the forensic pathologist at the Royal Eastern Hospital. We're handling the new Ripper murders. There's a van outside this building' – she jerked her head in the general direction – 'that was involved with one of the people involved in the investigation. It's hard to explain. Just let me say I had a hunch, found out the address of this building – where the van was – and came here to look around. I'm sure you understand.'

The policeman clearly did not. 'Why did you have to get in through the window, which is what I'm told you did?'

'The door was padlocked,' she said with sweet reasonableness. 'What else could I do?'

'Get a proper warrant and search that way,' the policeman

said. 'If you really are on this case.' He looked down at her pass and the glowering photograph of her on it. 'How do we know you didn't pinch this? That you're not just another villain?'

She smiled delightedly at him. 'Oh, thank you! I hate that picture – it doesn't look a bit like me, does it? I told Gus as much when I got the pass – Superintendent Hathaway, that is – and he said I do look like that and there was no need to fuss. But now you think maybe I pinched it – you've truly made my day.'

'Um, Jerry?' The other policeman, who she could now see was rather younger and clearly the junior of the duo, came forwards. 'There's something here that I –'

Jerry raised a magisterial hand and his colleague subsided. 'Pictures on passes are never all that good,' he said. 'This could be you. On the other hand, it mightn't be. And I still say, what proof have I got that you really are involved in this investigation?'

'Jerry,' the other policeman said a little more urgently, and this time his colleague turned and glared at him.

'What?'

'Um she called him Gus,' he muttered.

'What's that? She what?'

'She called him Gus.' The younger policeman looked a little braver. 'How'd she know that if she wasn't on the team?'

'Gus? What are you on about?'

'Superintendent Hathaway, Jerry. He was one of our lecturers at Hendon last month. He's called Gus. And she knew it.'

There was a little silence and then the other policeman turned back to George. 'Have you touched anything in here?'

She looked around and then pointed. 'That stuff over there on the bench. The blue and the green. Yes. These labels in this box here. But otherwise . . .' She looked around. 'That's about it.'

The policeman tucked his hat under his arm and began to walk around the room, looking at everything as his colleague and George watched him in silence. The old lady and her dog now sounded much further away, though the yapping could still be heard from time to time, and George stretched her ears, trying to hear whether any sounds were coming from the room in the corner.

When the policeman called Jerry moved the dust cover and then the screen she felt her heart literally jump a beat. It was a choking sensation and her pulse was so pounding she thought he'd be able to hear it, but all he did was rattle the door of the office, satisfied himself it was locked and then turned back to her. 'OK, lady. You come with us. I'll take you back to the station and we'll make a few calls to see if you are what you say you are. But Gawd 'elp you if you're not.'

Gus stood and stared at her, his face quite expressionless. She stared back, her hands shoved deep into her pockets, trying to look as blank as he did. She suspected, however, that she looked anxious and apologetic. She certainly felt it.

He sighed then, and went over to the glass wall that separated his office from the main incident room, which was buzzing with activity. 'Honestly, George, you make life hell sometimes. What were you thinking of to go snuffling around that way?'

'Snuffling?' she said. 'You make me sound like a dog. Oh, Gus, you should have heard that awful dog the old woman had. It really was –'

'George, shut up!' He turned on her and now he was far from expressionless; he looked exceedingly angry. 'Look, I bow to no one in my admiration for your cleverness. You get ideas and you make deductions that leave me breathless sometimes – even if they're wildly out, there's always something in them that makes sense. But you really have to stop being such a bloody loose cannon, rolling round this way.'

'First I'm a dog and now I'm a bit of armoury,' she murmured. She looked up at him but he was clearly in no mood for her feeble humour so she straightened her face. 'OK, Gus. I'm sorry. I was wrong. It was just that I thought there had to be some stuff there that'd help us, seeing the van's linked with the place. It made sense to me to go and have a good look round.'

'We'd have had a look round ourselves in due course, once we'd got a warrant! You know about warrants? Those bits of paper that make what we do legal and which make it possible for us to get evidence into court? Without them we're no better than a bloody police state. Which this country is not.'

She took a deep breath. This was as angry as she had ever seen him, and the degree of control he was exercising shamed her. 'I truly do apologize, Gus.' She meant it. 'I suppose I was impatient and it seemed something useful to do. And I discovered some stuff that does show the way to –'

'It's no use till we go there ourselves,' he said flatly. 'With a warrant. You must realize that.'

'Yes. But please let me tell you!'

He was silent for a moment and then threw both hands up and went back to his desk to sit down. 'So, tell me.'

She did, at length, and in spite of himself he became more and more absorbed in her account of her findings.

'So it's a commercial espionage operation. They get hold of original designs from expensive designers, copy the samples and then –'

'Sell them at inflated prices in inferior fabrics. Yes,' she said. 'And Alice Diamond has to be bang in the middle of it all. That's what she was bringing back from Italy, wasn't it? Samples of designer clothes. And the chap who met her at Heathrow and took them from her trolley is working for this Max Hazell chap. Which means she is too. You didn't seem to think much of that contact – I mean, all that stuff about the van just happening to be borrowed because it was available. I thought there had to be more to it than that. Which was why I went to look. And truly, Gus, I reckon one hell of a lot of money's going through that business one way or another. Once we find out what's in the office, it'll be easier.'

Gus tilted his head. 'What office?'

She blinked, pulling herself back from the brink of saying too much. 'Oh, the one in the corner. I opened all sorts of doors and there was one in the corner of one of the big rooms that I reckon had to lead to an office but it was locked. I'd love to see what's in there. It'd answer a hell of a lot of questions, I'll bet you.' She thought yearningly of Julie. Was she still there? Had she managed to get out? Should she, George, go back as soon as she could and see if she needed extricating? Or . . . Oh hell.

'How did you know where to go?' Gus said then.

'Mmm?' She blinked at him again. 'Well, I just sort of looked around you know. Worked out the geography of the place and went looking for a room to match the one where I found the fabrics and there was this door and –'

'No,' Gus said with exaggerated patience. 'I mean how did you know where to go to do your break-in? How did you get the address of Max Hazell's place?'

She stared at him and felt as though her blood was congealing in her veins. How did she know? How could she say without implicating Julie? And that just couldn't be considered.

'Um,' she said, aware of the way his eyes were fixed on hers and the tilt of his eyebrows, which spoke of deep suspicion. 'I – the computer –' She took a breath. 'You know how it is with computers. You hit the wrong key and suddenly you're into a whole lot of info you didn't really want. I was putting in my report and it happened.' At least her lying abilities were marshalling themselves. She didn't like using them on Gus, but sometimes a person had to. 'I thought I'd lost all the stuff I'd put in and I was nearly finished too, but then I saw that it was Mike Urquhart's stuff that I'd accessed by accident, and there it was. It put the idea into my head. I mean, you were busy here and there wasn't anything else I could do, so I thought, why not go over to Wembley and have a look around. And then I hit another key and this time I got my own copy back. It was a great relief,' she finished piously.

'Hmm.' Gus's gaze left her face and wandered off behind her head to the incident room on the other side of the glass. 'I see. That was how. Very fortunate, wasn't it?'

'Wasn't it just?' she said with enthusiasm. 'So, now you'll come with me and take a look too? As soon as you can get a warrant? And then after that, let me come with you to talk to Alice Diamond again –'

'Again?'

'You've talked to her before, haven't you?' She was on an

improvisatory roll now. 'So talk to her again. Only let me come along too, what do you say? I might be able to, well, you know, two women together. She might talk more to me.'

'I haven't the least doubt she'd talk more to you,' Gus said drily. 'If you shut up long enough to let her. I'll think about it. Right now, I have to talk to my team. As long as they're all there. I'll make a check and see where everyone is and what they've been up to.' He looked at her with eyes wide and smiling and George thought, he knows. The bastard knows I went with Julie and he's going to drop me right in it. And of course, get Julie. And I've no one to blame but myself.

She followed him out of his office into the incident room with her head spinning as she tried to think of a convincing tale she could tell to cover Julie's absence. It wasn't as though she was a member of the detective force; as a uniformed officer Julie's job on this team was station-based. She had no leeway to wander off the way CID people sometimes could to follow a lead they had picked up. The moment of her discovery was on her and it was, George reminded herself yet again, all her fault. She couldn't let it happen. She put out her hand to catch hold of Gus by the elbow and pull him back; she had to tell him the whole truth and trust to his innate goodheartedness to protect Julie. Not that she was too sanguine because she knew that when it came to matters to do with the Force, Gus was a sea-green incorruptible. But for all that, he had to be told.

21

He was through the door and into the incident room before she could reach him, and it was too late to pull him back. He had eluded her grasp expertly as though aware that she was trying to stop him and again she thought, he knows. The rocket's going to go up with such an explosion and I don't think I have any idea what I can do.

'Right!' Gus called loudly. 'What's everyone doing? I want a progress report. Roop – Rupert, let's go through the roll and see who's doing what and with which and to whom.'

Dudley, who had been head down over one of the computer screens, lifted his chin and sighed. 'It's getting a bit late, Guv.'

'It certainly is. So the sooner we get on with things the better.' Gus sounded sunny. Too sunny. George felt sick. 'Let's start with the uniformed lot, shall we? Then they can go home to make the best of what's left of Sunday and us poor CIDs'll work on into the midnight hours, hmm?' He showed his teeth in a great glimmering grin and caught George's eye, and she could have hit him. He was tormenting her and doing it deliberately, she was sure of it. 'OK, Roop, let's get on with it.'

Roop got on with it, trailing through the various members of the team and what they had been doing. They listened to accounts of long searches to find the people in the Creechurch Lane building and the painstaking collection of statements from them to add to those already collected from people living or working near the other murder sites. They heard of similar actions in the Market at Spitalfields and found that at neither place did anyone know anything at all about anything and certainly no one had seen either victim or anything that might have suggested a useful line of inquiry.

'Not that they was eager to help,' the reporting sergeant said gloomily. 'You'd think on a case like this people'd be glad to give you all the co-operation they could, but it's the usual business of "if you're talking to the Bill then act like you've got a terminal case of verbal constipation".'

'Then try again tomorrow,' Gus said briskly. 'People can be different when they're talking in their boss's time, at work, than when they're using their own at home. OK. What's next? Ah, yes. Victims' interests. The Committees and suchlike they sat on. And the family connections and their activities. Who's on that?'

'Margaret Chalice, Julie Bentley, Dave Bannen,' Rupert said. 'Let's hear from you, Bannen, first.'

Gus looked a touch irritated, George thought. He wanted it to be Julie first so that he could catch her not being here, and catch me out in a lie. She knew it as certainly as she knew she was sitting on the edge of the table, her hands clasped tightly between her knees to stop them shaking. Oh, but he's getting his own back, she thought. And what a row we've got brewing . . .

PC Bannen reported clearly and concisely about the three Committees he'd been investigating. 'The Building Regulations one had all of them on it except Scroop. Officially they were on it, that is, but as far as I could tell, the Bishop hardly ever attended the meetings. The others did, but apparently it was a pretty dull business. They were trying to match up our Building Regulations with those of Europe, you know the sort of thing.'

'We know,' someone muttered from the back of the room. 'If they had their bloody way they'd match us up too and we'll all be wearing flat-topped caps and shouting "*ooh là là!*" at the Toms when we arrest 'em.'

'Get on with it,' Dudley growled. 'Or we'll be here all night.' He glared at the grumbler. 'What about the other Committees, Bannen?'

'Drugs used in the NHS and the import thereof.' Bannen consulted his notebook. 'Here again, this one had CWG on it and the Bishop – he used to be a doctor, didn't he? I s'pose that was why – and Sam Diamond. It was a tricky one – rows kept on breaking out, especially between CWG and Diamond. CWG wanted all drugs to be on the NHS list however much they cost, and wanted the doctors to decide who should have what, and the Bishop agreed with him. Diamond said that cost too much and –'

'We don't need the politics, thank you,' Dudley said. 'And the other one?'

'The House of Lords one?' Bannen riffled the pages of his notebook. 'Here we are. This one is chaired by – was chaired by Lord Durleigh and included his brother. That got a bit of publicity when it was first announced because there was another relative on it too – CWG's brother-in-law, Lord Hinckley. He's got a huge estate in Yorkshire. His sister Marietta is CWG's wife – widow, I mean. And there are three other lords on it, as well as the Bishop of Droitwich.'

'Very cosy,' Dudley said. 'I can't see many changes being made when they've got so many of the people with vested interests on the Committee.'

'There are lots of others from the House of Commons,' Bannen said. 'I can tell you which they are.'

'Not now, thanks,' Gus said quickly. 'We can check on all of 'em tomorrow. OK, that's the Committee news. There are clearly areas here where our victims overlap. We'll need a lot more investigation into all the members in every one of those groups so that we can see if there's a logical link between any of them and the five victims.'

'Four,' Bannen said. 'Lord Scroop wasn't active on any of them. He was listed on the Building Regs. seeing he was once a trade union bod, but –'

'Like I said, tomorrow.' Gus rode over him. 'Now, who's next?' He bent his head to look at the list he was holding in his hand. 'Ah! Julie and Margaret to report.' He looked up and round the room. 'Now, where –'

'Here, sir.' Margaret Chalice bobbed up from her seat. 'I've been working with Dave on that stuff. He's reported for both of us really. But I've also been helping Julie with the constituency searches – seeing what we could find on each of their patches. We checked on all the local agents and the canvassers and so forth for the Members of the House of Commons; for the ones from the Lords, we checked on their local areas, if you see what I mean. They don't have to have agents or anything. They just do what they like really. But we collected a bit of stuff on Durleigh in Warwickshire and on Droitwich and –'

'Julie worked on that, did she?' Gus sounded cheerful. 'OK, Julie, what have you to report?' He lifted his chin to stare round the room and George looked down at her clasped hand and tried to remember to breathe.

'Quite a lot really, Guv.' Julie's voice came out of the crowd in a slightly breathless rush and George lifted her head and stared.

At the far side of the room, near the door, Julie was standing with her face flushed and her hair rather rumpled, but otherwise she looked as she should, her uniform neatly buttoned and her collar and chequered necktie perfectly arranged. She caught George's eye and grinned broadly and George positively beamed back. Gus turned his head to look at George, and at once she tried to compose her face, but it wasn't easy.

'Well,' Gus said. 'Quite a lot, you say?'

'Yes, sir. I discovered that Alice Diamond has another shop. Not just the one in Sloane Street, but another one.'

'Well, I'm not sure that's all that important,' Dudley began.

'Oh, sir, it is!' Julie interrupted. 'She's kept very quiet about it, hasn't she? And that's funny for a start. But it's not just that. She owns it, but it's run in someone else's name. And the best bit is' – she paused for effect – 'it's in Durleighton in Warwickshire.'

There was a little buzz of interest. 'A close link between Sam Diamond and Lord Durleigh?' someone said 'That's a breakthrough, 'n't it?'

'Why?' someone else jumped in. 'Unless you mean it was Alice Diamond what did both of them for some reason – the old man and the local Lord of the Manor – but what about the other three? Why should she go for them? That's the real –'

Gus held up both hands and shouted for silence. 'All right, all right, you lot. We'll have to digest that and get over to Durleighton and have a look round. Nice work, Julie. How'd you get hold of that?'

Julie looked back at him limpidly and George thought, she got that from prowling round the office at Wembley. Oh, hell, how's she going to get out of this one?

'A hunch, sir,' Julie said brightly. 'I thought, if a woman has one shop, she might have another. So in every place I was looking, I checked on local dress shops and who owned them. And I found this one in Durleighton.'

'A hunch,' Gus said softly. 'Well, well, a hunch. Well done, Julie.' He grinned at her, a wide rather mirthless look, then said over his shoulder at George, 'Nice work, hmm?'

'Very,' George said. 'Great. But I'm not surprised. It's the sort of thing a woman would think of. We do have our uses, don't we?'

Gus stared at her expressionlessly. 'I suppose you do,' he said, still softly. 'I suppose you do. Sometimes.' And turned back to the room to finish his round-up. Somehow, George thought, he's lost some of his excitement, and she could have hugged Julie. How she had managed to get out and back here George had no idea; but thank whoever it was one had to thank for such events for it. The ice had been horribly thin there for a while.

As soon as the round-up was finished she slid to her feet. 'I'll be back in a moment,' she murmured at Gus and escaped to the ladies' room. Not surprisingly, Julie followed her. Gus stared after them for a moment and then went back to his office to check the remaining documents he hadn't had a chance to go through.

'Tell the rest of them they can go, Roop,' he said. 'And go home again yourself, do me a favour. Tomorrow's also a day and I want you all as fresh as it's possible for you to be, seein' how overworked we all are. I'll see to the last crackin's here.'

'I don't mind finishing off,' Dudley said and Gus shook his head.

'Do me a favour, mate, go home already.' And he sounded so weary that Dudley didn't argue. Nor did anyone else. The big incident room emptied rapidly.

When George came back into the room she looked round, surprised, and then saw Gus at his desk. She made her way across the paper-littered floor and pushed back chairs to reach him. He looked up as she came in.

'You are going to go right over the precipice one of these days, my duck.' He said it in a conversational tone. 'It's not so bad when you get yourself in stück, but do me a favour, will you? Keep my people out of it.'

'I don't know what you're —' George began but he shook his head.

'I'm not as daft as I look. I know Julie was out and about this afternoon when she shouldn't have been. And it doesn't take Sherlock Holmes to know she was with you when you look the way you do when you're caught. This is me, remember? Old Gus. I can read your face like a bleedin' book. So don't try it on with me.'

She capitulated. 'I'm sorry, Gus. You're right. I shouldn't involve other police people. But to tell the truth —'

'The less I know the better,' he said wearily. 'Just give me the stuff you've collected and we'll say no more. But tell your friend Miss Bentley that she'll ruin her chances if she doesn't watch it. She's a bright girl and I've been keeping an eye on her. She'll make a good detective yet, but she has to do her slogging first. If you interfere you'll give her silly notions, understand?'

'Understood.' She sat down. 'So now what?'

'Where's Julie?'

'She'll be out of the loo in a minute.'

'I'll have to put a CCTV camera in there, I swear it,' he muttered. 'The way you females plot. Ah, here she is.' He got to his feet and went to the door as Julie, whistling between her teeth, came back into the incident room. 'As you can see, Policewoman Bentley,' he called, 'your colleagues have gone home exhausted by a hard day at the computer and on the phone, don't you know.'

'Me too, Guv.' Julie smiled at him, her eyes bright. That she was pleased with herself was undoubted. She seemed to shine.

'As I say, *they* were on the computers. But let that go. If you're tired, you'd better go home as well. But let me just say this, missy. I'm not as green as I'm cabbage-looking, as my old granny used to say. I know what's what, and I don't like being taken for an idiot, you understand me? This time you've got away with it. Another, you won't. Now hop off home and come in tomorrow ready to sit at that desk and really work. OK?'

'Sir,' said Julie in a small voice. She ducked her head and picked up her bag from her desk and then almost scuttled out of the room.

'Now we can talk,' he said as he came back to the desk. Let me have it all. And this time *all* of it.

When she had finished he nodded. 'So, when we get the warrant we'll have to check the office particularly well. Did Julie take anything away?'

George shook her head almost indignantly. 'Of course not, Gus! She told me in the loo. Everything was left exactly as she found it. She copied out the information she thought'd be useful. There was a list of customers on the computer there it seems, and she rolled through and spotted one called Sloane's in Durleighton, and that made her think. As she said, Alice mightn't be able to use her own name on this shop for some reason, but she'd still want to put her mark on it. And naming it after the place where her other shop is –'

'Tell me, when you girls go to the loo, do you do anything apart from talk?' Gus growled.

'Not a lot,' George said. 'And I have to say we spend at least as much time talking about men as you do talking about us in your john. It's what people use johns for. Gus, I'm sorry I misbehaved, but I'm not sorry we got what we found out. Are you?'

'Of course not. But we'd have got it just the same, you know. When we got a warrant and searched the place.'

'But *when* would you have got it? When would you have

looked? Not yet, I'll bet. Everyone thought the van had just been used opportunistically and that this chap Max Hazell had nothing to do with it.'

'He can't have had much to do with it,' Gus pointed out. 'Seeing he's dead.'

'I wouldn't even believe that for sure if I were you,' she retorted. 'That really is one hell of an operation they've got going on there. It must handle vast sums. Who knows what else they might be up to? When people have a good smuggling operation going they don't usually confine themselves to one sort of goods, do they? For all you know they might be bringing in all sorts of other stuff.'

'Now you really are running away with your imagination,' he said. 'I'll grant you you uncovered this earlier than we would have done. Now no more searching over dead ground. Let's plan tomorrow.'

She lifted her chin and looked at him hopefully, and he managed a grimace which was half grin, half frown.

'It'd be safer for me to take you along, I think, rather than to let you wander around loose. We'll go to Durleighton, see what's what there; I'll leave the rest of it here in London to Dudley. It's all straightforward routine and he's very good at that.'

'Listen, Gus, I may step over your rules sometimes but that doesn't mean you have to treat me like a child! Telling me you'll take me with you to keep me out of trouble – Jesus, man, I'm supposed to be helpful! And I thought I was!'

He gave up. 'Of course you are. Bloody helpful. It's only that sometimes you just don't stop to think. OK, we'll go to Durleighton together not just so's I can keep an eye on you but also because I'd value your input. And your hunches. All right?'

She smiled, completely disarmed. 'All right. Thank you, Gus. And I'm sorry too. I'll try to behave like a policeman, I promise.'

'Heaven forbid,' he said. 'A policeman is the last person I want to go into the country with. Because we'll go up tonight, stay over and be ready to start first thing. So go home and get our gear. By the time you get back here, I'll be ready. Hop it.'

22

In other circumstances Durleighton was the sort of small town in which they might have spent a long weekend, doing the things that visitors do in attractive small towns: wandering round the antique shops and secondhand bookshops, of which there were a surprisingly large number; taking morning coffee and afternoon tea in impossibly bucolic tea shops run by intense middle-aged women with a penchant for vegetarianism, alternative therapies and animal welfare (going by the noticeboards they displayed over their arrangements of home-baked scones and fruit loaves); and generally behaving like tourists. As it was, there was no time for such pleasures.

They took a room in a hotel-cum-pub in the middle of the town which prided itself on its long history and exposed oak beams but which provided a lumpy bed and decidedly inadequate bathroom arrangements. George, however, was so pleased to be with Gus as his partner in investigation that she made not a murmur of complaint about either, a fact which amused Gus greatly. He said as much over breakfast.

'Usually by this time you'd be groaning about your bruises from that bed. How come you're so quiet about it this morning?'

'Because I've other things to think about.' She bit into the rather soggy toast which formed the centrepiece of their meal. 'We're here for work, not fun. So, is there a plan of action?'

He laughed. 'Is this my George?' he asked the ceiling. 'Putting her creature comforts so far down the list? Who'd ha' thought it? OK. First thing is to find a better place to stay, because if you're not in the mood to complain, I am. And then –'

'Oh, Gus, stop it. This'll do well enough. Talk to them and ask for a different room with a firmer bed, if you must, but let's not waste time. I want to start looking around.'

'OK, OK, I'll suffer for my work. You want a plan of action? First off, I want to talk to the local nick. See if there's anything I can pick up from them. You never know. Then –'

'Well, I can't do that with you, can I?' She pushed aside her plate and set her elbows on the table. 'I'll tell you what. Let me go and look at the shops, hmm? I'll find this place Sloane's and wander in and see what's what. It makes sense for a woman to do that, anyway. Maybe I'll be able to dig out things that an interrogation, police-style, won't.'

He thought about that for a moment, sipping his coffee and looking at her owlishly over the rim of his cup. Then he put the cup down and nodded. 'Why not? I've got you here, so I might as well make the best use of you I can. Now, please, George, no going off half cocked. I don't want you discussing the case or giving any hint of why we're here. Not till I'm ready for that.'

'As if I would!' She was indignant. 'You know I pride myself on being discreet.'

'Discreet?' He laughed. 'You're as discreet as a pimple on a bald head. A bloody gifted liar, but discreet? Never. And that's the next thing. Don't get involved in too complicated a set of taradiddles, will you? Sometimes it's useful – I remember the way you made yourself into a gambling expert from Las Vegas when you were investigating those betting shops in Shadwell. It helped get me out of trouble, I won't deny, but was altogether too clever by half.'

'What a Brit you are, Gus!' She got to her feet. 'No American would ever say a person was too clever. We admire smart people. You'll just have to trust me. I'll be on my way then. Where shall we meet?'

He looked over his shoulder to the dining-room window, looking out into the main square of the town, which was beginning to play host to the cars parking on its ancient central cobbles. Durleighton was coming to life for the day, blinking in the late autumn sunshine of the morning like a tired old spaniel, but still with some life left in its old bones. He watched people greeting each other and standing to gossip for a few moments before bustling off about their business, and sighed. George could almost feel the moment of wistfulness in him, so common to city-bred people when confronted with the charms of a small town. Gus wouldn't leave his beloved London for anywhere else in the world, but he wasn't immune to Durleighton's peace and security.

Now he gave his head a sharp little shake and went on, 'I doubt we need to make any special arrangements. This place is so small, we'll hardly lose each other. I'll find you when I'm ready. Good luck and, sweetheart, be careful. There've been five killings in this case. There's a real danger. It's not just a fun game of spot-the-villain or a particularly devilish crossword.'

She lifted her face and kissed him swiftly. 'Bless you for caring. And I'll be careful. I do know the risks – didn't I do the post-mortems? I know viciousness when I see it, and there's plenty in this case. But I'll be safe enough here. Broad daylight and a place so sleepy it'd take an atom blast to wake it up. I'll see you around, then.'

He kissed her then, a little more thoroughly, and watched her go. At the door she looked back and he lifted his hand and snapped the brim of his non-existent hat with his thumb and forefinger, and she laughed and went, feeling warm and happy. Dear Gus, she thought as she came out into the street and looked about her. He puts up with so much from me. I'm a lucky woman. Then she walked across the square purposefully towards the narrow street entrance where there appeared to be some shops. She had work to do.

George took her time, wandering from window display to window display and peering in, sometimes going into the little shops to browse among the goods inside. At this time of year, when the weather was unreliable and the tourist season, such as it was, was dwindling to its close, there were few customers; and even if it had been the height of the season, she told herself, looking up and down the quiet street, nine o'clock on a Monday morning is never exactly boom time.

She remarked on the quietness of the place to the assistant in the grocery store in which she bought a pot of fiery mustard to take home; Gus loved mustard that threatened to drop through his chin. The girl looked up from her cash register and grimaced.

'Most borin' place in the world, this is,' she said, in a marked Midlands accent that George had to concentrate on to understand fully. 'Nothin' to do, not nowhere. S'always quiet 'ere.'

'As quiet as this?' George looked round the empty shop. 'Then how do you stay in business?'

The girl shrugged. 'Oh, it ain't *that* quiet. I mean, there's always the fancy people, like, buying their fancy stuff.' She looked at the shelf nearest her with some disparagement, and George followed her gaze, taking in the jars of asparagus, the row of olive oils in elegant bottles and the pots of country chutneys and jams. 'Real people goes out to the supermarket over towards Baston 'ill. This is for the weekenders and the rich ones.' She looked up at George consideringly. 'An' tourists, o' course. But I don't get to see none of my mates in 'ere.'

George could understand her sulkiness. It would clearly have been much more agreeable to have worked where young men might wander in for a packet of crisps or a pot noodle. She smiled sympathetically at the girl. 'What about clothes and so forth? Is there any worthwhile fashion shop here in Durleighton?'

'Fashion?' The girl laughed. 'Oh, if you've got a few bob to spend, there's always the fancy shops, but for the sort of stuff I like I 'ave to go all the way into Birmingham or sometimes Warwick to the market. But it costs, o'course, the buses being what they are. My friend Dawn's got a car and sometimes she takes me shoppin'. Otherwise it's like I said. There's nothin' to do not nowhere in this place.' And she hit the keys on her cash register crossly. 'Will there be anythin' else, then?'

'I'm afraid not,' George said. 'I wish I could buy more if only to cheer you up.'

The girl stared at her for a moment, then giggled and relaxed.

'It might cheer my boss up,' she said. 'Wouldn't do nothin' for me, would it?'

'What would cheer you up? Is there any other shop in the town you'd rather work in?' George settled for a cosy woman-to-woman chat. 'I always used to think it would be great to work in a fashion store. Somewhere they had really nice stuff, you know, and you could try things on?'

'My friend Dawn, she works in a place like that.' The girl leaned comfortably on the counter, clearly delighted to have the chance to talk. 'But it's not like you said. You can't go trying the clothes on – they'd 'ave a fit if you did that. You just 'ave to fetch and carry, like. It's not even as though Dawn gets to talk to the customers much. It's always the boss what does that.'

'Oh,' George caught her breath. Had she struck gold? 'What shop is that then?'

'It's a place called Sloane's,' the girl said. 'Over to the end of Market Street, just before you get to the church.' She pointed vaguely. 'Next door to that men's shop – whatsit, Adonis.'

George smiled brilliantly at the girl. She had indeed struck gold. The mother lode, in fact. 'Sloane's?' she said. 'Funny name for a shop, isn't it?'

'Funny? Not really. I suppose you bein' an American – you are, aren't you? Yeah, I thought so – maybe you haven't heard of 'em. They're from London, silly people what they call Sloane Rangers. They're always on about them,' the girl said with some contempt. 'So Dawn says. Only they're sort of old-fashioned now. But the shop's ever so old-fashioned, so I suppose it don't matter what it's called.'

George's heart sank. There was no way a shop owned by Alice Diamond could be unfashionable. 'Old-fashioned? But I thought you said it was a fashion store?'

'Oh, yeah, but not what *I'd* call fashion. They got all these tweeds and silks, like. There's a dress they've got in their window what's just black silk, nothin' special at all, but it's six 'undred pounds! Imagine, *six 'undred* . . . I seen better'n that in Warwick Market for twenty quid and I still wouldn't give them 'ouseroom! There's no *excitin'* stuff, like. No nice big clumpy shoes or anything.' She sighed. 'So Dawn doesn't mind not tryin' things on all that much after all. I reckon I'm better off 'ere. At least I don't 'ave to run around makin' cups o' coffee for the customers and bein' all smarmy all the time. I just takes the money and lets 'em get on with it.'

'What's Dawn's boss like?' George said casually. 'Nice person to work for?'

The girl made a grimace. 'All right, I suppose. Always on the phone to London, Dawn says, and thinks 'erself no end of a madam, but she's just workin' there like Dawn is and doesn't 'ave no cause to give 'erself such airs. It's not like she owns it, is it?'

'Oh? Who does?'

The girl looked at her sharply then and George smiled back vaguely. Careful, she told herself. Don't be too nosy. 'Some chap, I dare say. They really are the worst, aren't they? At least here your boss owns the place.'

'I think that makes 'im worse.' The girl allowed herself to be distracted, to George's relief. ''E thinks he can do anything 'e likes and so 'e can, I s'pose. Comes in when 'e fancies and goes on at me like you'd never believe. I'd be off only there aren't that many jobs in Durleighton now, not even at the supermarket. I'm on the list there, mind you, for a cashier.'

'Well, I hope you get the job.' George said heartily. 'Is Dawn trying to work there too?'

'No, she's happy enough where she is. Like she says, she can always get back at Mrs Morris, tellin' her she'll complain to the boss if she treats her bad. An' she would too.'

'Oh, does she know the boss, then?' George was as casual as she could be, busying herself packing her jar of mustard into her handbag, in amongst the make-up and change purse and assorted detritus. The girl seemed happier about answering now.

'Oh, yes. She comes to Durleighton sometimes. Got a shop in London, you see, as well. And in other places, seemingly.'

The door of the shop opened and a woman in a raincoat and with her hair tied up in a scarf came in. 'Good morning, Hayley,' she fluted. 'How are you today? Nice weekend, I hope?'

'Very nice, thank you, Mrs Charteris,' Hayley said straightening up. 'I've got your jam all ready. Mr Edmunds said you'd be in for it.' And she went slouching away to the back of the shop. George smiled vaguely at the new arrival and closed her handbag. 'Well, I must be going,' she said to no one in particular. 'Good morning. Goodbye, Hayley.'

The girl waved her hand from behind the counter and the customer herself smiled inquisitively at George. 'Visiting, are you, dear? How nice. I hope you find it pleasant here in Durleighton. We think it a charming place to live.'

'Oh, very, very,' George said and escaped. The last thing she wanted was to stay talking to a shop's customers. It was the staff who would give her the material she needed, and she set off for the end of the street in the direction Hayley had indicated, trying to make herself walk slowly. But she couldn't. So she stepped out with a swing, no longer looking in shop windows, and reached the end of the street in a matter of minutes.

Traffic was beginning to build up now and she stood at the side of the road and looked across at the shop as she waited for a couple of vans and cars to pass her. It was a handsome building and probably an old one, she thought, trying to remember what Gus had told her in the past about the differences between Queen Anne, Victorian and Edwardian structures. She came to the tentative conclusion that this had originally been a Queen Anne house, with its flat front and the small flight of steps that led up to the door from the pavement level. The shop windows, which were clearly a later addition, were set high and sparsely dressed. In one was the black dress about which Hayley had spoken so scathingly; even from here George could see that it was in fact a most handsome garment, beautifully cut and with a good deal of flair in its design. It stood in the window in splendid isolation against a stark white background. On the other side the window had been reversed, with a black background in front of which a white silk coat was displayed. The effect was dramatic and seductive and George wanted to go into the shop for its own sake, never mind the name on the fascia above the door, which read in discreet black letters, 'Sloane's.'

She was able to cross the road at last and did so at a fast pace, and almost ran up the steps of the shop in her eagerness. Inside it was precisely what she would have expected, had she thought about it. The big room that formed the showroom was lit with a large overhead chandelier as well as spotlights, the walls were a soft cream and dotted about were cream suede-covered chairs set in chrome, modern yet looking perfectly at home in the clearly old room, with rosewood and chrome tables between them bearing glossy magazines and flowers in silver bowls and ashtrays. Around the walls were mirrors, set at various angles, and here and there, on headless models, garments. There was in the far corner a curtain, made of cream and silver beads, and beyond it she could just see rails of clothes. The place smelled of hyacinths and coffee and was as relaxing as it was possible for a shop to be. She felt a stab of pure pleasure at it all.

The girl who popped her head out through the bead curtain was clearly Dawn. She had the same petulant look of her friend at the grocery store, George thought, but had been better advised about her appearance. Where Hayley had been undoubtedly over-lipsticked and -mascaraed, this girl had a discreet make-up and her fair hair held back by a velvet Alice band, rather than the elaborate cut Hayley had sported.

'Good morning,' she said with false brightness. 'CanIhelpyou?' It was clearly one word, which she used often, but contained not an atom of any real interest in giving assistance. George, however, smiled at her as though she believed it had been meant in all sincerity.

'Good morning!' she said. 'How kind of you. May I look around?'

'Oh, sure, yes,' the girl said, bringing the rest of her body out through the bead curtain. She was wearing a copy of the black dress in the window, George thought. It looked good on her because she had the young figure that such a garment demanded, and yet it didn't look quite the same. She took a deep breath.

'There now,' she said in her most American drawl, which she always found so useful on these occasions. 'If you aren't wearing that darling dress that's in the window! It is the same, isn't it?'

The girl giggled and looked down at herself. 'I wish,' she said. 'No, Mrs Morris had it copied for me. Just to wear here of course. I wouldn't wear it out anywhere.'

'But it looks perfect on you!' George said and was truthful. The dress mightn't have the special qualities of the one in the window but it looked fine on Dawn.

'Well.' The girl smiled at her in a rather mechanical way. 'It's not what you might call my style, really. But it's good for work. Is there anything I can show you? Mrs Morris'll be back in a minute if you want to wait. She said if anyone came in I was to say to wait for her, an' give you a cup of coffee or tea.'

'Oh, how very nice!' George promptly sat down on one of the suede chairs, which was not quite as comfortable as it looked. 'I'd just adore some coffee! How kind of you. I've plenty of time, so why not?'

23

By the time the shop door opened again to let Mrs Morris in, George had learned a lot about Sloane's, because Dawn needed only the most gentle of prodding to release a flood of chatter. Clearly the girl spent so much time alone in the shop that having someone to talk to was a major event in her life.

George realized almost at once from Dawn's artless complaining that the shop took very little money over the counter. The weekdays were almost invariably quite empty of any activity. George herself was, Dawn said, the only person she could ever remember coming in so early on a Monday morning. Not that they did no custom; the weekends could be busy, Dawn said. The rich people from the big houses round and about the town as well as some of the weekend visitors and tourists came in; Sloane's did a very nice business in costly designer clothes.

'We've got every famous label you could think of,' Dawn said with a sort of irritated pride. 'Though I have to say for my part I go by what a dress looks like, not what it says on the label. But seemingly there's a lot of people put a lot of store by that.' She looked alarmed for a moment. 'I hope I'm not speakin' out of turn. Maybe you –'

'It's all right,' George assured her. 'I agree with you. I've no time at all for label snobbery. But I do like nice clothes and you can see that the things in here are very nice indeed.'

'Well, I suppose. I like stuff with a bit more pizazz, m'self.' Dawn went pink for a moment. 'Ooh, you won't tell Mrs Morris

206

I was talking like that, will you? She'd be dead annoyed if she thought I wasn't saying our stuff was the best thing since sliced bread.'

'Not a word,' George assured her. 'Though I must say if she scares you that much . . .' and she waited hopefully.

She wasn't disappointed. 'Oh, she doesn't scare me! I just can't be bothered with her goin' on at me the way she does. She thinks she's God Almighty, that's her trouble, but she's only the manageress here, no matter how many fancy friends she reckons she's got. It's Mrs Dee what's the owner, an' I've got her phone number in London so if I ever need to tell her anythin' about Mrs Morris, I shall. Not that Mrs Morris knows that.' Dawn giggled then, and there was an unpleasant edge to the sound.

'Mrs Dee?' George said, trying to sound offhand. 'What does that stand for?'

'Stand for?' The girl was puzzled.

'Dee. What's it for? Dawkins? Donald . . . ?'

Dawn's face cleared. 'Oh, I see what you mean. No, it's not an initial. That's her name. Dee. Arabella Dee Ltd. That's the name of the company, like. I've seen it on the papers.' Again she gave a little giggle. 'Not supposed to, but I did. Oh' – she shook her head – 'I'm really talking too much, aren't I? My mum says I always let my tongue run away with me and one of these days it'll get me into real trouble. You won't say to Mrs Morris I've been chattering, will you?'

'Trust me.' George smiled brilliantly. 'I'm just the same myself. I was always being put down for being a chatterbox when I was a child. But I don't think it's so bad. It means I always know what's going on, because when you talk to people they talk back, don't they?'

'Yeah,' Dawn said and leaned comfortably against a mirror, clearly happy to go on gossiping as long as George wanted her to. Someone up there loves me, George thought.

'So do tell me, what is Mrs Morris really like? As well as going on at you?' She left the words invitingly in the air.

Dawn rose to them obligingly. 'Oh, a real bighead, that one! You'd think there was no one in the world as sophisticated as she is. Sophisticated!' That warranted a snort. 'She's got as much chance of being sophisticated as I've got of changing into a fella, livin' here. I'll be out of this town as soon as I've got a few bob together, off to London to live. That's the only place to really be sophisticated, 'n't it?'

'Yes, indeed.' George was touched by her adolescent small-town yearning. 'But you're fine as you are, Dawn. You needn't worry about being anything other than yourself. People who put on a show of being something different –'

'Oh, yes! Aren't they awful? Always goin' on about her famous friends and Lord Durleigh this and Lord Durleigh that. The way she carried on when he got killed, you'd think they'd been lovers or something. And I know they was never that close because I saw him once in the street outside and said, "Oh, there's Lord Durleigh," and she was out there like a shot and chattin' him up, and it was obvious he was dead bored. She just likes to suck up to rich and famous people, that's all.'

'I know the sort.' George's pulse had quickened. This was getting more and more interesting. 'It was awful about Lord Durleigh, wasn't it? Being killed that way.'

'Awful,' Dawn said with relish. 'Just imagine, a madman running about in London. Of course it makes my mum extra nervous. Every time I say I want to go and work in London she goes potty, and with all these killings – well, it don't help. But I say to her, it's only a madman. They'll catch him and then I'll be as safe as anywhere else. You can get terrible things happening in the smaller places after all. Think of Hungerford.'

Her faith in the police and their abilities to catch murderers, mad or otherwise, was even more touching, George thought. I must tell Gus it's not all hopeless in the police battle to retain public respect. She smiled warmly at Dawn. 'I'm sure they'll catch him, too. So, who else does she – um – suck up to?'

'Well, there's Mr Caspar-Wynette-Gondor,' Dawn said. 'He's Lord Durleigh's brother, like, and she's all over him too.' She stopped then, her head on one side. 'Of course now he'll be Lord Durleigh, won't he?'

'Will he?'

'Well, I suppose so. I mean the other brother got killed as well, didn't he? So it'll be Edward. Oh, there'll be no holding the old cow now. They really are a lot more friendly. Well, sort of. It's his mate she's friendliest with.'

'Oh?' George waited, smiling gently. 'What mate?'

'The bloke that works on the estate, you know. The agent, Mr Powell. Jasper. One of those fancy names.'

'Oh?' George said again, non-committally.

Dawn was well away now. 'Oh, yes, I think she might be having a bit of an affair with him, to tell the truth. They're as thick as they can be. Having lunch over at the Bald Monk and all like that.'

The Bald Monk was the pub where George and Gus were staying and she couldn't help but grimace at the thought of eating there on a regular basis. Fortunately Dawn didn't notice.

'I see them there in the evening sometimes, as well as lunch-times. Always got their heads together and chatterin' away like monkeys. I reckon that's how she knows so much about things up at Durleigh Abbey. Anyway –'

And then the shop door opened. The woman who had come in was tall, almost as tall as George herself, but a good deal larger, with an imposing bust and extremely handsome legs, a fact which she clearly knew perfectly well, because she was wearing very high-heeled shoes and a rather short skirt on her crimson suit. But the man who came in behind her was still taller than she was. He was carrying a pile of cardboard boxes and he stopped as the woman did.

'Oh, good morning,' the woman said. 'I didn't expect – Are you – um – being looked after?'

'Oh, yes,' George said with a wide smile. 'I've had lots of coffee and I've been looking through the magazines as well as at your lovely shop. Your young lady said I could wait for you, as you know the stock best, so I thought I would. I'm in no hurry.'

The woman's shoulders obviously relaxed and she produced a wide professional smile. 'I'm so sorry to have kept you waiting. If I'd known – well, it's my fault,' she said with an air of great generosity. 'I can't blame the girl for not sending a message to me, because I didn't say where I'd be, which was very remiss of me.' She looked up at her companion. 'My dear, *would* you mind taking those through?' She turned back to George. 'Now, what can I show you?'

The tall man looked at George as she glanced up at him. He was about forty or so, she decided, and undoubtedly good looking. He had widely set grey eyes, and his chin was so square with so definite a cleft that it was almost a caricature of a film star's jaw. Fortunately he was rather lined under his eyes, and his nose was a little crooked, which gave his face charm rather than perfection, and that was far more attractive. He tossed his head slightly so that a lock of thick dark hair which had fallen over one eye was thrown back. The movement had a boyish quality about it that added to his attractions. George, who had always been a connoisseur of male beauty, found herself warming to the woman now standing beside him; any woman with any taste at all would make a friend of someone like Jasper Powell. Because that was obviously who the man was. She could tell by the way Dawn's colour had come up as soon as she had seen him. It's never comfortable to be interrupted in the middle of a flood of gossip by the subject of your chatter, George thought, amused.

'A pleasure,' he said in a voice that was satisfyingly deep but which had a slight huskiness in it, giving it a rusty quality. He smiled at George. 'Good morning.'

'Good morning,' she said. 'You look very loaded there.'

'Oh, I can manage them.' He winked at the woman beside him. 'Daffy here makes sure I keep in good practice. In the stockroom, then?'

'Yes please!' Daffy said with a brilliant smile. 'Now, my dear, what can I show you? And would you care for more coffee while I get things out.'

'Oh, no, no thanks.' George, who feared she might be on the way to caffeine poisoning if she drank any more, shook her head and stood up. 'Dawn has been most generous with it already.'

'Oh, so she told you her name?' The woman looked sharp

suddenly and George could have cursed herself for being so careless.

'I asked her,' she said. 'I always do. I'm George Barnabas. Hi!' She held out her hand towards the woman. 'And you are . . . ?'

'Daphne Morris,' she said after a moment. 'How d'y'do.' But the sharpness had gone and George relaxed. 'So, what sort of things are you looking for?'

'Oh, I just don't know!' George looked rueful. 'You know how it is. I don't know what I want till I see it. I thought a dress – a party dress, you know? But one I can wear during the day as well if necessary.'

'Oh, dear me, yes,' Daphne Morris said. 'It's so difficult for businesswomen, isn't it? Having to attend meetings all day and then go straight on to a party.'

She's fishing, George thought. Wants to know what I do. And she smiled at her. 'You're so right. I suppose every working woman has that difficulty. So, what do you suggest?'

Mrs Morris moved across the shop towards the bead curtain. 'Well, I'll see what I think is right for your size. Let me see, twelve?'

'Something like that,' George said, knowing perfectly well that in some very sleek garments she felt better in a fourteen but not wanting to admit it. 'It depends on the cut.'

'Everything always does,' Daphne Morris said and went in through the bead curtain just as Jasper Powell emerged. 'I'll see you later, Jas?' she said quickly. 'As usual?'

'Of course.' He smiled down at her and looked about to bend to kiss her cheek but she shook her head slightly.

George was sitting down again on the suede chair, and she smiled up at him with as wide and ingenuous a smile as she could conjure up. 'Such a lovely day,' she said. 'A real joy to be in the country.'

'We've had better weather,' he said dryly, because the sky outside had indeed clouded over. 'But at least it's not raining.'

George, who had mentioned the weather only because she had been taught this was the polite way to start a conversation with a stranger in Britain, glanced at the window. 'Yes, indeed,' she said with vague heartiness. 'It's so difficult when it rains. Especially if you're delivering goods. Makes them wet. That must make life very hard for you.'

He laughed then. 'I'm not precisely a delivery boy,' he said. 'In spite of appearances.'

George showed a nice line in pretty confusion. 'Oh, I'm sorry. I saw you bring the boxes, so I thought –'

'Just helping a friend collect some stuff from the station,' he said.

'So you have a more interesting job,' she said brightly.

He looked down at her and the creased face closed a little more as he smiled, a long slow smile. 'Indeed I do. Like you, I dare say.'

Daphne Morris appeared at the bead curtain again and came out with a couple of garments over her arm. Her eyes glittered slightly as she looked from Jasper to George. 'Oh, I thought you'd gone!' she said with a tight smile.

'I'm just on my way.' He went over to the door and hesitated for a moment. 'See you later, Daffy. Take care.' And he went, leaving Daphne Morris staring after him, her face blank.

'He seemed very nice. It's so good to have friends to help you, isn't it, when you're in business?' George said.

'Mmm.' Daphne had clearly been somewhere else, deep inside her head, and now she looked at George. 'He just carried the boxes up for me from the station.'

'Of course.' George was a little startled at the sudden intensity with which Daphne was looking at her. 'It's such a help, as I say, having friends to join in. That's what's so good about living in the country, isn't it? In cities we're all just too selfish to care for anyone but ourselves.'

'Yes.' Daphne seemed to seize on that. 'You're so right. We are very helpful to each other here. Now, let's see. What do you think of this?'

This was a slender dress in deep blue. George looked at it, thinking of the last dress she had bought and how expensive it had been, and bit her lip, for it was clearly marked at four hundred and fifty pounds. Outrageous, she thought, but this is an investigation and sometimes you just have to do what you have to do.

The next half-hour was fun, and she became absorbed in it, almost forgetting why she was there. That somehow worked in her favour, because Daphne Morris became more and more relaxed and in consequence chattered more.

Not that George learned a great deal more than she already had from Dawn, who was now buried somewhere in the back of the premises, though she did get confirmation of some things. But none of them seemed to George to matter too much.

Mrs Daphne Morris was indeed a crashing snob of the worst kind, boasting steadily of the high social calibre of her clients and her friends. Listening to her, George had the impression that the first thing that Lord Durleigh's female guests did was rush to Sloane's to stock up their wardrobes; that everyone in the district who had any hope of being regarded as of any style at all shopped there too; and that Daphne Morris herself was *persona* very much *grata* everywhere she went. A regular guest at all the best houses, was how she put it.

George tried a little probing as she wriggled in and out of one lovely dress after another, chewing her lower lip as she pirouetted in front of the mirror, because many of them suited her exceedingly well. But she still managed to keep her goal in sight, and asked artless questions as offhandedly as she could.

Was Jasper Powell a person of local importance? Indeed he was; a close friend of Mr Edward Caspar-Wynette-Gondor, as was Daphne herself, of course, and indeed lived in the adjoining house to Edward, since he now worked as his agent. At one time, when Edward had first met Jasper, Daphne said, he had been one of London's top chefs, and he still cooked like an angel, whenever he could persuade Mrs Lyons, who looked after them both, to let him into the kitchen.

'She does get away with so much that an ordinary member of the domestic staff never could,' prattled Daphne as she circled George to look at the fit of a remarkable garment in dark brown suede trimmed with fur, which had a price ticket that ran into four figures and which, to George's relief, did not suit her at all.

'But she was Edward's nanny from babyhood, and you know how it is with those old-retainer types.' And she laughed prettily. George managed not to show in her face how ridiculous it all sounded. Old retainers indeed, in the last decade of the twentieth century.

'But she loves Jasper as much as Edward, almost, though of course not quite since he was always her favourite nursling over his brothers, and she lets him – Jasper, you know – cook for us occasionally. We have the most delightful supper parties!' She laughed merrily yet again as she displayed her highly superior lifestyle to her customer.

Eventually George felt she had to go. She doubted there was any more she could get out of Daphne; however hard she tried to bring the subject round to the actual ownership of the shop, Daphne slid away from it, and anyway she had Dawn to fall back on, she told herself. I'll tell Gus she has a phone number for the owner of the shop; that it's a different name to Alice Diamond, but not so different it couldn't be made up to cover Alice's identity, but not too carefully. Arabella Dee: absurd, she thought. But I'll hand all that over to Gus.

She had to choose something to buy, of course, and opted for a rather handsome confection of pleated silk in a deep amber shade that suited her well, and cost a mere three hundred pounds, which, compared with everything else she'd been shown, was downright cheap. It needed altering, however, since it was somewhat too big on the waist and hip (which comforted George absurdly, until she reminded herself she'd had to opt for a size fourteen to accommodate her generous bust measurement) and she made complicated arrangements with Daphne for this to be done and the finished garment to be sent to her London house.

It was close to eleven when she eventually left the shop. The sky was still overcast and she pulled her coat collar up to cover her neck because of the chill in the air. She would have to make her way back into the square to see if she could find Gus, and turned to the kerb to cross the road.

There were now several cars parked outside, with their rear ends to the kerb, noses pointing out into the street. The closeness

214

of them made it hard to find a place where she could get between them and across the road, so she walked along to where there seemed to be a vehicle parked further out than the rest, which would give her room to get over the road.

She reached her chosen crossing place with some difficulty, walking with her head down to keep the now really cold wind out of her face, and not looking at the big car that she thought offered her the crossing space she needed. She walked past the adjoining one and turned and then, as she did so, the big car suddenly sprang into life as the driver, whom she had not noticed was in it, switched on the engine.

He seemed to move with an amazing speed. The engine was no sooner turning over than he'd slipped the car into gear and it leaped – backwards. George, with the sudden rush of adrenaline that comes when danger threatens, jumped out of the way, but not fast enough. The back bumper hit her leg with a numbing blow and she felt the heat of blood trickling down it as she battered with both fists on the back of the vehicle, which was now pinning her to the wall of the sweetshop behind. She was completely unable to move and could hardly breathe because of the shock she was in. She had never been so alarmed in all her life.

24

Jasper Powell behaved like a man distraught. Her shouting had made him aware of something wrong and he had driven forwards to release George before switching off the engine and almost falling out of the vehicle to come rushing round to her; but it had made her hoarse and unable to say a word when he reached her side. She just leaned back against the sweetshop window and tried to catch her breath.

'Oh, my God, I'm so sorry. I didn't see you there. I can't imagine how I could have – Here, let me take you to sit down somewhere. We'll call an ambulance, get you to the hospital and –'

'No!' George managed. 'No. No need. OK.' And she knew she was. She'd had a very nasty fright and needed time to recover. But no bones were broken. Only the skin of her leg had been scraped, together with her tights, leaving a mess on her shin that looked, she thought, as she managed to gaze down on it, rather worse than it probably was. Her professional mind reassured her ordinary rather panicky one, and she took a couple of deep breaths to soothe herself. Gradually her pulse eased, her breath came back, and she was able to stand up straighter, though it helped to have his arm around her.

'I'm OK,' she said. 'I guess I should have made sure there was no one in the car before I tried to go behind it.' She looked up at the vehicle then and shook her head. 'Not that I'd have been able to see you, would I?' The car was a Range Rover, very high off the road and with its back window partly obscured by wire netting. He looked up and shook his head.

'I shouldn't keep that there, I suppose, but I need it for the dogs, and I usually use my wing mirrors very carefully. I just didn't think this morning. I'm so sorry. Here, we must get that leg fixed. It looks awful.'

'It isn't.' She was feeling better by the moment and by now embarrassed. It was so stupid to walk behind a parked car without checking that it wasn't about to be driven; all she wanted to do was get away to sort out her injuries in peace. 'I'm a doctor. I can fix myself easily. I don't need any ambulance.'

'A doctor?' For the first time he let his anxious expression relax. 'That's a comfort. Are you absolutely certain that –'

'I'm certain,' she said firmly. 'Now, let me just be on my way, please. I'll go back to the hotel and get it –'

'You'll do no such thing,' he said, urging her firmly towards the passenger door of the car. 'The least I can do is take you where you can sort it out in comfort. Come on.'

She really couldn't make the effort to disagree. It didn't seem important enough. She needed to be taken somewhere, and she might as well go with him as try to argue with him. 'Well, all right,' she said. 'A lift would be nice. We're staying at the Bald Monk.'

'It's as easy to take you home,' he said. He settled her in the high passenger seat and belted her in as though she were a child. 'Our Mrs Lyons'll be furious with me if I don't, when she hears what happened. And that really would be dreadful.' And he smiled at her and then hurried round to the driver's side.

This is so silly, George thought. It's like something out of a soppy romance. Handsome man nearly runs down heroine, insists on taking her home, and then what? She shook herself mentally. She must have been more shocked than she realized to be thinking so foolishly.

He checked his wing mirrors with a most exaggerated care, caught her eye and laughed and then let in the clutch and the car moved forwards smoothly. She felt odd, sitting so high, used as she was to Gus's road-hugging car, but the effect soon wore off and she looked out at the passing scenery in a slightly sleepy fashion as he drove through the town's narrow and now crowded streets. It was odd how sleepy she was, she thought, and then reminded herself of the way injuries led to the production of endorphins, the natural opiates that help control pain. She laughed softly.

He gave her a sideways glance. 'What's so funny?'

'Me, sitting here, feeling sleepy and working out in my head the reason for it,' she said. 'Endorphins.'

'Oh, the natural chemicals your brain makes when you're hurt or eat or exercise or whatever, and that make you feel euphoric? As well as sleepy?'

'You know about that?'

'Oh, I know a lot about such things,' he said. 'It's always been an interest of mine. Anatomy and physiology,' he added as he saw her puzzled look. 'I've got all sorts of books on it. I first got interested when I was a chef and had to learn how to handle various sorts of meat and fish and poultry. I thought it was extraordinary the way so many animals have the same interior arrangements – hearts and livers and so forth – that I started to cross-check with people. Riveting, it was.'

'Yes,' she said and stifled a yawn. 'It can be.'

'Ah,' he said then. 'I should have thought of this sooner. Hold on, I won't be a moment or two.' He pulled the car over to the kerb and got out to run into a branch of Boot's the chemists'. She watched him go and thought, he's after plaster or something. I really should have insisted he took me to the hotel. This is all getting too silly for words.

But when he came back and pushed a bag into her hand, before starting the engine and pulling out into the traffic, she found he hadn't been after wound dressings at all. The bag contained a pair of black tights and she turned the pack over in her hands and laughed. 'I see you got the large size.'

'Not everyone is blessed with legs as long as yours,' he said. 'I noticed 'em when we were in Sloane's. I thought it better to get them too big than too small.'

'You're quite right. I do need this size. Thank you for your trouble. What do I –'

'If you dare to ask me how much they cost and try to pay me back, I'm liable to get very stroppy indeed,' he said. 'I tore 'em, I buy 'em.'

She couldn't argue with that so she said no more and went on looking out of the window. They were out of the town now, on a narrow country road which, after another few minutes, narrowed even more as it curved into a bend. And then she caught her breath.

'Oh, come on!' she said. 'That really is ridiculous!'

He laughed delightedly. 'Isn't it just? I've said that ever since we moved in.' And she went pink with mortification.

'Oh, God, I'm sorry. Is this your home? I shouldn't be so rude. But it looks like – like –'

'Like a chocolate box, yes.' Indeed it did. It was a long low building crowned with neat thatch, whitewashed, with low diamond-paned windows, and a neatly hedged front garden that was crammed, even this late in the year, with colour from late asters and roses, Michaelmas daisies, chrysanthemums and variously brightly berried bushes. There was even a wisp of smoke emerging from a chimney and the scent of woodsmoke in the air. Everything but a woman in a crinoline, in fact, holding a parasol and hiding her face in a poke bonnet.

'It looks a lovely place to live,' she managed.

'I live in just half of it.' He came round the car and opened the door to let her out. She moved gingerly, for her leg had stiffened considerably and was far from comfortable. 'You'll see. Now come along. Lean on me.'

She did, and hobbled up the path – which was, of course, she noted with some amusement, made of bricks between which sprigs of thyme and other scented plants grew, filling her nose with their aroma as she trod on them – glad to have the help. The front door, which was, inevitably, painted a glossy black and bore several heavy brass fittings, opened as they reached it.

The woman who stood there was small and neat and had exceedingly black hair frizzed into an aureole round her narrow

219

face. She wore a good deal of make-up, with pale blue eye shadow, exceedingly red lipstick and pink cheeks, but she was obviously old; really, George thought, very old. Seventy or more.

'I saw the car,' she said, coming out to reach for George's other arm. 'What on earth is all this, Mr Jasper? Really, what has been happening to you, you poor soul?'

'I ran her over, Pushkin.' Jasper said. 'Backwards. She needs a bowl of warm water and some antiseptic and bandages of some sort. And don't try to do the dressing for her because she's a doctor.'

'Then she'll have the sense to let a good nurse take over what nurses do best.' The old woman grinned widely at George, showing teeth to match the rest of her appearance: that is, highly artificial in their white regularity. ''N't that right, doctor?'

George, who wanted nothing more than the chance to get her now very sore leg comfortably dealt with, smiled and nodded. 'I suppose so,' she said, knowing that arguing would get her nowhere. The old woman looked very pleased with herself.

'You see? I told you. Now you go and get my dressing box and then get out of the way. We'll sort this out in no time.'

She led George into a neat kitchen, which was surprisingly modern with highly reflective Formica work-surfaces and cupboard doors. George looked round, a little startled. The old woman laughed as she saw her face.

'I told him, I said, you can be as oldee worldee as you like everywhere else, my lad, but not in my kitchen. I want the most modern there is; I don't care if it *does* look like an operating theatre, and there's an end to it! So that's what I got. He spent a fortune on all the old stuff out there, he did, but not so much as he had to spend in here.' She laughed, a fat, self-satisfied sound and almost lifted George on to a high stool. The arms were remarkably strong.

'Now,' she said. 'I must find a nice bowl and some – ah, here we are . . .' She moved easily about her kitchen, collecting a glass bowl and filling it with warm water and adding a splash of something from a bottle she took from the box that Jasper brought in at that point.

'You hoppit, now, Mr Jasper. We'll be out when we're good and ready,' the old woman said. Jasper flashed a smile at George and obediently went without a word. Really, George thought, this is too feudal to believe, and had to say something about it.

'Jasper,' she said. 'I thought it was his first name?'

'It is,' the old woman said. 'He's Jasper Powell. Now, you'll have to get those poor old tights off, won't you? Ah, got another pair I see, very good. Here you are then.'

George went on talking as she stood up gingerly and hoiked up her skirt to get her tights away from her bottom before sitting down again. 'I didn't think anyone called people "Mister" and then their first name any more,' she said. 'It does sound . . .'

'Well yes, but it's better I think. He said just to call him Jasper, but since I call Edward "Mister", I can't be different with him, can I? Even though I've changed every nappy he ever wore.'

'Eh?' George stared at her. The old woman was helping her pull the tights over her feet and it helped to have her attention distracted, because the action hurt her injury.

The old woman laughed. 'I used to be his nanny, you see. Both of them.'

'Jasper and –?'

'No. Edward and Richard. Lord and Lady Durleigh's boys, rest their poor souls. Lord and Lady D., I mean. Dead a long time now they are. Only me and the boys left really. And now . . .' She shook her head, squeezing some cotton wool in the water in the bowl, and began with deft and practised movements to clean the mess on George's shin. 'Richard's dead. And David.'

'Richard,' George said carefully, almost unable to believe her good luck. She thought she'd struck a mother lode finding Sloane's this morning; but this! She wasn't sure what to say, and chose to be honest. 'I know,' she said and then, as the old woman looked up at her, seeming startled, added: 'The papers are full of it.'

'Yes, o' course. I forgot that. I never see them. Nor watch the telly. Not me. I like old films, that's what I like, and I've got my video that Mr Edward bought me and a lot of old films and that's all I watch, and very nice too.' She seemed determined to say no more about Edward, and for a moment George was nonplussed. She wanted very much to talk about him, and about his dead brothers, but knew perfectly well she had to walk on eggshells. She'd promised Gus, after all, that she wouldn't let anyone know that she was doing any investigating here in Durleighton. But she had to go on; to waste an opportunity like this when it had fallen into her lap would be lunacy.

'It must be dreadful for you, after so long with the family to have lost – I mean, two of them . . .' She left it dangling.

The old lady stopped her ministrations to George's leg and stood there, her head down, thinking. Then she said, 'Yes. It's not easy. But then, it never has been. Right from the start, it was problems with those two. Lady D. always said we should have called them Pharez and Zarah, but then she was always one for her Bible. And now David too.' She shook her head. 'What's done is done. No point in crying over what's happened. Now, you *did* make a mess of this leg, didn't you? Well, I'll get on with clearing it up and we'll see how we go.'

'Thank you,' George said, and left it at that, for the old woman had set her jaw and clearly had no intention of saying any more about the Durleigh family.

'I'm George Barnabas, by the way,' she said after a little while and the old woman looked up at her and nodded.

'Dr Barnabas. And very nice too. I'm Edna Lyons.'

'But Jas– he called you Pushkin.'

'Well, he likes to be the same as Mr Edward. When they was little they couldn't manage Nanny Lyons the way their mother said they should, and anyway Richard started calling me pussycat because he saw one on my lap one day and I said, "Say hello to Pussy," and he thought it was me, you see, that I was pussy and well, you know how it is with children. They get their pet names for people and they sort of stick. There now, that looks better! I'll just try a bit of our yellow magic. It's old-fashioned but it's good.'

She took a bottle of acriflavine from her box and dabbed some of it on to the injury, turning it a fierce saffron, and George was very amused, even though it made her wince momentarily because it stung. Aniline dye antiseptics were as old as the Ark. But it didn't matter; the graze would soon heal with it or without. She watched as Mrs Lyons smoothed a sticky dressing on top of the yellow, and then straightened her back.

'There,' she said. 'You pull them tights up and then we'll see about a nice cup of tea to complete the cure.' She called Jasper to fetch her box to return it to its place and he came back to the kitchen looking hopeful.

'Comfortable now?' He peered down at George's leg and nodded. 'I can barely see the dressing under the blackness of the tights. I hope they fit all right?'

'None of your business,' Mrs Lyons said sharply, looking scandalized, and they both laughed. 'Go to the sitting room, do. I'll fetch your tea in a moment or two.'

The next half-hour was extremely agreeable. The sitting room was as studiedly period as the exterior of the house, and Jasper took a good deal of pleasure in explaining to her how it had come about.

'There was a row of four cottages that were tied to the estate – farm workers got them as part of their job. But then, as agriculture turned mechanical, they got rid of the workers and their families and Lord Durleigh was going to sell these. But my friend Edward who is – was – Durleigh's brother, and who lived up at the Abbey then, said he wanted a place of his own. So he got them and converted them. It's two houses now – did you see there was another front door a bit of a way along? That's the smaller cottage. It's mine.'

'Yours?'

'While I live here.' Jasper smiled easily. 'I don't own it. It's Edward's but he wanted me to have it on a tenancy. I'll show you later – it's a bit smaller than this one. This has an *en-suite* bathroom upstairs alongside the main bedroom – very Tudor, my dear, couldn't be more!' He laughed then and looked at her sideways. 'As well as another bathroom for the other two bedrooms. Guest rooms, you see. Then there's this big room we're in and the kitchen and the utility room . . .'

The room they were in really was big, with odd turns to the

walls, and small areas which were reached by a couple of steps up or down, and a vast log-burning fireplace, in which at the moment a small fire was crackling in a cheerful manner. The period look was completed with lots of chairs, deep, squashy and upholstered in very bright chintz, ruffled lace curtains at the windows and a plethora of highly polished wood everywhere.

'And yours is the same as this?' she said, looking around. 'Very . . .'

'Very *not* me,' he said firmly. 'I think all this is right over the top but there you go. One man's meat and so on. I've done my interior in a rather more stark fashion which Edward hates. He won't come in there. But Pushkin doesn't mind. She cleans up after me as happily as she does in here for Edward.'

'Why did you bring me here instead of to your own house?' she asked, and he looked surprised at the question.

'Because I wanted Pushkin to look after you. And I knew she'd be here. Edward likes to drop in at home for lunch, so she has a busy morning. He should be here soon.' He glanced at his watch. 'It's almost twelve now.'

She sat up sharply. The hot tea and the cheerful chatter had made her unaware of all but her immediate comfort, but now she remembered. 'Oh, God,' she said. 'Gus'll be looking everywhere for me.'

'Gus?' he sounded curious, but not particularly so, and she almost told him, but held back just in time. Gus said to keep a low profile and keep it she would.

'A friend. We're staying at the Bald Monk and he said he'd find me around the town when I'd done my shopping. I really must get back.'

'Oh, do wait for Edward,' he said. 'I'm sure he'd love to meet you. You really are a breath of fresh air in a place like Durleighton. We meet very few interesting people here. All these country types – you'd think it was still 1955 sometimes, they're so stuffy.'

It was then and only then that George realized what a pit had been dug for her feet. She had met Edward Caspar-Wynette-Gondor, at the party at the House of Lords where she first met Lord Durleigh. It had been a brief meeting, but it had happened.

And if he came in now and remembered her, she'd have to admit that yes, indeed, she had been at the party with a superintendent of police and yes, they were investigating the murders including those of Edward's brothers, Richard and David. And how could she explain all that without displaying just how duplicitously she had been behaving all morning? Edward's sighting of her would surely expose entirely the fact that Gus was snooping around the town, and that could . . . She hated to think about it.

She got to her feet and said urgently, 'Really, I can't wait. I'd be most grateful if you could give me a lift back to town right away. I know G— he'll be most concerned at the delay. If you'd be so kind?'

'Of course,' he said. 'Be glad to. Just let me have a quick word with Pushkin.' He turned to go back to the kitchen and then lifted his head to listen. 'Well, wouldn't you know it? There's Edward's car now. I'd know the row that old banger of his makes anywhere. Just a quick hello then, and I'll see you back to town at once.'

25

She did what any woman does in an emergency. She asked for the bathroom and locked herself in.

This really was a mess, and for a change not one of her own making. She hadn't chosen to be run into by that socking great car, she told herself with a tinge of self-pity as she sat on the lidded lavatory and contemplated her situation. Gus can't say I'm up to my neck in trouble because as usual I've talked too much or deliberately gone where I shouldn't.

But that line of thinking didn't help at all. What she had to do was to try to convince Edward that he did not recognize her, and that he'd never seen her with a police superintendent companion. And that wasn't going to be easy. She knew she was a striking-looking person, with her hair piled on top of her head, her big glasses, her height and her –

She stopped then and peered into the mirror above the washbasin. With swift fingers, she unpinned her hair. There was a comb on the little shelf beneath the mirror and mentally she blessed Edward – or should it be Nanny Pushkin? – for such care of guests as she used it to fluff up her hair into as wild a look as she could, especially making a sort of fringe with side bangs to cover as much of her face as possible. Then she took off her glasses and peered at the hazy image in the mirror, wishing she'd brought her contact lenses out with her. To herself she looked exactly like herself, of course, but she thought she might just bamboozle a man who had seen her only once, so she took a deep breath, tucked her shoes under her arm to make them as unobtrusive as possible, slumped her shoulders and curved her body to reduce her height, and unlocked the door.

The two men were standing in the middle of the hearth rug in the living room, with their backs to the fireplace, talking quietly and intensely, and they looked up as she came into the room from the far end, where a set of small steps led up to the lavatory. The cloud was lifting now and as she saw the feeble splash of sunshine on the floor by the windows she moved that way, trying to get the light behind her. That might help.

Whether it was the hair, the sun or the absent glasses and shoes she would never know, but something had worked; Edward came forward readily, one hand outstretched in response to Jasper's introduction, and looked at her politely but without any hint of recognition.

'It was my fault as much as his,' she said, trying to sound as English as possible, remembering just in time that when they had met he might have noticed her American accent. 'How do you do.'

'I'm glad Mrs Lyons was able to help you.' Edward was still being very punctilious, but he seemed a little abstracted and she thought, busy man, wants to get on with his lunch, can't be bothered with a stray visitor: I've pulled it off! She smiled widely.

'She was splendid. And now I really must go. Thank you so much for your help, Mrs Lyons,' for the old woman was fussing around a small table which she was setting up for lunch in the hearth, 'I'm most grateful.'

'My pleasure, I'm sure,' she said and sniffed. 'You'll not be staying for lunch then?'

'Oh, no, not at all, thanks all the same. No, I really can't,' she added hastily as Jasper opened his mouth and seemed about to repeat the invitation. 'I truly must get back into town. Good afternoon!' And she made for the door.

'I'll be back right away then, Eddie,' Jasper said and followed her as fast as he could, but she was already out of the door and halfway down the path before he reached her side. 'Are your shoes giving you trouble?' He seemed anxious and she looked down and laughed, trying to make it sound natural.

'Oh, how silly of me! I took them off because they were making my feet ache – new ones you know – and would you believe forgot to put them on again! I'll do it in the car.' And she hurried through the open gate into the roadway, very aware of the chill against her nyloned feet.

Again he helped her in and then with a sort of bow took her shoes from her and fitted them on to her feet. 'There you are, Cinderella,' he said. 'I hope they stop pinching soon.'

'I'm sure they will,' she said. 'And now please, if you could get me to the Bald Monk as soon as possible?'

'With pleasure.' He drove fast and a little recklessly, pushing the vehicle through the narrow country roads and then the town streets as though there was no possibility of any oncoming traffic and consequently having to swerve once or twice. She held on grimly and was deeply relieved when at last they reached the front door of the Bald Monk.

The town was busy now, with lunchtime strollers in the square, but there was no sign of Gus and she was glad of that. The last thing she wanted was to start explaining to him what had happened while Jasper was around. Gus had a tendency to get rather pugnacious when people he cared about were injured.

Jasper tried to get out of the car to come round and help her down but she was too swift for him. She had her seat belt unbuckled before the car reached the kerb and the door open even before the engine was switched off. She was on the pavement and smiling up at him just as he tried to open his own door to get out.

'No, please, stay where you are,' she called quickly. 'I'm fine now, really. Thanks for your help.' She turned to go and then said over her shoulder, without losing step, 'And do thank Mrs Lyons again. Goodbye!' And she almost ran into the hotel.

Once inside she headed for the stairs and ran up them, only stopping when she reached the half-landing with the long window that looked out into the Square. She peered round the edge of the window-frame, keeping herself well back, to see what he was doing, and to her relief saw that he hadn't left the car, but had restarted the engine and was pulling out into the traffic. With a sigh of relief she finished her climb to the room she and Gus shared.

He was sitting on the bed, which was littered with papers, and as she came in he leaped to his feet, his face thunderous. 'George! Where in the name of all that's holy have you been? I've walked all over this bloody town three times looking for you and –'

'Gus, Gus, easy now, I'll explain.' She slumped on the bed herself, swinging her legs up and pushing the papers aside. He saw at once and pounced.

'What have you done to yourself? Here, let me see.' He took her foot in one hand and ran his fingers up her shin. The plaster could be clearly seen now, for she had pulled the tights well into place when she hauled them up.

'No need to panic,' she said. 'Not in the least, Gus. I've struck paydirt. Listen to this.'

He listened as he always did, in silence and concentrating hard; he was, she thought somewhere at the back of her mind, the most satisfying person to whom to tell a story. No silly interruptions, no failure to understand every word she said, and she finished her account with a flourish of one hand. 'There! What do you say to all that?'

He was silent for a moment and then shook his head. 'Sorry, ducks, but a lot of it isn't news.'

'Eh?'

'First of all, I've been talking to the local force. The woman who runs Sloane's – I've got all the lowdown on her because – well, you'll hear why – and it's not up to much. A silly woman who does as her employer tells her and that's as far as it goes. She doesn't know what her boss is up to. She only knows she's in major trouble if she talks too much about the business.'

'And her boss is?'

'It's actually a group of people, they reckon. But the one Morris reports to is Alice Diamond. The company's called –'

'Arabella Dee.'

'Oh, you found that out too, did you? Yes, so, there's her and your nice new friend Jasper Powell –'

'I was right!' she crowed. 'I knew they were too close! And what about Edward? Is he in on it?'

He shook his head. 'Not according to the local super. He's gay, of course, but we knew that.'

She stared at him, her head on one side. 'Oh! Yes, of course. Durnell mentioned that, didn't he? I should have remembered.'

'Why should you? Like I say, it's no crime and not particularly relevant in this case. Or am I wrong? Is the business of cutting off the genitalia and displaying them a homosexual thing?'

She was thinking hard. 'I don't think so. I have to say, I never saw it that way. In a curious sense I've never seen anything really sexy about these murders. I mean not like some where there's been signs of sexual activity by the perpetrator. I looked as I always do, of course, for any extra evidence such as semen, and blood that didn't match the victim, and you know there's been nothing. It's what I've said to you before, Gus. I've always seen these murders as being purposeful.'

'You can't get much more purposeful than slit throats and genital mutilation,' he said mildly.

'You know I don't mean that. I mean this isn't the business of a mad axeman who happens to have a hatred for Members of Parliament. They're being done for a special purpose, I'm sure. The murders have all been so – so tightly planned. Matching the old Ripper pattern, organizing in advance – none of the usual pouncing on a handy victim which is the hallmark of your Sutcliffe or Boston Strangler type.'

'Planned in advance,' he said slowly and frowned. 'You might have something there.'

'What?'

'I'll come back to that. Let me finish on the stuff I got locally. Edward seems to have no involvement with this Sloane's and Arabella Dee business apart from being Powell's lover – or so the locals tell me. It's common gossip seemingly in the town. And of course people can be lovers and still not know what their other half is up to. You mentioned the Sutcliffe case yourself

230

– she knew nothing about what her husband was doing. So Edward –'

'Hey, hang on,' she said. 'Jasper is Edward's lover? Then what about the way he is with this woman Daffy, Mrs Morris? They were very loverlike.'

'So?' he lifted his brows. 'Where is it written a man can't be AC and DC at the same time?'

She looked exasperated. 'Oh, for heaven's sake, Gus, I know that! What I mean is, he just doesn't seem to behave even remotely like someone who swings both ways. Women get to know the signs of that, believe me.'

'Well maybe he's just a good actor. But I tell you this much, my duck. If I'd known you'd got mixed up with them this morning, I'd have had kittens. Because it's my guess this is a dangerous man.'

'Why?'

'Because of this Arabella Dee affair. The local force have been quietly investigating because there has been a spate of robberies and fires in dress shops all over the country, and when they investigated, they found almost all of them restocked via a wholesaler called –'

'Arabella Dee? So that's how they get their gear on the market! A bit extreme though, isn't it, firing shops or robbing them? I wonder why they don't just sell their big label garments normally? With agents and salesmen or whatever?'

'According to the police investigators, they also use an element of blackmail. These shopkeepers aren't entirely stupid – they know the garments they buy from Arabella Dee are copies – but they have to be persuaded to sell them at top whack. The local Super thinks they've been using a combination of protection-racket threats and personal blackmail. He couldn't be more delighted that we've found the warehouse for the fake gear; it's more evidence for them. So we need to do some more careful checking on Madam Alice. Could she have polished off her Sam because he rumbled what she was up to, and was a risk?'

George opened her mouth to speak, but had to close it again.

Gus must not know of her illicit visit to Alice, so how could she tell him he was right and that Alice and Sam had indeed had a row over her activities?

'That could be a reason to kill Sam,' she now said carefully. 'A very good one. But why the other four?'

Gus shrugged. 'Edgar Allen Poe?'

'How do you mean? Oh!' she said. 'I see. If you've got something to hide, hide it among a lot of the same sort of thing.'

'You've got it. Only these are murders, not purloined letters.'

'It sounds possible,' she said. 'But is it likely? I have a problem with that. And if, as you seem to think, Jasper Powell's in on it with her, why should he risk killing so many people? One, maybe, but five? And in such a bizarre fashion?'

'We have to think about it. Because we've got even more on him than you might think.'

'What?'

'The *Courier*, have you seen it this morning?'

She looked disgusted. 'Oh, Gus, for heaven's sake. I don't read that rag! I didn't think you did either.'

'You'll read this copy,' he said with a certain grimness, pulling one out from behind the drift of papers on the bed and pushing it into her hands.

She bent her head to read the headline on the first page and her brows shot up. 'Good God!'

'In spades, sweetheart. Now read the story.'

The headline shouted, 'WE NAIL THE MAN THE POLICE MISSED!' And then in letters not much smaller went on, 'WHEN THE POLICE ARE BAFFLED, THE *COURIER* BIFFS 'EM!' And there was a photograph. She stared at it and then at Gus.

'What is this?'

'I told you, read the story. Page two. And three and four. They're like puppies with six tails over it.'

She turned the pages.

For a week now the Metropolitan Police, under the direction of the Slowcoach Superintendent, one Gus Hathaway, have been seeking the evil murderer who has been stalking the corridors of power, leaving blood-boltered bodies behind him. Five of our great and good men, including a Bishop of the Church, have died in a welter of their own gore, and what have the police done? *Nothing!* Our intrepid reporter, however, has been on the trail. He has followed suspects, watched the people the police watch, slipped between their echelons of uniformed plods to come up with the goods. And here they are!

First of all, we ask the police to study the photograph on the front page. As you will see, we have blanked out the face of the man in it, because he is the main suspect and we at the *Courier* will do nothing that could pervert the course of justice.

Police followed him as he met a member of the family of one of the tragic victims, at Heathrow, <u>and still failed to detain him</u>.

We filmed him, however, and have passed the evidence we collected on to the police.

The ball is now in their court. <u>Will they arrest this man</u>, who, we have discovered has been dealing in underworld activities in this country as well as in another foreign power's territory?

And that is not the only question we ask the Sleepsodden Super.

We want to know how it is we have uncovered WITNESSES at two of the murder sites who ACTUALLY SAW SUSPECT ACTIVITIES. How is it we could get this information when the Slothful Super failed?

We have passed this information on to him, however, because we at the *Courier*, we repeat, are law-abiding citizens. We want to see evil men caught and the cruel murderer of these leaders of our country <u>brought to justice</u>.

And if and when he is – and it all depends on the, dare we say it, Stupid Super – we will be campaigning for the ultimate penalty.

BRING BACK HANGING says the *Courier* . . .

She lifted her head and stared at him blankly. 'Ye Gods, Gus. What have they got hold of that we didn't?'

'The photograph, I'll grant you, is a real asset.' He said it almost savagely. 'We had only eye-witness reports from our people who followed Alice Diamond at the airport. Obviously one of their busy cockroaches was there with a camera and got this shot of the man who met Alice. And I've checked with Rupert and he says the print was sent to us this morning. After the paper hit the streets, of course.'

'And what about this stuff —' she prodded the paper — 'about finding witnesses?'

'Rupert swears to me they couldn't have, he checked like — well, I know how thorough the man is. That's what I most value in him. All I can suppose is that this bloody paper got to someone with a cheque book and nudged their memories, and that's what they've got hold of. Someone happy to oblige with any sort of tale for a few quid. It makes me sick!'

'They're after you personally, the sons of bitches,' she said. 'Christ, but I hate the British press!'

He shook his head wearily. 'It's only the tabloids. There are *some* good ones. Anyway, it's the price you pay for freedom, they tell me. Ah, sod 'em! I don't mind the abuse. They can dream up as many ridiculous bits of alliteration as they like. All I care about is getting the stuff they've got and talking to the people they got it from. And I want to look at that photograph, of course. From what Rupert tells me, I have a strong suspicion it's your Jasper Powell.'

'He's not mine!' she protested.

'Whoever's. Anyway, I suspect he's dangerous. And so it has to be back to town, right away. I would have gone a couple of hours ago if you hadn't — well, never mind. Is your leg OK?'

'It's fine,' she assured him. 'And yes, let's get going. We can talk more in the car.'

She had packed all their gear and was down at the desk paying the bill with him in a matter of less than half an hour. He'd arranged for some sandwiches to be made to take with them, 'because I don't want you keeling over with starvation halfway there,' he said. 'And I'm bloody starving too. Breakfast was horrible. The sandwiches can't be much worse.'

They were, of course, being dry, with an evil-tasting margarine and underfilled with ham that was so loaded with water all they could do was throw the whole lot out of the car to feed the birds, and then settle down to the long run home, with what patience they could, through heavy traffic. Neither of them talked much, after all. Both of them had too much thinking to do.

26

'Yes, that's him,' George said and put the photograph back on the desk. 'In spite of the cap and the shadows. You can't miss it. That's Jasper Powell.'

'And Alice Diamond is with him,' Dudley said, more as a statement than a question.

'Yes,' she said and then flushed as she caught Gus's eye.

'How do you know?' he asked sharply. 'You haven't . . .'

She hesitated, and then decided there was clearly no point in lying about it now. 'I'm afraid I did. I went to the shop in Sloane Street. Just to nose around, you know.'

'Yes,' he said savagely. 'I know. Now.' And George caught the smug look on Rupert Dudley's face. She wanted to bite her own tongue out. How could she have been so stupid? Gus looked at her witheringly and then returned to the photograph.

'That's the green van in the background. And the rear of the car Alice Diamond was driven away in,' Mike Urquhart cut in quickly, aware of the tension and wanting to dissipate it. 'And I agree – that's the chap who met her. No question of it.'

'So,' Gus said. 'We have at last a positive ID of one of the key people. That's a beginning. Now we need to talk to Mrs Diamond, I think. Yes. Most definitely, Mrs Diamond.' He caught George's appealing stare and hardened his jaw. 'Rupert, I want you to do that. Take Mike Urquhart as well as Tim here, who saw her with Powell and saw the business of the switch of baggage. Keep him in the background, and only wheel him into the interrogation to tell her he saw her with Powell if she gets stroppy, understand? And be careful. I don't want any pressure put on by those damned people at the House of Commons, they'll put it on if they can. Look after their own, they do, and they'll see the Diamond woman in that category. I'll go to Creechurch Lane and the Market in Spitalfields and check on this other stuff the *Courier* uncovered. Off you go.'

They went and George sat on there in Gus's office, watching the men disappear into the busy incident room. Then she looked at Gus. 'I know I don't deserve to go with you to Creechurch Lane and –'

'Haven't you any work to do at Old East?' Gus had his head down over some papers on the desk. 'Isn't it time you got back there?'

'You know perfectly well I've got a leave of absence,' she said. 'Alan and Jerry are holding the fort magnificently. They'll call me if they have any problems, I assure you. Please, Gus, I know you're sore at me for going to see Alice Diamond, but I thought it might help. And as for the Jasper Powell business, I wasn't looking to have my leg damn near knocked off. And be fair. You agreed I should go up to Sloane's, see what I could find out. And I found Powell – but I didn't go looking for him. He found me, didn't he?'

He lifted his head and sighed. 'Ducky, I'm delighted to get help from you. Your input is great, believe me. You have ideas. You get from point A to point X far faster than any of my guys, who always have to go all through the whole damned alphabet on account of that's what police work is all about. Having you as a pointer dog, a sort of direction-finder, is very useful. What I can't be doing with is when you go off on your own and don't tell me. That way you could get into trouble, and I couldn't get you out of it. Suppose you made the Diamond woman suspicious? Suppose Powell had been there at the same time? Suppose he'd tried to do something to shut you up because you'd stumbled on him? Then what?'

'And suppose the sky falls in? Honey, you cannot, you really cannot be so careful all the time! It's no way to get answers and –'

'It's only you I'm so careful about,' he said. 'Believe it or not, my love. Because that is what you are.'

She swallowed hard, more touched than she could have said and smiled brilliantly and a touch tremulously at him. 'Thank you, Gus. And I promise I won't do it again. Or if I do, it won't be my fault – like Jasper turning up . . .'

He stared at her for a long moment and then laughed, a huge rollicking noise that made her blink. When he'd recovered, he shook his head and said, his voice still a little spluttery, 'Oh, George, you really are the end! Even your promises are full of holes, made conditionally. No, don't look at me like that! Dealing with you is like dealing with an – with an eel. Oh, all right, I'll do my best to keep you safe and you'll do your best to help me. Deal?'

She was flooded with relief. 'Deal. And thanks, Gus.' She went over to his desk and kissed the top of his head. 'Can we go and see these so-called witnesses now?'

'When I'm ready. I've got some bits of paperwork here to sort out first.' He bent his head to his desk again. 'You can read this stuff if you like.' He handed over a pile of papers. 'It's interesting. Explains a lot.'

It did. What he'd given her was an account of the findings made at the warehouse in Wembley Park when it was searched under warrant. There was also an account of an interview with a bewildered taxi driver from Ilford who was the sole remaining relative of Max Hazell. It was clear from reading it all that the man had had no knowledge at all of his cousin Max's business or associates; he had, in fact, not seen him or heard from him for years, not since his dad, who'd been Max's uncle by marriage, had died, long ago. He'd been delighted to hear, after Hazell's death, and the lawyers' searches, that he was the residual legatee, and had been 'lookin' forward to pickin' up a bob or two. I've always wanted to buy a coupla cabs of my own and go into the business proper, be a real musher, like. But I'll tell you this much – I'll settle for the one I've got and go on pushing that around

237

London the way I already do. The last thing I want is to get mixed up in any funny business.' He had been quite forceful about it. 'Don't tell me nothin' about nothing. This ain't my business, and I'm keeping well out of it.'

So, she thought, turning the page bearing the cousin's statement, there's a dead end there. But maybe that's not so bad. At least it doesn't muddy the waters; no laborious hunting through the activities and alibis of members of the Hazell family.

The next page dealt with the way the Hazell business had been run and this really was, George decided, an eye-opener. Julie's search of the computer had found one shop that stocked clothes distributed by the warehouse; in fact, according to the work done by the police computer experts, who had spent hours with the floppy disks, there were several hundred such shops. A surprising number of them had names that linked with the Sloane Street shop: there were several called Chelsea Style or Chelsea Fashion; a couple called Hans Some (a dreadful pun, she thought, on the Christian name of Hans Sloane who had owned parts of the area back in the eighteenth century); and others which played on the initials of Alice Diamond – Audrey Day had been used for three establishments, as had Angelina Derry – and all of them sold designer-labelled goods at full designer prices though it was obvious from the accounts and the balance sheets that the actual cost of producing the garments was minimal.

In fact, George thought, running her finger down the columns, the amount of money spent by Alice Diamond on her trips to Italy and France and Scandinavia and the USA, obviously to collect her basic sample garments, was one of the company's major expenses. She always stayed in expensive hotels, and travelled first class. But everything else was done on the cheap. She had even – and this made George's eyes open even wider – she had even, it seemed, only occasionally actually bought clothes from the collections she visited. Sometimes there were photographs of several of them with swatches of fabric attached, but mostly it seemed, she had stolen them; there were neat brackets after the style numbers enclosing the word 'Donated' or occasionally 'Complimentary', and there could be no other interpretation. That would also account for the way she had used someone to 'steal' the extra luggage from her trolley at Heathrow. She wanted to be rid of it as soon as possible, to get it to Hazell's place. Concealing the provenance of the garments she copied was very important, and she had done it very successfully. George almost admired her for it.

She could see it very clearly now, she thought. Alice collecting her garments, either stealing them by simply slipping them off the rails in the hubbub of the hotel room where so often a collection of clothes was shown to overseas buyers – something George, like most people, had seen on T V programmes about the fashion shows in Paris, Milan and New York – and smuggling them home past an easygoing Customs man who was so used to her regular trips he mostly let her through on a wave; or, when she had to, settling for her photographs and swatches. And on the back of all that she had – with assistance from Jasper Powell and perhaps some others not yet identified – built herself a fortune.

How much had Sam Diamond known about it? George let the papers sit on her lap as she stared sightlessly out of Gus's window at the dwindling light of the afternoon. Had he been unaware of his wife's activities? Alice had referred to her dead husband as her partner, but that could be euphemism for husband; it didn't have to mean business partner. If he had known, it would have been exceedingly risky for him to carry on as an MP, surely? He would have been very aware of how difficult it is to hide such matters, especially in these sparkling new days post the Nolan Committee, which had laid down such stern rules about the behaviour and activities of those in public life, and particularly Members of Parliament.

A scenario built up in her mind. Sam, discovering by some accident what his wife was up to and appalled by the scale of it. Sam threatening to leave her, or take some other sort of drastic action if she didn't stop forthwith. Alice and Jasper, facing the loss of a massively successful business which was making a fortune for them both, conspiring to kill him. And choosing to hide his killing by doing the same to four other people ...

She shook her head decisively. That just didn't wash. Did it? And she became aware that Gus had lifted his head and was looking at her, his mouth lifting at the corners.

'You have a very speaking countenance, as they used to say in olden times, ducky. There you sit, thinking that Sam Diamond found out and was killed for his pains – but you just can't see why the other four. Right?'

'That's not all that clever of you,' she said. 'Seeing we talked about it before.'

'Well, I still knew what you were thinking at that particular moment, didn't I? And that's clever.'

'I'll think about it. Look, Gus, there has to be some other reason here. Yes, we've uncovered something very nasty in the woodshed of one of the victims, but how *does* it match up with the others? It doesn't.'

'One of Alice Diamond's associates, Powell, lives with – or certainly very close to – the brother of two other victims,' Gus pointed out. 'And you yourself said one of the five – Lord Scroop – looked to you like a dummy-run case, so he might be there just for that reason and no other. Which means there's only one victim left, the Bishop, who doesn't seem to be connected in any way. So I suggest that we concentrate on the Bishop's connection for a while and then look again at the CWG lot. I have to say that from where I sit, the fact Jasper Powell, who is gay, lives so close to a bachelor in his late forties who has never had any history of involvement with women – yes, we have looked into that – gives me furiously to think. Perhaps this is some sort of gay thing? I know you said the killings weren't sexual in your opinion, but I have to say that when I think of bodies with their male genitalia chopped off and a pair of suspects who are heavily into male genitalia, as you might say –'

'Stereotypical thinking,' George said firmly.

'Maybe. But that doesn't alter the fact that it's a *possible*. We'll check sexual orientations. Especially the Bishop.'

'What have we got on the Bishop?' she asked. 'Show me the documentation.'

It didn't offer a great deal. The Bishop was indeed unattached, but according to the notes this was part of a general asceticism. He had been married once, when he was a young doctor, but she had disappeared and eventually divorced him, abroad, and he had made no effort to find another partner. Furthermore, he seemed to be everything a bishop should be. Once he had been converted, he devoted himself solely and wholly to his Church work, abandoning his medical career altogether. She was interested in that. Had he been any good as a doctor, she wondered? And leafed back through the pages, looking for information.

She found it eventually and read it carefully. He had been a student at St Cecilia's, a London teaching hospital that had long ago been merged with its South London neighbour, an establishment which had not been as careful with the old records they inherited as they might have been. A terse note in what she thought she recognized as Mike Urquhart's handwriting said, 'All student info lost. No other useful info available.'

But Mike had picked up the trail later; probably, George thought, through the Medical Directory. The newly qualified young doctor had gone into practice as a GP and had worked first in a small Welsh village and then in a Lancashire mill town. In the very early fifties he had got a partnership in a small town in the West Midlands; she blinked as she looked at the name of it and then caught her breath.

'Gus!' she said.

'Mmm?'

'Would you believe I've found the link between the Bishop and the other victims?'

'What?'

'Do you remember, when we went to Durleighton, we used the B roads once we left the motorway, because there were roadworks on the other route?'

He lifted his chin and looked at her, clearly taken aback by the urgency in her voice. 'Yes?'

'Do you remember that place we went through that had a pub called the Frog and Nightgown and you said what a pity it was these silly names were spreading out of the cities and what was wrong with calling a pub the Red Lion or whatever?'

'Get to the point, ducks. We still have to get over to Creechurch Lane and the Market, and I'd like to get there before they all go home for the day.'

'What was the place called?'

'Oh, shit, I can't remember! Yes, I can. It was – it was Ardenford. Because I said to you that –'

'I thought I'd got it right!' she cried and thumped the paper she was holding on to his desk. 'Have you seen this?'

He pulled the paper nearer and read it from the top. And then looked up at her. 'You're right. The Bishop was a GP there forty-odd years ago.'

'And it was only fifteen minutes away by road from Durleighton?'

'Yes. Well, well. So there is a link between the CWG lot and the Bishop! And a link between Sam Diamond and CWG, via his wife's partner-in-crime.'

She sank back in her chair, almost in awe. 'Gus, do you think we might have the answer?'

'I don't know. The question is *why*? Why should a respected Bishop and ex-doctor have anything in common with a rip-off fashion business? And –'

'It doesn't matter!' George was jubilant. 'The important thing is there is a link. We've been looking for it all along, haven't we? Whatever there might be that would be common to all the victims? And here it is.'

'But it isn't,' he objected. 'These links are very tenuous, George, and not complete, anyway. They depend largely on one person – Jasper Powell. And even he doesn't tie all of them together. The Bishop sort of hangs on the outside in an accidental way. I mean, look at it.' He grabbed a piece of paper and made a quick scribbled drawing.

'See what I mean? This is a bit messy, but it explains. I've marked direct links with a line, and tenuous ones with a broken line. Jasper ties up with Sam Diamond through Alice, and Lord Durleigh and David CWG through their brother, but that's as far as he goes. Then Lord Durleigh and Edward are linked with

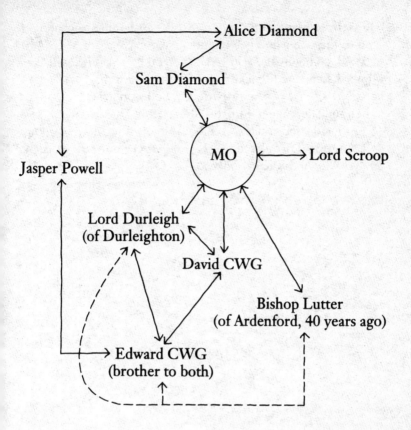

Bishop Lutter through a neighbouring town but a great many years ago, so that line needs marking as a very weak one, and it also leaves out David C W G who is like Lord Scroop – nothing links with him either, except of course the M O. Though we agreed that that could be because he was just there for the murderer to try his skills on.'

She sighed deeply. 'It is a very holey network. We need to see them tied together much more closely. Oh, hell, Gus. I really thought I was on to something.'

'You still might be,' he said. 'But it's not clear yet by any manner of means. Look, we have to go. I must get to Creechurch Lane as soon as I can. Are you fit?'

'I've been ready to go any time this past hour,' she protested. 'You're the one who's been hanging about.'

'Well, come on,' he said. 'And pick up young Julie, will you? I'll need someone to make notes for me, and it might as well be her. She's keen, as we know perfectly well, don't we?' He grinned at her and she hugged him, briefly.

'Put me down, woman! You'll have the whole nick gossiping.'

'Like they don't already? OK, I'll go get your new assistant. See you down in the car park.'

27

They reached the office building in Creechurch Lane remarkably rapidly; the traffic was for once thin and penetrable; Gus didn't even need his blue light and siren. Julie sat in the back, her hands tightly clasped in her lap, oozing excitement at being asked by Gus to accompany him. George could almost smell it and grinned companionably at her as they got out of the car together.

'Now's your chance, Julie,' she murmured. 'You do a good job here and who knows what mightn't be possible for the future.'

'I didn't bring you two with me to gossip,' Gus growled. 'Come on, and shut up. I'll do the talking. To start with at any rate.' And he winked at George, to take the sting from his words.

The guard who had been so grey and sick the last time George had seen him, the night that they had found the Bishop's body in the basement, was now looking a very different person. There was a sleek self-important plumpness about him that told George at once what had happened. Ever since the victim had been found he had made himself the centre of attention, the building's pundit on all matters to do with the killings. He positively beamed as he recognized George coming towards him.

'Well, well,' he said, rather loudly so that he could be overheard by the few people who were in the marble lobby. 'The police again? And what can I do to help you this time, Inspector?'

'Superintendent to you. And we're here to see if you could try telling us all I asked you to tell us last time.' Gus, who was much too old a bird at the game to be caught by any amateur, spoke not so much loudly as with a penetrating clearness. Several of the bystanders turned to look at him. 'Instead of blabbing it all to a cheap newspaper. How much did they pay you? I'm sure everyone would be fascinated to hear.'

The guard blinked and went a dark brick colour, opened his mouth to speak and then closed it again.

'And I see you've got yourself promoted from night duty,' Gus went on. 'With a rise in pay, I dare say. You're making a very nice thing out of this killing, aren't you?'

'Whaddya mean?' the man said with an attempt at bluster.

Gus smiled at him, his teeth looking very white. 'What I say. Now, you're –' he looked down at the notebook he had taken from his pocket – 'Peter Maxwell, right?'

'S'right.'

'On duty with Darren Cooper, the night of the killing. Where is he now?'

''E's still on nights.'

'That doesn't seem very fair,' Gus said, still speaking in bell-like tones. The people in the lobby stood silently, clearly enthralled. 'Seeing he was the one who found the body. But you talked more, I take it.'

'I answered all the questions as I was asked.' Maxwell was beginning to recover his aplomb. 'Don't you go blamin' me if them journalists asked better questions than what your lot did.'

Gus leaned over the big central desk to bring his face close to the man. 'It is the bounden duty of all responsible citizens in all cases of crime to tell the police all they know that may be of use to us in our inquiries, whether the said citizens are asked leading questions or not. And you clearly didn't behave like a responsible citizen, did you? You kept stuff back and then sold it to the *Courier*. How much did you get, hmm? An' how much of it are you going to hand over to the Police Benevolent Fund? Or do I have to take steps to get you punished for your thoroughly disgraceful uncitizenlike behaviour?'

Maxwell blinked and said no more, just standing staring at

Gus with his mouth half open, and Gus nodded, seeming satisfied.

'Right. Now we can talk, man to man. Julie, make notes.' Julie moved smartly forwards, her notebook ready. 'What did you tell those journalists?'

Maxwell looked over his shoulder at the people in the lobby and leaned forwards. 'It'd be easier to talk in the office like,' he said pleadingly.

Gus looked at him thoughtfully and then said in a slightly less plangent voice, 'If you promise I'll get every word out of you and get it fast, I'll consider it.'

'Yes, sir,' Maxwell said eagerly. He had begun to sweat now, and had a decidedly oily look. George felt quite sorry for him. 'This way, sir, this way.' He pulled a card from beneath his desk which read 'Temporarily away' and plonked it on the counter. 'If you'll come this way, sir?'

The office turned out to be little more than a cleaner's cubby hole, but it had a couple of chairs, so Gus could park himself, as he signalled to George to do, and Julie and Maxwell stood in what remaining space there was.

'Right,' Gus said. 'Out with it.'

'Out with what?'

'What you told the *Courier*, dammit!' Gus roared and Maxwell flinched slightly and then tightened his shoulders.

'Right, sir. Well, they was just standing nattering, like, the two of them. They come in about, oh, dinnertime it was, day before yesterday. I'd just got the management to shift me to days, on account of I'd got a nasty go of that post-trowmatic stress thing after what happened, and they sort of dropped in to find out who was on nights and were well pleased to find out they'd got it in one, like, with me.' For a moment he preened, then caught Gus's sardonic look and returned to his previous manner. 'So they said, what happened? And, well, I sort of told 'em.'

'What did you tell them that you did not tell us?' Gus was beginning to sound dangerous and the man swallowed.

'I said as 'ow there'd bin another coupla people around but I didn't think much to 'em.'

'And they were?'

'There was Maggie, who's the manageress up in the canteen. She's worked 'ere over thirty years. She went out last of all the staff – a good bit the last, she was. She'd been fixin' stuff up in the kitchen, she said. They 'ad a flood there, see, last week and –'

'I need no details like that. Just her full name and where she lives, if you know. Or where she works exactly. Tell my colleague here.'

He did, and Julie wrote busily. 'The sixth floor for the kitchen?' she said. 'Which side of the building?' He told her and George watched him as his eyes slid away from Julie and back to Gus.

'And who else?'

'Eh?'

'A couple of people you said. Who bloody else? And stop playing games with me. I know perfectly well that the *Courier* said that if you told anyone else at all they wouldn't pay you what they promised, but I'm here to tell you you'll lose a hell of a lot more than the few quid they'll come up with if you keep anything from me now. So, what else?'

'I don't know who he was,' Maxwell said sulkily, clearly giving in completely. 'It was just a bloke in overalls. Mucky ones. Carrying one of those old-fashioned tool bags – you know the sort that's got 'andles but when you puts 'em down and opens 'em, the bag turns out to be flat, with slots to fix things in.'

'When? Where? How?' Gus said.

'About, oh, I dunno exactly. It was well after Maggie had gone and before Darren got here. We – er, we used to sort of take it in turns to – um – get here a bit later, like.'

'Oh, my word,' Gus said. 'So you were playing that little scam, were you? Clocking in for each other so that you could get paid for hours you don't work. Pretty, Maxwell, very pretty, and I don't think. Stealing from your employer, that's what that is, you know. Or did you know? If I was to tell the boss, would he –'

Maxwell was sweating even harder now. 'Well, I s'pose – anyway that was why I never said to you lot, and I wouldn't have said to them *Courier* blokes neither, only a monkey's a monkey.'

'A monkey?' George couldn't help herself.

'Five hundred pounds,' Gus said shortly. 'I see exactly. Well, you'll get no monkey from me. Not so much as a lousy tanner. But you'll be in big trouble if you —'

'It was about half eight,' Maxwell said swiftly. 'I just happened to come out of the bog, to check the phone for any voice mail which I should pick up and there was this geezer comin' out of the lift.'

'So what did you do?' Gus snapped, for the man had stopped.

'Well, I say comin' out of the lift,' he went on as though Gus hadn't spoken. 'But to tell the truth I can't be sure. I mean the lift door was shut, like and he was sort of walking away. But he mightn't have come out of it. He might have been comin' from anywhere.'

'So?'

'So I says to him, "What are you doin' here?" and he looks at me an' sort of bobs his head and says, "Well," 'e says, "what do you think?" he says. And I says, "Was you one of the blokes fixin' Maggie's kitchen?" and he says, "What else would I be doin'?" and I says, "Fair enough but you should have gone when Maggie did," and he says, "Well, I would have but I had things to do." And then he laughed, all soft, like, and I laughed too, the way you do, and off he went. I don't reckon he could have done that 'orrible thing in the basement – no way he could have. He had such a soft easy voice, not a bit the sort that you'd think of cutting people – people's throats and that.'

He went pale again as he remembered what had happened and shook his head. 'If I'd ha' thought he was that sort I'd have told you even if it did mean trouble for Darren an' me with the management, but it was obvious he was nothin' to worry about. That mucky set of overalls and a proper worn-out bag – of course he was all right, what he said he was! A workman. Couldn't have been nothing else.'

'What did he look like?' Gus said, very sardonic now. 'Apart from his close resemblance to the Angel Gabriel?'

'Eh?'

'Oh, never mind! Just get on with it. What did he look like?'

'Well, sort of – ordinary, you know? He had these dark blue overalls over his clothes and –'

'How do you know?' George couldn't help cutting in and Gus looked at her sharply and then at Maxwell.

'Eh?' The response was getting monotonous and George too felt irritation with the man rising in her.

'How do you know he had the overalls on over his clothes?' she snapped. 'He might just have worn them over his underwear – some workmen do. In fact most of them, going by the ones who've been through my department after accidents.'

His face cleared. 'Oh, that. Well, he had that soft bunchy look, know what I mean? You can always tell. And galoshes over his shoes and –'

Gus lifted his chin sharply. 'Galoshes?'

'Them overshoes what you wear in the snow or when there's a lot of rain and bad weather an' all that,' Maxwell said helpfully.

'There wasn't any snow and it wasn't raining,' George said softly. 'But he might have needed to ensure that his shoes stayed clean. That he could get rid of any stains that landed on him without trouble. Mucky, you said?'

This time Maxwell's colour changed to a thick grey one and George jumped up and took him by the shoulders as he tottered. Julie too caught him and they lowered him on to the chair that George had vacated.

He recovered fast, once his head went down to his knees with George's hand firmly on his neck. He sat up again rather groggily and whispered, 'Oh, Gawd, could that have been him?'

'It's possible,' Gus said. 'The overalls were stained? Was it oil? Or what?'

Maxwell looked at him piteously. 'I never thought. I just thought, mucky. Like workmen usually are. Not that they were old overalls, now I think of it. Mucky, but not old.'

Gus looked at George and lifted his brows and Julie said, 'Can we check on purchases of overalls in local shops, sir?'

Gus nodded. 'Good idea, Constable. OK. Call that in as soon

as we've finished here. Now you, Maxwell' – he squatted at Maxwell's feet – 'I want you to think. The man's face. What was it like?'

Maxwell looked more wretched than ever. 'I don't know,' he said, almost whimpering. 'I mean I couldn't really see it, like. He sort of bent his head down, and he had this cap thing on.'

'Cap?' Julie and George spoke together.

'That's right.' He was now so eager to be helpful his words fell over themselves. 'It was like those old-fashioned peaked caps, only the peak was hidden under the cloth of the cap itself, like – Oh, it's hard to explain.'

'You don't have to.' Julie's voice was filled with exhilaration. 'The sort they wear in the country. And in adverts for country clothes.'

'That's right!' Maxwell looked pleased for the first time. 'You've got it. A dark green, I think, or maybe it was brown. Or it coulda bin black. Dark, anyway.'

'And his face?' Gus said, with an air of helplessness. 'Don't let me put words into your mouth, but because he kept his chin –' and he stopped.

'Down,' Maxwell said at once. 'He sort of kept it down, kept his head bent, talked to the floor. I never saw his eyes. He was shy, see. Knew he shouldn't be there, and was a bit bothered. But I'm not a hard man. Treat people as I find 'em, so I thought, let him get on home. But I never really saw his face. Not to say *saw* it.'

'And there was no way of knowing where he'd come from,' Gus said heavily, straightening up and brushing his knees. 'How long were you in the lavatory?'

'Eh?'

'Don't start that again!'

'Oh, sorry, sir, really, I'm very – well, I took the paper with me, like, and you know how it is.'

Gus took a sharp breath in through his nose. 'Ten minutes? Fifteen? More?'

'Oh, no, sir!' Maxwell sounded shocked. 'No more'n five or six at the outside!'

'Long enough,' George said. 'But when we looked at the body we both thought the same thing, that he'd been interrupted. If he was in the basement, and Maxwell was up here in the john, what or who interrupted him?'

They all fell into a silence, Maxwell looking from one to the other. And then Julie coughed. 'Er, sir,' she said. 'I just had an idea.'

'Well?'

She seemed a little subdued for he had snapped the word at her, but she took a deep breath. 'Well, sir, the boiler.'

'What about it?'

'Is it the sort that does things on its own?'

'It's a very old one,' Maxwell said, eager to please now. 'They done up the building but spent so much money on marble and suchlike they had to settle for the cheapest sort of heat system they could. It's an old one they put in. Secondhand, but it's good enough, sort of runs itself. You don't have to do nothin' to it. Every half-hour or so, it sort of sets up a roar when it blows through the system and lets off excess steam.'

'When does it do that?' Gus said sharply. 'What time?'

'Eh? Oh, about ten past and twenty to the hour, that is, roughly. I never has to worry about it, old though it is. Now and again we have to reset the level of heat when it gets cold – there's not the modern sort of thermostat, you see – but that's all. I always say the old ones are usually the best . . .'

'Well done, Julie,' Gus said. 'The boiler went into its act, frightened the crap out of him because he thought a person was there operating it, and he packed up and ran for it. And almost ran into chummy here. What time did you come out of the bog?' He had whirled on Maxwell.

'Oh, sir, I'm not sure. Darren was due in at nine, see, and I'd done my first round and, well, about –' He went white again. 'Twenty to nine, I dare say. About . . .'

'But would he let himself be alarmed by an automatic boiler, for God's sake?' Gus said. 'This man has been as cool as it's possible for a man to be, yet the sound of a boiler letting out a bit of steam scares him into making a dash for it, and a badly organized one at that. He meets a witness.'

'It can happen,' George said. 'However carefully they plan, they can be caught out in silly ways. There's a good deal of evidence in the literature —'

'Not now, ducky. Not now. We have to get ourselves over to the Market at Spitalfields and find out if anyone saw a workman with stained overalls over his clothes and an old-fashioned tradesman's bag. And, of course, galoshes. Come on.'

He paused at the door of the cubby hole and looked back at Maxwell. 'And as for you, not a word to anyone, you hear me? If I find out you've told the *Courier* you've spilt your beans to me, I'll spill your brains in the gutter, you understand? And never think I wouldn't. I know how to better'n most.'

28

In the event they were too late to go to Spitalfields Market. By the time they emerged into Creechurch Lane, it was past eight. Gus squinted up at the dark sky and swore under his breath. 'Even if we do go now, we'll have to go again tomorrow, to get all the people we need to see. So an early start, which means home now. Julie, you can go home too. Get cracking on that overall business as soon as you get in in the morning.'

'I've already phoned in about that, Guv.' Julie sounded demure but was clearly highly pleased with herself. 'While you were finishing off with Maxwell. Someone's starting by checking all the possible places they can be bought. We'll start around here, in the East End, and see how we get on.'

'I don't suppose we'll get too much out of that,' Gus said gloomily. 'It's important to try, of course, but they're pretty commonplace garments. And come to think of it, they can be bought mail order, can't they?'

'Yes, Guv,' Julie piped up again. 'I thought of that, and I've asked Jenny – she's at the next desk to me – to dig out some of the specialist firms that do them. We'll be well on our way tomorrow.'

'Good on you, girl!' Gus said. 'Now go home.'

She nodded happily, looked at George and almost winked, then turned to go to the car.

Gus called her back. 'From now on, P C Bentley, it's me you look to to help you on your way to promotion. There's no more

Dr B. can do. Just thought I'd mention it. Now, you'd better get the tube back, hadn't you?'

'Er, yes, Guv. Thanks, Guv,' Julie managed to mutter and, clearly mortified, turned and scuttled away, heading down the street as fast as she could. George looked after her and then at Gus.

'Gus, that was mean of you! If anyone's to blame, it's me, not Julie. And making her find her own way back – you might have given her a lift.'

'Do her good,' he said. 'Show her the errors of her ways. Come on. We'll go and get a bite o' supper. And not another word about Julie. She's my business, not yours, and from here on in, don't you forget it.'

If she had learned only one thing about Gus, it was the point at which it would be a waste of time and energy to argue further and this was one of them, so she said no more. But she was pleased for Julie all the same. Clearly Gus was going to treat her aspirations with respect, however firm he might be in the details.

They went to Gus's own fish restaurant in Aldgate. It was comforting to come out of the chill of the evening and the soft drizzle that had started to grease the pavements into the vividly lit, steamy, food-scented interior. The place was busy, with most tables occupied and the waitresses nipping between them like bees in a lavender patch. Gus looked round with deep pleasure.

'This one's the best, no question. It was the first Dad started, and he always said it'd make the most money. And he was right. Top out of nine can't be bad. Now, where's Kitty?'

The manageress, a plump and lively woman who had been running the restaurant for Gus ever since his father had died, came out from behind the desk where she took the money and watched over the waitresses with the sharpest eyes in the whole of East London. 'Well, well, and here was me thinkin' you'd gone over to hamburgers or something nasty like that. You haven't been in for weeks.'

'Go on, nag me. Make my life a misery,' Gus said, and slapped her rump. Kitty looked at George and threw her eyes up.

'The chances he takes, Dr B.,' she said amiably. 'One of these days I'll have him for sexual harassment. Come on, then. I've a nice corner table for you.'

'Eyes in her toochus, this one,' Gus said admiringly. 'Got her back to the corner and still she sees the people leaving it. As for sexual harassment, it's your own fault for having such a nice –'

'That's enough of that,' Kitty said firmly and led the way to the corner table. George laughed as she followed Gus and reached out to pinch his own bottom hard.

'Since when did you learn to speak American? This is your tooshy, not your however you said it.'

'Which only goes to show how wrong you can be,' Gus said as they settled at the table. 'Your version comes from the same source as ours. It's Yiddish for rear end. Now, what'll it be? Halibut or –'

'What else?' She peeled off her coat and settled comfortably into her chair. 'And some jellied eels to start with, please, Kitty, and a glass of the house Chablis.'

'When I think of how I had to educate her to understand good food, it makes you glow, don't it, Kitty, to hear her askin' for eels? I'll have the same, please. And brown bread and butter, o' course.'

'Would I forget it?' Kitty said in mock dudgeon and hurried away.

George leaned back in her chair and grinned at Gus. 'I have to say I do enjoy watching you at work,' she said. 'The way you handled that Maxwell man was . . .' She shook her head, seeking the right word.

'Oh, Maxwell!' He waved a dismissive hand. 'He's a type, believe me. Full of bluster and chat until you get him pinned down and then goes as soggy as a cornflake in a jug of hot milk. He's no trouble. I can only hope that Chummy, when we come up with him, is as easy. He won't be, of course.'

'Have you got a picture of him?' she asked. 'An image in your mind's eye?'

'You're the doctor, ducks. You tell me.'

She shook her head. 'I've told you before, I'm more a physical forensic type than a psychiatric. But I could have a go.' She leaned forwards and set her elbows on the table. 'As I see it, this is a man with hard reason behind what he does. He's an organized sort of person, traditional in his outlook, with a taste for history. That's the Jack the Ripper bit – and he does what he does with commitment. Otherwise he'd have sheered off from the last two murder sites when he found out, as he must have done, how thoroughly you were watching them. And he hangs on to ideas when he gets them – this man is so *organized*. He has to be to carry through a five-murder project like this. That's why I say he has some real motive for what he's doing. There may be flourishes about his MO that are meant to make us think of a serial murderer, but there's no way I can do that.'

'Why not? He's picking on the same sort of victims: all Members of Parliament. He uses the same method of killing and adds the same fancy touches – if you call posthumous castration a fancy touch – and to crown it all, puts himself to the trouble of aping Jack the Ripper. You see that as a taste for history, and a traditional frame of mind. I see it differently.' He shook his head with a sudden violent movement. 'That's what really gets to me. The bastard signalled where he was going to commit his crimes, and we still couldn't stop him. That gets up my nose more than anything else. Why, for God's sake? I mean why tell us where he'd be? So that he could escape us and show us up for idiots, that he was spring-heeled Jack come again or something? That was what the original Ripper did, they say. Wrote a letter, showing off. We've had no letter from this one though.' He sat and brooded for a moment and then sighed. 'Oh, well. I suppose we'll find out eventually, when we get him. And we bloody will!'

She looked away, with an odd sense of embarrassment. 'I wish I could be so sure.'

He was genuinely surprised. 'You're not usually so pessimistic about a case.'

'I know. But this one's intelligent. I keep telling you, I think he's killing for a reason.'

'It's true that you've been saying that all along, and I haven't paid much attention. But you're often right in these things, so I should. You still think it's political?'

'In a sort of a way it could be. I don't think it's *party* political. If you look at the MPs and lords who were killed it doesn't make any sort of pattern that fits party alliances. We've got one Tory member, one Labour member, one hereditary lord, a Bishop and a TUC guy, a life peer. There's a fair spread of attitudes, isn't there? Though I suppose there's a bit of a lean to the left with David CWG and Jack Scroop. I guess I could be wrong and it's not political, yet I can't get rid of the notion.'

'Well, if it's not a political motive, then what? A criminal conspiracy? I know we've uncovered one – or are in the process of doing so, to be accurate – but that only involves Diamond, and I suppose by association Lord Durleigh and David CWG. But it's a tenuous link. The fact that a man was involved with a victim's wife and is a friend of at least one of the other victims, and knows yet a third, is a link, but –'

'But it doesn't really make you jump up and down with excitement. Me neither.' She looked up as their starters arrived. 'I keep coming back to the politics of it – thanks, Kitty. That looks great. Oh, and you've got some Jalapeño sauce! Fabulous.'

'Vinegar, ducks, vinegar's all you need with jellied eels. Anything else is sacrilege.'

'I like my pepper sauce. You back off, buster, and eat your own supper.'

He did, and the next half-hour passed in agreeable and inconsequential chatter as they ate massive platefuls of fish and chips of the most delectable sort; as George told Kitty, yet again, she hadn't lost her skill with a skillet. At which Kitty, looking over her shoulder at her vast range of big up-to-the-minute fish fryers and hotplates, was highly amused.

Over their coffee, replete and relaxed, they returned to talking about the case. But somehow the edge had gone. That there was, somewhere tantalizingly out of sight, the clear link between all five of the victims, George was certain. That there would be found a solid and fully understandable motive for the deaths, she was equally sure. But what she couldn't be sure about was why she was so convinced.

'Maybe,' she said to Gus a little sleepily as he drove them home, 'someone said something to me that's gone deep into my mind and won't come out, but which I sort of know is the key. Could it be that?'

'How should I know?' Gus said as he steered the car into their driveway. 'Just let me know when you've sorted it out. But do me a favour, sweetheart. Not till I've had a night's sleep, which I will after that supper. I've at last got rid of the taste of the lousy food at that pub.' He shuddered. 'The Bald Monk! Starving Monk more like! Come on. Let's get to bed.'

That they had needed a good night's peaceful rest was made very clear by the way they were next morning. They were up, showered, breakfasted and on the road for Spitalfields well before nine, and remarkably, for a pair who usually woke in a thoroughly curmudgeonly mood, without exchanging one snappy word. Gus was whistling contentedly through his teeth as he steered his old car through the early morning clots of traffic, cheerfully cutting up other drivers whenever he could. There was nothing he liked more than a journey punctuated by indignant squawks from other drivers' hooters.

The Market was bustling when they got there, having managed to find a parking meter not too far away, somewhat to Gus's irritation. He much preferred using a single yellow line and then arguing the toss with the traffic warden who tried to ticket him; he reckoned that was a police privilege. But this morning he was in so sunny a mood he even put his coins in the parking meter without too much grumbling.

'We'll stay together, I think,' he said. 'If that wouldn't make you feel hard done by? Because I'm the one who has to do all the questioning?'

'That's OK,' she grinned. 'I'll do the thinking. Deal?'

'I should be so lucky! Right, we'll work as near to the storeroom as possible of course, to start with, not because I expect old Roop missed much but because now we know what we're looking for. The sighting of a man in overalls –'

'Stained, bunchy, and worn with a cap and galoshes,' she said. 'Then tally ho, old chap, and all that sort of thing, what?'

He laughed and pushed his way through the busy people setting up for the day, and the early customers coming in on their way to their offices and workshops, with her close behind.

The first hour went quickly and with it some of their good humour. All they found was that Rupert Dudley had indeed done a good job. There was no one among the established people at the Market, the shopkeepers and their regular customers, who had not been interviewed exhaustively, and no one had seen any more than they had already told Roop's team.

They used the second hour to widen the circle, talking to people who were not in direct lines of vision to the door behind which the body of Lord Durleigh had been found, which was, Gus had to admit, a pointless exercise really because unless someone was seen at the door, or near it, it wouldn't constitute real evidence, even if he looked exactly the same as the man Maxwell had described as being at Creechurch Lane. 'It's the most flimsy of circumstantial evidence,' he said gloomily. 'But I suppose it'd be something. So let's get on with it.'

But they got nowhere, and at twelve-thirty, with their early happiness quite disappeared and both of them feeling not only bitterly disappointed but tired, grubby and very thirsty, they looked at each other and, without exchanging a word, knew the time had come to give up. No witnesses had seen any suspect activities here at the Market, whatever the *Courier* said.

'Can't you slap some sort of order on the *Courier*?' George asked. 'To make them divulge what they claim they've got?'

'Oh, sure,' Gus said savagely. 'And make them crow at the tops of their voices about how the baffled police consulted them? It's one thing to have proof – like the statements Maxwell made last night – but quite another when we haven't a scintilla of evidence to back our demands. No, love, there's no joy that way. Listen, I'm as parched as the Commissioner's heart. I want coffee. Is there a place here we can get some?'

She nodded. 'I saw a sort of coffee shop back there – a canteen. I dare say I can find it again.' And she plunged back into the Market, leading the way.

The canteen was designed more for the stallholders themselves than for their customers, and many of them were sitting at small tables which were covered with slightly cracked oilcloth, eating lunch. There was a strong smell of toasted cheese and spiced bun beneath an overwhelming miasma of tea made in the really English style, thick and strong and very well laced with milk and sugar. George, who preferred her tea pale and milk free, sighed. It would have to be coffee, and everyone knew how dreadful English coffee could be.

George was right to be gloomy. She contemplated the beaker of muddy instant coffee that the man behind the urns banged down in front of her, then followed Gus to a table right by the entrance to drink it.

'This is gnat's pee,' he announced as he looked at the tobacco-brown mixture in his own beaker. 'But I'm thirsty enough to drink anything.' He began to gulp steadily.

George, still feeling gloomy, looked around. Most of the people at the tables had their heads together, talking quietly, or were reading newspapers. A rather stooped figure, bulky yet somehow lacking any sense of being weighty, was moving between the tables, muttering. Most of the people the figure stopped beside either ignored it, or made a flapping gesture with one hand to try to send it away. One or two reached into pockets and handed over something. A beggar, George thought, another of London's homeless, and felt the usual state of distress such sights gave her. Gus, catching the line of her gaze, shook his head.

'Try not to hand over all you've got,' he said. 'A bob or two'll be quite enough.'

'I'll spend what I like,' she said, reaching into her pocket for her purse and pulling out a crumpled five-pound note. She had intended to give the beggar a pound when it reached her – and she had to think 'it' for at this point she couldn't see what gender the bundle was – but Gus had tipped her over the edge into extra munificence. He laughed.

'Oh, George,' he said. 'It's so easy to push your buttons, sweetheart! No need for that, I'll muck in,' and he put his hand into his own pocket.

The beggar had reached them by now, a fairly heavy effluvium of old tobacco, beer and some very basic body odours signalling her; for that is what she turned out to be. A woman in perhaps her late fifties – though George knew perfectly well that the lifestyle of these street alcoholics could put twenty years on their real age – she had a grimy face, a nose pitted with blackheads and eyes that were reddened and watery.

'Got a few – Oh, ta!' she said, startled, as at once both Gus and George held out their hands. Her face lit up as she saw the five-pound note in George's hand and then, just as she reached out amazingly dirty fingers for it, she pulled back. ''Ere, what you want, then? I'm not doin' anythin' I shouldn't. I got enough trouble on me plate, ta very much, without any more.'

'It's all right,' George said as kindly as she could. 'I'm not asking for anything. I just want you to have it.'

The old woman quirked her head. 'Oh,' she said. 'You're a Yank,' as though that explained everything, and took the note so fast that it was a blur. With amazing speed she hid it somewhere beneath the bundle of garments in which she was wrapped.

She reached out again for the coins Gus was offering and he grinned at her, the wide white wolfish grin that he affected sometimes. 'I'm not so soft,' he said. 'I ask questions, I do, for my cash. D'you come here often?'

She cackled suddenly. 'Yeah! I likes the dance floor.' And did a sudden awkward pirouette, twirling round on lumpy booted feet. George and Gus laughed and the old woman did too, revealing surprisingly white teeth of her own.

'So, you see a lot of what goes on here?' Gus said invitingly.

'I sees what I wants to see. And ignores the rest.' She was holding out her hand again, looking at the coins in Gus's palm. There was a glitter about her that made her seem rather alarming suddenly, George thought.

'Heard about the murder here, did you, then?' Gus managed still to keep his offering tantalizingly out of her reach.

262

'Course I did! I'm not daft!'

'Any idea how it was done?'

''Ow d'you mean?'

'Locked door and all that. Didn't you hear? He got in through the –'

'Through the hinges. That's right.' She pushed her hand forwards more aggressively. 'Listen, are you givin' me that money or ain't yer? 'Cause if you ain't, I'm on my way. I got my own affairs to look after.'

Gus was looking at her sharply and suddenly said, 'How about some grub? It's all right. You can have the cash as well. There you are. But how about a bowl of that soup?' The man behind the counter had lifted the lid from a big pan at the back, and a waft of steam scented with onions and carrots and a hint of lamb and barley had drifted through the canteen. It was an agreeable smell to George who was not hungry, and the old woman, who almost certainly was, lifted her head and took it in, never taking her gaze from Gus.

'Why should I?'

'To give me a bit of info. Soup, and what's more, another fiver,' Gus said with a casual air, leaning back in his chair as if he couldn't care less. 'I reckon you see things around here and I'd like to hear just what. But it's up to you.'

There was a long silence, and then the old woman sighed, a bubbly sound. 'Might as well,' she muttered. 'Got through the rest of it already, di'n't I? Mean buggers, thinkin' they can do that to me. 'Undreds they said and then it was just a pony. So I might as well. But I wants the soup an' all, mind!'

'You shall have it,' Gus said gravely and moved along the bench on which he was sitting to make room for the malodorous old woman beside him.

29

George fetched the soup, together with a roll and butter and a slab of cheese, and together they watched the old woman hoover it up as though she had never eaten before. That she was half starved was obvious and George was worried for a moment or two when the woman stopped eating, and sat panting for a while. Had they overfed her, let her take too much, too fast? That could be almost as damaging to a starved person as going without food.

But she recovered and wiped the back of her hand across her mouth and again grinned, showing those white teeth. She had good dentistry once, George thought. How did this happen to her? But she had no time to pursue the thought because Gus was now leaning forwards to look into the dirty face and talk to her. 'So, what's your name, darlin'?' he said easily.

She looked down at his hand where a five-pound note had appeared between his fingers. 'Sally, if you must know,' she said, and snatched the note which also disappeared into the malodorous clothing. 'Sally Whittaker, tha's me. I was a dancer, you know. Yes, I was. A dancer. When I was a girl.' There was a little silence and then she sniffed unpleasantly and looked at George. 'What about a bit o' pud then?'

'I'm sorry?' George was startled.

'She wants a dessert,' Gus said. 'I saw apple pie, I think. If that'll do?'

'If there ain't nothin' better, it'll have to,' Sally said. George went and fetched some together with a beaker of tea.

Again they had to wait until she had demolished the food, and then she sat back, the cup of tea steaming in front of her and actually looked at them with an agreeable expression on her dirty face.

'Well,' she said. 'That was a bit of all right, that was. My lucky day, 'n't it? Had a few o' them lately. Maybe me stars are in the ascendant. I'm a Pisces. What are you?'

'I'm a nosy fella wants to know what happened with you and the *Courier*,' Gus said. He was taking risks, George thought. They might be wasting their time with Sally Whittaker (though there was no way they were wasting their money, she told herself. The poor creature deserved every penny she could get) and the only way they would know was, she realized, to go right to the point as Gus had done. She held her breath for a moment, waiting for Sally's response.

It wasn't only Sally who was having a lucky day, she decided. Because the old woman slid her gaze sideways to look consideringly at Gus and then she giggled. 'You're a smart bugger. 'Ow did you know I bin talkin' to them?'

'I didn't till now,' Gus said. 'Thanks for telling me.'

'Just guessin'? Pull the other one. It's got bloody tambourines on it, that one has. Someone tipped you off I bin seen talking to them.'

'Swelp me bob, I guessed.' Gus smiled at her. 'Listen, ducks, you're the first one I'd go for myself if I wanted to know what went on in the place. It's obvious you're a regular around here, the way you was goin' round the tables. So, I took a guess.'

'Oo are you?'

He hesitated. 'Detective,' he said at length. 'Been asked to work on this case.'

She looked at him, her eyes glittering. 'A private eye, like in the films? I was in one of them once. In 1967 it was. I was a woman in a crowd outside a courtroom. That Jason somethin' was in it, you know the one? Got a lot o' lines on his face, very fancy clo's, you know the geezer I mean.'

'Yes,' lied Gus. 'Of course I do. Very famous.'

'An' you're like him?'

'Not so good lookin',' Gus said. 'And no fancy clothes.'

She laughed. 'You can say that again. All right, I'll tell you what I was telling the blokes from the *Courier*. Two of them there was, promised me 'undreds of pounds if I told 'em all I'd seen and then when I done it, said it was only worth twenty-five quid, take it or leave it. Buggers!' She stared venomously at George as though she were one of the journalists who had cheated her, and George looked as sympathetic as she could.

'Wicked,' she said. 'But you can't trust some people, can you?'

'You can't trust them,' Sally said. 'What'll you pay me then? Hundreds, like they promised?'

'Not on your nelly,' Gus said. 'I only promise what I can deliver. I can give you another tenner on top of what you've got already. Can't say fairer than that.'

'Now, there's an honest man,' Sally said admiringly and winked at Gus alarmingly. 'So what d'you wanna know? Ask yer questions.'

'What you told them, first,' Gus said. 'Then we can go on from there.'

'Well.' The bundle of clothes shifted in the seat as Sally settled herself more comfortably. She was smelling worse than ever now, but it didn't matter. George felt a little wave of excitement lift in her. Perhaps they hadn't wasted their morning after all.

'Well, I was lyin' down in my usual place, right out there.' She gestured vaguely. 'By the entrance where they brings in the heavy goods, right? There's a hidden place there by a boiler house. Warm, really warm. It's my special place and I won't let no one take it from me, though don't think some of 'em don't try.'

She looked brooding for a moment, and Gus said quickly, 'So, you were there. When?'

'The night before that murder.'

Gus frowned. 'The night *before*? You're sure? What day was that?'

'Don't you ask me about days o' the week, ducks. I don't know one from another. There's nothin' to choose between 'em for me. But it was the night before they found that body. I can tell you that. Do you want me to give yer what I saw or doncher?'

'I do,' Gus said. 'I won't stop you again. I'm sorry.'

'Right,' Sally said with a somewhat grand air. 'Now I'm in charge, I'll get on. All right. There I was, in my place, and it was late. An' don't go askin' me the time on account of I don't wear a watch, right? But I do know it was well late. So, I'm lyin' there, an' suddenly I sees there's two blokes at the door. I didn't see 'em comin' there and I didn't hear 'em neither, but I was well wrapped up in my stuff so I suppose my ears was covered. But when I sees 'em, I uncovers my ears, very quiet and careful, so I can 'ear, but not so they notice me movin', like. I don't want no one interferin' with me, and I just keep still and I know I look like a pile o' garbage.'

She stopped then and gazed at George, and for a brief moment there was a look of utter hopelessness in her reddened eyes. 'Which is what I am, I suppose.'

George felt her throat tighten and she reached out and touched the old woman's hand. Sally looked down and then pulled her own hand away, almost pettishly.

'Well, like I was sayin', I was very careful not to move an' they didn't notice me. I'm in a shadowed place there, anyway. So I sees them because they're under a bit o' light in the porch place. And one of them says somethin' and the other one mutters back and then they open the door and the buzzer – the alarm – starts, then stops, an' I think, oh, it's one of them that belongs 'ere, on account of 'e understands the alarm, and I was goin' to settle back down again and then I thought, it's bleedin' cold tonight. It'll be a sight warmer inside. So I goes after 'em. They've shut the door, like, but it's unlocked, o' course. So I gets up quietly an' I follows 'em in.'

George was hanging on to every word, almost breathless with excitement and Sally Whittaker seemed to understand the effect she was having and began to take pleasure in it. She lifted her voice a little and made gestures as she spoke, adding a touch more excitement of her own.

'I walks behind 'em very quiet, and well away from 'em. I listens, but they was whisperin'. But I 'eard a bit. One of 'em was agoin' on about wantin' a fag. He was the Eyetalian one.'

'The what?' Gus said and she turned to glare at him.

'You got cloth ears? I said the Eyetalian one. 'E 'ad an accent you could cut with a knife. Not that I could 'ear much but enough to know. I used to go out with an Eyetalian once, when I was a dancer. 'E was a musician, and 'e came from Rome. Ever so good lookin' 'e was, too.'

'And you're sure that the man you heard —'

'I told you. 'E was goin' on about wantin' a fag. Anyway, they didn't talk no more and the other bloke — not the Eyetalian, the other one — goes up to the storeroom door and I sees 'im fiddlin'. It's not very easy to see, because he's got a torch an' I can't see much, but anyway, he fiddles and then they sort of squeeze in. I couldn't see as much as I wanted, because I was well back, o' course, outa sight. And they sort of shut the door and that was that. I went down the other side an' found a lovely soft sofa in one of the antique shops and I spent the night there. It was great. Woke up in time to get out of the way into the lavvy and then when the first few in did see me they thought I'd follered 'em in, and never said a dicky bird. And that's what I told the blokes from the *Courier*. An' if that ain't worth 'undreds I don't know what is.'

'Would you recognize either of these chaps again?' Gus asked.

Sally shook her head. 'Ain't you bloody listenin'? It was dark. They 'ad a torch, but they didn't shine it on theirselves. I did see one of 'em was wearin' a sort of cap, mind you, a flat one. But that was all.'

'And you're sure it was the night *before* the murder?'

'O' course I am! Because the next night, when I was sleepin' out in the back again, I was woke up by all the row when the police come and broke in and set off the alarm and found 'im and there's cars and ambulances and Gawd knows what else everywhere.'

Gus looked at George. 'So,' he said softly. 'That was how Durleigh got there. The murderer fetched him. Italian? Perhaps

Milanese? That was where Alice went a lot wasn't it? Though it was his companion who knew how to open the door. But could it be that we've already found the reason for all these killings? A *fashion* fraud, for God's sake? Five killings? It doesn't seem possible.'

'What you mean five?' Sally Whittaker said with sudden pugnacity. 'I told you what I saw about *one* of 'em. I don't know nothin' about five and I won't 'ave you sayin' I do.' She looked alarmed now. 'I shouldn't 'ave talked to you. I must be potty. Look, I'm out of 'ere.' She was shuffling along the seat, getting to her feet, and Gus reached for her.

'No, Sally, don't go yet, I want to ask you —'

But she was gone, shuffling off at an amazing speed through the now crowded canteen. Gus rose to go after her, but then sat down again. 'I suppose I can get her when I need her,' he said. 'She won't go far from here, however much I've alarmed her. Listen, George, I'm trying to remember. How long did you say Durleigh had been dead when we found him?'

She shut her eyes, trying to conjure up in her mind's eye the report she had written on Lord Durleigh's body. After a moment, to her relief, her old gift of an eidetic memory kicked in and she could see the page in her mind's eye.

'Twelve to fifteen hours was the nearest I could get,' she said. 'But as I wrote in the report, it's all very dependent on such things as the ambient air temperature, and the speed with which heat can radiate out of an enclosed space. That was a warm dry storeroom. He could easily have been there longer than I was able to estimate.'

'Up to twenty-four hours?' Gus asked.

'It's possible.'

'So we do have a witness, if we can ever get her to court. And if we ever find Chummy to get him to court. Oh, this really is a bugger. Come on, let's go and look around at the back, anyway.'

They found the door Sally meant without difficulty. It was a pair of double doors, in fact, that could allow large items ingress, and just inside it, some six feet up on the wall, was a heavy painted black box. Gus peered at it and then pulled on the knob.

It opened to reveal a board of keypads and clearly was used to control various internal operations.

'Whoever did this knew the code for setting the alarm and switching it off. So Rupert's got another major job on his hands. He'll have to check everyone here to see who knew the code and when it was changed and so on. I'll get him on to that.'

He reached into his pocket for his mobile phone and stabbed in the number of Ratcliffe Street station as George went out of the doors to look round outside. By the time he'd finished giving his instructions she had found Sally Whittaker's sleeping place.

It was just as she had said; a corner between the main wall and the boiler house, about four feet wide and ten feet long. There was a piece of grimy plyboard leaning against the opening and when George moved it, she could see at once how cleverly Sally had fixed herself up. Sheets of cardboard had been pushed in and shaped to fit the available ground and they in their turn were covered by several layers of newspaper. Over that Sally had thrown a heavy piece of old carpet she had found somewhere, and to disguise what she had done, had piled in some old black polythene bags bulging with what appeared to be rubbish but was mostly newspaper. The bags had the added virtue of keeping off rain and cats and other undesirables; it was, George thought, probably as snug and warm as a bed could be out of doors in London's inhospitable climate. Again her throat tightened at the evidence of the struggle that Sally had to keep herself going in a hostile world.

Gus had come up behind her and was looking at the arrangement as well, and then looked over his shoulder.

'She heard them easily enough,' he said gloomily. 'It's only fifteen feet away. That bit of roof over the porch would collect sound anyway, and she'd hear them better than they might hear any movements she made. It's a true bill all right. The old girl saw two men come in here, the night before the murder, one of them an Italian – though I have to say that's a bit flimsy. She says they were whispering and accents are notoriously hard to identify. Still, she saw neither of them leave, so we can't find out what time they did, or if only one left as we suspect or –

Oh, shit. We seem to find something and then it wriggles away almost at once. It keeps on happening.'

'Not really,' George said. 'One of the things that most puzzled us was how the body got there. Now we know. The victim was enticed first here, and then through a door – a narrow opening, admittedly, but he used it of his own free will. And was killed there. So this isn't any sort of a locked room killing of the fictional type. It was straightforward breaking and entering.'

'No, it wasn't,' he said. 'Not breaking. They walked in with a key and presumably he – the killer – got out the same way. Otherwise we'd have seen signs of entry. That was what made it seem so – so magical. And I doubt we'd ever have known, at least until the body began to stink, if the bastard hadn't sent that fax to show us where he'd left his fourth victim. Christ, but I hate him, whoever he is. Arrogant bastard.'

'You could call him that,' George murmured. 'Well, honey, now what?'

'Back to the nick,' he said. 'I have to feed all this info into the system and see how it fits in. I also want to check as far as I can all the timings we have. Who was where and when.'

'Whose timings?' She had fallen into step beside him as he hurried round the building to where they'd left the car.

'Eh?'

'I said, whose timings? I mean, who are your suspects?'

'I wish I knew!' He was explosive. 'Every one and no one. I'm going to see to it we confront Alice Diamond with what she's been up to, for a start, now I've got Roop's report on his talk with her. That has to be done now, no hanging back any longer. And I think I might check the times and whereabouts of some of those politicians in the Whips' offices – they're the ones who are supposed to know where everyone is, aren't they? That's their job. Well, we'll make use of their knowledge. Anyway, for all I know, one of them could be involved. That chap Marcus whatsit, I wasn't struck with him and he's a close friend of one of the victims, which puts him in the frame. That's worth a bit of time. And –'

'This isn't like you, Gus,' she said as they reached the car.

'You're not being concise. You're just thrashing about looking for anyone and everyone.'

'Weren't you listening to what I was saying?' he snapped. 'It's the only thing we can do. I prefer line fishing, going out with the right lures for a particular fish because you know all you can about him, but sometimes you have to go out with bag nets and trawl everything and everyone. This is one of those cases.'

He let in the clutch and moved in to the traffic and now was driving as fast as he could. George held on to her seat belt and said no more. Gus was angry now. This had stopped being just another case in his professional life but had become more of a personal vendetta. He wanted this perpetrator very badly indeed. And she shivered a little as she glanced at the way his jaw muscles were working over the side of his face.

The best thing she could do, she thought, was go on behaving like a line fisherman. There had to be, somewhere in all she had heard and seen in the case, something that would point to the killer more accurately than Gus's net-'em-all-and-drag-'em-all-in approach. All she had to do was find it. Somehow.

30

George knew that Gus had not set out to push her into the background, but that was what it felt like. He ran up the steps into the nick, barely noticing whether she was behind him or not, and into the incident room like a gust of cold wind. The people at the computer consoles looked up, startled, and Mike Urquhart, who was at the fax machine reading an incoming sheaf stared at him wide eyed, suddenly looking surprisingly young.

'Wha's happened, Guv?' He sounded hopeful.

'Not a bloody thing,' Gus said. 'Except I've found an eye-witness who tells me that victim number five walked into Spital-fields Market of his own free will, and went into the storeroom just as willingly.'

'Guv, that is fantastic!' Mike said, his face lighting up but Gus just bared his teeth at him in anger.

'Great nothing! She's a bloody wino who'd be as much use in the witness box as – as the bundle of rags she looks like. All we can do with her is use her as a lead. She says one of the men she saw was Italian . . .'

He explained, fast and reasonably coherently, and sent them all bustling: Mike to the House of Commons to talk again to Mary Bodling in her Whip's office; one of the constables to search out Rupert Dudley to send him there too, but to talk to the Opposition Chief Whip; and – here his voice became grim – Tim Brewer to bring in Alice Diamond for questioning.

'Tell him to take Julie Bentley with him, and to be careful.

273

It's the first time we've asked her in any hostile sense, and she'll be tricky. I can promise them that. This bloody woman's been dancing jigs under our noses and so far we've let her get away with it. But enough is enough. And I want to talk to Jasper Powell, too. But not until after we get her sorted. We're going to blow this fashion scam as wide open as a tart's drawers. Now get on with it!' And he slammed into his office and reached for his phone, leaving George in the incident room outside.

'Getting angry now, is he?' Mike said unnecessarily but sympathetically, and she grimaced.

'Tell me about it. This has really got under his skin. Anyway, I wish you joy of talking to Mary Bodling again. I hear she's a tough nut.'

'The toughest,' he said happily. 'But I'm no' scared of that one. I can give as good as I get. Now, who's coming with me?' He looked round the room consideringly. 'Gil, what do you think? Are you up to a bit of high-level interrogation?'

DC Gil Morley grinned and came round his desk with alacrity. 'I'm in the mood for anything but this Godawful paperwork. Lead me to it.'

Colin Twiley hovered unhappily outside the closed office door and blinked at Mike Urquhart. People passing in the corridor looked at him with huge curiosity, a fact of which he was painfully aware. The Opposition Chief Whip didn't usually show himself anywhere near this particular office door, as everyone knew. There were, Colin was sure, a few muffled shouts of laughter as people went on their way. He was a deeply wretched man. 'I don't see why you need to talk to us again at all, really. And now to say you want to talk to me at the same time as Mary Bodling, well, it –'

Mike looked sympathetic. 'I know she can be a bit difficult.'

Twiley straightened his back in a painful attempt to look strong and resolute. 'Oh, I'm not scared of Mary Bodling!' he said, almost twitching with terror as he said it. 'It's just that we're on opposite sides of the House, you see, and we don't generally –'

'This is police business, not party politics, sir,' Mike said with

274

a somewhat stern air, and Gil Morley, beside him, nodded his agreement. 'I'd ha' thought you'd be anxious, even eager, to help with our inquiries, seein' as it's five Members of this House that have been murdered.' He allowed himself the luxury of an extra Scottish burr on the word, making it sound even more horrid. 'Does that no' make your people a touch nervous?'

'Hmmph,' Colin Twiley said, himself clearly much alarmed by the whole affair. 'Of course we're distressed to see honourable friends . . . though in fact it's only been two of our people, the rest come from the Other Place.'

'And so don't matter?' Gil said over Mike's shoulder.

'Oh, no, I don't mean that, it's just that . . .' His misery deepened.

Mike wasted no more time and tapped sharply on the door, and then ushered Colin in ahead of him. 'We're here to see Miss Bodling,' he said to the young man sitting at a desk. 'You'll remember me, no doubt. I'm Sergeant Urquhart from Ratcliffe Street. This is DC Morley.' He showed his warrant card briefly, as did Gil. 'And you'll know Mr Twiley, o' course.'

The young man looked a touch scornfully at Twiley, who was doing his unsuccessful best to look relaxed and insouciant, and then at Mike. 'You didn't say you were bringing anyone with you when you made your appointment with Miss Bodling.' He sounded as accusatory as if Mike had committed some major act of insurrection.

'No, I didn't, did I?' Mike said sunnily. 'But there you go. Changed our minds. We were going to talk to you two sides of the House separately, but then we thought that was a waste of expensive police time, which you'd not like at all, of course, so it was agreed that after all Inspector Dudley would not come and that DC Morley and I would do the interrogations.'

'Interrogations?' Colin Twiley almost squeaked it. 'What do you mean?'

'Oh, just a few questions,' Gil said. 'Miss Bodling in there, is she?' He jerked his head at the door of an inner office and, without waiting for confirmation, marched over and opened it, and held it wide for Mike and Twiley. The young man, scandalized, leaped to his feet, but it was too late. Mike and his now almost visibly shaking companion had followed Gil in there.

Mary Bodling had been sitting with her head down over something on her desk and at the sight of Twiley she went an odd purplish sort of shade. 'What do you want, then?' she snapped. Twiley shook his head and looked from Mike to Morley and back again.

The policemen went through the business of identifying themselves as smoothly as usual and seemed unaware of Miss Bodling's furious glances. 'I need to check with you the movement of your members,' Mike said. 'Mr Diamond and Mr Caspar-Wynette-Gondor.'

'Again?' Mary Bodling cried. 'We've wasted enough of our time on that already. If you can't keep your records straight, young man, then don't come here and expect me to –'

'This has nothing to do with incorrect records, Miss Bodling.' Somehow Mike rode over her so easily that she actually stopped talking and Colin Twiley glanced at him for a moment, startled. 'It's a matter of corroboration. The more we can fill in the wee interstices in the evidence, you understand, the better the job we can do. Now then, I'll start with you, Miss Bodling. I'd like to know where you were at the relevant times.' And he looked at Gil who was sitting expectantly with his notebook open and his pen poised.

Now she seemed to go puce. 'Where was – Are you asking me – Do you sit there and –' She stopped, lost for words, and for the first time since Mike had dragged him so unwillingly from his own office, Colin Twiley smiled.

Mike looked at her with his brows up, as though surprised. 'But I have to ask, Miss Bodling. In a murder inquiry of this magnitude, you'll understand, every tiny fact is relevant. I'm sure you'll not mind telling me –'

'I'm not a suspect, Goddamn you!' Mary roared. 'And don't you dare to suggest for one moment that –'

'We never make suggestions, ma'am,' Mike said, and suddenly he sounded icy. 'We just ask our questions and collect our evidence. So, if you don't mind refreshing your memory –

perhaps check with your diary? – I'll get the same information from Mr Twiley here and then return to you.'

He did and Colin told him willingly, even eagerly, as Morley scribbled fast. Since there had been business in the House on all the relevant dates Mike quoted, he had no difficulty in pointing out he'd been here all the time. 'And,' he added, glancing at Mary Bodling, 'so were you, weren't you, Mary? I remember that because –'

'I am perfectly capable of speaking for myself,' Mary boomed, banging her desk diary open. She proceeded to give precisely the same information Colin had, watching Gil beadily as he wrote it down and from time to time spelling out the simpler words very slowly to assist him.

Mike remained sunny throughout the performance, and when she'd finished looked artlessly at her. 'There now, that wasn't so difficult, was it?' he said and again her eyes glittered with rage. He just smiled and then turned back to Twiley.

But he'd won. From then on the inquiry went as he wanted it to and Gil was kept busy with his notes. They corroborated their previous evidence on the comings and goings of their respective Members and Mike nodded happily, as though this was all he had come for. And when he'd finished, settled down to a little cosy chat.

'This must be upsetting your Members,' he said with an air of great sympathy. 'Seeing colleagues murdered in this inexplicable fashion. It must make them look over their shoulders all the time.'

'I can only speak for my own people,' Mary said magnificently. 'And they are much too concerned with the essential business of the Nation that they are here to carry out to bother themselves unduly with their personal welfare.'

'More fool them,' said Colin Twiley. He had been much encouraged by the way Mike had handled Mary and now sat beside him rather closer than was entirely necessary, as though he was sheltering beneath a particularly safe rock. Gil's presence behind him seemed an added strengthener.

Mary sniffed. 'You wouldn't understand,' she said. 'The sort of people *you* have to handle are shaking in their miserable shoes,

I imagine. Going in convoys of special buses to keep themselves safe, no doubt.'

'They are not!' Twiley said, stung. 'They're travelling like everyone else; by public transport, too, which is more than your people do. Even your Transport chap has to have a chauffeur-driven car to get around! Much he'd have to worry about the new Ripper!'

This was getting too silly, Mike decided, exchanging glances with Morley. He felt almost as though he were back in school. 'What I need to know,' he said in a loud voice, 'is whether you think there could be any political motives at work here. We outside the House know only what the papers and TV tell us, and God knows we get the impression you're all at each other's throats. But are you in a literal sense? Are there any issues simmering here that the public doesn't hear about, that could be linked with these deaths?'

Mary looked sardonic. 'Oh, come on, Sergeant! Use your head! We have over six hundred Members in this House, the majority of them extremely ambitious, or fired with strong convictions, or both. They not only have to take great responsibilities for the Welfare of the Nation, as I said, but also have to face the matter of being re-elected every five years. Of course there are issues going on here the public doesn't know about. And I'll tell you this much, they aren't going to. I can assure you that if I knew any reason why our Member should have been killed, I would tell you. I've already told you that I believe his – um – problems were more connected with his wife than anything here. Now, work on that and leave us alone!'

'Oh, dear,' Twiley said, looking at Mary with an expression that was part loathing, part amazement, and part a sort of respect. 'I think I have to agree with you. Uncomfortable though that has to be. David CWG's death too is much more likely to be linked with his family than it is with anything going on here, as I believe it is with most cases of murder. I mean, if people got themselves killed here for political reasons, none of us'd be around to tell the tale. We'd be dying like flies.'

With which, eventually, Mike had to be satisfied. As he said to Gus later, when he and Morley reported back to him: 'I did all I could to get more out of them but they were adamant. These murders have nothing to do with political business, they're sure of it. It's just a coincidence, according to the fearsome Bodling, that all the dead people are involved with the Houses of Parliament. It's strictly personal, she says. But then, she would say that, wouldn't she?'

Left alone in the incident room at Ratcliffe Street, George was restless. Gus had shut himself into his office to get on with a series of phone calls, for he had other problems on his plate as well as this case. After a while she sighed, stretched and told herself she ought to drop in at Old East and see what was happening there. She too had responsibilities other than this case, which she had, she reminded herself with a twinge of guilt, been neglecting. So, she put her head round Gus's door and hissed that she was going. He just waved his hand and didn't look up, so she slipped away. They'd meet again later in the day and exchange further notes, no doubt; right now, she could only leave him and his team to it, ache though she did to be doing more about the case.

She chose to walk to Old East, pulling her coat collar up and thrusting her hands deep into her pockets, for it was an icy day, though bright. By the time she had made her way through the narrow side streets she used as a short cut her eyes were streaming with the bite of the sun and wind combined, and she thought, we've been too close to this case. The thing to do is step back a little, stop thinking about it and let the stuff that is already in our heads cool, and then wait and see what comes up with the bubbles. It was a technique she had tried before and it usually worked, she told herself optimistically as at last she reached the rear entrance to her department on the fringe of the Old East site; surely it would again.

Jerry and Alan were genuinely glad to see her and plied her with coffee and questions about the case; she accepted the first and flatly refused the latter.

'I've thought, breathed, slept and eaten this damned case for ever,' she said. 'Well, it feels like for ever, though how long is it? Only a week. Anyway, I'm not going to say another word about it. I've had it up to my eyebrows and beyond.'

'Ah, you're rotten,' Jerry said. 'Here we are, gobbling all the papers, agog on the news and complimenting ourselves we had a hotline right to the horse's mouth, and when the horse comes in it turns out to be as useless a line as – as –'

'Forget the compliments,' she said firmly. 'Tell me what else has been going on here.'

Alan obliged, overriding Jerry who was clearly all set to go on complaining about George's uncommunicativeness, and she read reports, checked lists of costs, discussed the progress of various clinic commitments the department had and generally caught up.

'You've done very well,' she said. 'Too bloody well, dammit. Ellen Archer'll be telling the Trust Board they don't need me any more.'

'Oh, no she won't,' Alan said. 'First of all, she's a bloody good business manager but she doesn't know sucks about the real work that goes on down here, and second, she'd never risk having them cut her establishment by her most senior consultant. You need have no fears.'

George, who in fact had nourished no such doubts but had wanted to find a generous way to compliment Alan, grinned. 'Well, bless you for that. So, how're things otherwise? What's happening around the place?' She had as healthy an appetite for hospital gossip as anyone else, and had felt a touch deprived this past week, not knowing of the latest scandal.

'Not a damned thing,' Jerry said. 'They're still cutting the corners and counting the paperclips. If they try to squeeze any more money out of this poor bloody NHS we'll all go down with Kwashiakor or something. Starvation is what they're inflicting on us now, starvation.' He shook his head. 'The stress levels are dreadful,' he added, looking at her piteously. 'I feel like an overloaded camel.'

'Oh, you're breaking my heart,' she laughed at him. 'And as for feeling like a camel –'

'No,' shrieked Jerry. 'Wrong example! I meant an over-worked angel. Having to worry about the sordid matter of coin all the time, it's horrible.'

'Oh, do shut up about financial matters! That's going on all the time. Is there no *new* news about individuals we can chew over?'

He shook his head with mock misery. 'Only that Neville Carr over in Oncology's spearheading an attempt to make the place totally non-smoking, for our health's sake, *he* says. I think it's to stop us having any pleasure at all, miserable sod. I'd been thinking about giving up, but as soon as these bloody health fascists start, I get a mad bad urge to double my intake.'

'You're giving up smoking?' George patted his back. 'That's brave of you, my lad! A dollar gets you five if you keep off the weed for three months.'

'Five dollars? How many cigars would that buy?' Jerry said. 'I don't want to know otherwise.'

'You're on to a winner there, Dr B.,' Alan said. 'He'll never stop. It's true – there's no real news around the place at all. That's why we were glad to see you. We thought you'd have something enthralling to share with us.' And he looked at her sideways before rather ostentatiously reaching for a new pile of folders to work on.

She laughed. 'You're as bad as Jerry.'

'No one's as bad as me,' Jerry said proudly, 'and I can prove it. Dear Dr B., dear, dear delicious creature, tell us what is going on in the wilds of the Ratcliffe Street nick. You said not to ask, but I have to. I'm desperate for info! Tell us the pillow talk between you and your sexy superintendent.'

'Watch it,' she said warningly, and he had the grace to look embarrassed.

'Sorree! But you see how far you push us when you won't talk? What *is* happening with the case? Are you any nearer to catching the bugger?'

She gave in. She had to. 'Well, maybe.' And she told them of the conversation with Sally that morning, warning them both it was highly confidential and making them swear to tell no one else. They promised, solemnly, and listened agog to the whole tale.

'Italian, eh?' Jerry burst into an imitation of an Italian tenor, singing the lines from a TV ice-cream ad. 'Just one Cor ne-tt-o, give it to me. Just one Corne-tt-o and I'll kill thee.' He stopped singing and swept into a flurry of stage Italian. 'Yes, sir, you giva me da knifa and I cutta offa your lovely bitsa dissa and datta and den I –'

'That's enough!' Alan said. 'You sound about as Italian as a Welsh miner with a bad hangover. Dr B., what's the matter? Are you all right?'

George was sitting bolt upright and staring at Jerry with her eyes wide and her lips apart. She looked as startled as though she had just been bitten somewhere unexpected.

'Jerry!' she said. 'Jerry, do that again. Do it some more. Tell me about – about Neville Carr's new campaign. In that Italian style.'

Jerry looked at her and then at Alan, and shook his head. 'She's gone off her chump,' he said. 'Poor dear. It had to come, of course, but all the same, it's painful when it does.'

'Jerry, will you do as I ask you?' She almost shrieked it. 'Tell me what Dr Carr said about smoking. In that cod Italian accent. You *must*.'

'Oh, Gawd,' Jerry said. 'Well, I'll have a bash. Ahem ...' He was actually embarrassed, because now several other members of the lab staff had drifted over, fascinated by what they could hear of the conversation, and were staring at him. George leaned forwards and actually poked him in the ribs, commanding him to do it. So he opened his mouth and tried.

It took him a while to get going but when he did it was amusing enough stuff, if, as Alan said loudly, 'Bloody stereotypical!'

'I ama Dr Carr, you understanda, and me, I knowa a lotta dere is to know about de lightsa and de lungsa – ze big balloonsa you gotta hera.' And he smacked his chest. 'Even da fellas gotta de big balloonsa here, calleda de lungas. Anda if you smoka di cigarctta, den you –'

'I knew it!' George cried and jumped to her feet. 'I knew it.

282

Jerry, you are *wonderful*.' And she threw her arms round him and kissed him on both cheeks, hard. He stared at her as she held his face between her hands, and managed to say only, 'Eh?'

'I have to go.' She was jubilant. 'I can't hang around. Listen, you're doing a great job, a really great job. I'll be away for the next five days – that'll give me my two weeks – and I'm beginning to think we may be able to crack this by then. 'Bye.' And she was gone, pulling on her coat as she ran, leaving them staring after her in blank amazement.

'Gus, I have to explain to you!' She sat at his desk, his phone in her hand, her coat still bunched around her. 'I think I know who the Italian was – I mean I think I know what it was ... No, I know I can't tell you over the phone, but – what? ... Oh, all right. What time? ... Yes, I suppose it can wait, if it must but ... Oh, all *right*, Gus!' She cradled the phone with a small clatter and sat and stared at it, furiously.

The frustration was huge. That she had worked out what it was that Sally had heard, she was sure, but what it meant – that was something else. There were ways of checking, of course, but if Gus wouldn't let her tell him on the phone (and he was right; they knew only too painfully at Ratcliffe Street how vulnerable mobile phones were to interception, and Gus had been using his) she'd have to wait to explain. All the same, to make her wait till he got home tonight was almost more than she could bear, she told herself, and then grimaced at her own silliness.

'I don't have to wait for him,' she said aloud, staring out at the incident room. There were very few people there now. If they weren't out re-interrogating the people at the House of Commons they were searching for suppliers of overalls or busy on other routine jobs. There was certainly no one she knew well enough to accompany her; and she ached for Julie. If only she were around to help; together they'd show the rest of them how to solve this case. She was quite certain she was on the right road, and to see it stretching in front of her and not to be able to run it – or even walk it – was dreadful.

It was inevitable, of course. She knew she shouldn't. She knew Gus would be furious. But she also knew she'd get answers if she did it, and that would surely mollify him, wouldn't it? It'll be one in the eye for Roop, if I solve this one before he and Gus do.

It was that thought that did it. She *would*. She clattered away down the stairs and out of the back door of the nick into the car park as fast as she could. One or two of the other policemen and -women on the strength greeted her as she went by, but she was almost too breathless to respond to their friendly comments, and more than one noted her progress and were startled by it.

The car needs a fill-up, she thought, but there should be enough gas in it to get me there. She pushed it out into the traffic, her London A–Z atlas open on the seat beside her, and headed steadily north and west.

The traffic was horrendous and she crept through the City and on to King's Cross and then up the Marylebone Road, switching lanes feverishly until at last she realized it did her no good but only made surrounding drivers boil over with rage, and settled grimly to being as patient as she could. Things weren't much better on the Westway, but at least she could move a little, and at last, almost an hour after she had left Ratcliffe Street, she pulled off the A40 to thread her way down the Greenford Road to Harrow.

The trouble was, she didn't know exactly where she was going. But the place can't be that big, she thought. I'm sure people there will know the sort of set-up I'm looking for.

The needle on her petrol tank caught her eye and, cursing softly under her breath, she pulled into the next service station she saw, and filled up. The place was very busy for it was now almost six and the traffic was thick with eager homegoers, and she had to wait in line to pay for her purchase. But she used the time to look at the map she had thought to bring with her when she came in to pay.

Her heart sank when she realized just how large a borough Harrow was; page after page of her guide seemed to be covered by it and she could see no indication in any of the little markings of small nursing homes. And she had a distinct memory of that fact; it had been a small nursing home, not a major health establishment of the sort that was indicated on the map.

She tried asking the girl behind the counter as she at last moved forwards to hand over her plastic, but the girl, never taking her eyes away from what her hands were doing, just shook her head when George inquired if she knew of any private nursing homes in the district. 'Couldn't say, I'm sure,' she muttered. 'Sign here.'

Back on the road George followed the signs and at last reached the turn she had been looking for. Harrow was indicated straight ahead; Harrow-on-the-Hill to her left. She bit her lip, tossed a mental coin, and when it came down, turned left.

Someone up there likes me, she thought as she completed the turn. Somewhere there's an angel who is watching over me, because there, on the right just past a pair of school gates, was a well-designed entrance and in large letters on the wall, the word 'Hospital'. She indicated and cut in under the nose of oncoming traffic, wanting to cheer.

Her luck held. The excessively charming girl in the flower-decked reception area (Oh, thought George, the sheer luxury of the private sector!) was most forthcoming. A private nursing home? What sort? There were three she knew of for – um – psychiatric problems. One just up the Hill, another a bit further on.

George could have hugged her. 'One of them might be what I'm looking for. And even if they're not, they'll know of any others, don't you think so?'

The girl did think so and George set off again, bubbling now with real excitement. At last things were happening for her as they should.

But the first call was a disappointment. No, they had no such patient as the one she sought; no they could not suggest anywhere else. Oh, she knew about St Columba's? Then why did she ask?

She fled, leaving the receptionist staring after her, and once outside caught her breath for a moment. It was dark now, and it was hard to see her surroundings, but she was aware of large buildings and a great many trees. It would be pleasant here in good weather, she thought, and then, with an almost physical effort, made herself think positively of the next address she had, about a mile away on the other side of the Hill.

Yes indeed, it was a private psychiatric clinic, but of course it couldn't possibly tell her the names of any of its patients. That would never do, the woman at the desk said reprovingly. 'I'm sure you wouldn't like to think of failure of confidentiality if *your* relative were here, now would you?'

George's spirits became even lower and as always that made her irritable. She was also feeling very patronized, a most disagreeable sensation, and it made her almost snarl at the woman. 'I'm not asking for a failure of confidentiality. I'm just trying to find a patient I know who's in a nursing home in Harrow, somewhere, for an addiction problem, so that I can visit her.'

'Well, I'm sorry. If you don't know whether she's here or not, I can't possibly tell you who is,' the woman said firmly. 'It wouldn't be right. Now, if you'll excuse me?'

George could have wept with rage. There was something about the woman's behaviour made her suspect that she did have the facts that George wanted. She wondered, for a brief moment, whether a bribe would work, but dismissed the idea as unworthy. There was genuine concern here for a patient's welfare, or so there seemed.

And then she thought, I'm a fool. I've got a trump card and I haven't played it.

She reached into her pocket and pulled out her purse. Tucked into the back of it, to her immense relief (because she usually forgot to refill that section) was one of her professional cards.

She handed it over to the woman. 'Could you please ask the doctor on duty if I could have a word,' she said with an air of superiority. 'As one medical colleague to another, you understand. I'm Dr George Barnabas of Old – of the Royal Eastern Hospital. And it is on a matter of great professional importance that I need to speak to him.'

The woman looked at the card and then at George and sniffed. 'Well,' she said. 'I suppose I have to ask, although ... Well, I'll

286

see if you can be fitted in.' And she went toiling away up a flight of stairs on the other side of the rather gloomy entrance hall, carrying George's card by one corner as though it were polluted.

She came down a couple of minutes later and scowled at George, and went back to her desk without saying anything. George opened her mouth to speak, but then behind her a voice came down from the top of the stairs, a cool and very self-assured voice.

'Dr Barnabas? You want to see me?' The face was a square one, framed by neat dark hair, and beautifully made up. 'I'm Dr Susan Napper. What can I do for you? I understand you're interested in one of our patients.'

31

George sat in a deep armchair, staring across an expanse of polished desk to where Dr Napper sat in a matching though rather more imposing chair. The room was softly lit, had three or four bowls of fresh flowers dotted around and what appeared to be original paintings on the walls. It breathed expense and George felt her ire rise; years of working in a cash-strapped NHS had given her a certain amount of contempt for what she regarded as the overly cushioned private health-care sector.

The woman was looking at her coolly, but now she smiled, a rather wintry stretching of the lips that clearly she meant to be friendly. 'So, what can I do for you?' She looked down at George's card, which was lying on her desk. 'I see you're a pathologist. You told my receptionist you wanted to talk to me on a medical matter, but I am a psychiatrist. I'm not sure . . . ?' She left the question dangling.

George took a deep breath and decided to go in baldly. 'I'm a forensic pathologist as well as holding a hospital appointment,' she said. 'And I'm working on the so called new Ripper case. You'll have read about it, I imagine, or seen the coverage.'

The thin smile faded and the handsome face looked suddenly pinched. 'I don't have to read about it,' she said after a moment. 'I have a – you could call it an indirect link with it.'

George opened her eyes wide. 'You have? How?'

Susan Napper sighed softly and lifted both hands to her face and rubbed her cheeks in a way that made her cheeks crumple, giving her a vulnerable air. 'I knew the victims. One of them in particular, I knew very well. His wife and I are friends, have been for years. We were at school together. The others, well, my husband is a Member of Parliament, so –'

'Oh,' George said blankly. 'You're Susan *Napper*. You're married to Marcus?'

'Yes. How clever of you!' There was a ghost of a real smile there now and George responded to it as warmly as she could.

'I'm sorry, I didn't connect your name when I heard it. Of course I know about you, though I never heard you were a doctor.'

Again Susan produced that thin cold smile. 'My husband tries to keep quiet about me. He's deeply ashamed of what I do.'

'*Ashamed?* Because you're a doctor?' George's irritation with this woman vanished under a flood of fellow feeling. 'But why?'

'Not because I'm a doctor.' She moved her hand to indicate not just the room they were in but the whole building. 'Because I work here. In private practice. He's Labour, you see. And I'm not. Though we still manage to stay reasonably contented together.'

'I see.' George looked at her closely, not fully understanding. Could two people of such widely divergent opinions really be content together? But that was not important, she reminded herself. It was the case that she was here to discuss, not marital politics.

'I'd heard ... That is, I was told that David CWG's wife – I'm sorry, David Caspar-Wynette-Gondor –'

'Don't apologize. We all used the initials. It's a terrible name to be saddled with. He hated it, but he didn't think he had any right to change it. And in a way it amused him to have what he described as such an aristocratic handle to such an ordinary old tin kettle as he was. He and I got on very well, actually. He liked to tease me about my job, and I gave him a hell of a time over his politics.' She smiled reminiscently. 'Poor old David.'

'Well, yes ...' George was embarrassed now but pressed on. 'Anyway, we were told that his wife had called you the night he – the night he didn't return when she expected him.'

Susan Napper's face smoothed and went blank. 'Yes,' she said. 'I'm afraid I – I –' And now the attempt to control her expression failed and her forehead creased. 'I paid no attention. It was late. I thought she was all right really and I was a bit – brisk with her. She hung up on me, to tell the truth. But she said she hadn't been drinking, and idiot that I suppose I must be, I believed her. I meant well, but she hung up on me, which is always so maddening and – well, there it is. I didn't call her back. I should have done, but it was so very late and Marcus was tired and annoyed by the call, so I didn't. And then of course when David was found she –' She took a deep breath and seemed to recover some of her self-control. 'Well, not surprisingly she lapsed back into quite severe illness. She drank again, though she had been largely dried out, and that caused major problems, and then she went into a fugue. You know the term?'

George looked at her sharply. 'Oh, even pathologists know about fugues! We're not all limited to laboratories. Some of us have had clinical experience.'

'Sorry. It's just that not everyone does. I've had GPs who've looked blank at the word. Consultants too, come to that. They think it means music, not taking off and wandering about.'

George decided not to allow herself to be offended after all. 'So you think she went wandering, not knowing where or –'

'I'm quite sure she did,' Susan said. 'It was here she wandered from. I agreed to take her as a patient though I've usually refused to in the past. I never think it is wise for a friend to be treating a friend and, as I say, we go back a long way, to our schooldays. However, the family were very anxious I take her, so I did. But we don't operate a locked-door establishment here, and she took off in an hysterical state.'

'I know,' George said. 'I remember. There was a good deal of anxiety. She was in her nightwear, barefoot, I believe.'

'Yes. The police found her of course, eventually. In a shopping-centre doorway.' She gave a bark of a laugh then, painful in its harshness. 'She'd been there all night, but they'd paid no attention because they'd thought she was just one of the homeless. I ask you! Anyway, we got her back here the next morning and I did my best for her. It wasn't easy, since she was desperately angry with me. Her anger of course was due to the loss of David who had been the centre of her life, but I was the nearest target. I had a colleague treat her, but all the same . . .'

She sighed deeply and again rubbed her face with what, George realized now, was a characteristic movement. 'It was hard. I wasn't sorry when they decided to take her away.'

'Take her away? Who and where?'

'Her family,' Susan said. 'They'd brought her to me at first because I knew her, but then she became more ill and withdrawn. I had to tell them we were not being very successful. She'd made a botched suicide attempt, using a knife on her wrists. They said at first to keep her here anyway, but then they said they wanted her nearer to them. I didn't argue. In fact I was relieved.'

The woman's face went smooth and blank again and George looked at her consideringly. That she was in distress over her friend was clear, but that she was trying to behave professionally was also apparent. Poor thing, George found herself thinking and then, impulsively, said as much.

'Oh, poor you! What a lousy position to be in. It's hell being a doctor sometimes. I remember when my ma first developed Alzheimer's, we – well, I know how it is. I am sorry.'

Susan, who had been sitting with her eyes closed for a moment, opened them and said simply, 'Thank you.'

There was a short silence and eventually George spoke again, a little awkwardly. 'I don't want to harass you, but I do really need to know where she is. I need to find out where she was and so forth on certain dates. It's all tied up with trying to find the perpetrator of these killings.'

Susan bit her upper lip thoughtfully and looked at her for what seemed to George a long time and then said, 'I can assure you that it's exceedingly unlikely she can tell you anything about dates and times. When she left us, she was in a world of her own. I don't think she even knew she was moving from here. She was so withdrawn she was practically catatonic. So there seems no real point in breaking confidence, does there?'

'I'm also concerned for her safety,' George said.

Again Susan Napper looked considering, and there was another pause. Eventually she said, 'Safety? If it's in any doubt, why aren't the police here? Why just you? You're the pathologist on the case and I can understand your interest, but I didn't know pathologists got involved in anything more than autopsies and tests and the usual pathological stuff.'

George took a deep breath. Damned doctors, she thought, and then smiled at her own absurdity, and for a moment Susan smiled back, as though she knew what she was thinking.

'Oh, blast!' George said. 'O K, I'm going further than my remit, I can't deny. But I'm interested. I've got a couple of weeks off from the hospital and I'm so hooked into this case it's – well, I simply have to take part. And Gus – the Superintendent in charge – is a – um, special friend.'

'Partner?' Susan said.

'Yes,' George said after a moment's hesitation. 'And we do work together on some cases. I've helped with several so far.'

'Hmm.' Susan sighed, a deep, rather tremulous sound. 'Well, I don't suppose you mean any harm. O K, tell me precisely why you're after Marietta and I'll see what I might be able to do to help.'

George told her. It seemed the only way. 'We found a witness, Gus and I. A wino, homeless, saw two men go into the Spitalfields Market storeroom where the body of Lord Durleigh was found. Of course Marietta was married to his brother, and he had already been a victim. This witness said the men were whispering, and one of them was Italian and –'

'Italian? But what has that to do with all this?'

'Hear me out. The wino was a bright spark for all her condition, but she jumped to a conclusion: she said one was Italian and talking about wanting a smoke. And I thought, suppose what Sally – the wino – had heard was Lord Durleigh saying, "I want Marietta, where's Marietta?" Do you see?'

Susan stared at her and then repeated the words softly under her breath in a sort of whisper, 'I want Marietta. Where's Marietta?' And her face cleared. 'I'll be damned,' she said. 'Marietta, cigaretta. That really is *silly*.'

'I know,' George said. 'But it makes sense all the same, doesn't it? If you were an old woman who'd been abusing alcohol since God knows when so that your hearing was damaged by that as well as by age, and, no doubt, pretty filthy blocked external ears, couldn't you jump to the conclusion that you were hearing an Italian talking about cigarettes?'

'So have you any idea who might have been the other man?'

George looked at her and then made a small grimace. 'I'm not sure I should say.'

'Come off it!' Susan suddenly grinned a wide happy smile that transformed her. George thought, I like you, and grinned back.

'Oh, damn. All right. But for God's sake keep stumm. If anyone ever – Oh, hell, here I go again. Talking too much.'

'You'll have to. I won't tell you what I know about Marietta's whereabouts unless you do tell me.' Susan warmed to her theme. 'And I'm hardly a suspect myself, am I?' Her eyes sharpened then. 'Unless Marcus is. But that would be nonsense. He's more of a possible victim than a suspect. Anyway, that's what they all think.' She giggled. 'If you could hear and see them! They're all in a blue funk over it, thinking everyone they see has a knife tucked in his underpants ready to cut their throats.'

'Well, I suppose they're right. But you should be safe enough.' George was still uneasy, but the need to find Marietta was getting stronger by the moment. She had a deep conviction that in some way the woman was in danger of being the next victim. She didn't fit the pattern, of course, but she could be a direct link with the killer; he had used her name as bait to one of his victims, her brother-in-law, and she was the wife of another. It looked more and more likely that she was the factor that tied the whole affair together. In which case the murderer would need to get rid of her to protect himself. I have to find her, she thought, I have to.

So she took a deep breath and said, 'We've uncovered a criminal conspiracy as part of the investigations. A fashion scam that's made someone a fortune. We're not sure yet of all the people who are involved but we've got a pretty good idea of some of them. And I think the people in that might be after

Marietta, who may be in the position of knowing things she doesn't know she knows. If you see what I mean.'

'I do see what you mean,' Susan said. 'Well, will you tell me who these people are?'

'I don't want to. If I'm wrong it could be – well, you can imagine. I might start a huge witch hunt if you inadvertently let it out. And if I'm right and the killer finds out in some way that you know, then it'd put you at risk too, wouldn't it?'

'Oh, come on!' Susan said. 'This is daft. It means you're at risk yourself, if those are your criteria.'

'Oh,' George said, much struck. 'I suppose you're right. Well, so be it. That's a risk I'm prepared to take. It's a risk police take too, isn't it? And I'm sort of part of the police service. But you don't have to. Look, tell me where she is and I swear to you I'll tell you as soon as I possibly can what's happening. I can't say fairer than that.'

Susan looked at her and seemed to grow tired suddenly. 'Oh, what the hell,' she said. 'OK, I'll tell you. I had a phone call from her family saying –'

'Let's be clear. Which side of her family? Her own or her husband's?'

'Certainly not her own!' Susan said with a sudden harshness. 'Marietta hadn't spoken to her brother for years, and he and his wife and children are the only relations she has. She hated him because he got not only the title but every penny their father left, as well as the estate. The old man had this thing about keeping big estates whole for the heir, and wouldn't let his other child have any of it, apart from enough to educate her and to give her a sort of wedding present. And her brother's just as mean – even when David and Marietta were right on the breadline he wouldn't help them out. Said it was her own fault for marrying a Bolshie.' She laughed then. 'Not that David would have taken any money from him. If he'd even known she was asking her brother for help . . . Oh, well. It's all long ago now. No, it wasn't Marietta's brother who called. It was her brother-in-law.'

George tried to keep calm, to show no reaction. 'Her brother-in-law . . .' she said softly.

'Well, his secretary to be precise. That's what he called himself, though I gathered he was more of a personal assistant. He said Lord Durleigh – and I suppose we have to call him that now, don't we? He's the last of the brothers – was in Brussels as usual, so he had to make the arrangements. He said Lord Durleigh wanted her to be treated at home. That he had adequate care for her, a resident nurse – their old nanny, who is a sensible enough soul. I know her, of course, used to meet her on family holidays years ago. Anyway, he said Edward wanted Marietta to come home, and of course I couldn't hold her against her will. She wasn't sectioned or anything of that sort. If she wanted to go, she could go.'

'Did she want to go?'

'I told you she was so withdrawn she didn't care about anything. I told the secretary he had to come and ask Marietta herself what she wanted, and he did come. I was there when he talked to her. After a while she muttered, yes, she would go with him, though I told him I thought his questioning was a bit heavy. But there you go. I couldn't stop him, not legally. So, he took her away. And that's the last I saw of her. Or heard. I've phoned a few times, but the answerphone's always set and they never return any messages. So, there you have it. Go and talk to Edward if you want to know what's happened since then.'

'But it wasn't Edward who came for her,' George said, endeavouring not to let her excitement show. Her pulse was thick in her ears, rapid and heavy. 'The secretary, do you know his name, by any chance?'

'Oh, yes,' Susan said. 'Jasper Powell. It isn't a name you'd forget, is it? Rather old-fashioned, I suppose. Nice chap, he seemed. Very caring. Do you know the man?'

32

George drove back to London at a much easier speed than she had used coming out. It was now well past eight and the evening rush hour had petered out. When she stopped at traffic lights she could see people in their suburban living rooms at supper tables, or in front of the faint blue flicker of TV screens, and found herself thinking how comfortable it would be to be one of such a family, with no more to think about than the appetites of the children, the mood of a husband and the state of the housekeeping budget. Then, as she let in the clutch when the lights changed to release her, knew she was being foolish. The time would come for such activities; right now there was a puzzle to be solved and she had the heady sensation that comes just before the last pieces fall into place.

The plan of action, she decided, was to tell Gus all that she had worked out and then to go with him to Durleighton. The safest thing to do would be to reintroduce herself to Edna Lyons. She had shown herself to be a garrulous soul and if she were looking after Marietta, she would be sure to give the fact away, even if she'd been told not to. George remembered her conversation with the old woman and her lips curved a little. If I'm careful, I can coax her to tell me what I need to know, she thought, though I hope she does it without biblical quotes. I'm not as hot on those as I might be. She tried to remember the quote Nanny Lyons had used and the reason she had used it; but the memory eluded her. It wasn't significant anyway. It was more important to think about explaining to Gus why she had gone to seek out Marietta on her own when she'd promised him she'd do nothing in the meddling line ever again, or at least not until she had talked to him. But I couldn't talk to him, she told herself as she left the suburbs behind and took the slip road that led up to the speeding traffic on the A40. He wasn't there to talk to, was he? And I couldn't explain on the phone, because he was on a mobile and you can't trust them; radio buffs are always picking up stuff on police signals and it was a police rule that radio silence be observed on important matters.

So, she argued into the night as the car fled at ten miles an hour above the permitted speed towards the centre of town, I had no choice. In fact, I'm behaving very well; I could so easily have turned right on to the A40 when I left Harrow, and gone straight to Durleighton. As it is, I'm heading for home so that I can explain everything to Gus. He should be really pleased with me. And she bridled inside, as a child does, when contemplating the parental response to a good school report.

But she knew her lovely plans had all gone wrong as soon as she put her key in the door. He wasn't there. She could feel the emptiness out here in the road. The house was dark and quiet, with just one light burning in the hall, over the phone table, illuminating the sheet of paper which had been propped against the answerphone.

'Dear old B.,' she read. 'This is a bit of a bugger. I've been trying to call you all day, but you've had your phone switched off, or the battery's gone or something.'

She slapped her hand on her pocket and realized she'd gone out without her phone and felt the heat of shame filling her face. Of all the stupid things to have done! She read on.

The thing is, ducky, I have to go to Belfast. Panic you not, there's no big push on. It's just they're having a major summit-type get-together of police people to sort out some security stuff, and the Commissioner can't go on account of the old boy's promised his missus he'll be with her tonight for a dinner. In all fairness, it's their Ruby Wedding celebration, so you can hardly blame him, and seeing I'm his blue-eyed boy, smirk, smirk, I have to go for him. Roop's got the Ripper case in hand, knows what he's got to do and if you come up with anything, share it with the lad. He may be dour but he's dead reliable. Take care, my darling, I shall miss the warmth of your interesting anatomical parts against my back as I sleep, but I'll pretend. I'll phone you in the morning. I love you. Be sure to eat a good supper – maybe you can have eels again with Kitty? – and I'll see you on Thursday evening, with a bit of luck and a following wind.

PS Did I say I love you? I do!

She dropped the note on the table and scowled at it. Oh, shit, she thought. Now what? He's left no number and I can hardly try to track him down by calling Scotland Yard. They'd have a fit that he'd even told me he's going to Belfast, with their passion for secrecy in these matters. Gus had told her often enough about how important it was he kept a low profile as far as his movements were concerned and she understood that. So what could she do?

Call Roop? The thought stuck in her mind like a burr. It's what I should do. It's what Gus would want me to do. And if it was anyone else in charge but Roop, I might do it. But damn it, he's the one who's in charge and I know what'll happen. He'll take it right out of my hands, tell me he'll deal with it and try to send me home to be good and wait for Gus.

Well, to hell with that, or, as Gus would say, bugger that for a game of soldiers. It's my clue and if Gus were here he'd understand and agree we could both go to Durleighton to track it down. No Gus, so I'll have to go alone.

'And if you don't like it, Gus, do the other thing,' she said aloud. On an impulse, she went and picked up her mobile from her desk, where she'd left it under a drift of papers. She dialled their own number and when the phone rang, and the answerphone clicked, stood there watching it record as she left Gus her message.

'You'll be livid when you get this message, sweetheart,' she said. 'But there you go. Life's like that sometimes. I've found out who the Italian is, only he isn't an Italian, but someone we know well. And I'm heading north – well, northwestwards I suppose it is, to see what more I can find out. In case you pick up this message with your mobile, I'll say no more. I too expect to be home by Thursday evening. And who knows? I may have the case in the bag. Something for you to look forward to? 'Bye now. Oh, and I love you too.' She banged the key on her phone to end the call and watched the answerphone bleep, flash its light and then settle down. She felt rather like a rebellious teenager. Which was, of course, nonsense. She was just getting on with the job. Wasn't she?

She was on the road again within half an hour. She had the forethought to pack a change of clothes, a toothbrush and some odds and ends of make-up and so forth, and threw the bag into the boot with a flourish that was, absurdly, aimed at Gus, and set out to drive to Durleighton.

It was late, very late; and she realized even before she left the London suburbs behind that there was no hope of furthering her investigations tonight. If she turned up at the pair of houses in the lane outside the town now, she'd cause a great deal of consternation. She would have to spend the night at the horrid Bald Monk and go first thing in the morning. It was maddening to have such a delay, but once she accepted its inevitability it made the journey much more pleasant. She could allow herself to drive within the speed limit and even decided to stop and have some supper at a motorway café. Whatever she ate there wouldn't be as bad as the offerings at the Bald Monk, she told herself, and also took the precaution of phoning ahead to the hotel to book a room. To arrive and be turned away at midnight would be tiresome to say the least. If she had to find other accommodation, better to discover that now.

The woman on her desk took her booking with a reasonable degree of efficiency and George finished her journey comfortably, checking into the Bald Monk just before midnight. The woman she had spoken to was still on duty, so that eased matters. George was in her room and in bed within half an hour.

She slept uneasily on the uncomfortable mattress and woke early, grateful to find that at least it wasn't raining, but it was a cold dull day and she felt the heaviness in her mood as she dressed, glad of the extra warm clothes she had brought. She waited till she felt it was late enough to go visiting; to appear before nine would be strange to say the least. Half past would be barely tolerable.

All the way there, retracing the journey on which Jasper had taken her after the injury to her leg, she rehearsed what she would say, knowing the likelihood was that she would not use her planned words; somehow they never worked out right, but it was helpful to go through the exercise anyway. She needed some sort of mental activity because the elation of the previous afternoon had quite gone. She felt uneasy as well as oppressed by the weather.

The houses looked much as they had when she had first seen them, though somehow rather less charming. But at least there was, to her relief, a wisp of smoke coming from a chimney. That showed that someone was up and about, and she parked the car outside and pushed open the gate.

There was a slick of early frost on the path and she almost slipped over at one point, landing on the doorstep with a small gasp of dismay as she righted herself; and the door opened at once. She had not had a chance to ring the bell, or to compose herself. Clearly she'd been seen from inside the house.

The old woman was peering round the door, her face creased with anxiety. 'What d'you want?' she said with some pugnacity, though her voice was shaky.

'Oh, Mrs Lyons, good morning,' George said, trying to sound friendly without being gushing. 'How are you?'

The door opened a little wider and the old woman peered at her. Then her face seemed to clear a little. 'Oh, it's you, is it? The lady what had her leg all battered by our Jasper.'

Relief filled George and she beamed at her. 'Indeed it is. How good of you to remember me.'

'Well, you got a look that people would remember,' Mrs Lyons said, a touch ungraciously. 'Is it better now?'

'Oh, yes, thanks. Almost. I only need a small plaster now.' George held out her leg to demonstrate.

'That's all right then.' Mrs Lyons stood there, making no move to invite her in or to hold the door any wider open.

'Um,' George said, and opted, if a little uncertainly, for the direct approach. 'May I come in?' She reached a hand out and pushed gently on the door in as ordinary a manner as she could. Mrs Lyons gave way, clearly disconcerted, and George immediately moved forwards, till she stood on the inside doormat, beaming at the nanny as she pulled off her coat.

'What a lovely fire you have going here! May I go and warm my hands at it? Then I'll feel the benefit of my coat when I go out. It's a very chilly morning.'

She handed her coat to Mrs Lyons with all the aplomb she could muster and went over to the fire, smiling cheerfully. 'It is nice to see you again! You were so kind to me that morning and I did appreciate it.'

'My pleasure, I'm sure,' Mrs Lyons said, sounding surly, and dropped George's coat on a chair beside the front door. She came further into the room. 'There's no one 'ere but – Jasper and Mr Edward, they're not 'ere, you know, and what's more I don't know when they'll be back, so there's no sense in your waitin' for 'em, is there?'

'Oh, that's all right,' George said sunnily and straightened up. None of the things she'd planned to say seemed to fit in; she looked at the old woman and decided that this time guile had to be her answer. 'I didn't come to see either of them,' she said. 'It's Marietta I want to see. I heard how ill she is, poor dear, and I thought the least I can do is pop down to visit her. I'd have brought some flowers, only to tell you the truth, the ones I saw in the shop in the town were so droopy, I thought they'd be an insult.' She laughed merrily. 'But then I thought, Marietta won't mind. It's having visitors that people like when they're ill, isn't it, not just flowers?'

'I thought you was a stranger when Jasper fetched you here.' Nanny Lyons was staring at her, torn between suspicion and relief. 'You never said you knew none of the family. You never said you knew our Marietta.'

'Didn't I? I thought I did.' George looked her frankly in the eyes with a direct inviting gaze. 'Are you sure I didn't say how

I'd known Marietta for – oh, years? Through Susan, you know. They were at school together and my sister was at the same school.' Don't ask me which school, for pity's sake, she prayed inside her head, or I'm in deep do-do.

Nanny Lyons didn't ask. She produced a rather unlovely gap-toothed grin and nodded, allowing the relief to overwhelm her doubts. 'Well fancy that! And me never knew! So what would your sister's name be? And how come she was at school in England and you an American an' all?'

George took off on one of her wild improvisations at once, and at a deep level loved every minute of it, risky though it was. 'Oh, she was my half-sister, you see. My mother married twice. After he left my ma – you know how it is with divorce these days – he came to England and he married an Englishwoman and it was their daughter, Dorothy, who was at school with Susan and Marietta.' Dorothy? she thought. What possessed me to use such a Godawful name? If I had a sister called that I'd refuse to speak to her. 'Yes, indeed,' she said and beamed again. 'Darling Dottie and Marietta were very close.'

Nanny shook her head. 'I thought I knew all the girls who were her friends,' she said. 'Seeing she and them used to come to the boys' parties when they was little. But there you go. I dare say my memory's not what it was.'

'Oh, Dottie left England many years ago,' George said reassuringly. 'Went to South Africa where she married a lawyer. So I dare say you'd have forgotten her. Anyway, how is Marietta?'

Nanny Lyons accepted the question without any anxiety this time. 'Not a bit well, poor baby.' She shook her head. 'I do all I can, o' course, to get her talkin', but she just lies there. I've had to change her medication, now she's so deep in her sleep. He told me it would make her sleepy, give her a chance to recover, like, that she needed the rest, and I was to see she got it, no matter what. But, well, it's very difficult.'

She shook her head again. 'I can't get her to swallow a thing now. So I'm putting the medicine into a rectal tube, the way we used to do for the very sick little babies when I was a student.' She nodded wisely. 'If they can't swallow and absorb their food through the mucous membrane of the stomach then they can have it put into the rectum and absorb it through the mucous membrane there.' She said it as though she was reciting a learned lesson and her eyes, distorted behind her heavy glasses, were bright with an air of satisfaction as she did so. 'I can't get a lot into her that way, but she gets her fluids and she gets her medicine and that's the most important. I'll soon get her plumped up again when she improves and I can start cooking for her, poor lamb.'

'May I see her?' George felt the anxiety thick in her belly and had to concentrate hard to avoid conveying it to Nanny Lyons. She had to be relaxed, relaxed, relaxed, she told herself deep inside, very cool does it. 'I'm a doctor myself, of course, so I'd be glad to check her for you.'

Nanny Lyons beamed. 'I'd forgotten that,' she said. 'You did say you was a doctor, didn't you? Well, well, imagine me, trained as I am, forgetting such a thing! Of course, doctor. You come along with me. I'm sure he won't mind *you* seeing her, not at all, though they was very strict about no one else disturbing her, on account of her needing all this rest. That's what a rest cure is, after all!' She laughed, pleased with herself. 'But a doctor' different, o' course. He didn't think much to the doctors here in Durleighton and I can't say as I know them, but he'll be glad indeed to have a London doctor to see her. Jasper was saying only yesterday that he thought a London doctor might have to come sometime. And here you are! Well, well. Did he send you then?'

'Er, I'm not sure I quite remember how it was arranged . . .' she began, following Nanny up the shallow wooden staircase to the upper landing. Three doors ran off it and the old woman turned and peered at George when they reached the first of them.

'Oh, well, I know how it is,' she said indulgently. 'With the whole family worried about the poor girl it's natural enough. Now come along in. I'll open the curtains.'

The room was dim, and smelled of disinfectant. Dettol, thought George, and was taken back in an instant to her childhood when minor injuries were treated with the pungent stuff. It's the essential hospital smell, she thought, and watched as Mrs Lyons turned back from the window and looked at the bed. She's recreating her past. She's got a patient and she's trying to treat her the way she was taught to with Dettol and darkened rooms.

Now she too looked at the bed and managed somehow to keep her face expressionless. The woman who lay in it was on her back, her head and shoulders propped up on three pillows set in an armchair fashion. Her hands were resting on the covers, and her head was neatly centred on the pillow. And both hands and face were emaciated to a very marked degree. This woman, George thought as she moved forwards, is starving.

'How long has she been like this?' she asked sharply, bending her head and looking at Marietta's face more closely. There was a hectic flush on her cheeks, and the eyes were not fully closed, showing a white rim. Gently George raised one eyelid with her forefinger. The eye did not move, but stared sightlessly ahead. The woman was clearly deeply unconscious.

Nanny Lyons peered at her through her heavy glasses. 'Sleeping like that? Oh, it's been, let me see, three days now. I got fretted at first, I thought she was sleeping too much, but he said it was all right, she was supposed to be like that on this medicine.'

'Who said?' George asked, and her tone sounded sharp even in her own ears. But instead of it alarming Nanny Lyons, it seemed to make her stand more erect and become more professional than ever.

'Mr Jasper,' she said. 'He showed me the pills what the doctor in the hospital gave her, and I checked the label and it said they were for her.' She put her hand in her apron pocket and pulled out the bottle. 'Here they are. You can check, doctor.'

George took the bottle, opened it and spilled the contents into her palm. They were large gelatine capsules, half blue, half green, and she frowned, trying to remember what they were; they had a vaguely familiar look. The label read only, 'The capsules. Three to be taken every three hours.' The last phrase was the easiest to read, though in general the label looked old and rubbed. George frowned again.

'I said to him it was a heavy dose. I thought, I mean, I'm used

304

to two of anything every four hours, but like he said, times change and new methods are used.'

'This doesn't look like a new label.' George was talking almost to herself. 'It's undated, there's no name of the drug on it, and there always is now. This was how things used to be dispensed . . .'

She looked again at the capsules and then caught her breath. Tuinal, she thought. Tuinal, a heavy barbiturate. There'd been a suicide, she remembered, whom she'd autopsied, who'd taken a massive overdose using similar capsules that she'd had in her medicine cupboard for many years. That was when she'd last seen the drug. 'No wonder this label looks so old,' she said aloud. 'This drug hasn't been used for years because barbiturates are now known to be so dangerous. They're the last thing you would want to use for a deeply depressed patient.'

'I'm sorry, doctor?' Nanny Lyons said, unable to hear for George had spoken in a low voice. 'What did you say?'

'It doesn't matter,' George said. She put the capsules back in the bottle and turned to look at Marietta and put her finger on her pulse. It was thready, rapid and there were occasional missed beats. Not good, George thought. Not good at all. This woman needs special care and needs it fast. 'Mrs Lyons,' she said carefully. 'I'm very worried about her. I think she ought to be in hospital.'

The old woman's face crumpled as she stared back. 'In hospital? She won't get better nursing there than what she gets here! What modern nurse knows you can take medicines like that and open the capsules to dissolve the stuff inside into dextrose and water and give it per rectum? They wouldn't have the sense! They don't know, for all their university degrees. That was why Mr Jasper brought her to me. She was in a hospital and they treated her so bad she was wretched there. Doesn't she look lovely and comfy! Not a mark on her. Most people in this state gets bedsores, you know, these days. I've heard how they don't do proper back care any more. But I've rubbed her back and made rings for her heels and elbows so she don't get pressure sores there, and −'

'It's not nursing she needs,' George said gently. 'You're doing that splendidly. It's medical care I'm worried about. Please let me arrange for her to go to hospital.' And then she had a brilliant idea. 'You can go with her as her special nurse, if you like. I'm sure that'll be all right.' Anything, she thought, she would have promised her anything to get Marietta out of the house and into safe medical hands. 'Would you like that?'

Nanny Lyons looked unsure for a while and then at last, nodded. 'Well,' she said. 'If you're sure, doctor.'

'Oh, I'm sure,' George said with supreme confidence. 'I'm a specialist in cases like this, you know. I really do advise it. Doctor's orders, you see.'

'Well,' said Nanny Lyons, straightening her back again. 'Of course that's that then, isn't it?'

33

George carried Marietta to the car without too much difficulty. She was as light a burden as a human could be; if she weighs as much as forty kilos it's a lot, George thought, and gently lowered her into the back seat, alongside Nanny Lyons who was already ensconced there and looking very anxious.

'Now, Mrs Lyons,' she said. 'She's well wrapped up and I've got the car heater on full blast, but you make sure she stays well covered, and of course that her head doesn't loll too much. We have to keep her airway open.'

Nanny Lyons nodded seriously and put her hand behind Marietta's head to hold it forwards; she was clearly too occupied in doing as George told her and worrying about Marietta to think of anything else. And George, running back to the house to close the door and pick up her bag, and then hurrying back to the car, was grateful for that. Clearly Mrs Lyons had been told no one was to know Marietta was at the house, let alone allow anyone in to see her; that had been made clear by her behaviour from the moment George had arrived; soon she would remember her instructions and perhaps get agitated. And Marietta was enough for George to cope with at present.

She drove into the town carefully, checking Marietta constantly through the rear-view mirror. Nanny Lyons, in a very old nursing uniform coat and matching hat, which she wore well down over her forehead, sat beside Marietta very uprightly and holding her head steady with one hand while holding on to the unconscious woman's shoulder with the other to stop her rocking as the car turned corners. It was not a comfortable journey for George, either.

She found Durleighton's one hospital easily enough – it was clearly signposted – and parked the car outside on the gravel and ran up the steps to the main entrance. There was the usual surly man in the porter's lodge there who put his head out when George asked for the A & E entrance and shook it with a certain relish.

'Ain't got one here,' he said. 'You'll have to go over to Ardenford for that. We're just a –'

'Oh, for God's sake.' She let all the tension of the past twenty-four hours boil over and roared at him. 'Don't be crazy, man! This woman is dying, you hear me? Dying. I'm a doctor, and I have to get her into reliable medical hands right *now*. At once. So get me a senior doctor and get him fast.'

The man looked terrified, as well he might, for she looked and sounded like the wrath of doom, and bobbed back into his box to reach for the phone. She heard him mutter into it and then turned to look again out into the driveway where she could see Nanny Lyons still holding Marietta upright. She turned back, burning with impatience, in time to see a man in a grey suit come down the staircase at the far side of the hallway.

'I understand you're asking for A & E?' he said with careful courtesy. 'I'm sorry, we don't have that service here.'

'Have you got doctors?' she roared again, deliberately this time; it had worked so well before, after all. 'Have you got beds? All I need is a safe medical bed to take care of a woman whose life is at major risk. It's not that she's in need of desperately difficult care, it's just that –'

The noise she was making seemed to have galvanized the place. People were peering down the stairs and heads were coming out of doors on all sides. One such door, however, opened widely, and a large woman in a white coat came striding out. She was untidy to an amazing degree, with stockings that were in rings round her ankles and badly bagged at the knee, a skirt held in place in front by an oversized safety pin and sparse hair pinned into a misshapen bun at the nape of her neck. But her eyes were bright and very intelligent and she looked friendly enough. George whirled.

'You're a doctor?' she demanded.

'Neurology,' the woman said comfortably. 'That is, I run a small unit for geriatric patients with long-term neurological damage. What *is* the noise about? What can we do for you?'

'Save a life,' George said grimly and launched into an animated explanation, describing her own status, both medically and in police terms, and making much of the fact that Marietta was a woman involved unwittingly in the Ripper murders case. And then said, 'I believe her life is at real risk. She knows something that will incriminate the murderer, I'm sure of it. All I need is a safe bed for her under the care of a decent doctor. She's been appallingly overdosed with barbiturates – and that of course is the doing of the murderer. I know who he is now – but she's still alive and I believe we're in time to pull her back. Please, will you –'

'Will I!' the woman said jubilantly and turned to the man in the suit on the stairs. 'Charles, I've got an empty side ward on Hainault. Let me have it. *Now.*'

The man looked bemused. 'But Dr Kelley, how can I? Whose case is this? What's her address and post code? Is she coming in from a fundholder? Or on the local contract? You know that's impossible till next April, we're over budget as it is. Or is it an extra-curricular referral? Because, if so –'

'Oh, Charles, go and play with your computer,' Dr Kelley boomed. She had a voice that could be heard, George suspected, on the other side of the road. 'I'm taking this case. We'll worry later about who'll pay for it.'

'ECR,' George said swiftly. 'It'll be an extra contractual referral. I'll see to it. She lives in London usually. I'll make her health authority pay.'

The man called Charles seemed to cheer up marginally. 'Well, if it's going to be paid for, well enough. Here, Davidson, get a trolley will you? There's a new patient for Hainault Ward.'

George breathed a deep sigh of relief and went to fetch her patient from her car. Marietta's safe, she told herself, at last.

*

Dr Kelley proved to be a perfect ally. She threw herself into the business of both caring for and treating Marietta with an enthusiasm that knew no bounds. She had no objection at all to allowing Nanny Lyons to act as a special nurse, under the guidance of the ward sister on Hainault.

'She's always short staffed,' she said happily. 'So she'll be enchanted to have another pair of hands. Oh, this is a lovely change from the usual!' And she bustled off to chivvy Sister to organize an intravenous infusion for Marietta, who was going to need all the fluids they could get into her to deal with the overload of barbiturates she had been given.

By the time Marietta was settled, with her head lowered so that her circulatory depression was aided, an IV line in place to provide her with fluids, and a catheter put in to drain her bladder and maintain her kidneys, George felt a good deal better. The only risk now was pneumonia and, looking at Dr Kelley and Nanny Lyons, she knew that was not going to be a complication if they could help it. Marietta would be made to cough and deep breathe the moment she had any responses at all, and she was not in as deep a coma as George had at first feared. In time there was no reason why she shouldn't recover well.

'Fortunately she's had her overdose over a longish period of time,' Dr Kelley said. 'They tolerate that better than one massive dose, you'll agree, I'm sure.'

George, who had forgotten more about barbiturates overdoses than Dr Kelley was ever likely to know, was tactful and made it clear she bowed to her colleague's greater knowledge. Dr Kelley was, therefore, a very happy lady.

And so was Nanny Lyons. She had taken off her nurse's coat and hat to reveal herself in her usual overall, but it didn't look all that different from the nursing staff of the ward, about whom she was able to be very scathing indeed.

'Call themselves nurses?' she grumbled. 'And not a cap or a belt in sight. More like skivvies, if you ask me. It's a good thing I'm here to take care of the poor young lady.'

'Indeed it is,' George said. She was standing at the foot of the bed watching Marietta's breathing and trying to judge whether she was doing it rather better than she had been at the house. It was hard to be sure. Nanny Lyons followed her gaze and looked anxious.

'She's still having her medication, is she?'

'Um, no.' George thought it better to be honest this time. 'It turns out not to be the right one.'

Nanny sighed. 'I'm glad,' she said simply. 'I was beginning to worry. It was all very well for Mr Jasper to say it was prescribed, but I never met the doctor, did I? And she did seem to me to be ailing more and more.' She swallowed then and said with a little burst of confidentiality, 'To tell you the truth, doctor, my eyes aren't what they were. There was a time when I was known for my sharpness in every way. My hearing, my eyes and the way I thought things out . . .'

'I'm sure,' George said sympathetically and, unwilling to leave just yet, though she knew she ought to report this latest development to Rupert, sat down on another chair beside her. They both watched Marietta's frail chest lifting and falling with her shallow breaths.

'Tell me how it was in the old days, Mrs Lyons, will you? I'd love to know. I trained in medicine in the late seventies, you see, and early eighties, so I'm a bit . . .' Keeping Nanny Lyons happy was essential, George thought. And most old people loved reminiscing.

Nanny Lyons cackled at that. 'Jilly come lately? Well, it's nice of you to admit it. Not many does. What do you want to know?' She stretched her neck a little proudly. 'My memory's fine no matter how the rest of me may be gettin' a bit battered and worn.'

George smiled. 'Tell me what you used to do. The job you most enjoyed.'

'Oh, no question about that!' the old woman said readily and touched the hand of the comatose woman in the bed. 'It was midwifery. I always hoped, you know, as I'd be able to deliver this one's babies, the way I did her husband, but it wasn't to be. Miscarriages she'd had, any number, poor little girl. It'd break your heart. It's what turned her to . . . you know. Made her the way she is.'

George was looking at her, her mind running fast. 'You say you delivered her husband? David?'

'Oh yes! They wouldn't have no one else, Lord and Lady Durleigh, in them days. I'd been with 'em five years then, you see, and I was worried. I mean, it was one thing to be delivering babies when you was doing it all the time, but I'd stopped, hadn't I? I'd been with the twins, you see.'

'You're not being quite clear,' George said carefully. There was something important here and she couldn't be sure what it was, but she felt the significance; knew she'd already been told in some way, and couldn't quite remember what it was. It had been hanging about tantalizingly at the back of her mind for days now, and she still couldn't quite catch hold of it. Now she looked at the old head bent over Marietta, and stopped trying to remember. She concentrated on Nanny Lyons instead.

The old woman sighed a little impatiently. 'I was hired by Lord and Lady Durleigh when she was seven months pregnant with the twins. They guessed it was twins, she was so big – they had none of this fancy machinery that you can look at the babies with now.'

'Ultrasound,' murmured George.

'That's right. They didn't have it in those days. Just experience was all, and she said she wanted the best midwife she could get and sent to my hospital and they recommended me.' Her chest seemed actually to swell with pride as she said it. 'So, I come down to live in Durleigh Abbey and oh, but it was fancy in those days. Servants – even I had a little maid to look after me! – and entertaining and hunting meets and hunt balls, everything. Well, she got ill, didn't she, nearly at thirty-nine weeks she was. I checked her and the cervix was soft and a head engaged, and I thought she's going into labour any minute. But she just didn't really get going and I was worried about the babies. I checked the foetal heartbeat every half-hour – and we didn't have the fancy machines for that either, just our ears and experience.' She was proud again. 'And I'd had a lot of experience which was why the hospital sent me to Durleigh. Anyway, I got really worried. The babies' hearts seemed to me to be showing foetal distress – fast, irregular, the lot. And then there was some meconium in the liquor when her waters went and I thought, oh, no, that's it. I'm not hanging about. I wanted to do the delivery myself of course, I don't deny it, but I'm not stupid and never was. I sent for the doctor and oh, there was a panic! He said it was right to get him, that he had to do a Caesar right away. There wasn't even time to get her to hospital! So he did it there at the Abbey. We fixed up one of the small stillrooms and he fetched the anaesthetic and I did it for him – he started it, see, and then he got me to carry on with it, though not too much because all he had was ether and that's a worry with the babies, you see, and there you go. Big they were, considering. Richard, who was the first out, he was almost five pounds and Edward, he was only three ounces less. We put them on the kitchen scales, I remember. Bonny babies they were, so lovely. And she fed them both, she did, amazing woman she was. And I nursed her all through till her stitches healed and she was properly on her feet again and then one of the babies – Richard it was – for all he was the biggest and all that, he got enteritis and croup, so I stayed to get him well. It was as nasty a go of croup as I'd ever dealt with, and somehow I never went back to hospital. I stayed with them, and then when she got pregnant with David she swore no more Caesars for her, she'd have him natural and it was a high risk. But she insisted. I said she was an amazing woman, didn't I? Well, she was. And so I said, well, all right, I will stay. And it all went fine. David was a small baby but vigorous and did very well. And now here's this poor little thing, never going to have one of her own with him.'

The old eyes filled with tears and her thick glasses misted so that she had to take them off and rub them clear. 'And I always promised myself I'd deliver her.'

She was silent for a moment, seeming almost exhausted by the great tide of talk that had overwhelmed her. George sat and watched her and then looked at Marietta, once more to dig into her memory for whatever it was that was bothering her, but couldn't find it. There was something she had been told, and by this woman. It was getting late, she thought. Concentrate.

'Still,' Nanny said cheerfully then. 'There's always Lady Durleigh, isn't there?'

'I'm sorry?'

'Barbara, her name is. Lady Durleigh. She doesn't have much to do with things, either at the Abbey or on the estate, not like our Mr Edward, being she's a bit on the shy side, but she'd let me look after her, I'm sure. Not that we've ever talked about it, but I *am* almost family, aren't I? When the time comes, she'll agree. Poor thing. A widow and all, but at least she's got something to remember my dear Mr Richard by. Oh, he was a lovely baby and I'm sure she'll have a lovely boy too. That's another of the newfangled things I don't hold with. Knowing the baby's sex before it's born! It takes all the excitement out, doesn't it?'

'I hadn't thought about her,' George said. 'No one seems to have mentioned her much. She's Richard's widow, of course –'

'That's right. She was away when – when it all happened. When my darling boys died. Oh, I was so glad she was. Gone to visit her mother see, in New Zealand. While she could, I suppose. She'd not told anyone as she was in the family way, though I suppose Richard, rest his soul, I suppose he knew. Anyway, she's still there, and she told me, only said I should keep her secret a bit longer.' She looked up sharply then, clearly troubled. 'Oh dear, and here's me telling you, a stranger! But you won't say nothing, will you? It's only me and her mother in New Zealand knows, and –'

'Trust me,' George said, crossing her fingers behind her back. 'I'm a doctor.'

'Yes, o' course.' Nanny Lyons brightened. 'Hippocratic oath, so *that's* all right. I have my nurses' code too; we don't talk out of school neither. And she only phoned and told me she's pregnant to cheer me up, I think. And it did, oh it did!'

'I'm sure it would.' George sighed as she caught sight of the clock above the bed. 'I have to go.'

'Oh, must you?' the old woman said and went a mottled pink. 'Well, I'm sure you must, doctor, but it's so nice to have someone to talk to who listens, you know? Mr Edward, he's never got time and as for Mr Jasper' – she shook her head – I never feel quite . . . well, never mind.'

'Quite what?' George was diverted.

'Comfortable, I suppose,' the old woman said after a pause. 'He's a funny person really.' She shrugged. 'I can't say how, not really. I always think he's a bit like Agag who came unto Samuel delicately, putting on a show, like.'

'Agag?' George was bewildered now.

Nanny Lyons sighed. 'No one knows their Bible any more,' she said almost reprovingly. 'I was brought up on it. I don't believe every mortal word, mind you, but there's things in there, and it helps me understand.'

'Agag?' George said again with an upward inflection, wanting more information and Nanny Lyons sighed again, sharply this time.

'First book of Samuel, chapter fifteen, verse thirty-two. King James' version, of course.'

'Oh, of course.' George's head was spinning now, as the memory that had been tormenting her at last emerged, slowly and painfully. 'I think you quoted the Bible to me last time I met you,' she said carefully. 'To do with the twins and their names.'

'Eh? Oh, yes!' Nanny Lyons laughed. 'Genesis. Chapter thirty-eight, verses twenty-seven to thirty. It was Lady Durleigh, rest her sweet soul, who said we should have called them Pharez and Zarah, not me. But she was right, of course, not that it really mattered all that much. I mean, brothers are brothers, aren't they? They always look out for each other.'

For a moment George wanted to quote another story from Genesis, but she didn't. Quite apart from the fact that unlike the old woman beside her she would not be able to quote chapter and verse, she didn't want to alarm her. So she bit her tongue.

'Well,' she said. 'I must be on my way. I'll be back to visit very soon, but I think you'll find she's safe now. And she'll get better quickly. You will stay here, won't you? You won't call anyone or talk to anyone?'

315

'Oh, I won't.' Nanny Lyons sounded fervent. She reached out and took Marietta's flaccid hand again. 'She's my patient, isn't she? Of course I'll stay here.'

'Not – not even – well, not any one,' George said, and the old woman cocked her head at her.

'Hmm,' she said and then nodded and turned back to her contemplation of her patient. 'I s'pose so.'

And with that George had to be satisfied.

34

Back at the Bald Monk, George settled to the phone. People had to be told what had happened and be alerted to what Jasper was up to; and it had to be done fast. And by people she had to admit she meant Rupert Dudley. Who else was there she could enlist, after all? But she still felt unhappy about talking to him. Oh, Gus, she thought, where are you when I need you?

First of all she phoned home to pick up any messages on the answerphone, manipulating the remote control that played them back in her usual impetuous fashion so that at first the wretched thing wouldn't work. But at last it did. She listened impatiently to her own message to Gus, then held her breath, full of hope; and finally breathed out, miserable and angry with him. There should have been a message from him; why hadn't he picked up hers? He had a remote control too; he could have done, and then he could have told her where to reach him.

She slammed down the phone irritably, and sat there, gnawing her lower lip and at last, unwillingly, but knowing it was inevitable, dialled Ratcliffe Street nick, using the number of a line direct to the incident room. Roop, she was told, was not there. Could anyone else help? She wanted to cheer, and then was angry with herself for being so unreasonable.

'Yes, is Mike Urquhart there?'

'Sorry, no. He's out too.'

'Oh, damn,' she said. And then in a moment of inspiration, 'Julie Bentley?'

This time she struck gold and Julie's voice, welcome as a cold drink on a hot day, clattered in her ear. 'Hello, Dr B. How are things?'

'Extraordinary, Julie. You can have no idea. Listen, I have to report to Roop. Gus is away and I have to tell someone. I've found Marietta and –'

'Marietta?' Julie sounded puzzled. 'Was she lost?'

'Oh, it'll take too long to explain. All I can say is, if Roop comes in, *please* tell him I'm in Durleighton, that Marietta is here and that –' She stopped then as a faint click sounded in her ear. She realized almost as soon as she heard it that it was probably just the earpiece had tapped the side of her glasses, but it had been enough to remind her to be careful. 'Look, Julie, I'd better not say too much. This is a land line, but it's on an extension and you never know. The thing is, I know who the murderer is. He's been trying to kill Marietta, but I've got her safe now. I know what Sally meant when she talked about an Italian. So tell Roop, will you? Try to find out where he is and get a message to him. It really is important.'

'This isn't fair!' Julie almost wailed it. 'I'm trying to understand what you're on about and you won't –'

'Oh, Julie, please don't waste time! Try to find him. I'll give you my number here and you get him to call me as soon as you track him down, OK? Then first chance I get I promise I'll call you and let you know. But I'll tell you this much, the – um – the job we first did together, remember, is all part of it. And the second job too. That's where the answer lies. It's someone involved with that.'

Clearly Julie couldn't stop herself. 'Alice?' she breathed.

'I told you, this phone's on a switchboard in a hotel! I think we should be careful. So, do as I ask you, Julie, and call me back. But be *careful*. OK?' And she hung up.

All she could do now was sit and wait, and it was going to be difficult. She was prepared to fight every inch of the way with Roop to be allowed to stay on the chase, right at the front, until they'd got Jasper. She wanted to see him when he was arrested, wanted to talk to him if she could, to get the chance to find out the whys and wherefores of the killings.

That he had been making a great deal of money out of the fashion scam was clear enough. That he thought it was worth killing to preserve it, once Sam Diamond found out what was going on – and that had been the springboard of the whole series of deaths – was understandable. But why all the others? And why, above all, that method?

The others, she thought, sitting and staring sightlessly at the phone, were killed because – and the pieces clicked neatly into place in her mind – because Jasper was Alice's partner on the legal side. After all, Alice's business was an apparently kosher one; it had to be run legally, and she had used Sam's status as an MP to provide public assurance that it was. And that had probably been the way Alice had met Jasper, through some Parliamentary shindig or other, which brought in the CWG connection. Was Edward gay? The fact that Lord Durnell had said so that night at the Country Sports Association reception at the House of Lords was, after all, meagre evidence it was so. He was a wicked old gossip, the sort who liked to invest every situation with drama. The fact that Edward was a bachelor with bachelor friends didn't prove he was gay – and his particular bachelor friend was very much a womanizer, although, George told herself, that doesn't prove anything, any more than Lord Durnell's gossip did. Jasper could be the sort to hunt with either hares or hounds, whichever was the most profitable. So, possibly Edward was indeed homosexual, and that had been the heart of their relationship: the money or status Jasper got from whoever he was with. And she remembered how he behaved with the woman from Sloane's shop. So he'd have been close to Alice too; she, Alice, had recruited Jasper to her scheme – or had it been the other way round? Had Jasper been the criminal who, seeing Alice's business as a useful front for his own ideas, had scooped her up? It seemed possible. Either way, once his lover Edward found out and somehow let the information reach his brothers, that had been enough for Jasper to add them to his list of victims. As for the rest . . .

Again she chewed her lip. This wasn't working. There had been one dummy run, of that she was sure, she told herself. The killer had opted to get rid of Lord Scroop just to try out his method – but at the back of her mind a small voice argued; that's not good enough, just plain not good enough. No one would go to that sort of risk just to practise, surely? It doesn't make sense.

'Does any of it make sense?' she retorted aloud, arguing with herself rather absurdly. Why go to all the trouble of copying Jack the Ripper's crimes if all you want to do is get rid of people?

To make it look like a serial killer's work, she thought then and stared sightlessly down at the bedside table where the frustratingly mute phone stood, trying to see her way round that idea. It made some sense, in a horrible way. If a series of crimes makes the police think, serial killer, then surely they don't look at other possibilities. Like closer contacts, friends and families.

The same words went round and round in her head; she couldn't think clearly at all because of her anxiety, waiting for the call from Roop. Then her eyes, which had been glazed, focused again and she stared at the phone like a lovesick teenager who thought doing so would make it ring.

It was an old-fashioned handset, and it stood on a book, a dark blue cloth-covered one. She took it out from beneath the phone, just for something to do; and then was about to put it back on the bedside table, for it was only that inevitable fitting of a hotel room, a Gideon Bible, when she stopped. What was it Nanny Lyons had said?

She closed her eyes, staring back at her conversation with the old woman, trying to recreate the words in her mind. There had been two: one was about Agag walking delicately – well, that one wasn't terribly important. It was the other that mattered. Genesis. She could remember that, could hear the old woman saying it. And she strained her memory again, praying it would work for her aurally as well as visually. Would her eidetic memory work for something she had heard?

She squeezed her eyes shut, putting all her concentration on sound and then, slowly, there it was: Nanny Lyons' cracked old voice saying, 'Genesis. Chapter thirty-eight, verses twenty-seven to thirty.'

She opened the Bible and leafed through the pages rapidly. At least she remembered that Genesis was the first book of the Old Testament; and she found it easily enough. Chapter thirty-eight: 'It happened at that time that Judah went down from his brother's . . .'

'No,' she said aloud. 'Verse twenty-seven.' And then she found it.

27   When the time came for her to give
      birth, there were twin boys in her womb.
28   As she was giving birth, one of them put
      out his hand; so the midwife took a scarlet
      thread and tied it on his wrist and said,
      'This one came out first.'
29   But when he drew back his hand, his brother
      came out, and she said, 'So this is how you
      have broken out!' And he was named
      Perez.
30   Then his brother, who had the
      scarlet thread on his wrist, came out and
      he was given the name Zerah.

Slowly she put the book down and stared at the wall opposite, her head spinning. The language and name spellings were different in this Gideon version of the Bible – no doubt Nanny Lyons was accustomed to the King James translation – but it was obviously the right quotation, and it made all her other thinking about the case seem puerile. If the twins' mother had thought it apt to say she would call her boys after the twins in this story, it meant only one thing. That one of them had been a hand presenter and then . . .

'No!' she said loudly. 'Of course not. She *told* me what happened.' And again she heard the old woman's voice.

'. . . the cervix was soft and a head engaged . . . But she just didn't really get going . . . The babies' hearts seemed to me to be showing foetal distress . . . I sent for the doctor . . . There

321

wasn't even time to get her to hospital! So he did it there at the Abbey.' A Caesar.

The mother of Edward and Richard had had a Caesar after the head of the first baby was well down in the pelvis. Which meant that the baby that emerged first from her body had been Richard, not Edward, who had been the leader in the birth canal. Extracting him would have been more difficult because his head was so far down, so of course he was delivered second. And that meant that the child who was born to be the heir was reversed from what would have been the case had the birth been a normal one.

'Richard was the oldest by default,' she whispered. 'Edward should have been, but Richard was.'

And Richard had inherited the Abbey and the title and the money – because what was it they had told her? That old Lord Durleigh had strong views about keeping the big estates together. Or was it Marietta's father who had said that? Either way, it made no difference. The boy who should have been the heir was set aside for his brother.

That changed everything. It gave a motive for all the killings – or all but one, she corrected herself. And maybe that one will make sense once we've understood all the others. David and Richard, of course, because David would know the facts about the twins' birth (surely he would have been told sometime while he was growing up. Families often talk of such matters) and anyway – she remembered with a great rush of excitement – was working on a Bill to change the laws of inheritance altogether. If he succeeded, Edward might still lose his coveted place, even if he killed his brother Richard to get it. Sam Diamond probably for the original reason. He found out how money was being made illegally and was about to put a stop to it. The Bishop – and then her head felt as though it was about to burst and she reached again for the phone to call Julie – only to pull back as she remembered that it was an extension.

There had been phone boxes across the square, hadn't there? She ran to the window and peered out and there they were, two rather forlorn boxes on the other side of the road. She grabbed her coat and purse and ran, pulling on her coat as she went. At the foot of the stairs the receptionist peered at her blankly as she went by, and then someone in the glass box called after her. But George just waved a hand and ran on.

The phone box was, to her huge relief, empty. It smelled repulsively of old cigarette smoke, human sweat and urine, but she was too excited to care; she was just grateful that it took coins and not phone cards. She was trembling slightly as she put a pound coin in the slot and then dialled the incident room number.

It was engaged. She swore under her breath and tried to remember another of the relevant numbers; they had several. After a moment she managed to pull one out of her head and dialled again. This time she got a police constable she didn't know.

'I have to speak to WPC Bentley,' she almost shouted it. 'It's urgent!'

'She's on the phone,' the young voice said, clearly unintimidated by her demand. 'If you give me a number I'll see if she'll call you back.'

'No,' George shrieked. 'It's *urgent*, dreadfully urgent! It's me she's calling, probably. For God's sake! Interrupt her and tell her it's Dr Barnabas.'

He tried to argue but she shrieked again and this time he obeyed. It seemed like hours later that at last Julie's voice clattered in her ears again. 'Dr B., whatever's the matter! Davies said you swore at him.'

'I probably did. Listen, Julie, did you get hold of Roop?'

'I was trying to get you so I could tell you!' Julie sounded aggrieved. 'Only they said you'd gone out.'

'I'm using a telephone box,' she said. 'Safer. Now, listen, please. I was wrong about who I thought was the criminal. It isn't Jasper. He's involved, of course, but he just does as he's told. The murderer is someone else. I'm almost sure of it but I have to go and see someone to get another piece of information. And then I need you to do something. It's really important, Julie, so do it. I want you to check trains and timetables and planes and passenger lists and all that sort of thing . . .' She explained as fast as she could and when at last she hung up she stood trembling slightly. It was so tantalizingly close, the answer, and yet . . . and there was still Lord Scroop to wonder about . . .

But right now she had other things to do. She pushed out of the phone box to take a deep breath of the cold clean air outside, and then ran across to the meter where she'd left her car. It had a ticket on it because she hadn't stopped to put money in the slot when she'd left it there, forgetting she wasn't with Gus, but she just pulled it off and dropped it in the road. She had more important things to worry about than that.

She took the car out of the square at an amazing rate, squealing the brakes as she pulled sharply to the side to avoid a slow-moving van, but then she was on her way, heading for the hospital as fast as she could. She had to talk to Nanny Lyons and confirm what she suspected was the case. When she'd done that, and when Julie had done her checks and shown that he could have been there in every one of the places at the relevant time, as George was sure he had, the story would be complete. I'll have cracked it, she thought jubilantly. And to hell with Rupert Dudley!

The hospital car park was busy and she realized after a moment of frustrated rage that it must be visiting time; certainly there was a great deal of jockeying for positions going on. But again she was reckless, and just dumped her car where she could and got out and ran, ignoring the outraged cries from other frustrated parkers that followed her.

She was almost at the hospital doors when she felt the hand on her shoulder, and whirled to find herself staring into the face of a police constable.

'I want you, lady,' he said firmly. 'On account of several things. Like not paying at a meter, then throwing away a legal document, viz a parking ticket, and driving dangerously in the market square in the middle of the town, followed by exceeding the speed limit on the way here, and finally parking your car in a manner that makes it likely to cause an obstruction. These are criminal offences and I want you to come to the station to –'

'Oh, you idiot!' She almost howled it. 'Can't you see this is an emergency and that's why I drove like that?'

'There isn't an emergency department at this hospital,' the policeman said with sublime logic. 'So it can't be. Now, will you come along with me or do I have to arrest you?'

'Oh, go to hell,' George snapped. She tried to run away and up the steps, but he grabbed her.

'I arrest you on a charge of resisting arrest,' he said with relish. 'You do not have to say anything, but anything you do . . .'

They made her go back to the police station in the square under the windows of which she had been parked (which was why the police had had so clear a view of her various motoring offences) to show them her ID and make lengthy explanations before they at last agreed to let her go back to the hospital. By the time they did that she was almost frantic, convinced in the most absurd way that her quarry had somehow got wind of her activities and would either escape or do something dreadful. She was filled with foreboding and it took a great deal of conscious effort to convince herself that this was just the result of being kept from talking to Nanny Lyons, which was the thing she wanted to do most of all. But at last they said she could go, and that she'd be notified when she had to appear in court to answer the charges against her, and she fled into the square. It took her another ten minutes to get a taxi, for the small rank that stood there was quite empty, but at last she was moving through the streets, albeit at a maddeningly sober pace, on her way back to the hospital and Nanny Lyons.

It was getting dark now, the short autumn afternoon dwindling into a surprisingly deep cobalt blue, and she felt anxiety seeping away a little. She was just getting over-excited, she told herself. It was no more than that; there was no reason to get so agitated.

But when she got to the hospital, she found the bed in the side ward on Hainault Ward was empty, and Nanny Lyons and Dr Kelley were sitting there, the old lady in floods of tears, her eyes swollen so much she could barely see out of them.

325

'Oh, my God!' George said as she stood at the door and looked at the crumpled bed. 'What happened? Where is she?'

'Oh, doctor, doctor, I'm so sorry. But there was nothing I could do. He came in and said she was too ill to be in this stupid cottage hospital and that I was wicked to have let her be fetched here and I was sacked and never to let him set eyes on me again. And he took her away, he just picked her up and carried her off and there wasn't anything I could do about it. Oh, doctor, what shall I do? He said he never wants to see me again. My boy. My Edward, he sacked me, he hates me, he never wants to see me again. Oh, what shall I *do*?'

35

In the end they had to treat the old woman like a patient: admit her and put her to bed. She was in such paroxysms of misery that the only thing that could soothe her, said Dr Kelley, would be an injection of a tranquillizer.

'She's an old woman,' she said briskly as she wrote up the dosage on the notes. 'And she'll work herself into heaven knows what if this goes on. Let me bring her down, see to it she gets a night's sleep, and then, tomorrow, she'll be fit to talk. But not right now.'

'Please,' George begged. '*Please.* There's just one vital question I have to ask her. No one else will know the answer. I *have* to ask her. If I don't, I'll – well, I just have to know. There's Marietta out there with him somewhere, and God knows where, and I'm not even sure I'm right about his motives. I could be wrong about what's been going on, but I don't think so. Please, Dr Kelley.'

'What is it you need to know?' Dr Kelley set her head on one side and looked at George with bird-bright eyes. 'I have to believe it's important – you look almost as desperate as poor Mrs Lyons.'

George took a deep breath. There could be no harm in telling this person what it was; she was a doctor too, and would treat such matters confidentially. Wouldn't she?

George checked. 'You won't tell anyone I asked? In case I'm wrong?'

'Not a word,' said Dr Kelley solemnly and her eyes were even brighter. She hasn't had as much fun as this for years, George found herself thinking. That's why she's so helpful. Suddenly she knew she could trust her. Her curiosity wasn't based on anything at all threatening.

'One of the victims of the Ripper killings was the Bishop of –'

'Droitwich,' Dr Kelley finished. 'I know. I've read all about this case. Who hasn't?'

'Oh. Well, yes. But he wasn't always a bishop, you see, or even a Churchman. And I think his previous occupation might be linked with his being a victim.'

'He was a doctor.' Dr Kelley smiled at her before turning to the bed to swab Mrs Lyons' upper arm ready to give her the tranquillizer. 'But that was general knowledge, wasn't it? It certainly was in these parts.'

'Perhaps it was. I wasn't sure. And I need to ask Mrs Lyons if he – well, there's just one thing she can tell me and only she can. So *please*.'

'You'd better ask her fast,' Dr Kelley said, looking down on Nanny Lyons, who was still rolling her head restlessly on her pillow as tears ran out from beneath her closed swollen eyelids. 'This is intramuscular. It'll hit her like a poleaxe any moment now.'

George crouched beside the bed at once, setting her lips as near as she could to the old lady's ear, holding her head still with one hand under her chin.

'Nanny?' she murmured. 'Nanny Pushkin?' as the pet name came back to her mind, and the old lady tried to open her eyes and seemed to stop weeping for a second as she let her lips curl in a travesty of a smile. 'Dear Nanny Pushkin,' George whispered, '*do* tell me. Who was the doctor who did the Caesar when the twins were born? Where did he come from? Do tell me, dearest Pushkin.'

The jerky movements the old body had been making had slowed down and now almost stopped, and George was able to let go of the chin. The drug was working, and working fast as Dr Kelley had warned her.

'Please tell me, Pushkin,' George said a little more loudly, letting the desperation into her voice, and now the old eyes managed to open a little and stare into hers.

'Doctor from Ardenford,' she muttered. It was almost impossible to hear her. 'Doctor . . .' and then the eyes closed again and she was asleep, and no matter how often George murmured in her ear, it made no difference.

'She's away with the fairies,' Dr Kelley remarked with satisfaction. 'You'll have to wait till tomorrow now.'

'Oh, *hell.*' George scrambled to her feet. 'Hell and damn and – and –'

'That's pretty mild,' Dr Kelley said. 'You should hear me when I get going. Was it Dr Lutter you were asking about? I couldn't quite hear because you were whispering, but I did think, perhaps . . .'

George, who had been brushing down her knees, straightened and stared at her. 'You know – knew him?'

'Knew him?' Dr Kelley looked a little scornful. 'He was a houseman of mine for a while. When this was a general hospital and I was still doing general surgery. Let's see – that would have been about the middle fifties, give or take a year or two. Clever fella with his hands, I thought. It was a dreadful waste when he got religion and went off all evangelical, but there you go. He did all right for himself in the end.' She seemed to sober then as she remembered. 'Up to a point, that is. Short of being murdered, you understand.'

George closed her eyes in a sort of giddy relief. 'So he was capable of doing a Caesar in a private home?'

'On the district, you mean?' Dr Kelley nodded. 'Lord, yes. We were doing tricky emergency deliveries anywhere back then – long before the maternity reforms, that was. I seem to remember a couple of emergency Caesars done out in the depths of the country in those bad old days, so called. Oh, yes indeed. He could have done one. He was a GP, of course, not hospital based, but he worked here on shifts as a houseman. It was common practice then.' Dr Kelley looked wistful for a moment. 'It was a great time, actually. Before all these bloody reforms and ECRs and block contracts and the rest of that crap.'

George leaned forward and kissed her lightly on the cheeks. 'Dr Kelley, you're great, fantastic. *Thank* you. The last piece – but one – is in. I've got my case, near as dammit. Thank you. Take care of her, will you? I'll be in touch again as soon as I can.' And she turned and ran from the ward, leaving Dr Kelley staring after her.

She waited for as long as she could for a positive outcome, sitting in the same police station where she'd been interrogated and charged about her motoring behaviour, but this time as a tolerated representative of another force – but only just tolerated. No one spoke to her as she sat in the radio room at the back of the small station, listening to the crackling voices of the officers out in cars looking for a black Rover, licence Charlie Alpha Bravo … The number was called over so often that it seemed to have burned itself into her brain. As did their failure to find it.

'The house,' she said aloud for the umpteenth time. 'Why aren't they searching the house?'

'I did start to tell you, doctor,' the detective sergeant who was in charge of the room spoke with a heavy courtesy. 'One of the cars did go there, first call off, but there was total silence, no response. So –'

'But he wouldn't answer the door, for God's sake!' George almost wailed it. 'Not if he's hiding her there!'

'We don't have no warrant to search his house,' the sergeant said. 'And' – his voice rose as she opened her mouth to interrupt him – 'according to our Inspector Malvern, we've also got no call to apply for one. They're only looking for the car because Dr Kelley at the hospital said the woman is ill and might need further care. But I have to tell you, there's no law being broken here, as far as we can see.'

'But I told you! He's a suspect in the Ripper case!'

'We haven't been told that officially,' the sergeant said, sounding wooden. He was clearly unimpressed by George. 'And we haven't been able to get hold of this Inspector Dudley you mentioned, and the people on duty at Ratcliffe Street said they know of no call out to bring Lord Durleigh in and so –'

'But they wouldn't know!' George cried. 'I've only just found out it's him who is the killer! Once I get the chance to talk to Dudley it'll be obvious to him and to you that –'

'Well, doctor.' He was even more stolid. 'I'll be delighted to talk to the Inspector, and so will our Inspector Malvern, but we haven't been able to reach him, you see. I'm sorry.'

She gave up. She'd promised herself she'd leave it to the police, that she wouldn't meddle, that she would in fact keep her promise to Gus, but how could she leave things this way? That the search for Marietta being organized by this local force was perfunctory was obvious to her, and indeed the calls from the area cars were now becoming fewer and fewer. More of the calls were about pub brawls and domestic spats in remote villages than the search for the missing patient. So she got to her feet, tightened the belt around the waist of her coat, nodded icily at the sergeant and bade him a firm goodnight.

'You'll be leaving Durleighton then?' he said with obvious relief.

She stared coldly at him. 'No, I shall not,' she said. 'I'm going to do some looking on my own account. If Inspector Dudley is tracked down, you can tell him that I had no choice because you wouldn't – Well, tell him I had to. I'm using my car – you've got the number on file – so he can come and look for me. But I've wasted enough time here. Goodnight.'

She collected her car, moving quickly, thinking perhaps that in spite of his clear unenthusiasm for her company the sergeant might still think it wiser to keep her beside him, but the square remained silent and still as she let in the clutch and moved the car out into the centre. As she headed for the road that led to the two houses where she had first found Marietta, her mobile rang, and she cursed as she tried to find where she had put it. It was under the dashboard, and she reached it and slammed down the receiver button, and almost shouted, 'Hello,' into it. 'George Barnabas, here.' But all she got was a metallic voice intoning, 'You have messages. Call one two one.'

She parked the car neatly to take the messages. This was no time to get yet another ticket from these damned local police. She switched on the car's internal light and peered at the phone and cursed again. It showed a low power level in her battery and she was even angrier with herself for forgetting either to take it with her in her pocket or to switch it off when she left it in the car.

The battery only lasted long enough for her to get most of the first message, but it didn't matter. The message drove everything else out of her mind.

'Dr B.' It was Julie's voice, high with excitement. 'I'll try not to give anything away, since this is a mobile. Listen carefully. You were *right*. I've collected all the info on times and planes and tickets and yes, he did – he could have been there for every one of the events. Inspector Dudley had already thought of it – you see? He said you always have to think first of family – and that's why I've got it so fast. The checks were already done. Oh, and Inspector Dudley is –' Then the battery died. She tried to switch it on again to get the message back, but it refused to stay alive.

Anyway, it didn't matter. She had what she wanted. The new Ripper had to be Edward Caspar-Wynette-Gondor, now Lord Durleigh (and even as she thought that, a memory again knocked at her awareness and then skittered away; but she ignored it). He had had the opportunity, according to Julie, and with the exception of just one case, that of Lord Scroop, he had a clear motive. And at the moment he also had Marietta. She clearly had knowledge that would incriminate him. Probably she had known, as a member of the family, the true facts about the twins' birth and resulting seniority, and also that the three of them weren't nearly as matey with each other in reality as they put on a show of being, and had told him that she knew or suspected that he was the criminal. But the risk was clear. He'd used Jasper to drug her – but why was Jasper so helpful? So many questions! She had to find Marietta somehow and get her out of danger. And she was sure that she was at the remote house at the end of the lane, no matter what the police sergeant had said.

She chose not to take the car as far as she could along the lane. Better to stop well short of the house and then walk under cover of the dark to the back of the house; he'd surely be watching the front. So she coasted down the lane, her engine and lights switched off, as far as she judged was safe, then crept out of the car, leaving it unlocked and the keys hidden just under the driver's seat. She might need to switch on and get away in a hurry when she got back.

The geography and the weather were on her side. It was a clear night, but moonless, and just windy enough for there to be a steady soughing from the trees and a regular hissing and rattling in the hedges. Even if she did make a sound as she walked, it wouldn't be identifiable amongst the rest of the night noises, and she slid along under the lee of the hedge towards the darker bulk in front of her, which was the two houses.

Getting round the back wasn't too difficult either; the main hedge ran all the way round and on one side there was a high old brick wall. Kitchen garden? wondered George, who had visited her share of English country houses. Probably. And that meant the house's kitchen door wouldn't be too far away.

The wall was equipped with a door and she leaned on it gently and it gave way. Unlocked: someone up there loves me she told herself with a lift of excitement as she slid in through the smallest opening she could make (remembering suddenly with a frisson of horror the way Richard must have felt as he squeezed through into the Spitalfields storeroom) to find herself in a fairly narrow area of bushes and, underfoot, soft damp earth.

Great, she thought, and deliberately walked in the earth, using it to muffle her footsteps. The path, she could see, was brick and might make a noise under her heels; it didn't matter that tomorrow, in daylight, evidence of her visit would be clearly visible. All she needed now was silence.

It was, she thought with elation, incredibly easy. The back door was unlatched and she was able to push the door open and step inside. Here the floor was tiled. She looked down at it dubiously in the dimness and decided to risk it. In the event, the earth clinging to her shoes acted as a soft sole to her otherwise noisy shoes and she was able to cross the kitchen as silently as she had crossed the garden.

Outside the kitchen she could see a dull glow coming from the fireplace and felt its fading warmth. He *has* been here, she thought with a lift of pure joy. Otherwise, why the fire? Nanny Lyons hasn't been here all day to light it, so it has to be him. Or Jasper. And in the end we want them both. And if one or both of them are here, so is Marietta.

It wasn't till she got to the foot of the stairs that she found herself wondering what she would do if she got to the bedroom and found them both there. Edward and Jasper, together with Marietta. Tip her hat to them and say, 'Good evening, you guys. I've just popped in for Marietta,' and calmly scoop her up and take her away? She stood on the bottom step for a while, thinking. Perhaps she should have waited for the police after all; but then she shook her head. They had already refused to do as she had asked. How could she have trusted them to intervene? All she could do, now she was here, was to try to find Marietta without anyone hearing her, and then – suddenly her spirits lifted – then leave the way she had come and tell the police she'd found the girl and to come and break in at once. If she could assure them she'd seen Marietta with her own eyes, they'd have to believe her. Wouldn't they?

Encouraged, she began to move again, creeping up the stairs with as light a tread as she could, terrified of squeaking boards. But the house, though old, had been well built and was thickly carpeted. Not a sound did she make, and she reached the top of the stairs, breathing a little more rapidly, but still in full control of herself.

It was then she heard it. From across the hall came a faint mewing sound. She stood as though she'd been frozen but it wasn't repeated. She peered into the darkness to identify the source and saw a thinner blackness in the darkness ahead of her. The edge of the door, she thought, staring through slitted eyes to sharpen her vision. A half-open door, and whoever had mewed was on the other side of it. Mewed up, she thought absurdly,

Marietta mewed up, and wanted to giggle. Fear, she thought, makes you do strange things.

She took a couple of deep slow breaths to restore her self-control. It was all too easy to get hysterical in a situation like this. She had to relax; relax and think relaxed if she was to get anywhere. And after a moment she felt better and began to move again.

The door opened softly in front of her and her eyes, now well used to the dark, saw tolerably well. A bed, with the hump of a figure in it. And other furniture too. But no other figures, and she stood very still, listening to someone breathe, trying to hear if there were more than one person doing it. There wasn't, she decided and moved forwards to the bedside.

It was Marietta; she could have bent and hugged her. The woman was somehow less still than she had been; there was a sense of movement about her, rather than the dead comatose dullness that had so characterized her before. She was coming out of it, George's doctor's mind told her. Maybe she had had enough of Dr Kelley's treatment to start her off on recovery at least. I have to get her out of here and back to hospital; and that means I have to get the police here fast.

She got as far as the kitchen on her way back, could see the open back door and the garden outside, even got a glimpse of the door in the wall beyond it, and then it all collapsed.

He was behind her. She knew it as surely as she knew that her feet were cold and heavy with the mud on her shoes and that her pulse was beating so thickly in her throat it threatened to choke her. She turned very slowly, staring into the darkness and saw a shape. A human figure undoubtedly, but topped with a large flattened head. The cap, she thought. The flat country-style cap he always wore. The body, as far as she could judge, was bulky and soft and she stood and stared and thought, overalls. Flat cap and overalls. And then braced herself as the figure came towards her in a sudden rush.

How long she spent grappling on the floor she did not know. He cut her; of that she was very aware. Both hands, across the palms. She'd worked out where the knife was, and had reached for it, following a complicated thought process mixed with an almost instinctual awareness; knowing that she had to hold the blade, because even if it cut her palms, it wouldn't kill her there. Her blood was hot and sticky on her fingers and her hands slipped and she reached forwards again and pulled on the figure. This time, because there was no knife in his hands, he reached for her throat and she remembered just in time that he usually strangled his victims first and sliced afterwards. So why was he wielding a knife now? The thought whirled in her head and she knew it was stupid when what she should have been thinking about was finding the muscle power to fend him off. And though they were evenly matched for weight, for the body beneath the rough fabric of the overalls was quite slight, still she was losing. He seemed harder, tougher and altogether more determined than she was.

He had both hands round her throat and she was beginning to feel dizzy, the darkness threatening at the edge of her vision, when she heard it. The distant sound of police sirens. And at once he was gone, vanishing from on top of her, and she lay gasping, weeping soundlessly as the sirens got louder and closer. She couldn't have made a sound even if she'd tried to because her throat, she was certain, would never function again.

36

Gus held her so tightly that it hurt, but she wouldn't have told him so for the world. She just lay there, very aware of the ice pack round her throat, and listened to him. His voice was fortunately gentler than his grip.

'You're the biggest bloody fool there is,' he said. 'You go in bald headed where even a halfwit would have the sense to stay outside and mind her own business. You're not even a quarter-wit.'

'I've done pretty well for a −' she began and then stopped and swallowed. Her voice was harsh and painful; it was easier to let him go on insulting her.

'I know, I know. You worked it all out. But, ducky, so had good old Roop. No, don't shake your head at me. You'll knock the ice off and Dr Kelley'll have my guts for garters. He'd been beavering away in his dull old way and found out a good deal of stuff that bears out what you came at the brilliant way − and the dangerous way − just by stirring up your thoughts, jumping to conclusions, running into trouble and other daft athletic-type pursuits.'

'Shut up,' she managed. 'Just tell me what he −' And stopped again. This was frustration of a sort she'd never known. Not to be able to talk? It was a hell of the most excruciating kind.

Gus grinned hugely. 'Oh, George, George, who'd ha' thought it! My own little duck, speechless! Got to listen for a change! Oh dear, oh dear!'

She tried to pull away from him then, furious, but he held on.

'I'm sorry, sweetheart. I have to tease you, though. How else can I get over the horrible fright you gave me?'

She looked up at him and saw the brightness in his eyes and was filled with compunction. She lifted her chin and he bent and kissed her very gently. She had to reach up and pull him down towards her to show him that whatever her throat felt like, her mouth was still in excellent condition.

They sat quietly for a while then, she looking up at the ceiling of the small side room on Hainault's companion ward, Plaistow, very aware of the pain in her throat, but curiously detached for all that. Whether it was whatever drug Dr Kelley had given her to ease the pain, or a reaction to the tension and fear of the past couple of hours, she could not be sure, and she moved her neck gingerly inside its collar of ice and grimaced.

'Keep still,' he ordered. 'Dr Kelley said –'

'Bugger Dr Kelley,' she whispered. 'Tell me, for pity's sake.'

'OK, OK, I'll tell you. Dudley got the message you'd left about Marietta, and set out at once to get down here to sort things out. He didn't want to alert the local force because he wasn't sure what sort of relationship Edward might have with 'em. Even with properly trained coppers it can happen in small communities that old friendships get in the way of police procedures. Edward – all the CWGs for that matter – have been swells in these parts so long . . . Well, anyway, Roop set out to come down here. Then he got a message from PC Waverley, whom he'd appointed watcher of the computer data, that Julie had pulled off the computer the stuff about Edward's visits to Brussels and that you'd asked her for it – she had to tell him that to get the data – and he realized you'd got something on him. He'd suspected Edward from the start himself, simply because he was the brother of two of the victims, and, like we always say, us being old coppers, never mind the fancy stuff, look for the usual. Which is domestic crime committed by family members. Dress it up how you like, Roop said to me, this is one

338

of them. He might have a few other scores he's trying to settle here, but there's a reason for these killings.'

He stopped then and leaned over and looked down into her face. The lamp beside the bed, which was partly covered by a piece of pink fabric, threw a soft glow on his features and she could have wept for the sheer joy of having him there.

'You said the same, didn't you?' he murmured. 'That it was a crime with reason, not just a mindless set of serial killings.'

She nodded, closing her eyes in assent, and then looked at him again, her brows up. Learning how to converse without speech was getting easier.

He straightened up. 'Would you believe, even those politicians said the same. Mike Urquhart said that when he went to talk to Bodling and Twiley she said it had to be a family, not a political, motive. Oh, well. This time I was the one barking up the wrong tree, looking for a classic serial killer. I can't win 'em all.'

She grinned at him, but didn't try to speak. Or to crow.

'OK,' he said. 'So Roop set out to look for the sort of boring old police evidence that gets cases into court and to a satisfactory conclusion. First off, he got them checking on the man's trips to Brussels and, like you heard, he could have been in London for all the murders. It took a lot of planning, some jiggery-pokery with different names used in hotel registers, and a bit of his friend Powell posing as him and booking into hotels in his name, but he did it. He was available right here in London on *all* the relevant days at the relevant times. It took Interpol some time to compile the data, but they came up with it eventually. Not that that's proof, of course, but it *is* important that opportunity is clearly in evidence. Then Roop started digging into the C W G family history.'

Gus stopped and took a deep breath. 'I'll grant you, ducks, he hadn't uncovered this business of the twins born the wrong way round and Edward losing his inheritance in consequence. But he did find out the brothers had been at each other's throats – if you'll forgive the expression – all their lives pretty well, though they put on a great show of amity for public consumption. The old Lord Durleigh – the twins' and David's father – said in a letter Roop found among David's effects that public squabbling was "unseemly". He got them all to promise they'd behave "prudently". Nice word, isn't it, in the circumstances? Anyway, whatever the show they put on, it seems Edward never forgave his brother for being born before him. It was partly because of the poisonous atmosphere in the family that David turned so vehemently against them all. It made him a socialist of the first water.' He chuckled then. 'So it isn't all bad news. Or it wouldn't have been if the poor bugger had lived.'

She risked speech again. 'This was known?'

'Oh, there are always people who talk. Not the old girl here – they'd tried her. Sent someone under cover to chat her up, but she was stumm. It took you to get her talking. Well done you!'

Absurdly, she glowed. 'And then?'

He shrugged. 'So he – Roop, that is – began to look into the other victims' backgrounds. He, too, discovered the Bishop had once been a local G P here – he wasn't best pleased we'd made the same discovery before him! – and accepted that something had happened, he didn't know what, to get up our friend Edward's nose. And as for Scroop . . .' He hesitated.

Her eyes lit up. This had been the puzzle for her. 'Well,' she croaked. 'I must know, quick. Tell me.' And coughed painfully.

He tutted at her, looking worried, but the cough eased and he went on in response to the imploring look she gave him. 'He was an odd chap. You mentioned in the post-mortem report that he had undeveloped genitals. Remember?'

She wrinkled her brow and then nodded.

'Well, we've got a lot of this stuff out of Jasper Powell, who's been singing his heart out to Roop down at the local station. He was in the other house when Roop got there, *hiding*. A really repellent character that one. Always did what Edward wanted him to, no matter what it was, and especially when it coincided with his own interests. And they were always financial. Edward knew about his scam with Alice, and wouldn't have hesitated to turn him in if he hadn't co-operated. Even after Powell had enough evidence against Edward to have fought back he went on co-operating – he bought the barbiturates used on Marietta. I reckon he thought that if he helped Edward to his bloody earldom he'd get future cash rewards, via blackmail probably. He'd do anything to help Edward, even to the extent of engineering the accident to you. For that alone I could kill him myself, but I'll settle for squeezing him till his pips squeak for mercy, getting all the info out of him I can. Anyway, now he's terrified. He'll tell us anything we need to know in the hope it'll get him an easier sentence. He should be so lucky! Not that we're telling him that, you understand. We just encourage him to talk. Which he does. Oh, yes, he does.' He made a sharp little sound at the back of his throat. 'Which is how we got this stuff.'

'Why did he –?' To her relief he understood.

'Engineer the accident?' Gus said. 'He was suspicious of you, he said. Wanted to find out who you were and why you'd been chatting up the girl in Sloane's.' He chuckled then. 'And you fooled him, believe it or not. He decided you were harmless. You! The man's an idiot.'

'And Scroop?' She felt as though she had shrieked, but heard only a hoarse whisper.

'Oh yes, Scroop. Well, it seems that the boy Edward, who was always somewhat dubious about his own sexuality, hated Scroop because he'd deceived him. Or so he told Powell.'

'Deceived?' Her voice was still thick but a little less painful now. The injection Dr Kelley had given her a little while ago was biting at last, she decided sleepily. I certainly don't hurt so much but I must stay awake.

Gus sighed and made a face. 'I have to say this stuff isn't my idea of fun and games at all, but there you go. I dare say I'm just a boring old fart. There was a club they all went to, it seems. Gays, lesbians and the people who like their company. It was in the City, near Mitre Square, believe it or not. And Scroop used to go when he was younger and, well, better looking I suppose. Or maybe looks don't matter and Edward liked a bit of rough trade, and it was Scroop's working-class toughness that attracted him. Anyway, Edward fell for him like a plumb line, but then Scroop dropped him. It turned out that Scroop, who everyone at this club thought was transvestite as well as gay, was more transsexual. Or born with some sort of anomaly down there. Hell, you'll know more about this than I do!'

George wrinkled her eyes, looking back into her memory of the Scroop post-mortem. It had been a nasty one, for the body had been half rotted, of course. But she'd identified the empty scrotum, or what she had assumed was a scrotum, though she knew quite well it could have been overgrown labia minora, a sort of abnormal extrusion of the normal vulva. She'd also found what she had thought was the stump of a penis. Could it have been a misshapen clitoris? She tried hard to visualize it again, but her eidetic memory was stubborn. She had found some degenerated material on the shoulder, and because of the other cases had accepted that it was the excised genitalia. But suppose . . .

'Oh, hell,' she said in a whisper. 'He was a Klinefelter's.'

'I don't know what you call 'em,' Gus said. 'But according to the guy's medical records which Roop got hold of – don't ask how – this bloke had been a borderline case, registered as a male but . . .' He shrugged. 'I gather it's not uncommon for there to be such doubts about gender. And because Scroop never told Edward about himself, and just dumped him, Edward hated him. Always did. And according to Powell, it was the deception about his gender he had hated him for the most. He's a bit of an amateur psychologist, this Powell, and he spouted a lot of stuff about Edward having doubts about his own sexuality, and that, married to his rage about his birth experience and the way his mother failed to give him his birthright by not going through with a normal birth, made him hate women. And Scroop had been womanish. Anyway, Powell was clear, Edward hated Scroop. And then, it turns out, Scroop tried to get money out of Edward for old time's sake, he said, and Edward got mad. He arranged to meet Scroop at the shed on the waste ground, where they used to meet, years ago. It was a favourite haunt, apparently. That was why no one saw anyone arriving there in a van or whatever. They got in quietly as they always had. And Edward strangled him. He left the body there.'

'But why the Ripper? Was it just to bewilder us?'

'Sort of,' he said. 'That was part of it, we reckon. But not till after he'd done in Scroop. Edward realized after he'd strangled him that he'd left him in one of the Ripper's old stamping grounds. We think he must have gone back long after the strangling and done the chopping up and added the genital mutilation to assuage some personal need. It wasn't hard for him to do that. Cut throats and chop off organs, I mean. He was as keen a huntsman as aristocrats like him are supposed to be. Used to shoot deer, so knew how to gut them. He was good with a knife. And then he set to work to get rid of the rest of the people in the same way. His brothers, so that he could get the inheritance, especially the title, because he's always been a hell of a snob, we've been told, and to which he believed himself fully entitled. The doctor who was to blame for what happened when he and his twin were born – it was you who worked that out, of course. Sam Diamond, partly because, like his brother CWG, he was on the Committee trying to do away with inherited power in Parliament and partly to please his latest lover Jasper, who's a right bastard and who'd screw anyone for threepence and then sell the bits for candlewax. And of course, killing someone who was in Powell's way as Sam was, on account of he'd had a fight with Alice when he'd found out what was going on and he'd threatened to stop Powell as a way of getting *her* out of trouble – again, he should have been so lucky! – added to his hold on Powell. Or so Edward figured. The fashion espionage thing was all Powell's. He made a bomb out of it. So, there you have it. It's all explained, even the sending of the fax to direct us to the storeroom where Richard's body was. Once he'd started the Ripper thing he had to keep it up. It was the only way to keep us convinced a set of murders, including two which directly benefited him, were nothing to do with him.'

'He lured his brother to the Market by telling him Marietta was there and asking for him? I was right about that?'

'Oh, yes. You were right. Cigaretta, ye Gods! Anyway, it worked.'

'How did he get in?' she asked, coughing painfully once more.

'In his usual way: conning and bribing. Told a storeman at the Market he wanted to play a trick on a mate: gave him five hundred quid and got the back-door key copied, and the details of the alarm system. Roop managed to get hold of *him*.' He shook his head almost in admiration. 'I have to hand it to the bastard – Edward, that is. He did his job thoroughly: vetted all his sites; used 'em cleverly; got his victims where he wanted them. Scroop, of course, knew the hidden shed; he'd met Edward there before. As for the Bishop – well, we don't know yet how he lured him. But I imagine some tale of a person in trouble would work well enough. Dammit, the man was both a doctor and a committed Churchman. It wouldn't be difficult, I imagine, to play on his compassion. Getting his own brothers, David and Richard, to meet him almost anywhere wouldn't be difficult. Even though we now know they weren't on the good terms people thought they were, they were still brothers. Edward just had to invent some sort of crisis and they'd turn out. They wouldn't want to but they would. Edward used a sick Marietta as his bait, as you said. He only had one weak spot – Marietta herself.'

'Oh?'

'Yes, and it all got very dicey then. He suddenly realized Marietta knew the twin-birth facts – her husband had told her, or she found out through some casual comment – so *she* had to go. He used Powell to help with that. And was, I'm sure, all set to kill off his old nanny too, eventually, because she knew too much. It all fits, doesn't it? And while you did a hell of a good job of the case, you have to face the facts, my darling. Old Roop did all the dirty work. You had the fun.'

She touched her throat and glared at him, and then, after a moment, let her lips curve. 'You're right,' she whispered. 'I owe him an apology. Dammit.'

'That,' said Gus with a huge appreciation, 'is something I will have to see.'

'Is Marietta OK?'

'Fine,' he said. 'She's in another of these side wards here. This bleedin' hospital's packed with people from this case.' He chuckled appreciatively. 'There's some admin. type going around tearing his hair out over it. Wants to know who's going to pay for all these beds. I should worry!'

'I'll help him sort it out. It's not his fault. Listen, Gus.' George struggled with the words. 'It's all over? You've got Edward locked up? Does he get any privilege for being a lord? Which he is now, isn't he? Will he have to be tried in the House of Lords or something like that?'

'I've no idea,' Gus said. 'Right now, he's in a common or garden nick, lord or not. I imagine, by the way, that the event that prodded him into the whole set of murders, was his brother's marriage. It meant he might produce an heir, and cut Edward out for good and all – but what the hell! Let his lawyers sort out the rest of it. We've got bloody Lord Durleigh with enough evidence to swamp the House of Lords – What's the matter! For heaven's sake, what on earth's the matter?'

She was grimacing, her eyes shut against the pain and tears squeezing out beneath the lids as she tried to control the laughter that had suddenly filled her and realized that it looked very much as though she were weeping. She reached for his hand and managed to control herself.

'Oh, Gus,' she whispered. 'I just thought of something. He did all this mostly to end up as Lord Durleigh? Of Durleigh Abbey?'

'So I gather,' Gus said, mystified.

'Well, he's failed,' she said. 'He isn't Lord Durleigh at all. Just the Honourable Mr Edward C W G. Richard's widow is pregnant with a boy. Doesn't that mean that he'll be the new earl?'

'Do you know,' Gus said, as a smile began to spread across his face, 'do you know, I rather think you could be right.'

In the small hours of the next morning, when George had slept off the effects of Dr Kelley's injection, she turned and woke. Gus was still sitting at the side of the bed, his head drooping over his hands, which were holding one of hers, and she used her free hand to touch his hair gently, wriggling her fingers clear of the bandage. It sprang back under her touch and she felt a lift of pure delight at the look of it. He seemed to feel it, because he woke and lifted bleary eyes to hers.

345

She smiled at him. 'Hello, there.' Her voice was still thick but had lost the painful hoarseness. He grinned widely at the sound of it.

'Hello, ducks,' he said. He lifted one hand and flicked the brim of an invisible hat with his thumb and forefinger. 'How're you doin', then?'

'Fine and dandy,' she said. 'Fine and dandy.'

'Anything you want, sweetheart?' He sounded soft and warm and solicitous and she looked at him consideringly.

'Do you remember, right at the start of this case, you bet me I was wrong about it being deliberate motive-based murder? You said you'd give me whatever I opted for when it was time to collect?'

'I remember.' He looked cautious. 'Oh, Gawd, what do you want then? Something so bloody expensive I'll have to sell a restaurant to pay for it?'

Her smile widened even more. 'Probably, very probably.

'I thought, you know,' she added, 'that a baby might be rather nice. While we're both still in one piece, you understand. Is that something you think you could manage?'

'Manage?' he said. 'Oh, I think I could manage it. In fact, if you were a private patient instead of NHS, I'd manage it right now. But just let me get you home, my duck. Just let me get you home!'